WARRIOR WISEWOMAN 3

Edited by Roby James

Copyright © 2010 by Norilana Books and Roby James

Cover Images:
"Bust of a Woman" by Giuseppe Piamontini, 1688-1689; "A Classical Beauty" by John William Godward (1861-1922); "International Space Station Imagery" ISS007-E-13791 (30 August 2003), NASA; "The Trifid Nebula" NASA, JPL-Caltech, J. Rho (SSC/Caltech).

Cover Design Copyright © 2010 by Vera Nazarian

ISBN-13: 978-1-60762-061-7
ISBN-10: 1-60762-061-8

FIRST EDITION
Trade Paperback Edition

August 1, 2010

A Publication of
Norilana Books
P. O. Box 2188
Winnetka, CA 91396
www.norilana.com

Printed in the United States of America

ACKNOWLEDGMENTS

Introduction © 2010 by Roby James
"Driving X" © 2010 by Gwendolyn Clare
"Heart of Stone" © 2010 by Joel Richards
"Tourist Trap" © 2010 by Aimee C. Amodio
"Dinner For One" © 2010 by Bruce Golden
"The Race" © 2010 by Jennifer R. Povey
"The Envoy" © 2010 by Al Onia
"Bearer of Burdens" © 2010 by Melissa Mead
"What Lies Dormant" © 2010 by Swapna Kishore
"Katyusha's First Time Out" © 2010 by Susanne Martin
"Natural Law" © 2010 by Alfred D. Byrd
"Baby, Be Mine" © 2010 by Susan Tsui
"Mayfly" © 2010 by Gary Kloster
"To the Altar" © 2010 by Therese Arkenberg
"Sustain Nothing" © 2010 by Paul Abbamondi
"The Truth One Sees" © 2010 by Kathy Hurley
"Mater Luna" © 2010 by William Highsmith
"A Pearl of Great Price" © 2010 by Leslie Brown
"Dark Mirrors" © 2010 by John Walters
"A Bird In the Hand" © 2010 by Douglas Smith

Warrior Wisewoman 3

Norilana Books

Science Fiction

www.norilana.com

WARRIOR WISEWOMAN 3

Edited by

ROBY JAMES

CONTENTS

INTRODUCTION

by Roby James

In 1996, *Apollo 13* won the Hugo Award for best SF dramatic presentation of the year. Clearly, everyone loved it, and it was a masterful motion picture. The fact that it actually wasn't science fiction at all did not seem to bother anyone. It "felt like" science fiction.

"Feeling like" science fiction is a funny kind of criterion, but it's obviously a valid one—at least in the annals of the Hugos. In the case of *Apollo 13*, however, there was a reversal of the normal cause of the feeling. In most cases, the fiction is real and the science is the "feels like" part. For *Apollo 13*, the science was real, and fiction was the "feels like."

Nevertheless, it was a clear case of a mainstream movie convincing the Hugo voters that it was actually genre. Or else the voters made an exception to the norm because they really liked the film—or because they felt like making the exception.

As an editor, I identify with the "feels like." I cannot personally testify to the soundness of the science in many of the stories that are submitted, though I can usually discern if the key to the story depends on something that can only exist in the realm of fantasy. I've been fairly rigorous in accepting only those stories that had a science edge or basis to them. Eighteen out of the nineteen stories in this volume fit that criterion. One is really stretching it, but there was something irresistably "science-like" about it. Accepting it was great fun.

I'm delighted that almost half the stories in this volume (nine out of the nineteen) were written by men. I wasn't actually aware of that until I had the final list of stories I wanted to accept. When a story arrives, I read it without making a note of who the submission is from. If it looks like the story may be a possibility for the volume, I let the author know I'm holding onto it, and that is the first time I usually see whether the story was sent by a man or a woman.

I get query letters from men asking whether I'll even look at stories by the male of the species, and that is a dead giveaway that the person asking the question has never looked at a copy of the anthology. In volume 1, two stories out of twelve were sent by folks with a Y chromosome (16.67%); in volume 2, four and one-half stories out of fifteen had that source (30%). Here in volume 3, we're up to 47%.

I'll be fascinated to see what happens when the reading period opens for volume 4.

In her book *The Warrior Queens: The Legends and the Lives of the Women Who Have Led Their Nations in War*, Antonia Fraser has noted that the Oxford English Dictionary definition of "matriarchy" is: "That form of social organization where the mother, not the father, is the head of the family, and in which descent and relationships are reckoned through mothers not fathers."

That definition of "matriarchy" says nothing about ruling countries or nations, nothing about writing the laws that govern society. So even in a book ostensibly about reigning monarchs with armies behind them, the value of femaleness is anchored in the home and the family when it's written by past convention.

That isn't necessarily the case in the present, and it may be even less so in the future. Yet family figures strongly in many of the stories in this volume. In some, it's because of genetics; in others, it's because of emotions. Those stories, and all of the others, including the one that was irresistably "science-like," are presented for your enjoyment.

There are many stories about futures in which women take over. Most of those futures are times when women want to have the power. But what happens in a world in which the dominance of women is forced upon them by circumstances that nobody wants?

DRIVING X

by Gwendolyn Clare

Carmela wouldn't have stopped if she had known that the kid was still alive.

She spotted the body lying under a creosote bush, maybe ten yards from the road, and she hit the brakes. She grabbed the roll cage of the old dune buggy and pulled herself up, standing on the driver's seat to scan in both directions along the unpaved road. A dust devil twirled a silent ballet off to the southeast, but hers was the only man-made dust trail in evidence for miles. She raised her hand to cover the sun and squinted into the bleached, cloudless sky—no vultures yet, which was good, since vultures attract attention. Minimal risk, she decided.

The dune buggy itself wasn't that valuable, but the newer-model solar panels powering it would be enough to tempt any sane person, and the carboys of potable water were worth a small fortune out here.

Carmela swung out of the dune buggy and jogged over to check out the body. It was tall but skinny, with the not-yet-filled-out look of a teenager. Pale skin, a tint of sunburn, brown hair cropped at chin-length. The girl was lying face down in the dust, so Carmela rolled the body over and checked her front pockets for anything of interest. A month ago, she would have felt ashamed, but scavenging was the norm down here; after all, dead people don't miss what you take from them.

Carmela was rifling through the kid's backpack—shaking her head about the nearly empty water supply—when she heard the girl moan.

She froze, one hand still buried in the bag. She should gather up the loot and make a run for the dune buggy before the girl came around. The kid was probably a goner, anyway, she told herself. Instead, she leaned in closer, looking at the face plastered with sand and sweaty clumps of brown hair.

The girl's eyelids peeled back and stared up at Carmela with the glazed slowness of delirium. Her cracked lips parted and she said, hoarsely, "Mom?"

Nobody had ever called Carmela that before. She bent and slid her hands under the girl's armpits, to lift her.

ை‍‌‌‌‌‌

S winging her legs, nine-year-old Carmela knocked her heels lightly against the side of the exam table. Mama sat in a plastic chair, flipping through a magazine the way she always did when she was getting impatient. Carmela's test result had come in, and for some reason that was beyond her, Mama was really nervous about it. And the doctor was running late.

Carmela didn't know why Mama was all bent out of shape over the non-Mendelian genetic test. To be fair, she wasn't entirely sure what "non-Mendelian" meant, except that it was something bad that your genes could be. Driving X was a chromosome that was bad that way, and pretty much everybody had it, but for some reason you had to get tested for it anyway. That's what Carmela knew.

Dr. Tanaka entered the exam room, holding a manila folder to her chest. "Afternoon, Ms. Perez, Carmela. Sorry to keep you waiting."

Mama dropped the magazine on the floor next to her chair and stood, fingers knotted together nervously. "Well?"

Dr. Tanaka opened the folder, took out a single sheet of paper, and handed it to Mama. Mama stared at it for a long minute, like she couldn't quite see it properly. She made a choking noise.

In her tight, mustn't-cry-in-public voice, she said, "I'll be right back." She left the paper on her chair and hurried for the door.

Carmela hopped off the exam table and picked up the sheet of paper. It had a lot of gobbledygook on it, but right in the middle, in bold, it read, "$X^D X^D$."

She didn't understand what the big deal was. Pretty much everybody had the Driving X allele on at least one of their X chromosomes. What did it matter if she had it on two?

With a gentle sympathy that Carmela found unsettling, Dr. Tanaka said, "You're a double Ex Dee, Carmela."

She crossed her arms. "So what?"

"Well . . ." The doctor sat down and leaned her elbows on her knees. "When someone's gametes—that's eggs and sperm—are getting made inside a person's body, an Ex Dee beats out a regular Ex about three quarters of the time, and it beats out a Wye ninety-seven percent of the time."

Carmela rolled her eyes. "Yeah, and it's some kind of big problem that we're running out of Wyes. So *what*?"

"So, when you're older, and you want to go to a repro center to get pregnant . . . well." She sighed. "You've got a one hundred percent chance of passing on the Driving Ex. They're not even going to let you in the building."

"Oh," said Carmela.

"I'm really sorry, sweetie," the doctor said, as she picked up the GID gun from the counter, "but I've got to give you your genetic identifier now."

Carmela folded the piece of paper, creasing it between her fingers. "Is it going to hurt?"

"Not at all. It might tingle a little."

Carmela reluctantly climbed back onto the exam table. The GID gun looked larger and nastier than the immunization guns she remembered from previous visits. "Okay," she said.

"Give me your arm, sweetie."

She held out her arm and squeezed her eyes shut.

∽⃝⃞⃝∽

Carmela watched the girl sleep. She looked maybe fourteen or fifteen, too old by several years to be Carmela's child. How stupidly sentimental, wasting her water on somebody else's kid. She had a little cash left, but she'd heard they didn't take money in Old Tucson any more, and she had nothing of value to trade. Nothing she could part with, at least. How was she going to replace the water she wasted on some dying stranger?

The cave she found was a hollow worn out of the rock by a combination of rain, wind, and sand, barely deep enough for the dune buggy, the girl, and herself. Outside, the glaring midday sun bleached the color from the raw stone and the crusted, desiccated earth. Heat rose off the ground in palpable, viscous swirls. Carmela took a deep breath and, even in the shadow of the rock, the air seemed to burn in her nostrils.

The girl moaned and shifted, and Carmela wondered if she was going to wake up. It would be easier to get fluids into her once she was conscious. Carmela decided to pour some water into a pair of tin cups, then added a little powdered soup stock for the salt. When she looked again, the girl's eyes were open. "What's your name?"

"Shannon," the girl said. Even roughened from the dehydration, her voice was low and mellow.

Carmela introduced herself and handed over one of the mugs. "Dumb thing to do," she commented. "Old Tucson's another two days on foot."

Shannon shrugged. "I almost made it."

Carmela didn't know what to make of that. No sane person crossed the desert without supplies, and preparation, and a damn good reason. She rubbed absently at the inside of her right forearm, where the phosphorescent GID mark lay hidden in her skin.

Shannon eyed her. "I hear, in the city, you can buy a graft off someone."

"What?" asked Carmela, a little too sharply, pulling her hand away from her arm.

"In the city. You can get somebody else's GID grafted on, if you've got the cash. That's what I heard." Shannon took a long draught of soup. "So you're a double Ex Dee, huh?"

Carmela just said, "I don't have that kind of cash."

"Double Ex Dee." Shannon nodded. "That's what I thought."

Carmela's right hand tensed around the mug, and she felt a strong urge to slap that smug, knowing look right off the kid's face. Instead, she asked, "So what about you? What you doing wandering around the desert? Besides lying face down in the dirt, I mean."

"Going the same way you are. Mexico."

"Nobody makes it to the border on foot," she scoffed. "Double Ex Dee, or what?"

Shannon laughed. "Yeah, something like that."

"There isn't anything *like* double Ex Dee but double Ex Dee."

"Trust me, you're better off not knowing."

ଔୠ୧ଵ୨

Carmela parked the car and looked at Rosita out of the corner of her eye. "Ready, *hermanita*?"

Rosita took a long, nervous breath before she nodded and unbuckled her seatbelt. Climbing out of the car, Carmela caught a whiff of brine carried on the cool, humid breeze. As they walked from the parking lot to the front entrance, she reached for Rosita's hand and held it in her own.

Carmela always felt stocky next to her waifish little sister, but she didn't mind. She liked feeling solid—an anchor for fragile, flighty Rosita. She gave Rosita's hand a reassuring squeeze.

The main entrance of the Bay Area repro center was a set of automatic glass doors, tinted a shade of blue that evoked a feeling of medical officiality. Carmela was surprised to see only one guard posted outside; she would have expected tighter security. Maybe the male-rights radicals were starting to give up hope, or at least give up their ill-conceived attempts at taking over the repro centers.

Carmela and Rosita reached the entrance, and the guard stepped away from her post to position herself in front of the doors. She wielded a GID reader as if she wished it were a police baton.

"Your GIDs, please," the guard said. Her flat tone made it clear that the "please" was company policy, not personal politeness.

Rosita held out her arm for the guard, and the "XD" mark phosphoresced in response to the reader, two letters glowing like a moonlit tattoo. The guard turned to look blandly at Carmela.

"Oh, I'm not here for anything," Carmela explained. "I came with my sister."

The guard kept blocking their way. She was tall and big-boned, made bigger by her riot gear. Here, for once, was a person who didn't look at Carmela with pity; she looked at Carmela with boredom and indifference.

"Your GID, miss," she said again. "No exceptions."

Rosita started to get worked up. "I want to talk to your supervisor—"

"It's okay," Carmela interrupted. "You just go ahead."

"I don't want to do this by myself, I want you to come with me!"

"Rosa, I am sure they're used to helping first-time mothers, and they're going to take good care of you."

"But—"

"It's going to be fine," she said, her tone firm and chill. "I'll wait in the car."

೮೦೮೩೮೦೮೦

Carmela agreed to take the kid as far as Old Tucson, and then Shannon would be on her own. They very nearly made it there without incident.

It was late afternoon, and an intermittent wind pelted them with sand, stinging their faces. A deep wash, dry at the bottom but choked with mesquite, snaked along beside the dirt road. To the north, Carmela could make out the cracked, asphalt ruin that used to be I-10, sprawled like an enormous black snake along the horizon. So close.

Three sandcars roared up out of the wash, just a second after Carmela passed them. They kicked up billows of dust as their tires fought for traction, and there could be no confusion about the drivers' intentions. When Carmela squinted over her shoulder, she wasn't checking to see *if* they were raiders, she just wanted to know *which* raiders they were.

"Damn!" One glance had been enough to recognize the orange war paint down the sides of the sandcars, the long black hair whipping in the wind. "Tohono O'odham. You know how to shoot?"

"Sure thing," Shannon shouted back.

Not that Carmela could really blame them; the Tohono O'odham had plenty of reasons to be angry. Now, of course, all the men were kept in repro centers, but back when the government was still squeamish about male rights, they took the non-citizens first. The Native Americans hadn't forgotten.

As much as she might like to sympathize, Carmela wasn't about to give up her water supply as blood money for something that happened before she was born. She reached underneath the seat and pulled out a long-muzzled pistol.

Shannon took it from her, found the magazine release, and checked to make sure it was loaded. Then she grabbed the roll cage and leaned way out to the side, aiming around the pile of cargo and solar panels that obstructed her view of the sandcars behind them. She fired three shots, taking a pause between each one to aim carefully; at least the kid knew to conserve ammo.

Shannon sat back in her seat and said something, but Carmela's ears were ringing from the gunshots. "What?"

"Why aren't they shooting back?" Shannon shouted again.

"They want the dune buggy intact," she said, jerking the steering wheel to dodge a large rock in the road. "They'll try to pull up next to us and shoot me from the side."

"That's comforting," Shannon replied sarcastically. She leaned out to take aim again.

They reached the outskirts of what once had been the suburbs of Tucson, where the houses were reduced to black marks in the dirt. Whether from arson or wildfire, Carmela didn't know, but either way there was not enough water to waste on firefighting. The sight made Carmela's chest tighten, her breaths hitching with an edge of panic. There should be people living here—she and Shannon should be safe here. Instead, the suburbs were just another desolate landmark in a bleak, indifferent world.

Shannon fired off another shot and whooped with excitement. Glancing over her shoulder, Carmela saw one of the sandcars careen off the road into a patch of bursage shrubs. She couldn't tell whether Shannon had hit a tire or the driver.

Squinting forward again, Carmela could make out the city wall, a patchwork barrier composed of salvaged parts from outlying buildings. As the dune buggy wove back and forth along the rough, unmaintained road, a few odd panels in the wall seemed to blink at them with reflected sunlight. Carmela tightened her grip on the steering wheel, the plastic beneath her fingers sticky with her sweat.

Shannon threw herself back into the seat, ducking low, and flinched at the metallic clang of a bullet ricocheting off the roll cage. "I thought you said they wouldn't fire back!"

Carmela slouched lower in her own seat and locked her eyes on the road ahead. "If Old Tucson's got guards posted on the wall, we're almost in range. A damaged haul's better than nothing."

Shannon muttered something under her breath that Carmela couldn't quite hear, but suspected was a string of colorful expletives.

With the Tohono O'odham's gunshots rattling her eardrums, Carmela floored the accelerator. The suspension slammed them against their seats like they were riding a jackhammer, metal screeching against metal as it bottomed out on the uneven terrain. Every curve in the road, every obstacle avoided, was an attack on the tires' traction, and the dune buggy threatened to spin out with the slightest twitch of the steering wheel. Carmela blinked hard against the dust, knowing that a mistake would be her last.

The city wall loomed up in front of them, and she glimpsed a few desert-camo-clad figures atop it, illuminated by the late, golden sunlight. Suddenly, as if there were an invisible line they could not cross, the Tohono O'odham skidded to a halt in a violent cloud of dust.

"Jesus," Carmela said, easing off the accelerator a little. "That was close."

At the gates, the city guards were hard-looking women, rifle-toting and desert-worn. Carmela worried that there might be trouble, but the guards seemed welcoming enough and took news from the west as her entry fee. Still, Carmela had a healthy wariness of authority figures, so she and Shannon passed through as quickly and politely as possible.

Pulling away from the gates onto a street lined with more-or-less intact buildings, Carmela allowed herself to feel a modicum of relief. She steered with her left hand so she could roll her right shoulder, trying to work the tension out of taut muscles.

"You got one," she said. "That was some okay shooting back there."

Shannon slouched in her seat, letting the pistol hang from loose fingers. "Yeah, well, I could've gotten more if your driving didn't suck so much. I think you hit every pothole in a five-kilometer radius of town."

Carmela was a better-than-decent driver, and she'd been pushing hard. "You can be a real bitch, you know that?" she snapped.

Shannon looked surprised, and then she laughed. "I try."

രജ്ഞ

Pressing the cashmere sweater to her face, Carmela inhaled the lingering scent of perfume. How long would Jeanette's smell cling to the soft fabric, before this last reminder faded into obscurity? Sage and lilac perfume—it smelled like kisses on Fisherman's Wharf as the evening fog rolled in, like explosive tempers in Jeanette's tiny kitchen in the heat of summer, like slow sex. Like love.

Jeanette wanted the sweater back. She had left three phone messages; Carmela had returned only one, swearing that she couldn't find it. The sweater was a departure tax. After all, Jeanette could buy a new sweater, but Carmela couldn't buy a new Jeanette.

The worst part was that she didn't disagree. She wanted to hate Jeanette—for being wrong, for being selfish, for being able to forget and move on when Carmela herself could do neither—but the truth was that they were both X^DX^D, and Carmela had always known they wouldn't last forever because of it. Jeanette deserved to be with a single Ex Dee woman who could give her kids; Carmela knew that, but she ached with the old, familiar unfairness of it all. Jeanette left her nothing, not even a justification for righteous anger. Nothing but the hollow ache in her chest.

And a sweater.

∽◯◯◯◯∾

They found an abandoned building with a slope of rubble leading down into the basement. After testing the way on foot, they drove the dune buggy down into relative safety. The basement was chambered like a heart, rooms connecting to one another directly, without hallways. They passed through the gaping, dark apertures of a couple of wide doorways, and Carmela wondered what the building had been designed for.

The floors were bare concrete, dusty and sandy. The room where they holed up had narrow, high windows, smudged with dirt to near-opacity and much too small for a person to fit through. The air was stifling, hot and stagnant, but the concrete would be cool when they lay down on it. Carmela nodded to herself, satisfied.

Without having to ask, Shannon filled a pot with water from one of the carboys and took out some food rations to start them rehydrating. Carmela leaned against the side of the dune buggy and stretched her stiff knee, watching Shannon. It had been a while

Shannon rolled his eyes. "Think about it. What do I got in abundance that everybody wants? The New Tucson repro center's got to be more'n a hundred kilometers away."

"What? You—you can't!" Carmela was abruptly afraid, but it came out sounding like anger. "That's too dangerous! If anyone finds out about you—"

"Relax, I didn't tell them who it came from."

"And I didn't save your ass out in the desert just so some Tucsonite can rat you out to the border patrol for the price of a pint of water."

"It's going to be fine," Shannon said, turning quiet and serious. "I can pay you back, now."

೩೪೫೯

Carmela knew she shouldn't stare.

The little girl's short, black hair stuck up from her head in all directions, each braid ending with a brightly-colored plastic clip.

With the seemingly preternatural protectiveness common to all parents, the girl's mother swiveled in her seat to catch Carmela's gaze. The woman looked wary, hawkish, but as she took in the lines of gray beginning to streak Carmela's hair, the crow's feet at the corners of her eyes, her expression shifted to one of pity.

Carmela clenched her teeth together, suddenly furious, though she wasn't sure whether she was mad at the woman for pitying her or at herself for staring at the girl in the first place.

She would dye her hair black and get the wrinkles taken care of, she decided, and she would stop staring at other people's little girls.

೩೪೫೯

"It was better when I was younger. I mean, it's not like they stamp it on your forehead or anything. But at my age . . . with no kids? Everybody knows." Carmela sighed. "I'm just sick of people looking at me like I'm a walking corpse."

They were at the water station, refilling an empty carboy. Carmela leaned against the side of the pump, her right hand hovering near the pistol nestled in its leather thigh-holster. The station had a handful of guards, but she had learned not to be too trustful.

"Do you still want a kid?" Shannon asked, as he hooked up the water filter. "I mean, you did save my life; it's the least I could do."

"No," Carmela shook her head. "I'm over it. I just want to live someplace where people don't look at me like that. South of the border, there's whole communes of people who've never even gotten a GID. You know that?"

"That's what the word is. You speak Spanish?"

"Claro que sí," she said. *"Y tú?"*

"Más o menos." He smirked. "Anyway, I guess I'll learn pretty quick. Don't really have another option."

They lapsed into silence. Carmela worried about how a white boy with a handful of Spanish would get along by himself south of the border. How long could he possibly last? Even if he made it to Sierra Pinacate, which didn't seem terribly likely. It was before noon, and his face already shone with a persistent slick of sweat. The desert did not treat travelers gently.

After a few minutes, he quietly said, "It used to be a boy's name, too. Shannon." He kept his hands busy with the water filter. "Least, that's what my mom told me."

"Must've been something, trying to keep you hid." She couldn't begin to imagine how it would be done.

"Yeah, she was pretty much a force of nature. A real 'if there's a will, there's a way' kind of person."

Carmela noted the "was," but didn't comment on it. She cleared her throat. "Well, I think we should hole up until the worst of the heat's passed. You can get some sleep and head out by twilight. Safer at night if you're going on foot, you know."

"I'll be fine," he said, and Carmela wondered who he thought he was fooling. "Really."

She bit her cheek against a sharp retort. Better for them to part quietly, with the fatal truths left unmentioned. Abandoning people was, after all, a talent Carmela had cultivated.

ೋ ❀ ೋ

"**I** don't know, Rosa. Maybe I'll just keep driving. I've heard nice things about Monterrey . . . or maybe Veracruz," Carmela joked, smiling. She took another drawer from her dresser, dumped the contents on her bed, and began sorting through them.

"This is serious!" snapped Rosita. "You've seen the reports coming out of Los Angeles. There's no government in So Cal anymore, it's all water barons and highway robbers down there."

"No need to get all dramatic about it." She threw a pair of nice khakis onto the Salvation Army pile. "I'll trade the car for an off-road vehicle before I hit L.A., then head east. I can steer clear of So Cal altogether and cross the border near Old Tucson."

"Hey, Mama gave you that!" Rosita cried, snatching a green cardigan with frilly cuffs off the pile of clothes to be donated. She hugged it to her chest indignantly.

Carmela sighed. "I can't take everything. It doesn't fit me, anyway."

Softly, Rosita said, "But I liked being able to borrow it."

"Well, you can just have it, and then you won't have to borrow it anymore."

"It won't be the same."

Carmela put her hands on her hips, not knowing whether to feel exasperated or touched. "You've got your own family now. You don't need me for anything."

Still clutching the cardigan but with an air of defeat, Rosita turned to go. In the doorway, she said, "I'll always need you, *mi hermana.*"

"You'll be fine," Carmela said. *You'll be fine if I go, but I won't if I stay.*

When she inverted the last drawer over her bed, the sweater that had been stuffed in the bottom landed on top. Jeanette's sweater. What should she do with it? She would have no use for cashmere where she was headed.

⊲⊱⊰⊳

The afternoon sun blazed with a scorching, blistering heat that penetrated into the deepest shadows, turning their hideout into a hotbox. The desiccated air kept Carmela's skin dry, but her evaporated sweat left salt behind, stinging her wind-chapped face.

Crouching beside the dune buggy, she flipped the latch and lifted the lid of her sand-worn steamer trunk. Slowly, she began unpacking: dry rations and cooking supplies, an electric lantern, rolled-up clothes that were stuffed around the bulkier items. Searching, digging. And there it was, hidden at the bottom—her one frivolous possession, using up precious space that should be assigned to something more practical.

She took out the cashmere sweater. The scent of Jeanette's perfume was long gone, but she lifted the fabric close to her nose and imagined that she could still smell it. There were some things she couldn't let go. If she tried, she'd leave a piece of herself behind with them. She folded the sweater carefully and tucked it away again.

Carmela meticulously repacked the trunk, stood, and dusted off her knees. She walked over to where Shannon lay sleeping and looked down at him, his sunburned cheeks and scraggly brown hair and cracked lips, parted slightly to breathe. Reaching into her pocket, she fished for the dune buggy's starter key. She had wasted enough time in Old Tucson.

Loudly, Carmela said, "Rise and shine, kid."

He groaned and cracked an eyelid, looking up at her with confusion. "What?"

She dropped the starter key on his chest. "*Vámonos*. It's a long drive to Sierra Pinacate, and you've got first shift at the wheel."

Modern tools and the ability to use them give even the old-fashioned a leg up in a competitive world.

HEART OF STONE

by Joel Richards

I didn't have to stick around for the memorial service. The obituary had listed the cause of death as aortic valve calcification, and that made it beyond dumb to do so. That obit would get results fast, and I was clearly electing to live with the consequences.

The room was filling up, and it made good viewing. Conrad Wilkerson had done his bad, perhaps evil, work in high establishment circles, and that made for fashionable mourners. The paladins of North American power and money made up this assemblage, but the suits and dresses had French and Italian lines and labels. The secret service guys were an austere counterpoint. Their suits looked like they had been cut from the same bolt of cloth, and perhaps they were. The tailoring was designed to conceal holsters rather than excess flesh.

Before us and chatting with a Supreme Court justice and the attorney general was the officiant, minister to an inside-the-Beltway congregation and a television constituency that extended his reach into the national consciousness. Silver hair went well with the robes and the position. The minister had that, and a tongue to match. I was looking forward to the burnish he would put on a life of naked steel, wielded ruthlessly.

A whiff of Florentine cologne preceded the visuals. I was looking from my seat at a pinstriped Brioni pant leg. I brought my gaze up to French cuffs secured by silver links in a studded shield motif. Higher still was the face. It featured strong planes of prominent cheekbones, and piercing eyes whose intensity would always fall short of mine. His hair was gold, lined with silver in tight short curls that hugged his scalp.

I had never seen that face before. Of course not. I had won the last round, and this was the new avatar.

"Hello, Percy," I said.

"Ah," he said, and settled into the empty seat I had saved beside me. "I guessed right the first time."

"I didn't try to make it difficult," I said.

"No you didn't. And I'm beginning to wonder why."

"Later," I said. The minister was signaling for quiet, and the sound of high-voltage babble was starting to die down. "Time to reflect a bit on mortality."

He smiled and turned his gaze forward.

The service was brief. The minister did a polished job of summarizing the superficials of a life of industrial empire-building, crowned by a too-short venture into public life. The empire was in the realm of defense contracting, building what the government would label weapons of mass destruction when amassed by its enemies. The mourners heard none of that. Nor did they hear of the solicitation and sale (through sham offshore subsidiaries) of those same weapons to this country's avowed enemies. They were told of thousands of jobs created at home, nothing of the tens of thousands of lives obliterated abroad. They heard of philanthropic gifts of millions from an estate of billions. They heard of the friendships with black, Hispanic and Asian industrialists and politicians—many here today—of a man whose social clubs never had more than token representation.

And then the family. The fine, upstanding helpmeet, sitting stoically in the front row, an example to her children, who looked more cowed than in mourning. Her face and rigid body were already settling into the role of a monument to dedication. How many servants and personages, of whatever rank, had been broken on contact with that marmoreal splendor! But she couldn't match me in splendor of a more sensuous measure, nor in the excitement I had offered her husband.

The minister finished with further embellishments on the theme of a life cut short—the cabinet appointment of two years ago, the talk of a run for the Senate in furtherance not of vanity but of the advancement of principals that remained mysteriously unarticulated.

We rose at the end, and Percy turned towards me. "Your place or mine for our business?"

"Ever the man of action, Percy. I've made myself easy to find. Now indulge me. Let's have a drink at the bar and catch up."

Percy's responding smile was more of a grimace. But he couldn't force the issue with that heavy-duty security in place. He nodded.

The elevator to the downstairs lounge was a crush of forced intimacy. Percy's leg was jammed against mine. How strange to feel the press of Italian silk rather than a leather scabbard. Times had changed, and the object of this exercise and its outcome would rest on which of us had adapted better.

We found a dark and quiet booth at the rear of a lounge whose leather-dominated décor had not changed in decades. Percy sniffed appreciatively and patted his seat before sitting down. This was the real stuff, and I knew he would appreciate it. How he must have suffered in the naugahyde years of the seventies!

"It's been more than 150 years, I think. Delmonico's in the 1860s, wasn't it? This brings it back." He paused. "Thank you, Duse."

"You're getting perceptive, Percy. Even sensitive. That's a good sign."

The waiter appeared, took our order, and left. He was used to discussions of power and import and knew the value of a brief interruption.

"You were a Union cavalry officer then," I said. "Your last chance to wear a sword. What are you packing these days?"

"What the time and place allows and dictates."

"A gun," I said, and he nodded. "But not here."

"Of course not. I could never get it past security on this state occasion. No doubt you've been counting on that."

"And we're in a crowded room," I said. "I wouldn't imagine that you've figured out how to override your programming against performing in public."

"And you have? You've clearly adapted in some ways. That short wig couldn't conceal much. But, being Wilkerson's mistress, perhaps pubic hair would work as well."

"It won't do to turn men to stone in this age," I said. "Surely you realize that."

The waiter showed with our drinks. I admired the rich bourbon color as I raised my glass. "To adaptability, Percy. I've found another way."

He raised an eyebrow. "And you'll tell me?"

"I'll show you. Then you'll do your thing. That's the point, after all—at least as you still see it. But all in good time."

He nodded silently.

"But how about adaptiveness in the realm of behavioral psychology? Do you think this tableau must be played out every time we meet?"

"It's what we're fated for," he said.

I shook my head. "Percy, Percy. Fate. That's so old school. It's programming, and why act according to some long dead deity's will—century after century—if we can learn to override it? Minerva made me what I was. She took away my beauty and gave me a death-dealing power. But she's dead, and look at me now."

"You've got your beauty back, I will admit."

"And how about Orestes? Didn't he teach you something?"

He looked puzzled.

"The Furies were denied," I continued. "A new form of justice, tempered with mercy, emerged. Why should it stop there? I don't kill indiscriminately any more. Wilkerson was a man of power the gods might have loved. But he needed killing, I killed him, and there are no gods or Furies potent enough to stop or punish me."

"There is me," Percy said.

"I'd hoped you'd done some thinking and made some changes, but I suspect that thinking led only to a change in weaponry. Even there, you seem to have stalled out in the twentieth century. But this is the twenty-first. I'm disappointed, Percy."

"I don't know what you're talking about. I'm not a thinker, Duse. I'm a traditionalist and a man of action. You said so earlier."

"Too bad for you, then. If I'd seen progress, I'd spare you this time."

He smiled. "You're that sure you'll win this round?"

"Take a look, Percy." I set my elbow on the table and made a fist, flexing and rippling the muscles of my biceps. "I took back my beauty, but I've built up my strength. Without our artifacts, we're an even physical match. And beyond that I've adapted my powers to channels you haven't yet imagined."

He seemed more amused than impressed. "A superhero?"

"Biomorphism, Percy, not guns. I move with the times. Look at me again."

He did, and I opened my nictitating eyelids. He took my laser-enhanced gaze straight on, held by me in rigid stasis. I let him unlock after thirty seconds.

"Wilkerson got a lesser dose, over time," I said. "It took six weeks for the calcium to build up in his heart."

I stood up. "You'll last half an hour."

Living in a world to which people come to die creates great challenges, and one of those can be being vulnerable enough to love and choose life even in the face of death itself.

TOURIST TRAP

by Aimee C. Amodio

Another father whose name she wouldn't remember gave a nod, tears streaming down his cheeks. It was time to let the sea take the child.

Suicide-by-sea was the most peaceful passing available to those who could afford the trip to Endless Summer. This particular family had paid Visitor Medical Services well for the private tour boat and that particular guide.

Haryn [victory/survivor/h-symbol/first wave] pulled the deaffers off the boy and held them loosely in her hand. It didn't take long for the sea's song to catch the child, turn him in his mother's arms, and draw him out onto the thick spray shield on the edge of the boat. The father choked out a name. A grandparent murmured a curse or a prayer.

The boy didn't look back as he slipped over the rail.

&CR&&

Very few families lingered after a passing. Endless Summer was largely of interest to two types of people: those with the money to waste on an exotic vacation and those who needed a peaceful release from life.

Haryn left her charges at the main port to wipe their eyes and share comfort while they waited for the next ship out. She was halfway back to her boat when her AP throbbed for attention, then beat out the pattern of an urgent message.

Another tour. Immediate.

Her fingers flicked in a local expression of vulgar exasperation. Most of the tourists milling about wouldn't understand the gesture; another tour guide did and laughed sympathetically.

That told her the guide was a newcomer: he laughed aloud, rather than with his hands. Those who'd survived the first few colonization waves tended to use hand-speak almost exclusively among residents.

[Best-padded/job/here] he signed.

She flickered her fingers in amusement. [Best-padded/pockets but no-time/for-shopping]

Endless Summer had two main industries: tourism and water. Work in the water refineries was hard and thankless, reserved mainly for folks fresh off the ship who had to earn a precious scrap of land and criminals that nobody else in the system wanted to deal with. Working with tourists was thought of as cushy, but it was a job earned by years of hard labor.

Both industries kept the spaceports busy.

Haryn's AP pulsed again, signaling her to check the arrivals board. Her newest charge was landing.

∞

Processing was slow, boring, and rote.

"Welcome to Endless Summer. I am Haryn."

"I'm Zevach. Nice to meet you."

She acknowledged the pleasantry with a curt bob of her head. "By law I am required to review the information from your travel packet. Did you receive and review your travel packet en route?"

Haryn paused long enough for his assent, then continued the legal script over his attempt at conversation. They all tried to be friendly, to break the shell between tourist and guide.

"Your travel packet should have included a pair of deaffers." She indicated her own pair of noise-canceling headphones on a complicated arrangement of straps. "You will wear them at all times when you are outside of a sealed, soundproof room. They are your best defense against seasong."

Zevach pulled his deaffers out of a pocket and turned a helpless look on the tangle of straps. "Couldn't quite get them sorted out."

She deftly unknotted the stretchy material as she continued the legal spiel. "Once you leave the spaceport, you are officially classified as a Newcomer to Endless Summer. By law, any full-time free resident of this planet is allowed to command a Newcomer. This is for your own safety. You will immediately follow the orders of any resident, regardless of what you may think, feel, or want. If someone tells you to sit, you sit. If someone tells you to move, you move. Do you understand?" She lifted the deaffers and slipped them over his head, sliding the straps into position with the practice of many years.

He grinned. "Yes. Thank you."

Much of the lecture was designed to limit the legal liability of Visitor Medical Services—the largest tour sponsor on the planet—and scare off as many tourists as possible. It worked well enough on the casual travelers, and VMS still got to keep a sizable package deposit.

"The flight crew should have helped you with that." It was a departure from the script that she chalked up to being overworked and underslept. "They also should have fit you with a temporary Alert Pulse."

Zevach nodded. Alert Pulse. The locals had other names for it based on where it was placed. His AP was adhered to his lower back, low enough to be considered part of his gluteus maximus. The locals generally had theirs implanted.

"I will now test it for proper function." She touched the transmitter box clipped to her waistband and his AP throbbed. "For the duration of your stay on Endless Summer, the AP will be your most important form of communication. If you need to get someone's attention, use your transmitter. If you feel your AP go off, pay attention. Do not under any circumstances touch a native uninvited. Most residents consider an uninvited touch a serious offense." She eyed him for a moment. "I've seen arms broken over a tap on the shoulder." It was another departure from the script, but it earned her a smile.

"I'll keep that in mind," he said.

"Have you familiarized yourself with the handspeak included in your travel packet?" Most travelers said yes, but never did.

He opened his mouth to answer, thought better of it, and lifted a hand clenched into a fist: the handspeak for yes.

That earned him a small smile. "Most of your tour will be conducted aloud. The deaffers are designed to strip away seasong and other background noise before transmitting vocalizations. Still, there may be times when handspeak is useful. If you learn only one gesture, let it be this: deference/apology." Haryn pressed her palms together and brought her hands towards her chest. "If you piss someone off, you'd better start making this gesture so they don't kill you." A third departure from the script. She fully expected the VMS auditor to comment on it at her next review.

Zevach imitated the gesture.

"Keep your fingers pointed skyward. Thumbs together, not crossed." When he was groveling to her satisfaction, she nodded. "Once you leave the debarkation area, you are a Newcomer on Endless Summer for the duration of your stay. You are bound to follow the laws and customs outlined in your travel packet. If you choose to depart, a shuttle is ready to leave within the hour. Do you wish to continue?" She could pick a stayer from a quitter within thirty seconds of the spiel.

He raised his fist and backed up the gesture with the spoken word. Haryn gave a faint nod. No scaring this one off.

⋘⋙

The table in the hotel suite had been laid for breakfast. One wall of the sitting room was window, offering a panoramic view of the legendary singing seas of Endless Summer. Haryn sat with her back to the vista. Zevach occasionally remembered to eat as he stared.

"Will you teach me the symbol for your name?" Most Newcomers weren't good with silence. Haryn treasured it: every moment of silence meant she was still alive.

She gestured agreement and set her plate aside. Both hands sketched a series of figures in the air. As she repeated the sequence more slowly, she explained each part. "Victory and survivor, because I fought for my place here. It's more a title than an actual part of my name. The h-symbol because my spoken name is Haryn. And the last part signifies when I arrived on the planet." She said the last in a tone designed to discourage questions.

He asked anyway.

"I was in the first wave of colonists."

The travel packet informed vacationers in a distant, clinical way that many of the colonists in the first and second waves of settlement hadn't survived when the sea woke up and started singing. The few who resisted the siren call had carved out silent spaces to protect future arrivals.

Uncomfortable with the question, Haryn fell back into the safety of rote tour guide script. "Today will be your first encounter with the sea. I am required by law to review the information from your travel packet before you leave this room."

He nodded and forked up a mouthful of compote made from imported fruits. Tourists always ate well.

"The singing seas of Endless Summer are alive. The water is populated with organisms that in certain numbers can produce a sound that resonates with the human brain. It acts as an aural sedative. Within seconds of hearing the seasong, the average person will be drawn towards the water." Her tone made it clear that she thought everyone was sub-average. "The water itself is not caustic to the human body. As the music lulls you into a state of contentment, the organisms will be digesting your flesh. Burning will feel like bliss, and you will continue to walk forward even as your body disintegrates. The sea can consume an adult male within minutes."

Haryn let that digest as she took a bite of bread. Processed algae, dried and powdered for baking. [You/eat/me, I/eat/you.] Underneath the table, her fingers moved through the refrain of the survivors.

ఴᏨᎡᏰᏰ

S he stood at the controls of the boat, giving him the opportunity to admire the expanse of the ocean, the colorful clouds on the horizon, or the sunlight gleaming off the receding spires of the resort. But he wasn't looking at the views. Haryn could feel his gaze in the prickle between her shoulder blades. She indulged herself in a tiny sigh, quiet enough that it wouldn't trigger the deaffers to transmit the noise as conversation.

Racing over the waves was usually one of her favorite parts of a tour. Even the dance and snap of her long, sun-bleached braid in the wind couldn't crack her foul mood.

The plait caught on something, and she glanced back. Zevach was lunging forward, hand outstretched toward her head. The tail end of her braid slipped through his fingers.

Haryn whirled, white rage flaring behind her eyes. One hand went to his wrist to block; the other caught him under the chin. Off guard and off balance, he fell backwards into the bottom of the boat.

"You don't touch them. Not ever!" The receiver went to work, stripping the seasong out of the transmission and directing it to his deaffers. "They're life and death out here. Anybody else would break your wrist for it."

The moves had been automatic, self-defense. The words had exploded out of her, accompanied by a blur of handspeak the tourist wouldn't follow. But even through the adrenaline and anger, she could see the moment when he finally understood: the deaffers. Even if he had intended play, the move could have dislodged her ear protection, leaving her vulnerable to the ocean's song.

"You want my attention, you use the AP." The first heat of anger settled into a cold fury. Hands clenched into fists, she turned back to the boat controls.

She felt the thrum of the AP at the small of her back. When she turned, Zevach made the gesture of deference and apology, then fumbled his way through her name.

Her hands tightened on the boat's controls, knuckles white. Even in play, it could have meant her life. Still, he was trying. He seemed willing to learn.

Her fingers flicked a gesture that looked like dismissal: [Needless.]

ଔଔଔ

She couldn't sleep. Every night, they parted ways: Zevach to his cushy hotel suite, Haryn to the austere cell used by tour guides. Same hotel, but a world away in feel. The suite was soft, and warm, and welcoming, with expansive views of the ocean. The cell was spare, bare, and uncomfortable, even in the most generous of descriptions.

On every other tour she'd given, Haryn had no trouble falling asleep on the lumpy mattress, in the narrow bed.

It was Zevach keeping her awake. She could admit it to herself in the dark, fingers whispering out a conversation she couldn't see. It was all the questions he asked. Not the usual tourist questions. He had a terrible habit of asking sharp questions that poked through the shell that divided her from off-worlders. He asked things that drilled past Haryn-the-guide and tricked her out of the comfortable routine of tourspeak.

What did she want for herself after her guide days were over? Would she ever leave Endless Summer? Did she think about the families of the seacides she had guided? Did anyone ever come back to commemorate the passing of their loved ones?

They were the sort of questions no tourist ever asked before. On every other tour, she'd made it impossible to crack the tourspeak routine.

Zevach smiled, slow and lazy. "Yes. Because you understand. You love and hate and respect the ocean as much as they do."

She narrowed her eyes; her fingers spelled out a curse on the boat's controls. "You do it, then. If you have enough money to waste on a tour, you've got enough to buy a plot."

There would be no more gathering the bits of shell and walling herself up inside, after that. He'd had too good a look inside.

ೞ૭൧ЄᎤൔ

Hours later, long after he'd done his snooping and they'd gone to bed, Haryn woke alone. She found him outside the soundproof suite, tied to the balcony railing with his deaffers on the deck.

"I have given many to the sea," she raged, double-checking the seals on the door before taking off her deaffers. Zevach was wild-eyed, blinking uncomprehendingly. "None quite as stupid as you." Her fingers flicked vulgarities, far stronger words than stupid.

"I wanted to . . ." He shook his head slowly. Haryn knew from experience how the seasong would be echoing in his memory. "I needed to hear it."

More expletives. "Why?"

"To see if I was strong enough."

That set her off again, storming around the room with her hands flying.

"Haryn, if you want to yell at me, you'll have to talk." His voice was calm, but distant. His attention kept drifting back to the sea beyond the window.

"You have something to prove? It's a test, a game to tie yourself out there and listen to the song. You never had to watch your friends walk into the water and sing with you while they were being eaten. Never! You come here for adventure and novelty and leave again for the next one. One thrill after another. But you're not—" She cut herself short with a hand at her mouth.

"I'm not what?" His gaze finally found hers.

"You're not a lot of things." She sighed, fingers speaking the things she couldn't say aloud. [Not first/wave. Not/native.]

He must have recognized enough symbols from her name to start to understand. "Too many people left you." Colonists, seacides, thrill-seeking tourists. "I could stay."

Hand and voice spoke the negative. "What, for the song? You can't play with the ocean. It always wins. But you don't get that. You've seen every scar on my body, every place the ocean has tasted, and still you play games with the song. You think you're stronger than it is? You think you're stronger than me?"

Haryn whirled and went to the balcony doors. She slapped her palm on the control and broke the seal to let the oceansong in.

The pull at her chest was familiar. The desire to follow family and friends into the water was a constant companion. The promise of bliss was an old temptation. Haryn took the first step forward before she could command her body otherwise.

Muscles quivering, hand gripping the door frame, she turned to watch Zevach rise from the couch and cross the room. In just a few steps, he was close enough to touch. She wrapped her free arm around him, holding them both back from the ocean.

Her lips were at his ear as she spoke, louder than the song only by proximity. "I have given too many to the sea because they wished it. If you want to be let go, just ask."

The song battered at her common sense. She fought it with the faces of friends from the first and second waves of colonists, people she'd worked with, struggled with, and loved. Too many gone to the sea.

"The ocean has already taken everything that mattered from me," she said, her lips tickled by his short, dark hair. "I will give you away, too, if that's what you want." Someday, when she had no more anger or hurt to throw at the song, she would give herself to the ocean.

While the sea sang, she whispered the name of every person she'd lost into the water. Colonists first, then tourists—some who'd been there specifically for seacide and some who'd just been stupid or careless or fearless. As much as she wanted to forget, she remembered every one who had died.

The last two names in the litany—his and her own—were cut off by an urgent pulse from her AP. Her fingers flexed on him, squeezing out curses she didn't speak as she dragged them both back into silence.

⊰⊱

"**W**hy didn't you tell me?" The pulse had been from Visitor Medical Services.

Zevach—for once—had no words.

VMS generally only called during a tour for one reason: to confirm or deny clearance for suicide-by-sea.

"You came here to die." Her voice was hoarse, a combination of overuse, rage, and unshed tears.

"Maybe. Yes." He trailed off, fumbling for the truth. "I knew I was sick. I didn't know how long I'd have."

It had to be her imagination, but she could hear the ocean under his words. Haryn exhaled a long breath and threw herself into an armchair. "Why here?" It was a question she had never asked any of her tourists.

Zevach crossed the room in a few steps and crouched in front of the chair. "I've been waiting for that question from my family, my friends. You're the first to ask." He smiled, heavy shadows showing beneath his eyes. "I wanted to be able to choose. I don't want to be scared and hurting. I want to go with joy."

Joy was something she had never associated with the living ocean, luring friends and family into its hungry depths with a siren song.

⊰⊱

Less than a week later, he woke her in the middle of the night. "I'm ready now."

The dock was quiet. The sky was quiet. Under the protection of the deaffers, everything was silent; yet all around them was a sense of life. The ocean, ever moving. A light breeze stirring the hair. The stars dotted across the stretch of sky.

Zevach noticed small details, murmuring them to her through the deaffers. The way the deck vibrated beneath his feet, even though he couldn't hear the engine. The wisps of hair that continually escaped her long braid. The shimmering spray kicked up by the boat's passage and deflected away by the wide saucer around the perimeter. The play of starlight on ripples of wake.

Haryn noticed the big details, but didn't voice them: how dark the sky was between stars. How much it hurt that he was leaving.

"What are you going to do now?" The deaffers stripped out the seasong and sent his words across the deck, an intimate whisper.

Haryn shrugged, fingers moving automatically through the survivor's refrain. [You/eat/me, I/eat/you.] The unending cycle. A prayer, a curse, a way of life.

He moved forward to stand beside her at the console. "You could do something else." Haryn wasn't sure if he was trying to be funny. "You could go somewhere else."

She blinked at him, hands moving. The look of incomprehension on his face had her speaking, instead. "This is all I have." He didn't look convinced, so she tried again. "Can you see me fitting anywhere else? I have fought for this, and this is home."

ଓଔଞ୭୭

Eventually, she stopped the boat and let them drift.

"Do it, Haryn, while I'm still brave enough. I wait any longer, I'm going to back out and waste away." Zevach leaned in, touching his forehead to hers.

She waited a breath, studying his eyes as if they held the answer. Maybe he had been giving her answers all along, breaking down her shell so she would be ready to move on. To build something new. A place for healing.

few more hours before she would be home, where a rare treat awaited her. She was going to eat steak tonight—real beef steak, not soy byproducts or compressed vegetable matter, but real meat. She hadn't had a real steak in . . . she couldn't remember exactly when it had been. The failure of so many farms and ranches made such delicacies expensive. This one time, though, she had saved enough to indulge herself.

She could almost hear it sizzling under the broiler. She imagined the aroma and the flavor of the meaty juices as they flowed over her lips. She had some seasonings somewhere. She'd—

"Leander? Where are you?" A familiar voice interrupted her culinary reverie. "It's always so darn dark down here. Violet, are you down here?"

It was Walt, one of the roving security monitors. He came to the basement whenever he wanted to take an unofficial break. He was a misguided oaf who jabbered incessantly, but Violet endured his visits because . . . well, because they helped break up her day. Besides, she didn't have much choice.

"Of course I'm here, Walt. Where do you think I'd be?"

"I dunno," Walt said, lumbering down the stairs. "Sometimes they got you cleaning upstairs. Oh, there you are. It takes a while for my eyes to adjust."

Walt sat at the foot of the stairs, as he usually did, and pulled out a candy bar. Violet was continually amazed that the stench never affected his appetite. "It's sure a hot one today," he said as Violet continued to work her mop. "You're lucky you're down here where it's cool. It's a zoo upstairs. They're always busier when it's hot. The crooks come out of the woodwork when the weather's like this—God forgive them. You know this world would be a better place if everyone found God. You too, Violet. You'd look at things a whole lot different if your spirit hooked up with the Holy Ghost."

Violet ignored Walt's spiel, as she always did. She strained to visualize the steak again, but couldn't concentrate. It wasn't long before she found herself tuning into the pious windbag's diatribe.

". . . ozone's getting worse. Them radiation levels, or whatever they call 'em, are going up. I heard a report there'll be even more mutants being born because of it. As it is now, Beth and I don't let the kids out 'til after sundown. But where's it safe to let kids play after dark with all those hunger riots?

"Hey! I've got a new family photo, one of them 3-D jobs. Here, take a look."

Violet stopped her mopping and pretended to glance at the picture, but she didn't want to see Walt's family. She didn't want to be reminded.

"See, that's little Timmy and Peggy Ann, and me and Beth, of course. You got any family, Violet?"

"No!"

The terse reply silenced Walt for a moment, but it didn't keep him quiet long. "Yeah, I guess I asked you that before. You know, children can be a real blessing, Violet. Of course, Beth and I thought long and hard before we decided to have kids. What with all the mutants being born and the Antarean refugees crowding in everywhere. Our alien brothers do tend to be extremely prolific— God bless them. But we prayed over it and decided that God put us on this world to be fruitful and multiply, so what the heck."

"Damn aliens and their droids are everywhere," said Violet. "You can't walk down the street without bumping into one. It's not as if we don't already have enough immigrants from all the gutter countries."

"I know what you mean, Violet. Though it's not very charitable of me to say, I'm sure our offworld visitors are contributing to all the shortages. It seems like our monthly allotment is never enough. Just last week one of them random blackouts hit Timmy's school, and they sent all the kids home. You used to be a teacher, didn't you?"

Violet flashed him a look that said she wasn't going to answer, so Walt went on.

"You know, I understand some of those Antareans have heard the word of God. Born again right here on Earth. It's enough to make a man get down on his knees and shout 'Hallelujah!' I truly believe in live and let—"

Walt's com-flap squawked with static at that moment, and Violet was tempted to thank a deity herself.

"Walt, you there?"

"Right here. What's up?"

"We've got a toilet gone berserk on the fifth floor. The whole place is flooded. Go down to the basement and get Leander up here."

"I'm on it." Walt stood up. "Well, you heard him, Violet. Looks like they need you upstairs, and that means my break is over." Walt started back up the stairs and Violet jammed her mop into the water bucket. The only thing she hated more than cleaning up garbage was cleaning up after filthy degenerates.

ᘓᑫᔥᕟᔥᘙ

Emerging from the Hall of Justice, Violet traded the reek of garbage for the grimy smell of smog and the stink of dried urine. Outside, a familiar billboard greeted her—a monstrous sign, 80 feet above ground and a good 50 feet across. It featured a well-covered citizen, a blazing sun, and the warning "Mega Watts not Mega Burns." It was an old sign, one that seemed superfluous now.

The real sun was about to drop below the horizon, and the tableau of reds, yellows, and oranges combined with the smoggy haze to give the city a hellish hue. To shield herself from its lurid glare, Violet covered her eyes with dark glasses and stepped out into the teeming multitude. Compared to the basement's quiet seclusion, the clamor was almost deafening. It was all she could do not to cover both ears with her hands and shout for silence.

The streets reminded Violet, more than anything else, of where she was and what she'd lost. Sidewalks swarming with humanity and its galactic offshoots, streets choked with bikers, skaters, and all manner of rollerboarders. She despised them all. The crush of bodies was even more overwhelming, considering only those who had to be out would be. Those who could, would remain inside the safety of their homes. Streeters would be seeking shelter in whatever shady refuge they could find. They wouldn't come out until dark, when hunger drove them like rats.

It was still hot outside, much hotter than Violet remembered from the June evenings of her childhood. She wondered if it was the dwindling ozone, or only her fading memory. But there were things she didn't want to remember, so she didn't wonder for long. Street vendors and pedi-cabbies and beggars called to her. She ignored their mercenary cries and hurried to catch the next solarbus. As she pressed through the wall of bodies to get in line, her skin began to itch; it always did in such proximity. Too many people. Too many germs. A festering population of cranks and freaks and wireheads. She cursed them and wished they'd all go back to where they came from.

Ahead she saw a woman with sunken nostrils and no lips. Violeet thought she also might have a third breast, but couldn't be sure. The sight of the mutant was all the reminder she needed to turn up her coat collar. Like everyone else on the street, she was fully covered despite the heat. Hats, umbrellas, overcoats had all become commonplace with the rise in solar radiation.

Violet reached under her tattered cap and scratched at the itch behind her ear. As she did, someone bumped into the mutant woman, or perhaps she tripped and fell on her own.

She didn't say a word or make a sound, and the dense flow of pedestrian traffic kept moving around her, creating a momentary pocket. Violet hurried by, pretending not to notice.

She got into line as a group of children who'd disembarked from the solarbus passed by. Her eyes scanned their faces, a bit too eagerly, trying to see through the shadows created by their little parasols. But she didn't see who she was looking for. She never did. She scratched her neck and shuffled forward a few feet as the line gained momentum. She tried to concentrate on what awaited her at home—tried to ignore the stifling throng. It was what she did every day. Even those days when she had nothing to go home to.

03CRSO80

Violet took a deep breath and released it as she closed the door behind her. Her hunched shoulders relaxed as if she were tired of holding them up. She activated the door's locking mechanism and set the alarm.

The day had faded, and there was little light coming through her solitary window, so she reached up and began to furiously rub the glowbulb in the wall next to the door. The friction soon built up enough of a charge for some faint illumination.

The heat inside was oppressive, but she knew she couldn't afford the air conditioner's drain on her allotment. She began peeling off layers of clothing, all the while trying to convince herself it wasn't that hot.

She thought about the meal awaiting her, the steak she would broil to perfection. As she disrobed, she walked to her tiny bedroom and dropped the clothes onto the bed. She looked at the picture frame on the wall, as she always did. It was a nice frame, with an intertwining black and gold design—expensive, and empty.

She kept meaning to take it down, but she could never bring herself to do it. Each time she looked at it, she tried to imagine Kevin's face. However, with each passing week, the mental picture she carried of her son grew a little less vivid.

A crashing clatter from outside her window, followed by the bellow of an argument, caught her attention. Most of the time she was able to block out the steady hum of street noise, but at times it was too loud to ignore. She decided to utilize a portion of her allotment on some music. That wouldn't expend much energy. She chose a soothing ensemble of woodwinds and waterfalls, and went to the kitchen.

She rubbed up another glowbulb until it had a good static charge and opened the refrigerator. There it was, not too large, but worth every dollar she'd spent. She began unwrapping it, inexplicably gratified by the thick texture of the butcher paper. Her nostrils caught the faint, almost forgotten smell of beef, and she began to imagine how it would taste with the salad and red potatoes she'd saved to go with it. It was the first steak she'd had since . . . since Alan had taken Kevin and gone away. He'd told her the city was too crowded, too infested with criminals and perverts, but she'd insisted she couldn't leave her job. She told him teaching positions were hard to come by, and that her job gave them some security. She hadn't realized how determined he was, how little he must have cared about her. Damn him! He'd taken everything, even all their pictures.

The grim joke was, she'd been so distraught over losing her husband and son, she'd lost her coveted job. That was more than two years ago, and she was still looking at empty picture frames and keeping the world at a bitter distance.

A little garlic salt, she thought, some pepper, a dash of cumin if she had any. Most nights she wouldn't bother much with dinner. She'd radiate some pre-packaged, ready-to-serve meal and be done with it. Tonight, though, would be different. Tonight it would be a labor of love.

When she was done preparing the steak she placed it gently in the oven, punched the broiler setting, selected medium rare, and turned to prepare the rest of the meal. Almost immediately the music stopped and she heard a familiar dying whine issuing from the refrigerator. She'd lost power.

A quick glance out her window told her it wasn't a regional blackout, so Violet hurried to her residential powerpack and discovered her last cell completely drained. She cursed the world and slammed the powerpack as if she could she could bash it back to life. Still two more days until she'd get next month's allotment, and, without refrigeration, the steak would spoil. And even if it wouldn't, she didn't want to wait two days. She'd thought of nothing but that steak all day, and she was going to eat it tonight if she had to break up her furniture and burn her books. She was angry enough to do it—but the building's flame sensors would have immediately doused her cooking fire and sounded an alarm for which she would pay a sizable fine. You couldn't even burn a candle in the city any longer without special dispensation. She wanted to lash out and break something, hurt someone. Life had become a multi-limbed miscreation that bound and suffocated her, whipped her until the pain made her numb. It was the numbness that reminded her how useless her outrage was.

There was only one thing she could do. She figured she might have enough money to buy a power cell. She'd never bought a blackmarket cell before, though she knew it was a common, if illegal, transaction. She wasn't sure exactly where to go or who to ask, but she knew someone on the street would be selling. She hated the idea of going outside. It was bad enough during the day. At night it was no place for a civilized person. But she was going to eat that steak if it was the last thing she ever did.

෴

The sun had retreated, and the low-pressure sodium lamps lining the streets had begun to shed their orange pall over the city. There were still plenty of people out, but most were streeters with nowhere else to go. More and more began to emerge from their daylight havens. As their empty bellies began to growl, Violet knew they would gather and grumble and fume. Emboldened by numbers, they would spread through some unlucky neighborhood, demanding food that was not theirs, food they had not worked for. She didn't have much, but at least she earned what she had.

It was a warm night, like so many nights seemed to be now, and most of the people Violet saw had shed their protective daylight apparel for less modest garb. Now that they could display their wares, a host of tawdry hookers had taken up positions along the sidewalks. From what Violet could see, business was brisk.

Squads of police began arriving at standard staging areas, encased in protective body armor, carrying tear gas launchers and stun weapons. They ignored the hookers. They had more volatile problems to deal with. Maybe Alan had been right. Maybe she should have quit her job and left this festering hellhole of humanity. Maybe . . . but it was too late for maybes. He and Kevin were gone, and she was here.

The moon peeked over the horizon, bright with the promise of cool radiance. With sunlight now toxic, the moon's glow had become a symbol of purity. It was even the focal point of a new religion. *Just what the world needed,* Violet had thought scornfully when she read about the Lunarians and their rituals, *more crazies.*

She fought against her own repulsion to approach several strangers, but the conversations proved fruitless. They either couldn't help her or wouldn't. She was ignored or brushed-off or threatened. They were animals, and she detested them all.

Just when she thought her spite might get the best of her, a woman walked out of the shadows, adjusting her minimal skirt. It was obvious to Violet she was selling it . . . or *he* was. One look at the size of her arms and Violet wasn't quite sure—another pervert.

"Hi, honey," she purred, "want to have some fun?"

"No thanks," growled Violet, still trying to decide what might be under the skirt. "I'm looking to buy a power cell. Do you know where I can, uh, get one?"

"You don't need no juice, deary. I can give a charge right here." She moved closer as if to touch her.

Violet did a quick backpedal.

"No, sorry, no."

"Okay," the woman said, her sugary inflection replaced with boredom. "You want Roblevo. He's always got juice for a price."

"Where can I find this Roblevo?" "Down there, honey," she said, pointing, "corner of Mollison and Third. He always shows up there sooner or later."

ଔଓଈଓଃଔ

When she arrived at the intersection she saw a street vendor unsuccessfully promoting his wares to a passing couple. Violet hesitated, then walked up to the vendor.

"Are you Roblevo?" she asked.

"No, can't say that I am," replied the vendor jauntily from behind his portable stand. "The name's McCloud—Big Loud McCloud to my friends and clients. The Roblevo you seek does hang in these parts. No doubt he'll be along soon. But in the meantime, friend, let me show you the latest in solar powered timepieces." He held up a wristwatch that didn't look much different than any watch Violet had ever seen.

"I don't need a watch," said Violet sullenly.

"This isn't just a watch, madam. No, this is not the antiquated sundial of your glorious ancestors. This is a chronometer of the finest caliber, featuring the latest technological advances acquired during mankind's quest for the stars. This scientific wonder not only calculates the time for any time zone on or off planet, it can do so in four different languages. Meanwhile, it's keeping tabs on your heart rate, blood pressure, body temperature, and—"

"I said don't need a watch," Violet interjected abruptly. She wished this Roblevo fellow would show up soon. She was getting hungry, and she didn't like being outside so long.

"I understand, friend," the vendor continued, undeterred. "You're obviously a woman who isn't ruled by time. Not to fear, I have a wide assortment of items for your perusal.

"Perhaps a pocket pouch made of the finest synthetic leather, or one of these handcrafted dolls for your child? No? I have concert tickets, theater tickets, tickets to balls and ballgames. I have—"

"Do you have any power cells?" asked Violet, interrupting the spiel again.

"I am shocked and chagrined, madam," the vendor said with as much sincerity as he could muster. "Surely you know the unauthorized sale of P-cells is illegal. Big Loud McCloud is a reputable merchant who adheres strictly to all civil and moral codes.

"Perhaps, though, I can interest you in the power of the Lord, good miss. I have some pocket bibles printed on the highest quality paper, guaranteed to provide you with spiritual enlightenment up until the day you receive the call."

Violet shook her head and impatiently shifted her feet.

"I'll tell you what, friend. With any purchase, I will give you, free-of-charge, a personal aura reading. Surely I must have something you'd like to take home with you."

"Aura? What aura?"

"Your aura, friend, is the light of your soul. During a spiritual journey I once took through Tibet, I learned how to read and interpret the aura that envelops each of us. And I must say, friend, the dark gray hue of yours is a might distressing. Are you ill?"

"I don't want anything, and I don't want my aura read!" snapped Violet. "I just want to find a power cell and get home."

"You lookin' for juice?"

Violet turned at the sound of a bellowing voice. A hulk of a man stood there, his long, thick arms dangling at his sides. There was a dull expression on his face, and his clothes looked like something a streeter would throw away.

"Well, you lookin' for juice or what?"

His size and demeanor made Violet a little apprehensive. "Yes, I need a power cell. Are you Roblevo?" The expressionless giant didn't reply, but he motioned for Violet to follow him.

As she trailed behind the brute, wondering if she were being foolish, Violet noticed the dark street getting even darker. She looked up and saw a thick cloud bank moving in, blanketing the sky and blotting out the moonlight.

The giant stranger led her a short distance to a spot where there were few people about. Waiting for them was an Antarean. It was shorter than Violet, though its diamond-shaped head gave it the appearance of being taller. It was leaning against a wall, smoking a cigar.

The fact that it stood on two tentacles and waved the other two about like arms didn't make it any more human in Violet's eyes. She fought back an impulse to turn and flee, and choked off a cough when she got close enough to smell it—not the cigar, the Antarean. They all had that same smell.

"Lookin' for juice," said the giant, taking up a position behind and to the left of the Antarean.

"Roblevo," said the voice from the alien's mobile translator. *"What may I do you for?"*

"I need some wattage for a residential power pack," said Violet.

"How much you need?" asked the Antarean, its grotesque mouth wrapped about the cigar as its translator did all the talking.

"Just one power cell."

One of the thing's thick black tentacles reached into its pouch and pulled out a cell. It extended the cell to Violet, who took it gingerly, cringing when her fingers brushed against the clammy, scaled appendage. She looked it over. "How do I know it's fully charged?"

The Antarean stared at her for a moment, its two black eyes burning with what alien emotions Violet couldn't begin to guess. *"How does . . ."* Static squawked from the translator. The Antarean reached up and slapped it. *"How does the wind know which way to blow? How does a chicken know how to fly?"*

Violet shifted her feet uneasily. "Chickens don't really fly," she said.

The Antarean moved closer, tilting its pointy skull slightly towards Violet. *"How do you know I won't have my friend Geek here cut your throat and take your money?"*

Violet glanced nonchalantly to her left, trying to determine a direction in which to run. "How much?" she asked, her voice trembling.

"Twenty."

"Twenty?" repeated Violet. "For one cell?"

"It's primo juice," said the Antarean, seeming to shrug its version of shoulders.

Violet didn't want to argue. She paid for the cell and moved on.

In her haste to get away from the Antarean and its henchman, she didn't pay attention to where she was going. It wasn't long before she realized she was lost. She wasn't used to being on the streets, especially at night, and now she was completely turned around.

As she searched for a familiar landmark she heard something behind her. Had the Antarean sent the one called Geek to follow her and take the rest of her money? *It would be just like an Antarean,* thought Violet. Well the joke would be on it, because she didn't have enough left worth stealing.

Maybe they were lunatics who'd kill her for sport. Or maybe it wasn't the Antarean at all. Maybe it was some desperate streeter, or one of the mutant gangs she'd heard about.

There was another noise, louder and closer then. Violet panicked at the sound and took off running. She hadn't gotten far when she hit a dead end—a wall scarred with graffiti phrases like "Mutants Suck" and "Kill me or feed me." She searched the darkness for her pursuers, listening to the silence as she tasted her own sweat. Hearing and seeing nothing, she slowly retreated until she found a way she hoped would lead her out of this hostile maze. She moved carefully, avoiding the piles of refuse in her path. She thought maybe she'd lost whoever was after her. Yeah, she thought, the street trash would be the type to give up easily. They'd lose their appetite for trouble if it became too much work.

She followed a chainlink fence for some time and began to relax. She still wasn't sure where she was, and was trying to decide which direction to take when something came at her out of the blackness. A massive dog, barking bloody murder, threw its forepaws against the fence, making clear its intentions to tear out her throat.

Violet backed off the fence and ran. She knew she had to move fast. The barking would attract the scum who were after her. She ran until she was gasping for air, until she saw lights and heard the clamor of shouting. She ran for the lights. As she got closer the pandemonium grew louder. Suddenly, as she emerged into an open area, she collided with another body and went sprawling.

Momentarily stunned, she struggled to her feet and found herself being swept away by a mob of angry streeters. It was all she could do to maintain her footing as she was pushed and bumped from every direction. It was bedlam. A swell of noise engulfed her, distraught screams punctuated by angry shouts. She saw some people making a futile attempt to organize the mayhem, but they were swept away unheeded. Glass shattered nearby and she ducked down out of reflex.

"You are ordered to disperse," bellowed a machine-like voice. *"All those not leaving the area at once will be prosecuted to the full extent of the law. You are ordered to disperse immediately."*

Violet couldn't tell where the voice was coming from, but she knew she had to get away. She knew what would happen next. She'd seen the video reports all too often.

"We want food! We want food!" The shouts began somewhere off to Violet's right. There were only a few voices at first, but in seconds the cry spread through the rabble like a virus, and thousands were chanting, "We want food! We want food! We want food!"

She heard several explosive pops and suddenly there was a surge of movement in the crowd. Panic created a domino effect, and a wave of bodies slammed her and dozens of others to the ground. Those who weren't knocked down began to run, though no one seemed to know which way was safe.

Once she was back on her feet, Violet could see the gas clouds and the brilliant eruptions of flash grenades. All around her was disorder and confusion. Before she could decide which way lay escape, an excruciatingly bright burst of light materialized at her feet.

Violet grabbed at her eyes and cried out. She fell backwards but bumped into something that kept her upright. Her eyes burned and her head pounded with a rogue rhythm. She tried opening her eyes, but all she could see was light, a blinding, brilliant glare and nothing else. The pain and the loss of sight unhinged her. She thought that she was blind. She staggered off, calling out, "I can't see. Help me. Please, I'm blind, help me." But her cry was one of hundreds.

She kept moving as best she could, and after a short time the chaos seemed to have shifted away from her. She realized she was easy prey now. The thought fed her hysteria, and when she tried to move faster she stumbled over some unseen hazard. Exhausted, her head and eyes still throbbing, she kept going, prodded by the dread of her own imagination. The longer she couldn't see, the worse it became. She stopped calling out, afraid of whom her cries might attract. She was sure someone would see her soon, but who would that someone be? Using a wall she had come to as her guide, she felt her way along, taking one step after another until, abruptly, she took a step into nothingness.

She plunged downward, hitting hard and tumbling headlong over uneven concrete. When she hit bottom she was only partially conscious. She lay there for a long while, assessing her injuries. She hurt, but wasn't sure if she'd broken any bones. She tried to open her eyes. The painful flash was still there.

"Hello?" It was a child's voice. "Are you okay?"

"I need help. I'm blind," called Violet. "I fell down here and I need help getting up."

"I'm not supposed to talk to strangers."

"I'm not a . . . please, I need help."

She waited and listened, but there was no response. "Are you there?" Nothing. "Where are you?" *Damn little rodent has gone off and left me here,* thought Violet. *Probably an ignorant streeter kid, a wild little animal.* She tried opening her eyes yet again, and this time instead of one bright blaze she now saw several brilliant dots. In between there was only blackness.

"See. Down the stairs. She says she's blind." It was the child's voice again.

"You down there." This time it was a man's voice. "What's wrong?"

"Something blinded me, a flash grenade or . . . I don't know. Then I fell down here."

"Can you get up?"

"I don't know. My ankle might be broken."

"Well, see if you can get up. I'm coming down there, but don't try anything or I'll gut you. Iris, you stay here."

Violet managed to get to her feet, and when she did she thought she could see something moving. She was banged up, but now she didn't think any bones were broken. "Okay, there are stairs right in front of you," he said. She could feel him next to her now. "Step up and I'll help you."

It was slow going, but when she eventually reached the top she could tell her vision was returning. There was a sudden reduction of the glare, and despite the spots she could see more clearly. She looked up, saw the clouds pulling back from the moon, and breathed a sigh of relief. "I think my eyes are clearing up."

"That's good," said the man.

"I was scared I'd never see again," she said, still looking at the moon through blurry eyes. "Thank you for your help."

"Don't thank me, thank my daughter, Iris. She's the one who found you."

Violet looked at the little girl. Even through her fuzzy vision she could see her imperfections. She had no hair, not even stubble, and both her ears were swollen and disfigured. Her father appeared normal enough, a streeter from his clothes. But the genes passed on to the daughter had obviously been damaged. *Too much exposure*, thought Violet.

"Thank you, uh, Iris. I don't know what I would have done if you hadn't come along." She turned to the father. "If you could direct me back to Third Street, I won't bother you any more."

"It's right down there," he said, pointing behind him.

Indeed, she'd gone almost in a circle. She could see the street vendor still in place, hawking his wares.

"Well, I uh . . . thanks again." She checked her pocket as she walked away, limping only slightly. The power cell was still there. It had been a long, hellish night, but she'd have her steak after all. She passed by the vendor who recognized her and called out.

"Get your juice, friend?"

Violet nodded.

"Well, good night and good living to you then."

Violet had anticipated having to dodge another hard sell, but the vendor had apparently given up on her. Like Violet, he knew a lost cause when he saw one.

Lost cause—that's what she was. That's what this world was, her world, empty and barren.

An odd feeling came over her then. It was an urge she hadn't felt in a long time. It was so unexpected, she didn't even question it.

She turned back towards the little stand and eyed the vendor's merchandise.

"Change your mind, friend? Something I can show you?"

"How much for one of those dolls?"

"For you, only three and a half."

"Oh. I've only got two."

"Two it is. *Sold* to the power seeker with the limp." The vendor made the exchange, looking at Violet as if trying to be sure of what he saw. "Your aura, it's altered. Very unusual for that to happen so fast. I see a little color in it. Looks like you might be a healthy blue with a little work."

"Yeah? Well, thanks."

Instead of turning towards home then, Violet made her way back to where she'd fallen. A short distance from there she found Iris and her father. They seemed surprised when she approached, but didn't move.

"This is for you, for saving me," she said, handing the doll to the little girl. Then she asked the father, "Are you two alone?"

"Just us," he replied.

"Well, uh, my name is Violet, Violet Leander."

"Ross Bellows," he replied.

"Mr. Bellows, I'd like to find some other way to thank you and Iris. Who knows what would have happened to me if someone less charitable had come along."

"We are who we are," he said, shrugging.

Violet thought about it for a moment, and then asked, "Do you like steak?"

How do we honor our parents? Would a woman's way be different from a man's?

THE RACE

by Jennifer R. Povey

"We need to bring the port in now!" Elayne's voice echoed a little against the metal of the walls.

"We didn't in the simulation," Charlotte grumbled, but she was moving quickly.

"Simulations aren't perfect. That's why we do the live run, and you know it. If we're going to win . . ."

"I'm on it. Sheesh, woman! Can't we trust the computer?" Charlotte's voice rose in petulant anger. It seemed, of late, that she showed nothing towards Elayne except that very note.

"Nobody's ever won without direct manual. You know it. You gotta have the feel."

"I got the feel, all right. Right in my back muscles." Charlotte was leaning against the line now, supporting it, her harness barely keeping her in place.

"Enough." Inertia caused the boat to slant just a little, made the way in which things move shift.

In front of them, the heavy transparent metal screen showed the stars. They could not see their sails, but they could see the speed at which the sailboat turned. Feel it.

Two women, who looked almost identical. Elayne was maybe a fraction taller and a little heavier in the face, but they were otherwise cut from the same mould. Dark blonde hair, blue eyes, an ancestry that spoke of Germany or Scandinavia.

"Do we have enough power?" Elayne asked. She had her hands on the steering controls, which had been made to resemble a tiller. That was for feel as well.

"I think so. I almost wish this was a three-person craft. One to port, one to starboard. Would be easier."

"Harder to coordinate. Release the port."

Charlotte fed the line through her hands. "The only thing that matters to *you* is winning the prize money."

"Even the bonus for best amateur would be enough . . . okay. She's running straight now, belay." Elayne had detected the bitterness in Charlotte's tone, but put it down to her being tired.

"Got it."

Nobody had ever won using a computer. Several people would try. Several people tried every year. Elayne thought of Charlotte's suggestion of a third crewmember. Except whoever it was would either be rich and useless or demand a share of the money. Besides, they could not add a third securing point in time.

They needed the money for the next race. Of course, it was not just about the money. It was also about pride.

Their father had taken a crew out and won the big one—the Europa run. Once. The second time, the sisters had begged to be included. He had turned them down. His boat had never come back.

Of course, if they were going to do Europa, they would need a crew of at least six, probably nine. This race was much shorter.

"You still want to try for Europa?" Charlotte asked, her voice dangerously soft.

Elayne frowned. "Not in this boat. We need a bigger boat and more crew. For that, we need to win."

The amateur bonus would cover their expenses. It would not also buy another boat. They needed to win.

They needed to prove to their father's ghost that they could do it.

ର୍ଷ୍ଟିକ୍ତ

It was not a long race. A loop around the moon. Their 'markers' were virtual, set up using the same satellites that provided cellphone coverage on Luna. Those satellites also relayed footage to the people who watched. Sailboat racing, a grand maritime tradition.

It was inevitable that the second lightsails were perfected as a means of propulsion, people would start racing them. People raced everything, starting with their own two feet.

Elayne thought that when faster-than-light travel was finally perfected, people would race starships to Alpha Centauri. It was inevitable.

She stood, now, outside the hangared *Starbird*. She would feel bad about trading her for a larger boat, but they needed one. If they were going to do the Europa run.

If they won any money at all, they could keep racing. If they won first place, then they could do the Europa run. There was nothing else for her right now. Nothing else for her or for Charlotte.

Their father had won. Once. Then he had failed. They had to win it, they had to finish the race he had not finished.

She thought that she would hire an all-female crew. It would attract attention, and it would add something to the name all three of them bore. Only one all-female crew had ever completed the Europa Run, and they had not won.

She forced her mind back onto the race at hand. She walked a circle around the *Starbird.* With her sails collapsed, she was a small thing. A fragile thing, sitting in the hangar. It was a racing machine . . . a short-range one. All there was was the deck and the controls, the sails and the small thrusters that served as an auxiliary. Thrusters that could legally only be used for docking and undocking. Any other use was a disqualification. Automatic. They could not afford to be disqualified. Or to be sabotaged.

They kept the ship in a locked hangar. Nobody from any other crew would get close to her.

Maximum crew was three. They would have a better chance of winning with three. But no chance of winning at all if a third crewmember was a stooge, or incompetent. Or worse. She had heard of at least one instance of a crew planting somebody to be hired on by a rival; the planted crewmember then threw the race to give the crew of origin a better chance. Cheating was rampant. They could run with two.

And as a woman captain, she had faced just about every kind of proposition there was. Yes, she decided. She would hire only women for the Europa run. It would make for good publicity.

It would put the *Falcon* name—the name of their father's ship—back on the map. Their father had named the *Starbird*. Elayne's new ship would be the *Falcon Reborn*.

Smiling at her decision, she turned and left the hangar. She carefully locked the door behind her. For the rest of her inspection she needed Charlotte and the ship undocked so they could extend the sails. The sails were the most important thing. If they were damaged, the *Starbird* might not be able to race.

The competitors' lounge was in its usual state. Vague chaos. She noticed Paul Morton getting quietly drunk in the corner. One of these days he was going to be caught flying drunk and suspended. Space was a big place . . . until you had five or six sailboats trying to get as close as possible to the same marker at the same time. She hoped he was caught flying drunk before he hit anyone.

At another table was Charlie 'Rock' Britton. So-called because he apparently had no emotion whatsoever.

She shook her head. As usual, she was the only woman here. The few women who sailed tended to avoid the lounge, partly because they were the first target of the men who sailed. Elayne refused to allow herself to be intimidated. She had as much right to be here as any male. Thinking that caused her to put a bit of a swagger into her walk as she went over to the bar.

Looking right at Paul, she ordered an iced tea . . . and no, not the Long Island variety. She was going to keep her head clear, even if she was the only one here who managed that normally simple task. Seriously.

After the race, win or lose, she would get dead drunk, she promised herself. Either in celebration, or in . . . she was not sure what she would call it. Commiseration? If they made no money from this race, the *Starbird* would have to go into mothballs for months. At best.

Do the Europa Run as somebody else's crew? Charlotte would do that. Elayne? She was a captain and she would remain so even if that meant she had to stay beached.

She sipped her tea and looked around the room. As she did, she saw two young women come in. She did not recognize either of them. Rookies just moving up to this level of competition, perhaps? Well, as long as they didn't wreck . . . either in space or in here. She turned her back on them for a moment. Although, a small voice told her, she and Charlotte would need more crew for the Europa Run.

∞⬡∞

The *Starbird* eased out of her docking berth on auxiliary. Her sails were currently completely within the outer shell. She floated out into space.

Elayne did not look at any of the other boats being moved out. She was focused entirely on the *Starbird*. "Ease out port and starboard."

Charlotte had her hands on the controls, standing in a central point from which she could somewhat readily reach both. "Aye."

At least she seemed in a better mood than she had been during practice. Maybe it had been pre-race jitters. Space knew those were common. Elayne had them herself, although she tried to keep them firmly locked inside.

"Ease out to forty-five."

"Aye."

The sails would not, quite, catch in the shadow of the station, but bringing them part of the way out now would save time when they hit the first marker. For now, Elayne kept one hand on the throttle of the auxiliary. They floated, nudging out, and then there was the sun. It appeared from behind the station and behind the earth.

The charged particles of the solar wind would come at an angle to them. "Starboard to sixty."

"Aye." Charlotte was unsmiling, that same vaguely bitter and uncertain expression marking her face. On a run this short, there would be little time for conversation.

Then the *Starbird* leapt forward. Elayne took her hand off the throttle. "Ease off. Let's not jump the start."

"She's feeling good," Charlotte said. "Wind's strong today."

The direction of the wind never varied. Its strength did. And when one got in the shadows of worlds, there were eddies. It was possible to become becalmed. "Good. I'd rather have that than too much calm."

Throttled down, Elayne flicked a red band across the auxiliary. If that band was broken at the end, they would be disqualified. You only used the auxiliary if it was a matter of life or death . . . yours or somebody else's.

They were bearing down on the starting line. It was a rolling start. She saw the other ships. Morton's *Rolling Thunder* was distinctly too close to them. She adjusted the tiller, steering them past him. He was probably not drunk. He was almost certainly hung over.

Elayne shook her head. "The man's a disgrace to the sport."

"The man's going to get himself killed," Charlotte predicted. "I'm going to ease out starboard a little more."

"Do it." That way, they would not be pushed into Morton's path if they got a gust, but rather away from it. If they crossed in front of anyone, she wanted it to be a competent captain. Morton's mate, a Chinese man who never spoke, was no more competent than he was.

One of these days, they would get suspended. Pile on one safety violation too many and that would be it. She hoped it would not be today. As much as she wanted him gone, she didn't want her race ruined by his actions.

And then they were leaping forward again. The start. The trick was to get the sails trimmed perfectly as you came in. They did not quite have it right.

A corporate boat, *Redstar's Dancer* was ahead of them. Elayne made a face. So-called professionals. In truth, they were servants to their sponsors; the crew could be fired at any time. At least her failure would be her own. If she lost *Starbird*, it would not be because somebody decided she had not placed high enough often enough.

It hurt that the corporates, with their much higher budgets, won so often. Another of them was next to her. An Indian boat, the name on its bow in some non-English characters. But *Starbird* was ahead of the other amateurs.

Not good enough. They needed to win. It was a straight run to the first marker. It was all about speed right now, and the stars that streaked past, and the power in the sails. She glanced at Charlotte, who was leaning against the stays.

No computer had ever won. Elayne wondered who was trying it this year. Somebody always did. Somebody was always convinced that their algorithms could beat the human feel for things. 'It's not like Earth' was the explanation they invariably gave. Earth, where the wind came from all directions, sometimes more than one at once. Where no algorithm could predict it, not at that scale. Yet it had been tried and tried and tried and had not worked. Perhaps that said something about the limits of artificial intelligence. One day, Elayne supposed, somebody would create a sentient AI . . . but that, in her mind, would not really count as the same thing. And it might not want to sail.

Straight, still, the boat was like an arrow shot from a bow. The corporates were still ahead. Of course they were. In straight-line speed, it was the quality of the boat that did it, not the skill of the sailors. There was a reason there was a special prize.

But she did not want that special prize, that lesser acknowledgment. "Come on." The *Starbird* edged ahead of the last corporate boat, but only for a moment. A brief moment, and then they were behind again, but not by much.

If she and her sister were the better sailors, they could get inside the corporate boats at the first marker. Charlotte was already adjusting the sails. No specific orders from Elayne. That was a good crew. They could read each other's minds. They could feel each other. The tension that had dominated the last few months faded away.

And they got inside all but one of the corporates.

"Woot!" Charlotte called, as the boat turned, tacking against the wind. It might always come from the same direction, here where they were out of the shadow of earth and moon, but it still took skill, training and practice to use it effectively. The first ships to sail on it had only been able to run with it. What use was that? Getting cargo to Mars had been about the shape of it, and then only when the conditions were favorable.

The *Starbird* accelerated towards the second marker. Elayne found herself leaning forward. A slalom towards the moon. Then the difficult stretch around the moon, where the wind might drop off to almost nothing, or threaten to blow them onto the lunar surface. With no atmosphere, that could happen. It had happened. Racers got killed that way. That was part of the risk. Elayne found herself tensing. No. She would not think about it, and that would not happen to them.

They fell into a rhythm. If you got the first marker right and kept your rhythm, the rest would follow. Now some conversation was possible.

"You saw Morton's start?" Charlotte asked.

"The man's a hazard on the course. Those two rookies did it better." Elayne kept her hands on the controls, her eyes on the course, not looking at her sister.

"Are you sure they're rookies?"

"I checked. First full race for them."

"If they do well . . ." Charlotte left it hanging.

They would be easy to hire on; as rookies they would be less likely to have ambitions of doing the run themselves, Elayne mused. If they did well. They would have to prove at least some competence in her mind. "Worry about the race we're in."

Charlotte fell silent for a moment, then, "I am."

"We're ahead of any of the other amateurs. We're ahead of most of the corporates. All we have to do is look for an opportunity to get ahead of *Dancer*."

"Let's not wreck trying," Charlotte cautioned.

"I'm not stupid. I wonder who's even flying her this year."

"Some asshole. Redstar only hires assholes for captains." Charlotte's words were borne out by history.

Then they fell silent, focusing on the rhythm, focusing on the run. The shadow of the moon lay ahead of them.

ങ୦୫୫ଅ

The wind died as soon as the shadow struck them. Not completely, but into eddies that barely caught the *Starbird's* sails.

This was the first tricky part. You had to have enough inertia to fly right through the doldrums and trim the sails to catch any wind there was.

There would be boats dropping out now, trapped in some eddy. Eventually they would have to give up, use their thrusters, and be disqualified. It was not dangerous to one's life, only to one's chance of winning. This was not the skim, when one wanted to get as close to Luna as possible without being captured by her gravity well. That was where sailors died. Not every race, but one or two boats a year would make new craters in the moon's pitted surface.

Morton's *Rolling Thunder* was closer than she would have liked, coming up behind them, sails spread. But he had misjudged it. He did not stop as suddenly as it appeared, but he hit a dead zone and was abruptly left in their wake. She hoped he did not find his way out of it. The man really was a hazard to navigation.

But *Dancer* was pulling ahead, sharply so. They clearly had found a better route. They were the boat to beat, and Elayne found her vision tunneling in on them. Nobody else was at all close; whether they were behind or just out of immediate sight, she could not be sure.

"Port out . . ."

"Already on it," Charlotte said, a little smugly. She liked to anticipate things.

Elayne realized that sooner or later they were going to be wanting a second boat, so Charlotte could captain her own craft. Perhaps sooner, with the way things had been going between them. Maybe she could buy a large boat, do stuff like the Europa Run with it, and let Charlotte run *Starbird*. If they did well enough, maybe they could buy two more boats. Maybe they could have the Falcon Racing Team her father had dreamed of. "We need to set up a team."

Charlotte grinned at her. "Of course we do. We can't do the Europa Run without one." She seemed pleased.

Elayne put it down to her being right. Charlotte needed her own boat. They were out of the doldrums and darting around the far side of the moon. It felt as if the race had lasted minutes, not hours. It always did. Time changed when one was focused like this. Minutes, hours, a lifetime.

Dancer was still ahead of them. Blasted corporates. They had all the money, and *Dancer* in particular had a lot of expertise. They built much larger sailboats. The ones that took people to Mars. They raced for public relations. Because it looked cool.

They were going to beat *Dancer*. Elayne was determined.

"They're awfully low," Charlotte said.

Elayne calculated the distance. Undercutting was not smart. The corporate boat, perhaps aware that it had another craft on its tail, was playing it very fine indeed. Even here, the wind could change. Not all the way, not in such gross direction, but gusts happened.

"Oh my god," Charlotte exclaimed. She never swore.

Dancer was going down. The corporate boat had been struck by the wind, and it was obvious from here that they would skim too low, that they would hit the lunar gravity well. In theory they had a chance of survival. The crew capsule might survive impact intact, and they probably had a beacon, though it could be a while until their corporation mounted a rescue.

"Elayne . . ."

A good sailor can feel the wind. The wind that took them, that lifted them away from *Dancer*. A good sailor knows what it will do. The *Dancer*'s captain had made a potentially fatal error.

The *Starbird* was closest. But: "We stop, we lose."

"We don't stop, they die." Charlotte said, releasing the sheets. She could not move towards her sister, not in the harness, but she could fix her with a look that bored through her skull.

"We lose, we don't race again."

"Nobody stopped for our father."

Time stood still for Elayne. Their father's ship, the *Falcon*, losing one of its sails, flying off course. At least three boats had gone past without rescuing him. It might have been too late anyway. They would never know. But it might have been in time.

"Starboard . . ." A breath, in, out. ". . . in." Had they already left it too late? "Quickly!"

There were two other boats sweeping up behind them. She knew those boats. They would not stop, not slow. They would go right through *Starbird* if they thought their boat would survive the collision. They were the type who had left her father to die.

She dropped beneath them. She had to get the angle precisely right. Precisely. They called it drafting. You could pull another boat after you if you did it right.

Low, and passing over *Dancer* so close that they could almost see, through the transparent metal, her captain's eyes.

"Full out! Now!"

Charlotte's eyes were wide, but her expression was that of somebody who had just won the Europa Run.

The two boats almost touched. Kissed against one another like lovers, and then the *Starbird* was pulling up—and the *Dancer* was with her. Barely, skimming off the lunar gravity well, and then free into space.

"Full in." And the *Starbird* lifted in her hands, bucked away, leaving the *Dancer* free. In one piece. Her crew alive. Elayne felt adrenalin flow through her.

The *Dancer* did not leap away, as she could have. She paced the *Starbird*. "Port out forty-five. Starboard out sixty," Elayne said, calmly.

Calmly. As if she had not just thrown away the race they needed to win. Needed to. As if they would still have the money to race again.

࿊ⱅⰓⰔⱅ࿊

The *Starbird* and the *Dancer* crossed the finish line in perfect synchronization. In fifth place. The small amount of money would not be enough, and all Elayne could think was, *What did I do?*

Then Charlotte stepped across the deck and hugged her. For the first time in so long. Elayne knew, then, what she had done. She had regained her sister's respect, and that was worth a great deal of prize money.

"We'll manage," Charlotte said, finally. "There's more important things."

"Don't say it. You're not a walking cliché factory." Elayne laughed, though; she knew for sure what Charlotte meant. The code of the sea had not been adopted, whole, when sailing went to space, but perhaps it should have been.

Docking was an anticlimax, a mechanical activity. The boat slid into her docking place on thrusters.

Elayne wondered if she would even fly again. The only chance she had now was to go begging to one of the corporates. The microscopic fifth-place money might have been enough for entry fees and thruster fuel had they not shared it with *Dancer*. But she knew the corporate boat had held back so the *Starbird* would at least have something.

That was not the way it happened. They were supposed to be cutthroat, to care only about winning. Had she cared only about winning, the captain and crew of *Dancer* would probably be dead. Had she cared only about winning, though, like the others, she would not be wondering if she would race again. But she would be remembering that no one stopped for their father.

Then they stepped into the pilot's lounge, where the prize ceremony would take place. Somehow, it seemed, everyone was there. Even Paul Morton, who had probably been disqualified. Somehow it seemed the place was full to the very brim. And as Elayne stepped in, Charlotte a step behind her, there was a moment of hush, of stillness.

And then all the sailors in the room were on their feet.

Elayne blinked. Even those who, she knew, would never have stopped. Even the Rock, who had not stopped for her father. As if what she had done had reminded them of something older than the need to win a race.

A sea captain did not ignore a ship in peril. Yet she would have. It was Charlotte who had reminded her about stopping.

Then the captain of the *Dancer* was stepping towards them. "This is for you." He offered her the cheque for half of the fifth place prize.

She shook her head. "I can't take that. It's not even yours to give." He might get a bonus, but he did not get to keep the prize money. That went to the owners.

He brushed it off. "I won't let you have to stop racing. I promise."

Did everyone know about their financial straits? Was he in a position to help? Or to have the corporation help? His 'I promise' resonated in her. He went on holding out the cheque.

⋙✦⋘

The *Falcon Reborn* launched into space, her sails catching the wind as she flew away from the station. They spread wide, casting their own shadow, which another boat had to change course to avoid.

Seeing that on her instruments, Elayne laughed a bit. "Come on, girls. Let's show them what we can do."

She had offered Charlotte the captaincy, but Charlotte had refused. Do this run, together, and then they could split up, run their own boats.

Redstar had helped them. And not just Redstar. When the news of the rescue had hit, the newsies picked it up, and there had been a queue of people wanting to sponsor their Europa Run.

The *Falcon* streaked out into the dark, a good captain at her wheel, and a race to run. But also a vow, sworn among her crew, that if they had to stop, they would. You saved more than lives when you did.

Yet if you could win—you saved your honor, and that was more important than any prize.

This is the first of several stories in this volume which explore the price of peace in a time of war. The women in the stories make very different choices. Who is to say one is better than another?

THE ENVOY

by Al Onia

Envoy Martina Keng stepped from the airlock into the station. She leaned against a wall and slid to the floor. She crossed herself, "Sisters, give me strength." Her palms stank of grime from the walls of the clandestine facility.

She checked her watch. Pursuit was at least eighteen hours behind. For the moment she was the lone human aboard; isolated between two sworn enemies.

The aliens' retreat ships were the only ones she saw docked. Her prep team had left as planned, well ahead of the Earthcorp militia.

A voice scratched over the speakers. "I have been waiting two days in this hell-hole. You are precisely seventeen hours late."

It took all of Martina's will to push herself back to her feet. She took a series of short breaths before responding, "My apologies. You must be the Rix Ambassador, Tolan. Is the Mellainian representative listening?"

A smoother voice answered, purring, "I welcome you, Envoy Keng. I trust your delay means nothing untoward."

Martina said, "We had complications with the selection process. And I had to take a few detours."

The Rix said, "Envoyance should have been prepared. They gave us little enough time to get here for this . . . exercise."

Martina stretched her cheeks tight with her hands, trying to find still-active nerve-endings. "I will interview you in your quarters in twenty minutes, Ambassador Tolan. I need a short time to prepare."

"More delay? Interview? Very well, twenty minutes. Do not force me to wait longer."

"Mellainian representative, I do not know your name."

"You would have difficulty pronouncing it with only one tongue. *Mellainian* is acceptable. I find it curious that despite the physiological differences, you can accommodate both of us."

"I will interview you after I meet with the Rix. We can discuss the procedure in more detail then." She exhaled. "Cabin directions, please."

A line glowed in the floor, and she followed it to a stark cabin.

Martina sat on the narrow slab extruded from the wall. She loosened her high collar enough to scratch her neck, thankful no mirrors were present.

Though she could not see her collarbones, Martina could feel the wounds with her fingers. The drugs were blurring her memory of how they got there. Implants? That was it. Implants to facilitate the hosting. She was exhausted by the last-minute cancellation of the designated Envoy, the rush of surgery to prepare her own body and mind for the assimilation. Instead of marshalling her energy, she had had to study the history of the Rix-Mellainian conflict while she shuttled from ship to ship, outrunning Earthcorp. She closed her eyes and tried to think only of the goal.

After a quarter of an hour, she rose and fastened her cloak. Following the floor guide, she found the Rix's quarters.

"Come," was the simple order that followed her rap on the door.

"Ambassador Tolan, I am ready to conduct the interview." The pictures did not portray the true height of the Rix. Nor how predatory every movement seemed.

The avian paced, pausing only to tap a reverse-claw against the deck. "I had issue with humans offering this 'meeting,' but I've done some research on your species." He bent low to her eye level, then placed a talon on her breast. "A female."

The touch startled her. She had thought those feelings were gone. This physical familiarity paled in comparison to the pending invasion, but she tasted bile rising in her throat.

Martina stepped away from the Rix and sat on the floor, back snug to the wall. "I am a woman."

The Rix resumed his pacing. "Humans, judging us. It is outrageous. I have read your histories—millennia of uninterrupted warfare. How you survived beyond your planet is an enigma. And you now choose to meddle in our internal affairs."

"Enforcing an embargo on the Mellainian system is hardly *internal*. I will not debate your right to empire, Ambassador; I am here at the petition of your leaders. The dispute with the Mellainians has beggared you. The Envoys exist to mediate these disputes. Envoyance's goal, through me, is to help you see the other side." It was too early for the rest.

She thought the Rix smiled. His chitinous upper lip crinkled.

"I will learn what I will of the Mellainian psyche, to Rix benefit. What does this interview hope to accomplish? I have waited two days, and they send a *female*. You are here to serve our purpose. I have been poked and prodded until my feathers molt. The time for testing is passed. Proceed with this abomination."

"Not yet, your eminence. This is the final test, to see if you are suitable for me. My order does not share this technology lightly. I alone must judge the chance of success."

Martina hugged her arms to her chest. "I am a woman. If you studied our history closely, you'd know the women have often been the peacemakers, the conciliators." She thought of her sisterhood. Was it worth it? "And when those failed, we were the martyrs."

"I looked up 'Envoy.' Your rank is beneath Ambassador. I am superior in position and species. Go interview the Mellainian."

Martina did not move. "Ambassador, you have a choice. Return home and admit to your leaders and your people that you did not have the courage to attempt this." Offer him a glimpse? "Or you can answer my few questions and be on your way in less than a day, with more understanding, even compassion."

"And when your government troops arrive?"

"The Envoys have no immunity from Earthcorp. We are . . . non-commercial. But you and the Mellainian are guaranteed safe conduct back to your worlds."

The Rix dropped on one knee. He hissed air in and out. Finally he said, "Ask."

Martina pressed her hands to the floor, shifting her weight. "Are you a warrior?"

"I fight battles each day against those who would denigrate the Rix tradition."

"But not a soldier?"

"There are wars everywhere, not just on battlefields."

"Have you ever been in physical danger in your duties?"

"The Mellainians hold no threat to me."

"Are you willing to lead?"

"Of course. I am destined to lead."

"Will you lead the Rix to peace?"

The Rix hit the wall with an arm; feathers floated down slowly. "We are weeks away from victory."

"Every week costs more lives. Don't impose your propaganda on me. My mind may be dulled by drugs, but I know Rix public opinion cries for an end to the body count."

"I admit nothing. My presence here with that . . . Mellainian is proof enough of our commitment to this process."

Martina knew that was true; Envoyance had lost two emissaries before making contact with the upper echelon of the Rix government. "Ambassador, what will happen to the Rix if I say no?"

Tolan was on his feet in a flash. Martina tensed her arms and tilted her head away.

"We'll win."

"Are you willing to accept the cost of victory?"

A few feathers sprang into the air from the Rix's neck. He bent at the waist and brought an eye level with hers. "Do you know how close you just came to death?"

"Death is merely one end. A defeat to be feared, or a release to be embraced. I do not fear you."

The Rix's talons sheathed.

Martina continued, "Earthcorp is already supplying you with advisors. Do you know what they'll demand in return? Win or lose, they will take what little you have left and the Rix will be in no position to object. Now, are you willing to accept that?"

"We will crush Earthcorp after we have dealt with the Mellainians."

Martina stood, "Do you speak for yourself, or for the Rix command?"

The beak crinkled again. This time it was no smile. Tolan's feathers rose, then relaxed. "Any more questions?"

Martina shook her head, looking up at him. "What would you ask of me?"

The Rix knelt. "How can you allow yourself to do this? To subordinate your own personality?"

"Experiencing your enemy's suffering is a step to open discussion. My order has a long history of facilitating peace. It is no loss of dignity to save lives. That drives my decision."

Martina stopped at the door. She brushed her fingers across deep gouges in the jamb. The Rix apparently had tested the security. She said, "I must interview the other."

"Very well. It annoys me to be nested here with you and that Mellainian." The Rix squatted on the floor and closed his eyes.

"Do not dismiss *me*," she said and stepped into the passage.

She pounded her fist against the wall. *Damn fool*, she told herself. *If all Rix are like him, why save them? What was Envoyance thinking? What was I thinking?*

She stomped her way to the next meeting. "Calm down, Martina. Don't lose your temper." *Easy to say*, she thought. *Harder to do*.

ക്കൗജ

In contrast to the Rix's bare quarters, the Mellainian's room had furniture like her own. The alien's meter-long form curled in a chair.

"I bid you welcome, Envoy. How was your interview with the Rix? A true savage, is it not?" The Mellainian groomed his fur with a forked tongue.

"I cannot discuss that."

"Where's the harm? Soon, the Rix and I will be sharing the deepest, most intimate confidences."

"I have not yet made that decision, Ambassador." She took a moment to study him.

"Is everything satisfactory, Envoy?"

"Excuse me for staring." Martina blinked her eyes twice. "You look different from the pictures I was given." Her guts tightened. "You are not the Ambassador. But I have seen your face." Martina searched her memory, but it was hard to concentrate. Her recall was decaying with her personality. She summoned all her will, knowing it meant a heavier dose of drugs later. "You are the Mellainian Overlord."

Her host stopped grooming. "I am."

She relaxed. "That is excellent."

He sat back in his chair. "You are not disturbed by the deception?" His lip drew back to reveal badger-like teeth.

Martina leaned forward. "Our success rate is barely one in three when anyone but the leaders themselves are involved in this process. It is hard for even the most respected representatives to convince their leaders of the intensity of the experience."

"I see. Get to know your enemy."

"Get to know yourself through your enemy."

"And your success rate when both leaders participate?"

"Close to ninety."

"Have you hosted a leader and a lesser personage, such as the Rix?"

Martina shook her head. "No. Are you not afraid of the Rix gaining advantage?"

"I am confident he will learn nothing I do not wish."

"I admire your courage, Overlord."

"Yours is the greater courage, Envoy Keng."

Martina asked, "Do you desire peace?"

"We only defend ourselves. We approached you. Envoy, I understand some of your order's motivations. What are yours?"

She recalled another face. Much like her own. "Earthcorp conscripts young men and women into peace enforcement. Sons and daughters who don't come home. Mellain will be another *altruistic* mission. I have no one left to lose, but others do. How did the prep team miss your identity?"

The Overlord's fur changed color, and he flattened his ears. "Disguise is a gift we have." He came close to her. "Am I acceptable?"

Martina stood, her focus wandering with the intensity of the interviews and the drugs taking control of her system. What was real? The Rix's behavior was aggressive but straightforward. But the Overlord was all deception and disguise. Were the Mellainian's motives as shifting as its appearance? The Overlord's gamble needed examination. "I must make my decision in private."

The Mellainian nodded at the door. "You may go."

Alone in her room, Martina longed for advice. The decision was harder than she thought possible. It was too late for her own peace. This mission was to save others from her turmoil. The Rix lived to prey on others, but she could not fathom the Mellainians' true goal, if it was different from that of the Rix.

She focused on her family, and the pounding in her head abated. Able to think more clearly now, she realized. *I am the vessel to show them the path. Forget their motives, I will show them mine.*

☜❦ɩɩ❪☞

Martina did not feel the pressure points in the recumbent chair. Gravity, for her, had ceased to impose its burden. She looked objectively at Martina Keng, the personality she had been, the training and commitment she had endured. She unzipped her robe to the waist, shocked at the changes to her flesh wrought by the operations and drugs. She had tended such ravages on others, but had repressed those memories. Their eyes were harder to forget.

Her evaluation was interrupted by sounds from the speakers. The Rix and the Mellainian were ready.

She said, "Thank you both for your temporary sacrifice. Your worlds will benefit."

"This is more painful than the 'discomfort' your prep team promised, Envoy."

"Ambassador Tolan, please be stoical. The pain will end once the transfer is complete." Martina plunged the first jack into her chest. She found herself airborne.

The Rix screeched inside her. She felt disoriented as he tried to take wing. Then she saw with the iridescent vision native to their species. Martina shut her eyes, but the bright colors remained, burning paths to her brain.

She screamed. "I did not expect—the intensity. Ambassador, calm down or I will have no room for the other." *Or myself,* she feared.

Tolan's panic diminished enough for Martina to regain focus. She said, "Flight is the freedom you fight to preserve. Let the Mellainian see this." Then she battled her human fear of falling and braced herself for the second invasion. "Overlord, are you ready?"

It was long moments before a response came, and it was from the Rix. "Overlord? What trick is this?"

Martina said, "No trick. The Mellainian leader could not ask anyone else to do this." When she still heard nothing from the Overlord, she asked again, "Overlord, are you ready?" No answer. "Have I wasted my ordeal for only one transfer? Will you allow Ambassador Tolan to be the brave one?"

After a moment, the Mellainian finally said, "You may proceed."

Martina watched the shiny needle lift in her hand. She felt the Rix squirm, then she drove home the second jack.

The Mellainian brought an image of swimming to her. Coiling around submerged logs, chasing and capturing fishlike creatures, savoring the succulent flesh of prey.

The Rix gagged. "Can't breathe. Water crushing me."

The Overlord asked, "Do you not hunt? I see your ancestral technique of diving from high above ground. Prey is prey."

"I admit no parallel. Air is different." The Rix spoke uncertainly.

Martina's voice was weak. "Don't look for differences. Find the similarities." How could she get past their prejudices? Her training had not prepared her for the instinctive hatred and fear the two species harbored. She had to overcome her own fear of failure. She could not lose this one chance. Rix and Mellanian families were suffering as she had. *Show them how*, she realized. She beat down her own barriers and let them experience her war memories. The scant remains of a loved brother, a life extinguished in an instant.

Tolan said, "Human, I must convince my Chancellor to experience this. You will be the honored host for two great visionaries."

Martina searched for the right words. "I cannot fulfill your request, Ambassador."

"You refuse? Your mission is to serve."

"You did not search deep enough in the varied definitions of 'envoy.' It also means 'the conclusion.'"

The Overlord spoke, "We are trapped? No return to our bodies?"

The Rix lashed out. "This is unconscionable. You deceived us with your manufactured sorrow. How can you ask for our sacrifice? Too high a price."

The two of them tore at her, seeking escape. Martina hissed, "No, the experience for you both will be as promised, and we pray, successful in settling your conflict. I ask that you spend the next twelve hours understanding your enemy, until Earthcorp intervenes."

They believed her. She knew it at once when they calmed.

The Rix said, "I am amazed by the parallelism I sense already."

"Envoy Keng, as Overlord I pledge my protection when your fellow humans arrive here. You will be in no danger, I assure you. If you desire, you may accompany me to Mellain."

"Or to Rix."

Martina said, "I have set the automatic return transfer sequence. Your offers are humbling, signs that you can progress toward peace. However, you should know that the host's mind does not survive the reversal." She thrust her guests aside and thought of the sisters she had nursed. Their eyes, pleading for a way out. Some ego lingered in those spent hosts. Now she shared their fear. Afraid of only one thing—the loss of self.

The aliens returned to her consciousness. Martina tried not to read their feelings and said, "That is the price my order is willing, no, *I* am willing, to pay."

Anais Nin once wrote that she had made herself responsible for everyone she knew. She meant it metaphorically. But what if it happens for real?

[signature: Melissa Mead]

BEARER OF BURDENS

by Melissa Mead

"John Donne was a liar," the painter muttered under his breath at his first sight of his client.

A naked woman. He'd known that the mysterious Bearer of Burdens was female when he came to the Planet of Golden Sands to paint her portrait. He'd imagined a slender, silk-clad beauty out of the Arabian Nights. Now he stood speechless while his mind readjusted. Not a portrait; a landscape. This woman had foothills and terraces. Her breasts were just another stratum in the folds of her body. Rolls of flesh sagged from her like lava pouring from a volcano. Her belly, buttocks and thighs merged into an apron of fat that hid her lower body to the knees. Her thick legs splayed apart at a painful angle, and the bare feet at the end looked curiously small and vulnerable by comparison.

To his mortification, the enormous woman had heard him. She laughed.

"Not necessarily! He said that no *man* is an island. He didn't mention women," she said in English, the painter's own language. She said something in Calish to the dozen fully clothed attendants sharing the tent with her. The oldest, a graying woman, frowned. The youngest, a round-cheeked girl, giggled.

"Where are you from?" the girl asked the painter.

"Earth, like the Bearer. I didn't realize that she had children serving her," said the painter. "How old are you?"

"Eight." The little girl looked disdainful. "And I'm not a child. I'm a Hand. I get to help with the Intimate Mysteries!"

"You get to pour the wash water," the Bearer translated, smiling. "But you do it very well."

"Why do you want to paint our Bearer? You're not going to call her Jabal's Hut and make her mad, are you?"

"Because . . . um . . . Jabal's Hut?"

"The last applicant collected twentieth-century science-fiction films," said the Bearer dryly.

"Jab . . . Oh!" The painter's face burned. "No, of course not. Um, I thought your Community forbade offworld technology."

"It does. I cited his wristwatch computer as my reason for throwing him out with his waterskin only half full."

The painter swallowed. The Bearer looked him over. Under her scrutiny, he felt like the naked one.

"Let me give you the conditions," she said. "Besides the no modern conveniences rule, you'd have to stay within the compound walls until the project is finished. You'd live in the Foreigners' Quarters, which is the spartan cell next to this tent. Payment on project completion, schedule at my convenience. If I find you rude, crude, or otherwise objectionable, you're out. No pay. If you harass the girls in any way, you're out without pay or a waterskin, and it's a long walk to the next well. Still interested?"

"Absolutely."

Her dark eyes twinkled. "No return ticket?" When he looked away she said, "Of course not. That's no trip to make on a whim. Did you bring your portfolio?"

"Yes."

"Give it to one of the Hands." A young woman stepped forward to take it. She passed it to the Bearer, who studied the drawings inside while the painter sweated and tugged at his collar.

"Nice work," said the Bearer at last. "I particularly like your view of the Ash Barrens. Most people wouldn't consider an abandoned planet picturesque. You've managed to bring out a certain stark glory, yet you don't pretend the place is pretty."

He breathed again. "One of my first art lessons went like this: the teacher put a teacup in front of the class with the handle facing away, and told us to paint it. Half the pictures had cups with handles, even though we couldn't see one, just because you *expect* a teacup to have a handle. The teacher told us to paint what we see, not what we expect to see."

She looked thoughtful. "Did your teacup have a handle?"

"No."

"Good." She held out a hand. "If you still want the job, shake on it."

Puzzled, he did. When that plump hand engulfed his, the eldest Hand cried out in protest. The Bearer frowned.

The painter jumped. "Did I do something wrong?"

"Not as far as I'm concerned. Now that you've touched me, you're technically considered a Hand. That'll raise eyebrows, to say the least, but otherwise you're just a Foreigner, which means we'd all be stuck calling you Painter. I refuse to work in close quarters for weeks with someone without knowing their name." When he just stood there, she added pointedly, "My name is Amberlynn Delaverde."

"What? Oh, Edgar Morris. Ed. Why do they call you the Bearer of Burdens?"

"Set up your easel and watch."

Ed looked around the tent. The Bearer's mattress, braced with a complicated iron framework, took up most of the floor, and the Bearer took up most of the mattress. The Hands swarmed around her, braiding pearls into her hair, rubbing her feet, and chatting in Calish all the while. They stepped around a clutter of cushions, bowls and miscellaneous odds and ends as they worked. A pile of notebooks sat by the bed. Rolled-up sleeping mats heaped one corner. A small table held folded cloths and a chessboard. The baking-hot air smelled like talcum powder and cumin.

"I'm supposed to paint in the middle of this chaos?"

"At my convenience, remember? I'm not going anywhere, and we all have jobs to do. Your job," she added pointedly, "is to paint."

Ed set up his easel in the least crowded corner. The Bearer gave a quiet command, and the Hands lined up before her. She paused, and then pointed to the child and a young woman. They squealed and hugged each other, then stood at solemn attention by the Bearer's shoulders, one on each side.

The eldest Hand pursed her lips in disapproval, but called out something in Calish, and two men in white Community robes entered the tent. They bowed to the Bearer, then turned on each other and started arguing. The Bearer sighed and raised a hand. The fight stopped at once. The Bearer spoke with each man in turn, slowly and with deliberate patience. Ed had a feeling that this was a longstanding feud. Still, both men seemed satisfied with the Bearer's replies. They gave a plate of small cakes and a pottery bowl that exuded an aroma like curry to the young woman, who placed them on a table next to the Bearer. With an air of great ceremony, the Bearer ate one of the cakes and smiled. The painter's stomach growled, and he licked his dry lips.

All morning people came in, sometimes arguing, sometimes joyful, sometimes, as far as Ed could tell, just to chat. No one looked surprised at the Bearer's nudity. All brought some kind of edible offering. In the rare pauses between visitors, the Bearer sipped water and wrote rapidly in one of her notebooks.

At last Bearer Amberlynn raised a finger, signaling "Enough." The oldest Hand closed the tent flap.

"What a day," the Bearer groaned. She turned to Ed for the first time in hours. "I think half of them just wanted a glimpse of you."

"I didn't think anyone even realized I was here."

"Oh, everyone knows. An off-planet shuttle, landing here? That hasn't happened since I arrived. It would be rude to ask about you directly, but anyone with an offering and a plausible excuse could at least get a glimpse of you. I'm just surprised the Mandators . . ."

As though summoned, five older men in red-and-black-striped robes shouldered their way into the tent. The Hands cried out, and even the Bearer looked startled. The men's gazes swiveled at once to Ed. One picked up his portfolio and started riffling through it.

"Hey! Put that down!"

The man ignored him, but the Bearer upbraided the stranger with a stream of Calish that scorched Ed's ears, even though he only caught one word in twenty. The man put down the portfolio and glared.

"Ed, would you kindly show the esteemed Mandators that you have no electronic devices about your person?" said the Bearer, never taking her eyes from the men.

Ed turned out his pockets and rolled up his sleeves, but to his humiliation the strangers insisted on patting him down. They seemed disappointed at not finding anything. They bowed stiffly to the Bearer and left.

"What the heck was that about?"

Bearer Amberlynn smirked. "The Mandators are angry that I hired you without letting them vet you first. But inside this tent, the Bearer makes the rules. Oh—as a nominal Hand, you can eat some of the offerings. Help yourself."

While Ed attacked a plateful of curried lentils and flatbread and drained the water pitcher, the Bearer introduced the Hands. The little girl was Nima, the other chosen assistant was called Amira, and the disapproving older woman was Sabeen. Most of the others spoke at least some English and introduced themselves with formal courtesy, but their names soon swirled together in his head, thanks to the heat, the crowding, and Nima's excited chatter.

"Can we see the picture of Bearer Amberlynn?" Nima begged.

"There is no picture. I've just primed the canvas. I haven't started painting yet."

"Good." Seizing a loop of stout rope that dangled from an iron grid overhead, Bearer Amberlynn heaved herself fully upright. Ed froze, transfixed. He'd relaxed while she was talking, drawn by her animation, her rapport with her petitioners, and the comfort of hearing his own language again. Seeing that massive body in motion, falling toward him like an avalanche, sparked sudden discomfort, almost fear.

"You can't paint the Bearer of Burdens yet because you're not seeing her yet, just an alarmingly fat naked woman," she said. "Go take a walk, anywhere within the walls. Leave your supplies here. One of the girls will come for you tomorrow."

Ed trudged back to the unfurnished sandstone cell the Bearer had called the Foreigners' Quarters in disappointment. This wasn't the adventure he'd imagined, painting some exotic beauty while living in a silk-draped palace. Chances were he'd slip up, offend someone, and be stranded in the desert without a coin to his name. He'd pretty much called the Bearer an island, after all.

CREDO

"Painter?" said a low voice from the doorway.
 He looked up and blinked. There was the beauty he'd imagined. Standing there alone with the desert sunset behind her, she looked like royalty stepped out of a painting.

"Ah, come in. Um, you're . . . Amira, right?"

"You remember well. I bring you some comforts," she said in clear, yet charmingly accented English. A fragrance of spice and sandalwood followed her into the little room. She strung up a net hammock and draped a colorful blanket over the doorway. "To keep insects out. Here also are a cushion and blanket and a waterskin. You will be comforted now?"

He smiled. "Very. Thank you."

"No. Thank you. Now we will have a picture to remember Bearer Amberlynn when she is gone. And maybe you will save her."

"Save her? From what? From whom?"

Amira sighed. "This is a hard duty, to be the Bearer. She must take everything in our hearts to herself: all grief and joy, all troubles and secrets. With this she must accept the offerings. It weighs on mind and body."

"Yeah, I noticed."

Amira didn't seem to pay attention to his tone. "Yes! She is the best Bearer ever. Most Bearers die before they are so large, but

Bearer Amberlynn I think is near a thousand Earth pounds. The Mandators thought we would not trust one from Earth, but her father was of the Community. She understands. We all trust her."

"If everyone loves her so much, why does she need saving?"

"She is strong now, but soon the burdens will be crushing her. You can take her where gravity is lighter. The Mandators do not rule you."

"What? Whoa. I just came here to paint."

"You are a Hand now. We do for the Bearer whatever she needs."

"Well, I'm not giving her a sponge bath," Ed joked.

Amira's look turned pitying, disdainful. "Good night, Painter."

છૉૹ૭ৄ

S abeen came for Ed the next morning.
        "Is Amira, um, upset with me?" he asked.

The oldest Hand didn't answer; Amira didn't react when they entered the Bearer's tent, but the Bearer herself smiled.

"So, you stayed! The few others who got this far either decided they'd do better on a more hospitable planet or tried to seduce Amira. She tells me you didn't, so this just might work out."

Now Amira did catch his eye and gave him a defiant look that he couldn't fathom.

"Ah, I certainly hope it will, Bearer."

"Amberlynn, please."

છૉૹ૭ৄ

A s soon as Sabeen opened the tent flaps each morning, people started arriving with offerings of hot lamb stew, stuffed dates, pastries . . . and the most intimate details of life in the isolated compound. The more his Calish improved, the more Ed felt like an eavesdropper, hiding behind his canvas while people confessed secrets or confided their deepest longings to the Bearer.

"It's like a soap opera," he muttered. The other Hands looked blank, but Amberlynn, recording the latest saga in one of her notebooks, chuckled. Sabeen announced that she needed to fetch water and left the tent.

"What's her problem?" Ed asked.

Bearer Amberlynn chuckled again. "You're from Earth. To her, that's reason for suspicion."

"But you're originally from Earth yourself."

"Exactly. That makes me full of irreverent impulses, like proposing modern medical care and a library, or getting the Mandators to permit a portrait by an offworlder. Sabeen's been serving the Bearers since she was Nima's age. She's always disapproved of me," said Amberlynn with a tolerant smile. "I question too much. But I Rooted faster than any Bearer in living memory, and since a Bearer's size is a reflection of her compound's trust in her, she had to admit I was dedicated."

"Rooted?"

"Became our Bearer forever," said Nima from where she snuggled between Amberlynn and Amira.

"That's the Community term for realizing that you can no longer get out of bed." Amberlynn's smile took on a wry twist. "I've always made a point of being very good at what I do."

"So you haven't left this tent . . ."

"In eight years." She waved a hand at her colossal body. "However much Sabeen—and the Mandators—object to my improper requests, they can't deny that I've done my job exceptionally well. Bearer Samar, my predecessor, barely topped seven hundred pounds when she died. Heart failure."

The question that had been simmering in Ed's mind boiled to the surface. "Why?" His artist's eye had noted the darker tone of Amberlynn's legs, the bluish tint to her fingernails and lips. Now he recognized the signs of an overworked heart straining to pump life through an ever more massive body. "Why do you do this to yourself? Why do this at all?"

The other Hands looked indignant. Bearer Amberlynn sighed. "If you'd been raised in the Community, you'd understand. Becoming the Bearer is the highest possible honor."

"You weren't raised here."

"No," said Amberlynn with an unaccustomed scowl. "I was raised in a place that considered me undisciplined, unattractive and unacceptable for weighing less than a third of what I do now—regardless of my education, achievements or any other qualities. To the Community, I'm a role model, a symbol of trust and cooperation."

"But your health . . ."

"I know. It's part of the job. Ed, do you speak French?"

"Mais oui," he replied, puzzled.

"Excellent." The Bearer switched languages with ease. "This is the next best thing to privacy. Haven't you wondered why I commissioned this portrait? Show me what you've done so far, so the girls won't get too suspicious."

"Um . . . historical record?" Ed guessed, turning the easel so she could see.

"Very nice! No, although that's the official reason."

"Bearer, your Hands can't understand you," Amira said.

"Ed is a Hand, remember?" the Bearer retorted, and went on in French. "Ed, I'm asking you to paint a recruiting poster to duplicate and spread to Community compounds on other planets. This compound was without a Bearer for six months after my predecessor died. It was chaos. A compound without a Bearer doesn't exist, as far as the intergalactic Community is concerned. The Mandators plan to prevent that chaos by having our next Bearer already chosen when I die. Even if she's just a child."

"A child?" Horrified, Ed glanced toward Nima.

The Bearer pointed at the canvas. "Don't look at her. Look at the painting. Yes. And I have no authority over what happens after my death."

"The Hands would allow that?"

"They get their status through me. But some would encourage it. Spoil the girl, feed her treats, keep her entertained so she doesn't run about and get thin—and nudge her to think that your friends are her friends, too. Eventually you've molded her to think like you, and you can speak through her mouth. You can wield the authority of the Bearer and still be able to dance at the Cloud Festival."

"I can't picture S—the oldest Hand dancing."

Amberlynn looked stunned. "Her? She's a stickler for protocol, but she's devoted her life to the Hands. She knows the importance of maturity. She knows how wrong it would be to ask this sacrifice of a child. She even told the Mandators so once." Amberlynn winced. "If Hands weren't appointed for life, even I might not have been able to keep the Mandators from exiling her. No, not her." The Bearer's gaze shifted a fraction.

Toward Amira.

"The next Bearer will be an adult. One with some idea of what she's committing herself to, and the tradition she serves," said the Bearer of Burdens. "It's a great honor, but it's one that should go to someone who's old enough to understand what she's undertaking. Intellectually, at least."

Ed stole a glance at Nima. "Can't you send her away or something?"

"Send her where? Into the desert? Nothing leaves this planet but trade shipments, through the Mandators. I've fought with them for years." She sighed. "If it weren't for the technological ban, it would be easy to recruit someone else. Believe it or not, I'm an advertisement for a thriving Community. If we had computers . . . As it is, this portrait is the best chance I have."

"I'll do my best, Bearer Amberlynn."

"Thank you, Ed." Amberlynn closed her eyes. She looked weary and drained, like a melted candle.

⊰♡⊱

The painting took shape. Now that he understood why he was painting, Ed made a point of studying the compound and its surroundings. He understood why no one had been offended at his "island" remark. The Bearer was, in a sense, the soul of her compound, her land. Knowing this, Ed tried to paint an echo of the rolling golden dunes in the Bearer's abundant flesh, the clear dark of the night sky in her eyes. He painted her hands open, welcoming all who came to her, and tried to capture the wry, amused quirk of her smile. All the Hands admired the growing portrait. Even Sabeen unbent enough to bestow a grudging nod of approval. Amira pronounced him a genius—and doubled her efforts to get Ed to take the Bearer "somewhere safer."

Despite himself, Ed found himself nodding when Amira spoke. Now and then Amberlynn let slip glimpses of the previous Bearer's last days: gasping for breath, unable to sit up. Amberlynn deserved a few years of comfort after giving so much. Now and then Amberlynn spoke of her green homeworld with longing. He could take her to a green planet. He could bring her such joy . . . whether she wanted it or not.

Ed was painting pearls into Portrait-Amberlynn's hair and wondering whether the real Amberlynn would prefer a waterworld or something more Earthlike, but with lighter gravity when a young woman rushed in, wailing. Amira barely stopped her from throwing herself on the Bearer. Nima cried out. Bearer Amberlynn spoke softly to the newcomer, questioning. The woman sniffled and nodded.

Nima hugged the woman, who clutched the child to her heart and rocked back and forth, murmuring and sobbing herself empty. Then she released Nima, who was crying, too. The woman said something earnest to the Bearer, and walked out calmer than she had come in, leaving a cloth bag on the offering table.

"Nima, sweetheart, give me one piece of her offering and keep the rest for yourself," said the Bearer gently.

"But Alya's my friend," Nima said, wide-eyed. "Is it true, what her mama said? Did Alya really die?"

"Yes, sweetheart. The candy was supposed to be for her when she got better, but sometimes people don't."

"I don't want Alya's candy," Nima wailed. "I want her to be alive!"

The Bearer held out her arms and Nima rushed to her, pressing against the cushion of her body for comfort, and sobbing.

"Why did you stop that woman?" Ed whispered to Amira. "Amberlynn wanted to hug her back. I saw it."

"Only Hands may touch the Bearer." Amira frowned. "Amberlynn should not indulge Nima like this. She is weakening."

Amberlynn held Nima and stroked her hair until the little girl fell asleep, and Sabeen put her to bed on a mat in the corner. Amberlynn sagged with grief.

Ed motioned to Amira to follow him to the Foreigner's Quarters. "That does it. I'm going to tell the Mandators I need a special mineral for my paint and get permission to leave the compound. Then I'm going to arrange for a transport shuttle to land right outside the gates, and this is going to stop."

"Oh, Ed, I knew you would do it!" Amira threw her arms around his neck, but he turned his face away and she only kissed his cheek.

⊰⊱⊱⊰

Ed and Amberlynn had been speaking French so often that Nima gleefully greeted him with "Bonjour" every morning, and he was afraid that the older Hands would start picking it up. He could not take the chance of speaking more openly about what might happen when his task was complete.

Ed's hand shook when he signed the finished portrait. It had been hard to keep painting and to arrange for the departure without giving anything away. Amberlynn had been eyeing him purposefully for days.

"Thank you, Painter," she said, as she counted gold coins into his hand. For the first time since he'd arrived she was clothed, draped in flowing white fabric. Less formally, but with more feeling, she added. "It won't be the same without you, Ed. Where are you off to next? I suppose you'll be switching to a cooler palette for a while?"

He shrugged. He wasn't about to remind her of the forested green hills of her distant homeland. No point in adding to her burdens. Especially not now. "Bearer, forgive me."

"For what, Ed? Leaving us? I told you—staying put's part of my job."

The sky roared. Everyone looked up. Amira clapped her hands. The Bearer frowned at her.

"He did it!" Amira shouted over the rumble of a descending shuttle. "Bearer, you're going to be so happy. Everyone, help me move her . . ."

"Did I ask to be moved?" Amberlynn looked thunderous. "I'm not going anywhere!"

Amira's triumphant smile vanished. "But, Bearer, you must!"

The other Hands stared at Amira in shock. Ed sidled toward the tent exit.

"Amira," said Amberlynn, "remember that you're my Hand."

"Always, Bearer! And I do for you whatever you need."

"What you do not do," said Amberlynn in a voice that chilled the sweltering tent, "is decide for me just what it is that I need. That is my choice, not yours."

Ed stood with one hand on the tent flap, transfixed.

"Ed!" Amberlynn bellowed. He jumped and glanced toward Nima's empty sleeping mat. Amberlynn gave him an almost imperceptible nod. "Get out of here, Painter. Get off this planet. Get—" She clutched a hand to her heart and gasped.

The Hands clustered around her at once. Ed slipped out unnoticed in the chaos and ran to the waiting shuttle. Sabeen stood beside it, with Nima slumped at her feet.

"She will not sleep long, Painter. And you will never be welcome back here. The Mandators will never trust foreigners again."

"I know. But the new recruits will all be Community, right? And older than Nima." Ed scooped up the sleeping girl. "Tell me you think it's right to have a child as Bearer. Tell me that's what Amberlynn wants. I'm doing this as her Hand, and you know it."

Sabeen bowed her head. "I serve the Bearer, as always. Go."

Ed ran up the ramp and buckled Nima into a seat, grateful that the little Hand had not witnessed her Bearer's supposed heart attack. The thunder of takeoff roused her, and she looked around in panic.

"Bearer Amberlynn? Amira? Bearer Amberlynn!"

"It's all right, Nima. We're just taking a little trip."

She tore at the restraining belt. "I don't want to go! Bearer Amberlynn, help!"

Ed winced, but the shuttle pilot was either deaf or remembering a lecture from Sabeen.

"Nima, listen to me. Do you want to be like Bearer Amberlynn?"

"Yes." Nima sniffled.

"Well, she's very wise and learned, and she wants you to be, too. I'll take you someplace where you can go to school like she did. But first I need to get more paints and paint lots of pictures of Bearer Amberlynn to send to other Communities. She asked me to."

"Then that's our job," said Nima in a mournful voice. "Because we're Hands."

"And we do for the Bearer whatever she needs," said Ed, half to himself. "Nima, I'm going to send Bearer Amberlynn an offering. A book."

"She can't eat a book!"

"To feed her mind," Ed said and smiled. "She wanted a library. It's a start."

One book wasn't likely to change Amberlynn's fate. Even if the Mandators never discovered her deception, her body could not hold up much longer. But the change just might give her successors more options.

"Soon we'll come back with lots of books," Nima said.

Ed said nothing. He could never go back, and if Nima did, she'd find her world changed. But Amberlynn had wanted this. She knew what she was doing; he was sure.

Almost sure. He'd carry that burden of uncertainty forever.

He'd just have to bear it.

When does a woman being used by others, being outcast, being hated, turn around and stand up for herself? And if she does, what form will that take?

WHAT LIES DORMANT

by Swapna Kishore

I was gazing at the sands outside, sun-bright despite the smoked windows of our bus, when I heard Sunil's low hiss of frustration, and his mother's swift reprimand, also low, also wary. I did not want to join any argument. I wanted to stay wrapped in my daydream, where I was still in my Mumbai school, topper amongst special-track girl students, and far away from the reality of our rushed exit. Away from those pressed-together lips of Mother when I asked her, "Why Tilaknagari, isn't that, like, the pits?"

But voices possibly sound louder the more you ignore them, and finally I turned to face my family. Mother and Auntie were both staring at Sunil, looking even more like sisters than they usually did. Uncle was distant, resigned, and I knew he would never side with his son in an argument. Men had little say in gatherer families. My sister, Deepa, looked at Sunil with a wide-eyed wonder only a five-year-old can have.

"I don't see why I can't break off," Sunil said. "I can just ignore that I'm a—"

"Shh." Auntie looked around; luckily for us, a couple of empty rows separated us from our fellow travelers.

"Everyone has to complete Intercity formalities." Mother's tone was curt. She patted the nape of her neck to confirm that her sari covered the telltale blue of the implant. "Your papers reveal that you are, well . . . what we are."

Sunil turned his face away, but he said nothing.

I tried to resume my daydreaming, but the sands outside no longer presented an infinity of possibilities. Instead, they were textured with shadows of villages and cities our bus-route skirted around, places overrun by species gone wild because humans had been knocked off by biobombs. Decades ago, people in protective suits must have walked here, controlling officers and my ancestors, the gatherers, who were to harvest lifeen—life energy—from the collapsing men and women. Thinking of the present was no fun, either—that was full of Mumbai mobs three streets away from our house, their shouts and jeers spreading like waves, their hatred saturating the air even as we rushed to the Intercity terminus, dressed as commoners.

At least I had my books. I let my fingers brush the reader strapped to my stomach. The device, the only part of my school-life I managed to smuggle out in that dash for safety, was hidden by my tent-like salwar suit. It contained all the books I loved, even two new ones I uploaded just days before this calamity—Yusuf's 2020 classic, *Genetic Modifications and Life Energy*, and Subramanium's *Advanced Work on Unified Field: Papers published 2030 to 2050.*

I was drooling at the thought of the books when Sunil plunked himself near me.

"With false identities," he said, "we could have started afresh in Tilaknagari, even though it is a dump."

I glanced at the bulge of Mother's implant, straining against the held-in-place edge of her yellow sari. Sunil followed my gaze. "Okay, so they can't hide. But I don't have an implant, and neither do you." He paused. "Not yet."

"I'll re-submit my exemption application." That might not stop them from implanting me after my menarche, but at least I could become a researcher instead of a gatherer. "When my new school uplinks to my Mumbai school-records, the—"

"They didn't tell you?" he asked softly.

"Who? Tell me what?"

He did not speak for a few moments, and I felt uneasy as I waited.

"Maybe you should break free, too," he finally said. "Maybe if we get the gold they are carrying . . ." His gaze shifted to Auntie. "A distraction . . . yes, I think . . ."

"Tell me *what?*" I asked again. "It's about Tilaknagari, right?"

I didn't remember the details, but my sociology textbook described it as a throwback medieval dump, the poorest of the Cities, a City that survived only because the then-still-existing Indian government used it to prototype the City Shield. Obviously, Mumbai's textbooks praised Mumbai and criticized other Cities, I had told myself; Mother and Auntie chose Tilaknagari, so it must be good. But something was wrong; Sunil, usually extrovert and cheery, had become maudlin.

"Your studies—"

"Meera didi, I'm boooorrred!" Deepa tried to prop herself on my lap; I ruffled her hair and firmly moved her away. She loved to snuggle against me, and I didn't want her to notice the strapped reader.

She turned to Sunil. "Let's play." He nodded, pulled out the board for *Warring Presidents*, and handed out the tokens.

We spent the next few hours squinting at the simplistic model of the world. Deepa became Apple Pie Mom President; Sunil, the Dragon Lady Roars; and I was Deep-into-shit Brownskin, for the rest of the world that tried to place City-Shields for protection while biobomb-rich America and China ran amok. I hated such trivialization of the devastation, and played unwillingly, mechanically, while wondering what Sunil wanted to tell me. He avoided eye-contact now, and seemed pre-occupied.

When we reached Tilaknagari and Deepa ran to pester Mother, I pulled Sunil aside. "What—"

"I'm going to try, and maybe, if you—"

"Meera!" Mother beckoned me. "Help us with the bags." She did not give Sunil any responsibility, though he was nineteen, six years older than me. It was her way of showing displeasure.

The reception lounge was pathetic with chipping paint, torn upholstery, and desks loaded with paper files. No computers. Inked pads for thumbprints. I was pressing my inked-purple thumb on my form under the supervision of the officer when a loud bang shook the building and the lights snapped off. A massive short-circuit? Sunil had mentioned a distraction.

When the lights returned, sure enough, he was missing.

Mother noticed Sunil's absence, too, because her face went rigid; she whispered something to Uncle, who paled. She peered through the crowd, probably looking for Auntie, but just as Auntie and Deepa caught up with us, Deepa said, "Where's Sunil Bhaiyya? Where's his bag?"

Mother said, "Shh," and Auntie's eyes glazed in a shocked understanding.

I said nothing, just let the loss roll in my stomach. I held Deepa's hand as we boarded the bus to take us to the allocated apartment in the gatherers' colony. Our bus wove along convoluted roads, and I squinted through the window. Would I spot Sunil walking? Did he have a plan? What had he tried to tell me?

We reached a shanty-town.

"We get off here," Mother said, brisk and energetic, but she wrinkled her nose.

Even she had not expected it to be this bad.

છૢ☾☙ય

After we unpacked and tried to fit our stuff in our single-room apartment, Mother told me, "You will look after Deepa during the day; your Uncle is unwell most of the time."

"What about when I'm at school?"

Mother blinked hard. "Meera, girls here can't attend school after grade five. Tilaknagari reacted rather strongly to the women Presidents who biobombed the world."

I think I took an eternity to let that soak in, and then some. All those nights that I slogged to top my class. All my dreams of shiny labs, and papers presented in conventions. *No school?*

"See, you are thirteen," Mother said. "Your periods will start, you will get implanted and become a gatherer."

"I don't want to gather," I retorted. "I don't want an implant. I want to study." But the implant was unavoidable. The monthly medical checkup at school identified girls to be implanted. *No, wait.*

"If there is no school," I said, "then no one will know when my periods start. I can avoid the implant."

Mother turned pale. "No, no, without a controller, you could harm people. I've never been tempted to, but even the thought that I might ever do so is so horrible that—Believe me, implants are good, you harvest only when . . . let the controllers decide." She took a deep breath. "We were talking about Deepa."

"You should have chosen another City," I said bitterly. "You knew how important studies are to me."

"We had one hour to leave Mumbai. One hour to pack and rush and catch a bus. At least these people need gatherers. At least we are alive."

"Mother," I said, trying to sound reasonable, but squishy with panic inside, "let's buy false identities and move to another City. No one need know."

"Meera, we are gatherers, and our implants need to be managed. And you and Deepa will need to be implanted when you get old enough." Her arm rose, and I thought she was going to hug me, but she drew back.

⊗⊙⊗⊙⊗

L ife fell into the texture of nothingness soon enough, except for the time I hoarded for myself on my daily shopping trip.

That day, after Mother and Auntie left for work, our tap-water reduced to a trickle before the scheduled one hour. Uncle had not yet showered; he snapped at Deepa when she clamored for a game of Ludo. She burst into tears. I checked my watch and was relieved that it was time to go shopping. When I picked up the grocery list, Deepa said, "Take me along, Meera didi."

I shook my head. This daily trip kept me sane. I would head for a derelict outhouse, where, latched in safely and sitting on a stinky throne, I read my secret cache of books.

"Please, didi."

"I'll take you out in the evening," I promised her.

Returning a few hours later, clutching my bag of provisions, what struck me first was the searing heat. I was a few lanes away from home; I paused, surprised. Then I heard the crowds shouting. *Something was wrong.* I quickened my pace, my mouth dry with primal fear. People were ganged around our shanty-town. Huge licks of heat danced macabrely in the air. Shouts mingled with the hiss and spit of fire. Where were the fire-engines? Surely even this wretched City had them! *Deepa!* I rushed forward.

Someone pulled me back. "Let them roast," he said.

"But—"

A child stumbled out of a burning structure, its face a smudge behind the smoke. A man stepped forward. I thought he would pull the child to safety, but he thrust a pole out to push the child back into the inferno.

"A curse on these abominations," said a woman near me.

Hand held over my mouth, I registered the hatred round me. My legs wobbled. This fire was no accident. A hand fell on my shoulder; my stomach lurched. Someone must have recognized me. I was no easy prey. I would claw back if they pushed me into the flames, I would tear at their eyes—

A woman shoved me aside, her face twisted with fury. "You!" She shook her fist at the flames. "You deserve every death, you . . . my grandfather, when he died, you . . ."

She crumpled to the ground, sobbing hard; I did not stay there to watch her. I was shaking, all hollow inside. I slipped through the lanes 'til I was far enough from the woman. The flames blazed red against my closed eyelids, blotched black with the silhouette of the child pushed back. I should have taken Deepa to the market with me. Maybe also told Uncle to take a walk in the park.

I leaned forward and threw up.

Mother and Auntie were at the hospital, on gatherer duty. I had to tell them.

I do not remember weaving down the warren of roads, but there I was, standing inside the walled compound of the hospital. It was quiet—no mobs, nothing. I walked slowly, holding myself steady, past the entrance, towards the wing where gatherers worked. Calm. Too calm. I entered.

Bodies lay heaped on the floor, guarded by a solitary policeman. "Yes, child?" he asked.

"My mother . . ."

"Your mother works here?" He frowned as his eyes moved to my neck, searching for an implant. He gripped his baton.

"No." *I must deflect his attention*, I thought rapidly. "My mother's worried. It's my father . . . I mean—"

"Oh!" He chuckled. "Don't worry, no one's arresting the men. We made sure we arrived after they completed their work. Your father must be celebrating."

Celebrating. I choked back the animal cry rising in my throat. I did not dare look at the policeman, so I stared at the bodies. I was suddenly aware of the buzz that sang on my skin, a quicksilver sharpness around me. Lifeen? A broken collecting jar lay near the bodies. I had not been affected by jars in Mumbai, but those were sealed jars.

"Didn't help them in the end, did it?" the policeman asked, following my gaze. "They drained it from our dead, and then they died."

I took a step forward, fascinated.

"Stay where you are, girl," he said sharply. "The maintenance men haven't repaired those jars yet. It kills the likes of us if we touch it directly."

Ah, yes. Only those with gatherer genes could touch lifeen directly; others needed feeders. My behavior had almost betrayed me. I turned and left.

The hatred-etched faces haunted me all day, as I skulked around in a daze: the woman gloating over the burning shanty-town, the man pushing the child back into the flames, the policeman expecting celebrations. The smells had settled deep inside me: the smoke, the soot, the sickly burning flesh, the antiseptic hospital smell that should have spelled safety. Ash clung to my skin.

I had survived only because we were newcomers and no one recognized me.

Come evening, my feet led me to the still-smoldering shanty-town. Stupid, I knew, but how could I not go there?

No crowds any more. The fire-engines had arrived late—a formality, I suspected—and the bodies had been removed, but their stench thickened the air and clogged my lungs. My eyes smarted. I stepped carefully, keeping my breathing shallow. Embers scalded my shoes and burned my feet. I was near where our apartment had been when I heard a sneeze. A looter?

I flattened out of sight just as a shaft of moonlight struck a face. It was Sunil.

I stepped out.

His head shot up; his body tensed. Then he recognized me and gave a tremulous smile. "Meera? Are the others okay? My mother? Yours? Father? Deepa?"

"No," I whispered. "Any idea why suddenly—"

He touched my shoulder; his breath reeked of whisky. "The Consortium of Cities forced Tilaknagari's government to outlaw gathering; all other Cities had done so already. As soon as the law was passed . . ."

. . . *the hatred burst out*, I thought, completing his sentence.

The day-long wandering had dulled my fear into despondence. So the people hated us, in Mumbai, here, everywhere. I knew that. The energy crisis caused by the biobomb wars was over. Crop cultivation had resumed outside the shielded Cities, and lifeen was not critical to survival. So, sure enough, everyone suddenly detested gatherers for 'robbing' their dying relatives, ignoring the fact that governmental controllers had forced gatherers to harvest.

I carried those hated genes.

"Where can I go now?" I asked Sunil. "They will kill me if they know."

"Come with me. I work as a daily wage laborer; you don't need papers for temporary work." He held out his hand. There were calluses on his palm. Earlier, his hands had been so tender that Auntie often teased him, saying he should have been born a girl.

I nodded.

"They had gold, no?" he said. "If we find it . . ."

Had he come to pay homage, or for the loot? I hated myself for having doubts. He had offered to help me, no?

He poked the ashes. He did not find anything, of course; he was searching at the wrong place. I would tell him about it later, once I was sure.

CRECO

The trader gave me a packet to deliver. "Walk down this road 'til you see a yellow board with a painted chicken, and then . . ."

"Then?" I squinted at the scribbled address.

"Boy, you can read?"

Sunil had warned me to stay low-profile as an illiterate errand boy. "No," I said, nervous. "Just looking."

"A pity," the trader murmured. "I prefer a boy who reads and writes."

I hesitated. A week of running errands had exhausted me; I definitely preferred a job that depended on reading, not muscles. What was the harm in admitting I could read a bit? It was not as if I was confessing I understood complex science. Or that I was a girl. Or, God forbid, a gatherer.

"For what?" I asked.

"Accounts, records. High-paying jobs."

Sometimes one must take risks. "I can read a bit."

"Read this." He pointed to the address, and I read it out. He nodded. "Now I need your identity papers."

What a fool I had been! Sunil had warned me that, without papers, one could only do manual jobs. Fear clawed my stomach. "I can't read all that much, I—"

He leaned forward, and for a moment I thought he could see that, under my thick, coarse shirt were strips of cloth tightly binding prepubescent breasts, and that he connected this with my thin voice and my habit of using only the privy with a working latch. I could barely breathe.

"Now, here is what I suggest," he said. "You do my accounts. I will not pay a single paisa more, but maybe, just maybe, I will not report you as illegal immigrants. I know where your cousin works, and I know where you boys live. Just a hint to the local policeman and . . ."

"As you wish," I said, cursing myself for ignoring Sunil's advice.

As I slogged over his ledgers the rest of the day, adding numbers till they danced before my eyes, I promised myself that I would find a way out of this bind. I was supposed to be an unusually intelligent girl, and creative, too. All I had to do was ignore crippling emotions. I tried to shut out the burning shanty-town, the heaped bodies in the hospital. I fought the memory of that smell permeating my lungs, the soot and burning flesh. I tried not to think of the dingy hovel Sunil and I shared with five men, where I barely slept at night, scared I'd betray myself by my screams when the inevitable nightmares came.

It was only after I put in weeks of meticulous work that the trader stopped watching me suspiciously. My gaze remained lowered in a docile way, but I observed all I could. *Patience*, I told myself. *Gather data, think, explore.*

Then one day I heard a customer ask the trader whether his new identity papers were ready.

Sunil returned late as usual that evening, enveloped in the perpetual mist of alcohol. I led him to a secluded corner.

"Sunil, suppose we get identity papers?"

"Are you mad? Do you think we can trust anyone enough to ask?"

"The trader's ledger has—"

"Don't you dare let him guess you can read!" He gripped my shoulder; I jerked free, disgusted by his stale breath.

"If we buy . . ."

He guffawed. "If I had even a rupee more, I'd get myself a drink."

This was pointless. I would talk to Sunil after he sobered up.

But days passed, and he did not change.

Then my periods started. With the cramps of the flow, I thought of Mother and her insistence that implants protected us, and I was scared about the changes that would start in my body, and how I would handle them without anyone explaining.

The changes started soon enough. I was walking back from work, the streets a crush of men and women, and my skin crackled as if with static. I halted, too alarmed to react. It took me a few moments to connect this with my experience near the hospital's broken lifeen jar. The sense of being surrounded with static grew until an immense urge to scratch gripped me. My skin burned. I tried applying water and balms, but the burning stayed. It vanished a couple of days later, leaving my skin cool and normal.

The cycle repeated itself every three or four days. My skin, I figured, picked up stray lifeen from the people or air around me, and when I was overfull, I discharged spontaneously, like an out-of-control power generator. It unnerved me.

So this was what Mother meant by saying implants helped. An implant probably switched this affinity to lifeen off and on. I could not get implanted, though. I tried to control the sensation by staying physically distant from people. I discovered that discharges were slower and less traumatic when I was calmer, and accumulation less hurtful to the skin. I wanted to remove my sensitivity to lifeen, but my books only described the biochemical and electrical mechanics of storing and disbursing lifeen using implants.

Perhaps Sunil could help me. Like all men, he was insensitive to lifeen. The Y gene neutralized the ability of the X gene (an approach I could not use), but he might know something useful.

I cornered him on a day when he seemed relatively sober. "Sunil, I am already thirteen."

"So you are." He looked me up and down. "So you are."

I suppressed my discomfort; he was my aunt's son, and therefore, a brother. "My genes—"

"Don't talk to me about them. I hate this whole gatherer business."

He could afford to dismiss the problem; it did not affect him. But if all we did was move away from this crowded room, I'd find life easier to handle. Surely he would like a better life—a life other than breaking stones or pouring tar on roads. I understood enough about the trader's work to fake identity papers for both of us. "About my future, our future . . ."

"No woman would come to me if she knew." He took a swig from his bottle.

"Get a grip," I snapped. "We can get identity papers . . . and Mother and Auntie had gold. If we get it—"

"Gold?" My words had obviously jerked him out of his drunken haze. He held my chin up. "We'll go to Mumbai. We will marry."

"*Marry?* But that's *wrong!* We are cousins—"

"It's logical. Our community marries within itself because we can't spread the genes, and we are the only two left." He shrugged. "Cousins marry in some communities. I feel lonely at times; don't you?"

"Not like this," I said firmly. "You may be nineteen, but I am only thirteen, remember?"

His face stiffened. "It was a suggestion. It is not as if . . . as if . . ."

This is how disillusionment comes, I thought. *This is how a friend and brother becomes a stranger.*

The next day, I went to the burned shanty and dug out our half-melted box of jewelry and gold coins. I 'borrowed' stationery and stamps from the trader's stock, and spent the evening creating appropriately soiled birth certificates, the sort the merchant made. They would be good enough; this back-to-stone-age place had no sophisticated methods to check identity. No biometrics here, thanks to Tilaknagari's technology-hatred reaction to the biobomb wars. I made myself one identity as a Mumbai boy, Rahul Kakade, and another as a girl (of course, not a gatherer) with my real name, just in case I got sick of acting as a boy. For Sunil, I created an identity as Sameer Srivastava, from Mumbai.

Now I had to wait for an appropriate opening.

A few weeks later, I saw an advertisement from the Records Office of Tilaknagari, saying they wanted residential apprentice-clerks, the only selection criteria being a dictation and an interview. How difficult could that be?

That night, I bundled whatever I owned. I left part of the gold for Sunil, along with his new identity papers, and a note explaining that he should change his location because the trader might harass him. I crept out of the hovel when the sky was barely tinted with dawn pink. I was painfully aware that, regardless of its miserable state, this had been 'home' for months now, and that I could not return to it whether or not I got the job today, because Sunil would be gone, and the trader, alerted by my absence, would be searching for me.

ಐ೧೨ಬಿ೧೮

Ten other candidates, all men, all older than me. A supervisor read out three texts for us to transcribe—one an excerpt from a history book, one a legal case, and one from a biology textbook that I had studied three years ago and could have scribbled without prompting.

Then interviews. The supervisor frowned as he read my answer-paper. My stomach curdled. I had failed. I had made a blunder. Maybe I had signed my real name by mistake.

"Can you use computers, Rahul?" he asked.

I hesitated. Would I get into trouble if I admitted I knew how to use advanced (by Tilaknagari standards) technology? I peered at his face and saw no wile or cunning.

"Yes, I can use computers."

"You are underage." He glanced at my forged certificate. "Your guardians?"

"Dead." I sensed his fleeting relief. "I live on the streets, doing odd jobs to survive."

"Your transcript was error-free. Mumbai must have good schools."

I said nothing. He was an official, not a policy maker.

Along with a couple of other recruits, I was led through a complex of buildings, until we reached a section comparable to a modern Mumbai building. Air-conditioned rooms. Shelves stacked with books on just about every topic, and enough book-readers to service an army. Rows of computers. Men working. Such activity and energy was unusual in Tilaknagari. There were no women, though.

More interviews and tests. I answered the questions as well as I could, too far into this to behave half-heartedly. The interviewers debated amongst themselves, and finally, a middle-aged man called me. "I'm Madhur Bhatia, your new team leader," he said. "Do you know about lifeen gathering?"

My aptitude scores must have been higher in this area because of all I'd read. "I thought gathering is banned," I said cautiously.

"We may want genetic modifications in future. We want to study the lifeen experiment to see why it failed."

Failed? Lifeen had helped society through a critical phase; funny how everyone forgot that.

As Madhur explained the project objective and scope, my apprehension began to transform into excitement. Because of this project, I could access data on my people and our history. I might learn how my body was different and, perhaps, how to escape what my genes seemed to dictate.

Over the days that followed, in addition to doing assigned work, I grasped knowledge with desperate hunger. I read sociology, law, science. I read history to see why, despite lifeen being essential, the public never accepted gatherers. I read religion and politics to understand how leaders used religion to manipulate public opinion for vote-banks. When our team debated pros and cons of genetic modifications, I reminded myself to stay on the periphery. I was only a junior data-digging drudge who fed raw numbers to statistical programs.

Late into the night, though, I often thought of that awful day when my family was killed—all except Sunil, whom I had lost to dejection and drink anyway. I worried that my lifeen affinity would betray me some day. By then, I had trained myself to sense when a discharge was imminent so that I stayed away from people, but I was shaky about the secrets my body held. If I found a dying person, would I be tempted to draw out lifeen? The very thought repulsed me.

Life was further complicated because I was a female. As I reached the age when voice-breaking was common for boys, I increasingly feared detection. Perhaps they would have mandatory physical examinations. My breasts were bigger now; to hide the contrast of my bound breasts with my flat stomach, I wrapped cloth around my midriff, ending up as a thick-bodied youth with thin, non-muscular arms.

As our project progressed, the discussions left me increasingly uncomfortable. Gatherers, according to my seniors, were a modified species because they used changed chemical and biological processes to capture and discharge lifeen. Implants, though they adversely impacted gatherer health, were justified for controlling these 'engineered subhumans' because they allowed controllers to monitor use of the ability. I thought the team's bias against gatherers was affecting their scientific rigor, and the team leader, Madhur, was no exception.

I watched in silence, and kept studying.

One day, I spotted a small blue box on Madhur's desk—oblong, with a small antenna and a clamp. My breath quickened as I recognized it: an implant for gathering. My heart thudded wildly as I picked it up and rolled it in my hands. I switched it on. My skin turned cold and numb, and the implant started glowing. So this was how Mother and—

"What the—"

I jerked my head up and saw Madhur's startled face the same moment I noticed gloves on the table. *So implants are considered unsafe.* I dropped the box onto the tabletop; it sat there, glowing bright blue.

Madhur's jaw had dropped. "You—you—only a gatherer can . . ."

I won't harm you, I wanted to say, but my mouth refused to form words, and as I straightened up, he retreated and tripped, falling on the sharp edge of a steel cupboard. A gash slit the side of his face, right down his neck. Blood gushed out.

I could not move for a few moments. Then I managed to squeak, "Help!" Again, louder, more firmly. A few colleagues rushed over; one man said, "I'll call a doctor," while others stood around, looking scared and helpless. Waiting for help. But this was Tilaknagari—ambulances took time. Madhur's face blanched from loss of blood, and I sensed his lifeen seep out.

Lifeen. That was the key.

Feeders used to dispense lifeen were designed to power equipment and food synthesizers. No feeder had been designed yet to pour lifeen into people—but if people died when they lost lifeen, a reverse flow could restore health.

I could at least try.

I moved near Madhur and held my hand up to catch and deflect back his lifeen outflow. His face remained pallid. I discharged whatever was stored under my skin. Not enough. I needed more lifeen to pump in—where could I get it from? The room had no jars. There was only one other source, a source I had never tried tapping—I had never heard of any gatherer tapping it—my own lifeen. I focused and drew it from the very marrow of my bones, and channeled it into the wound. My skin burned, then became ice-cold; my vision turned hazy. I squinted at the wound and pinched it shut before I slumped near Madhur. Slowly, very slowly, color returned to his face. My dizziness reduced.

The impact of my action sank in as I heard the horrified whispers around me. "Gatherer," they were saying. In saving Madhur's life, I had betrayed mine.

"Call the guards," a man said.

I would not allow them to arrest me. I glared at the men and headed for the door. No one dared follow. All was not lost, I told myself. I still had my faked certificates; I could head for Mumbai, maybe as a girl—I was tired of pretending to be a boy. I fled back to my room.

As I shoved my clothes into a backpack, I was surprised to admit to myself that I did not want to leave. I wanted to ask the men *why* they feared me even after I saved Madhur's life. These guys were studying the 'lifeen experiment'—but even they behaved like I were an alien, a monster.

Emotions ran deeper than academic knowledge. People feared and hated what they did not understand. Heck, even I feared myself at times.

I was only fifteen. This was not how I wanted to live my life, always afraid of what others would do to me, and afraid of what my abilities would make me do.

But why was I scared of my abilities? Mother had implied that, without the implant, gatherers would crave lifeen and might hurt people, but I had never felt such an urge. Had implant designers encouraged this myth to make gatherers submit to implants? Lifeen gathered from dying people had been considered essential to tide humanity over the energy crisis, and controllers must have used the implants to "regulate" gatherers for such harvesting. It might never have occurred to them to explore other uses for lifeen affinity. After all, we were not normal people.

I strode through the corridors, arranging my thoughts into coherent, persuasive arguments. The committee that decided the projects *had to* give me a hearing.

I had used lifeen to heal, and now I was offering myself up for study.

୪୦ଓ୫ୟ

The morning phonecall had been unexpected; by the time I reached my already-established appointment at Mumbai Super Specialty Hospital, I was disoriented. I stopped outside the ward for a couple of deep breaths, put the thought of the call away from me, then entered. The patient, with an end-stage cancer, had been reduced to mere skin stretched over bones. His vital signs were deteriorating, and his organs had started surrendering. The Mumbai doctors were presenting me the toughest possible challenge within the parameters of cases I accepted.

The doctor-on-duty glared at me as I reached out for the patient's frail, almost translucent hand.

Mother must have stood near such beds fifteen years ago, but under the supervision of a controller who switched her implant on only when he wanted her to harvest lifeen from the dying to store in feeders. My implant was different; it let me control when and how much lifeen I gathered and when I disbursed it for healing. Using skills practiced over years, I connected with the patient's feeble lifeen flow, then adjusted a dial to pour my stored lifeen into him.

Ten minutes. Twenty. He gave a feeble sigh.

"That's all for one session," I told the doctor.

I recorded the methodology I had used, the units of lifeen consumed, the before-and-after readings of the patient's vital signs.

"That lifeen you used," the doctor said. "Did you extract it from me?"

"From you?" I gaped at him. "If you've read our published papers, you know we don't extract lifeen from people. We just store what is in the air." The healing implant allowed storing plenty of lifeen subcutaneously; discharge occurred only when initiated by the gatherer.

"You gatherers used to take it from the dying," he said. "You take it from the living now."

The prejudice hadn't gone. "Gatherers were forced to take it from the dying by their controllers," I said. "Now we only draw what is spare and would go waste anyway."

"But you *can* draw lifeen from people, right?" He paused. "And you could even throw it out of you, punching someone with it. Who will protect people from you?"

"When have I harmed—"

"Others could, once more freaks are reintroduced."

The doctor did not know, but there were already others like me. After I offered myself as a subject for study, the authorities managed to locate five other gatherer girls, safe because some non-gatherer families had hidden them. In the initial years, in addition to participating in experiments, I continued to work as a junior, but as I became proficient in science, I got involved in designing the healing implant. The implant had received reluctant acceptance from Tilaknagari doctors. I was now demonstrating it to Mumbai doctors, hoping to involve them in the project, but proud Mumbaikars refused to accept that Tilaknagari had done something better than them, and kept voicing apprehensions.

And then, there was this bias against us, despite scores of published papers.

"When gatherer genes are reintroduced," I said, "every female capable of lifeen harvesting will be trained using a standard curriculum."

He shrugged. "You cannot control rogue elements."

The truth was, there could be no rogue elements. We were six female gatherers living in a well-guarded Tilaknagari house, and none of us had, under any provocation, tried to misuse lifeen to harm others. The very idea disgusted us.

I had a theory about it. I had come to believe that the modifications enabling gathering also strengthened social empathy to a degree that made it impossible to deliberately harm others. I had compared gatherers and non-gatherers for incidence of hurtful actions and found this true. It also explained why earlier implants harmed gatherers—when women were forced to extract lifeen from the dying, the act clashed with their innate empathy and caused stress. Unfortunately, more studies were needed before my theory could be proved and announced.

I did four healings under the watchful eye of frowning Mumbai doctors, and, by evening, my reserves were low. I was relieved to return to the hotel.

Except that there was one more thing to do. I had to meet the morning's caller.

The man in the hotel lobby had a receding hairline rimmed with grey, and a body thick with flab. His face was pudgy. If I hadn't been given his name—Sameer Srivastava—I would not have recognized him as Sunil.

"You are famous," he said, his smile formal and stiff.

I sat opposite him. "Sort of. You live in Mumbai?"

His arm shook as he patted his face dry with a handkerchief. "Yes. I have a business here. My family . . . ."

"Yes?" I prompted.

"I have a daughter, Radha. My wife's dead."

"Sorry to hear that," I murmured.

"Meera . . ." He looked around nervously, then continued, "You are in this business, but for most people, gathering is evil. My wife never knew about me. My girlfriend, she really hates gathering, and if Radha shows any signs of . . . Anyway, no woman wants to bring up another woman's child."

Why tell me this? "You expect me to talk to your girlfriend?"

"*No!*" He bit his lip in an obvious attempt to control himself. He said, "Shruthi doesn't need to know, it's not like she wants children. But if Radha is living with us . . ."

"So you plan to send your daughter away?" To an orphanage, perhaps, or a residential school.

"I can't. Wherever she is, if she shows an ability to gather, everyone will know." He gestured towards the entrance. "Take her with you."

A girl of around seven stood near a couple of potted palms; she looked a bit like Deepa. My niece. But taking her along meant I would have to get her included in our project.

"The law is not clear on females with full or part gatherer genes," I told him. "Implants will probably be made compulsory—"

"Implants are fine, no?" Sunil grinned. "They keep us safe from women like them, and—" He broke off, embarrassed.

As a child, I had admired Sunil's outgoing, jovial nature, and considered him affectionate and considerate. But perhaps I had seen only what I wanted to see. Sunil hadn't got much of a track record in facing difficult situations; he ran off without a plan when we reached Tilaknagari, and though he helped me after the massacre, he soon sheltered behind drink. Even after getting a break using the identity papers I gave him, he married without telling his wife the truth, and now he was abandoning his daughter.

Sunil called his daughter over. "Radha, this is your Auntie Meera."

She folded her hands in a docile Namaste.

"Will you come and live with me?" I asked her, smiling.

The child darted a look at her father, who smiled a bit too broadly at her. She turned back to me, uncertainty flitting across her face. I held out my hand. She did not take it, just studied my face, and she finally nodded solemnly. "Okay, Auntie."

"I will get her bag." Sunil sprang up, as if scared I might change my mind. "It is in my car outside."

Men with gatherer genes had no visible traits like implants nor were they vulnerable and resourceless like gatherer children. Other men like Sunil probably survived the massacre and re-established themselves using false identities. They married and had children. Their sons carried no gatherer genes; their daughters carried one modified X gene. If a girl had one normal X and one modified X, would she sense lifeen?

"Here." Sunil held out a bag. A quick nod, and he strode off.

I gaped after him. No tips on the child's favorite foods or teddy bear or bedtime story, or other parental cautions. No card with his address or contact number. I looked at Radha; again I held out my hand. This time she grasped it and gave me a nervous smile.

Radha and I left for Tilaknagari at dawn the next day. The airplane fascinated the child. She noticed the bright yellow on the airline brochure, delighted at the samosas on our snack trays, and giggled at the cartoon movies. Her sense of delight made me long for my lost childhood years, when wonder came easily. But after a while, she lapsed into silence. When she turned to me, her eyes seemed moist. "Auntie," she said, a tremor to her voice, "why did Papa give me away if I am a good girl?"

I imagined days and weeks and months full of her questions and tears. She was so young, and Sunil's abandoning her would have traumatized her. How would I handle this? My work was my mission, absorbing all my energies, and I was always looking for more things to research. Even meeting Sunil and Radha had stirred in me the outline of a new study—identifying male survivors with gatherer genes and studying the gathering ability of females with only one modified X. Where, in the midst of all those proposals and deadlines and papers, would I rear a child? She would need cuddling and love. There would be the arguments that growing up inevitably brought. I tried to remember my own childhood, and how perfect I had expected my mother to be.

Then I remembered Sunil's relieved expression as he hurried out after leaving his child. That was not the sort of person I wanted to be.

I have inside me a special gene, I reminded myself. I am connected with the energy of life itself; my empathy is so intrinsic to me that I cannot dream of harming anyone. Of what use is such a gift, if I cannot embrace and love my own niece?

Radha was looking at me, wide-eyed; her lower lip was quivering.

I ruffled her hair. "Your father knew I want a daughter," I said softly, and pointed out of the window at the sprawl of Tilaknagari, bright and fresh in the morning sun.

"That's home," I said. "Our home."

Even in a post-apocalyptic world, motherhood may be the strongest drive of all. And a teenage girl can still rebel against it.

KATYUSHA'S FIRST TIME OUT

by Susanne Martin

Olga surfaced from her shallow sleep gasping for breath. In her dream, oxygen had been scarce, and she had felt her airways constrict in a way that made her chest burn. She sat up and gulped the air in the sleeping hall. Stale and heavy with body odor, it was still good breathable air. This wasn't the first time Olga had had a nightmare like this, but today it took on a more sinister meaning. She had been dreading this day for a long time.

She sat up and saw that her daughter Katya's cot was empty. The others had left as well. Normally Olga was an early riser and was gone before everyone else was up, but she had been kept awake by worry most of the night, only slipping into an uneasy slumber just before morning. As she looked around the deserted room, she was relieved that there was no one around to offer an opinion on the argument she had had with her daughter the previous evening.

Olga hurriedly pulled on her clothes. She picked up her breakfast ration at the canteen and ate it on the way to the suiting chamber. She was grateful to have avoided the morning rush. Even nodding to the few stragglers who lingered at breakfast felt like a chore. Olga often found the obligatory cohabitation of the commune stifling. The cramped, close quarters didn't allow for personal space. In the past, she had dealt with the lack of privacy by keeping busy. And there had always been the opportunity to go out. But by venturing outside so often, she had given Katya the wrong impression. She had given her the impression that going out was no big deal. And three days ago, she had discovered her daughter's name on the roster, signed up for her first outing.

The suiting chamber was a hub of activity. Long ago the room had served as the shipping and receiving area, and the space had never lost its impersonal atmosphere of transition. No one lingered here. Even the younger crowd, always looking for nooks to make out in, didn't come into the suiting chamber. Lockers and shelves had been lined up against the concrete walls. Benches stood in the middle. Someone had draped sheets of fabric over a metal frame to set up a changing room. Some people strode back and forth with purpose, while others were in the process of getting into their suits. Olga quietly slipped through the half-open door. And even though the small sound of her entrance was drowned out by the commotion in the chamber, amplified by hard surfaces and high ceilings, Olga's arrival didn't go unnoticed. She was aware of the attention she received; it did not feel entirely benign. She stepped to the side to look for her daughter and saw Alexej Vadimovitch Gribennik wave at her. Normally Alexej would have been assigned to be her partner for the outing, but today he was going with Katya.

Olga walked over and gave Alexej a pat on the arm before turning to her daughter. "Hi," she said, looking at Katya's young, unmarked face. It would soon bear the scars of chemical burns that marked all those who ventured outside. Olga's own features were crisscrossed with faded lines, and a few angry welts attested to her recent outing.

Katya was in the process of pulling on a suit. Olga reached out to help her with the sleeves.

"Mama, don't fuss, please," Katya hissed in lieu of a greeting and pulled away. Olga thought it best to ignore the cold welcome.

"Katyusha, I wanted to wish you luck for your first outing." She knew she should just go and get ready, but the afterimage of her vivid dream still lingered.

"May I?" she asked Alexej. After receiving his nod of permission, she reached for a breather. Her daughter rolled her eyes, but didn't push her away. Adjusting Katya's gear, Olga repeated the mantra every forager was taught: "Your breather is your body's connection to the outside, your tracer is your connection to your community; you need to take good care of both. And stay close to your partner."

"I know, Mama, I'm not a baby."

Olga was satisfied that her daughter's breather had been cleaned thoroughly, and the tracer did emit a strong signal. Everything seemed to be in good working order. Except her relationship with her daughter, whose glares left her as short of breath as her nightmare had.

She gave Katya a thumbs-up, but received no response. This was nothing new. In the last few weeks, Katya had barely spoken to her and had been furious when she learned that Olga had gotten herself assigned to the mission that was to be Katya's first.

Olga had tried everything in her power to postpone the moment her daughter had to venture out into the poisoned atmosphere. Katya hadn't been thankful for the effort; on the contrary, she had whined about being left behind when her peers had long completed their first, second, even third round of outings. Olga had abstained from instilling a fear of the outside in her daughter as some of the other parents had. In her opinion, fear didn't accomplish anything. What if the commune couldn't support them any longer? What if their scarce supplies started to dwindle? What if something went wrong? There had been a lot of what-ifs for Olga since the Melt, and she didn't have any answers. Even though the commune often made her feel claustrophobic, she did appreciate its safety. Collectively they might find ways to keep surviving, day by day.

"Don't worry, Olga," Alexej assured her. "I'll take good care of Katya."

"Thank you," Olga mouthed, but no sound reached her lips. She turned away to get ready. Performing Katya's security check had cost Olga valuable time for going over her own equipment, but she wasn't worried. She was somewhat of a veteran when it came to going out, especially since she had taken extra shifts that should have been Katya's. Olga had never been assertive in anything, but when Katya's medical form had come back with a check-mark in the box 'cleared for outside missions,' she had approached the commander to persuade him to let her take Katya's turns. She felt that there was little she could do for her daughter other than keeping her safely inside, since she wasn't the kind of mother who could tap into closeness and intimacy without discernible effort.

The commander, Ivan Vassilyevitch Bondarchuk, was a strict and imposing man who had taken charge during the chaos of the Melt. No one addressed him by his first name—even his last name was seldom used. For most of the members of the commune, the title had become inseparable from the person. The commander rarely strayed from protocol. He enforced the order that every adult with full lung capacity had to participate in outings. Even medical personal or techies, who had the important task of rebuilding the communications system that might enable them to make contact with other survivors, were not exempt. Going out to collect organic matter and other valuables was the only way to sustain life in the commune.

To Olga's relief, the commander had agreed to her deal. She told herself that this was due to her excellent track record and field experience, and that sharing his bed had been totally unrelated to the special treatment. Just last night, he had invited her to his quarters. She had been tempted; the commander's room offered privacy and a higher degree of ventilation, allowing for a better rest than the communal sleeping hall. But she had felt fragile on the night before Katya's first outing, and in that state it wasn't a good idea for her to seek solace in someone's embrace. Especially when that someone was a man like the commander, who valued courage and strength above all.

Olga stripped and pulled on the protective suit. When she straightened up, she found herself face to face with her partner, a young techie from Katya's group of friends.

"Sergej Alexandrovitch Gromov," he introduced himself stiffly. Rather than offering a handshake, he held out her tracer and breather.

"Olga Evgenyevna Baranova," she replied with equal formality and tried to remember what Katya had told her about the skinny young man who wouldn't meet her eyes.

⋐⋑⋐⋑

K atya watched from across the room as Sergej handed over the breather. With a pang of alarm, she remembered how she had gushed about Sergej a while back when she had still communicated more than the bare minimum with her mother. She hoped her praise had been forgotten. For the first time, she was relived that her mother wasn't a good listener. She never had been, and Katya often felt the need to raise her voice in order for her words to hit the mark.

Katya turned away; she didn't want to witness her mother appraising Sergej. What would Mama see? Long and greasy hair falling over a face covered with pimples? A body without a substantial muscle mass? Just thinking about it made Katya ill. She knew that Sergej was a wonderful person; he was kind and caring. He had invited Katya to join the group of techies she now called her friends. Katya wasn't good with technology. She wasn't good with anything, really. Maybe that was why she felt the need to go outside. She was hoping to find something she could excel in. And of course, she had looked forward to a chance to be alone with Sergej for more than a few minutes, something that wasn't possible in the commune. But her mother had prevented that. Her mother had used her influence to switch partners, arguing that Katya, on her first outing, would need to have the benefit of working with an older, seasoned forager. Katya was still annoyed at the interference. But her anger had cooled to a smolder, and now she cringed when she thought back at the words she had hurled at her mother when she had realized that she wouldn't go out with Sergej. All of a sudden, Katya felt that she should say something to patch the rift that had become so deep between them. But there wasn't any time.

Suited up, the team of eight foragers, two drivers and a navigator lined up at the big sliding doors. There was no fanfare to

going out, but with new foragers on the team, it was customary for
the commander to wish them luck. The commander entered the
suiting chamber and briskly strode towards the group. Katya was
nervous and barely listened as he recited the official farewell. She
wanted to sink into the floor when she saw the commander step
closer to her mother. They only exchanged glances, but Katya saw
that everyone was watching them. She was deeply embarrassed by
her mother's affair with the commander. Together with her group of
friends, she often observed people getting together and then
breaking up again. Sometimes they had laughed about seemingly
impossible matches. Katya had never thought that her mother, so
solitary and unapproachable, would find someone. And anyone else
would have been more suitable, even kind-hearted Alexej
Vadimovitch, who was the closest her mother had to a friend. And
in Katya's opinion, it would be more fitting to the commander's
position if he kept strictly to himself, as he had always done before.

The members of the team adjusted their breathers, pulled down
their goggles and went through the airlock. Katya's heart beat with
excitement as she stepped outside. The heat was stifling. Since the
Melt, the high air temperatures had never dropped to a comfortable
level. Katya knew about the cool arctic climate of Murmansk before
the catastrophe, but to her it seemed more myth than memory.

She felt disoriented in the thick, chemical-laden soup that
passed for air. She waited for Sergej, and together they walked
towards the Vodnik, the trusty armored vehicle that had survived
the Melt and seemed immune to the toxic atmosphere. Katya
thought that it looked like a heap of junk covered in slime, but it
served them well as a shuttle for the foragers. She climbed into the
vehicle and took a seat next to Sergej, who reached for her hand.
Her mother sat across the aisle, and Katya wondered what she
might think of them sitting together like this.

Their destination was Gorelaya Mountain. The shuttle's engine
started with a roar, and Katya craned her neck to see out of the
small, high windows. But even if they hadn't been coated by a film
of grime, the fog would have obscured any landmarks they were
passing. Sergej offered to switch seats, and from her new position,

Katya could glimpse a small frame of the driver's window. At first the Vodnik followed a well-worn track and made good time. But upon entering unfamiliar territory, it slowed to a crawl dodging the ruins of various structures that appeared before them seemingly without warning. The light beams barely penetrated the chemical fog, and the driver had to navigate by GPS. During every detour, an insistent beeping reminded them that they were off track. Katya's nerves were on edge from the unfamiliar sound, but her excitement to be included on the team hadn't abated. She had waited for this opportunity for a long time and had prepared herself well. She knew that the commune's surroundings had been depleted of resources, and the foragers had to go further away and stay out longer, making the missions more dangerous. Their breathers were only good for a limited time. In weather like this, they lasted for about five hours. Each outing was meticulously planned by the commander. Katya might not have listened to his words of farewell, but she had studied today's itinerary. Two and a half to three hours of collecting time were scheduled in addition to the one-hour round trip, allowing a buffer of about an hour, in case there was a problem. It did happen occasionally that teams got lost or the shuttle broke down. And foragers perished. It wasn't exactly advertised, but everyone knew.

When the vehicle came to a stop, it was Katya's turn. She turned to Sergej and squeezed his arm. He leaned close and breathed, "Katyusha, good luck." She followed Andrej Vadimovitch out of the vehicle and turned around to see her mother wave to her. She raised her arm, but the heavy doors had already slammed shut and the Vodnik rumbled on.

ଓଃ🙙🙚ଃ୦

Olga stood up to look through the back window and saw the yellow-tinged fog swallow the slight form of her daughter. She wished with all her heart for Katya to be safe.

Olga and Sergej were the last pair to leave the shuttle. Olga marked the drop and got her bearings. There was a sprawling structure that could have been the ruins of a shopping mall or medical center right below them and the rubble of smaller structures on higher ground. The shuttle moved away over the remains of a street that ran parallel to a concrete fissure that had once been a highway. Olga pointed to the smaller structures, but Sergej was interested in exploring the ruins of the mall. Of course, he was a techie and probably hoped to come across unfused metals or alloys. But Olga knew that the commune was in desperate need of organics. Again she pointed to higher ground, but she shrugged when she noticed that Sergej had already turned away. It didn't matter to her if they split up. It would give her a chance to work quickly and monitor the activity of the group. Of course, she was supposed to limit reception to her partner, but she kept all channels open in an effort to catch a snippet of communication about Katya's whereabouts. That depleted her charger and put her own tracer at risk, but it wasn't herself Olga was worried about. After all, she had been outside more than a hundred times, and in worse weather than this.

She set off through a maze of pillars and wire that were the ruins of the highway. She crossed the melted concrete to the other side and found nothing. Luckily the visibility was better up here and she could make out what looked like the remnants of houses. On the far side of a small ravine, she found her first batch of organic matter. It wasn't much to look at—just a fissure filled with slime that was thicker, more substantial than the usual coating of chemicals. But Olga had enough experience to know that the material would make a valuable addition to the nutrient film nourishing the commune's hydroponics. She scooped as much as possible into her container and searched for more.

Olga guessed that she had been collecting for the better part of the second hour when she noticed a change in weather. From the moment she had stepped outside, she knew that they were dealing with one of those low-pressure systems that were harbingers of dangerous turbulences. She had hoped that the weather would hold, but now the oppressive heat was close to unbearable. Her suit stuck to her skin, and droplets of chemical-laden humidity crept into the cracks between goggles and mask, mixing with her sweat and causing her skin to burn.

She clambered to the top of the highway structure. There she saw the storm front approach and received the call to move out. At that moment she realized that she hadn't heard anything from Sergej since they'd split up. She switched the tracer to two-way communication.

"Sergej Alexandrovitch, come in," she said, but didn't get any answer. She tried again, with the same result, and she switched to open channel. "This is Olga Evgenyevna, have you heard from Sergej Alexandrovitch?" There was no reply. "This is Olga, please respond." She tried one last time, but no answer came. Although she could listen in on other communications, no one seemed to hear her call. Tracer malfunction was not unheard of, especially during storms. But how could she still receive, while being unable to transmit?

She blocked out a hint of worry by taking action. Once she and Sergej met the shuttle, the tracer glitch wouldn't matter. She quickly went back down to the drop mark. Sergej wasn't there. She would have to go to find him and hopefully make it back before the shuttle arrived. Setting out in the easterly direction, she headed to the point where she'd seen Sergej turn into the mall. Still no sign of him. Again she heard the move-out call over the radio and, for a moment, considered hurrying back to the drop zone. But Olga imagined her daughter's expression should she return without Sergej and decided to keep looking.

First she climbed back to the top of the highway. The fog had started to shift, and she saw movement below at the same time as she heard the approaching Vodnik. She frantically waved her arms to draw attention to her new location. Just as she was sure that they had seen her, the storm hit. The shuttle was battered by a gust of wind and pushed against the mountain before veering away towards the city. Olga didn't pause to think about her fate, but scrambled down the slope to where she had seen the movement. When she approached the spot, she was disappointed to see that it was only a bit of colored cloth flapping in the breeze. She reached to grab it and discovered that it was attached to a pole that disappeared into a crevice.

Switching on her light, she could see Sergej crouching at the bottom.

"Sergej Alexandrovitch," she called. "Are you alright? Sergej?"

"Yes, I'm okay," he answered. "I just can't make it out."

"Hang on, I'll get you up."

Olga took out a length of rope, standard equipment for every forager, and tied it to a piece of metal jutting from a foundation. Sergej started to haul himself up the steep wall of the crevice. When he got closer, Olga grabbed his hand and pulled him the rest of the way. Without giving him a moment to recover, she urged, "We have to go. We have to get up higher."

"Higher?" Sergej wheezed. "Why higher?"

"The storm is here, and we've missed the shuttle. No time to explain, grab the rope, let's go."

She dragged him to his feet and pulled him up the mountain as fast as she dared. It was hard to move against the current of air. But they pushed on until they came to a shelter that might have once been a restaurant with a view of the city. She went through the enclosed space. When Sergej stopped, she pulled him further, onto the remnants of a viewing terrace.

He looked at her and spoke, but the wind ripped the words away before she could make them out. Only when they were huddled against a low wall could she understand.

"Inside," he said. "Let's stay inside."

She shook her head and removed the breather. Sergej's eyes widened with shock.

Olga covered the lower part of her face with a cloth before she explained.

"Turbulence. The turbulence distributes the toxins over a greater area, making the air breathable, especially up here. Take off your breather. You'll need it later. We don't have much time left until the filters become clogged."

Sergej did as he was told and took a tentative breath. The tainted air irritated his airways, but it didn't make him cough or choke.

"How did you know that this would work? Have you done it before?"

"Not in a long time," Olga answered.

"So what are our chances?" Sergej asked.

Olga paused for a moment before she replied, "Honestly? Not very good. But there is some hope that we can make it. They won't send a search party until the storm dies down. As long as it's blowing hard, we can breathe without the mask. We'll just have to sit here and wait. But when the storm lets up, we only have a short time before the breather gives out. And we still have to get down the mountain to the last drop mark. That's where they will be looking for us."

They sat side by side on the platform. The storm had thinned the grey-yellowish curtain of fog to an insubstantial layer barely obscuring the ruins of Murmansk. The city had boomed in the decade leading up to the Melt. The slowly rising temperatures world-wide had made real estate in the largest city within the Arctic Circle very valuable. The resulting multitude of high rises in the downtown core had been turned into seared skeletons, and the wide highways had left a crust of melted asphalt over the battered earth. Olga thought it was ironic that life should still survive here, among the high concentration of man-made poison, rather than in the countryside where organic matter would be more plentiful. But there was no indication that anyone had survived in the country, at least not within their limited communication radius. It was a fluke that a minor quake had buried a large part of Murmansk Ryba, a fish processing and packaging plant, a few minutes before the Melt. The earth had shielded all who were inside from the lethal spike in temperature. It was ironic that they, working the most menial and lowest of tasks, and their children, attending after-school care adjacent to the smelly plant, should have survived. The robust industrial cooling and air filtering system had soldiered on through the catastrophe and allowed the group of humans to hold on even longer to the threads of their lives. They had come a long way from those early days after the Melt, but the easy abundance of the days before had forever disappeared, leaving them to struggle day by day and making it necessary to forage in the ruins for organics and scraps of material.

A small choking sound startled Olga from her contemplation. Alarmed that Sergej might be suffering from an allergic reaction she turned to him, but his breathing was fine.

He pointed to the spectacle below and said, "This is beautiful. I know the fog is terrible, but like this, it's beautiful. And to be breathing without a mask and watching this—it's almost worth dying for." Olga made to interrupt him but he shook his head and said, "When you're inside all the time, you're working with the technical equipment and searching for signs of others who might have survived. But you can't really imagine what it means to be alive. In a time like this, in a place like this!"

"It's going to be tough today, but then, staying alive has been a struggle for a while. I wouldn't waste my breath on words about death," Olga replied.

Almost immediately she was sorry she had spoken so harshly, and she touched his arm. Without turning his gaze from the city, he said, "All right. If we have a chance, we're going to try and make it."

Gradually the wind died down, and the fog returned. The air started to sting with every intake of breath, setting their lungs on fire. Sergej looked at Olga and reached for the breather, but she held up her hand to indicate that they should wait for two more minutes, 120 endless seconds. Sergej tried. He made it through all of 23 seconds before gasping and pulling on the breather. He drew in a few breaths and said, "Sorry, I couldn't wait. It burns."

Olga nodded. She waited out the full two minutes before putting on the mask. "OK," she said. "Let's go down. Slow and steady. Don't rush. Try to measure your breathing."

Carefully they plodded down the slope. When they passed the ruins of the highway, Sergej grasped Olga's arm and pointed. His breather's indicator had gone from green to yellow.

"Keep going," she told him. "When we came out, it took us just over twenty minutes to the drop. They might have left the commune already.

When they reached the mark, Sergej collapsed against a slab of stone and closed his eyes. He started to wheeze and said, "Twenty minutes? I'm never going to make it."

"Calm down," Olga said. "This is what we are going to do. We'll switch breathers. Mine is still at four per cent. All I ask is that you stay calm and breathe slowly."

Sergej sat up, "No, you keep your breather. At least you'll have a chance."

Olga shook her head. "Listen to me, switch on three. One, two, three."

Her tone of voice didn't invite any further argument. They switched breathers and Sergej gulped the filtered air. Olga lay down. Time seemed to creep by very slowly. Eventually, the breather Olga was wearing flashed a red warning. She went into a wheezing spasm that lasted a few seconds before she could control her breath.

Sergej moved closer to Olga and shook her. "Switch," he yelled. "Switch!"

But Olga shook her head and whispered, "Quiet, preserve your breath."

Sergej leaned back against the concrete, noting that his breather's light had gone to yellow. The rhythm of their ragged breathing echoed in their skulls leaving no room for anything else. With an effort Sergej leaned forward and said, "Olga Evgenyevna, I'm sorry. I am so sorry. I fiddled with your tracer. Katya asked me to. We didn't want to hurt you, just give you a scare. You're always so confident. You have no idea how hard it is for Katya to live up to that." Tears collected in Sergej's goggles as he whispered, "I'm sorry."

But there was no reply. Neither of them heard the drone of the shuttle as it approached.

⋙⋘

The door flew open almost before the Vodnik had come to a full stop. Katya jumped out crying, "Mama, Mama, Sergej!"

She ran to her mother's side, closely followed by the commander who barked, "Oxygen, vitals. Now!"

The team fitted the two prone figures with oxygen masks and moved them into the vehicle. Sergej responded immediately. He drew in a couple of deep breaths and his eyes flew open.

"Olga Evgenyevna," he said before going into a coughing fit. When his breathing became stable, he asked, "Is she alive? Is Olga alive?"

Katya reluctantly left her mother's side to come to him. When Sergej repeated the question, Katya was silent. She fought back tears and reached for his hand. Finally she found a few words, "Mama is . . . she is breathing, but she is still unconscious. There might be some damage to her lungs and maybe—" Katya couldn't bring herself to finish the sentence and shook her head.

Sergej said, "I'm sure she is going to make it. She is tough, you know." Then he added, "Your mother saved my life."

"I know she's tough." Katya replied.

The commander turned to the driver and ordered, "*Davai, davai!* Let's move. We can do more when we get inside. Go!"

Katya drew a relieved breath. She had feared that her mother would be left behind. There was no room in the commune for the infirm. She shifted the oxygen tanks, clearing a space to allow her to sit in the middle. She was grateful when the commander pushed her mother's stretcher closer and took a seat on the other side. He checked that Olga's mask was secure. A faint beeping assured them that a whisper of breath still remained in her battered and burnt lungs. As the Vodnik plodded its way home, Katya rested her palm against Olga's shoulder and grasped Sergej's arm for stability.

Only the doctor and a few assistants received them in the suiting chamber. They stored the containers and the equipment and helped the team out of their suits without asking any questions. Olga was whisked away to the clinic. Sergej refused to get back onto the stretcher. He walked to the doctor's office leaning on

Katya's shoulder. When Katya heard that she was not allowed to enter, she settled down on the floor of the hallway to wait.

When Sergej came out, Katya jumped up to hug him. "Any word about Mama?" she asked.

He shook his head, "They have a curtain up around her. I only had a physical. It seems that I'm OK."

He waved a slip of paper. "I'm ordered to go and get some food."

The canteen was quiet. They picked up their rations and huddled in the corner. They were both tired and didn't have much of an appetite.

Suddenly Sergej leaned close and said, "I expect that we have to talk to the commander soon. He always investigates when something goes wrong outside. What do we tell him about the tracer?"

Katya said, "I don't know. The accident could have happened even if the tracer was working, right?"

Sergej shook his head. "Katya, I fell and your mom didn't get to me in time because I couldn't communicate with her. I did a stupid thing disabling the transmitter. But there's no need for anyone to find out that you knew about it, OK?"

Katya tried to speak, but Sergej pressed on. "I'm not just doing this for you. Katya, your mother saved my life. I don't want her to wake up and hear that you are partly responsible for this mess." Katya looked away and wiped at the tears trickling down her cheeks, but Sergej pulled her hands away, "Look at me, Katya. This is for the best. Please tell me that you're going along with my story."

"OK," Katya whispered. She felt exhausted and said, "I think I'm going to lie down."

In the sleeping hall, Katya slumped onto her cot and fell into a deep and dreamless sleep. She awoke to darkness. Getting up quietly, she managed to leave without waking anyone. The corridors were lit with dim emergency lights, and she found her way back to the clinic. The double doors were locked. She was about to knock when she realized that she didn't want to disturb the patients. She pressed her ear to the crack. There wasn't much to hear: the beeping of the heart rate monitor, the rise and fall of rhythmic breathing, the scraping of a chair being pushed into position. These small sounds calmed her, and she leaned forward as she would into the embrace of a friend. Suddenly the door opened and she was falling. She landed in the arms of the commander.

"What are you doing here in the middle of the night?" he asked, holding her at arm's length.

"My mother," Katya said, trying to see around his torso. "How is she? Nobody has told me anything since we got here."

When he didn't respond, Katya started to cry. Ivan Vassilyevitch Bondarchuk, after a moment's hesitation, held her close. He said, "You're not allowed to come in. But if you stay by the door, I'll turn on the light so you can see her. But you have to promise me that you'll calm down and go back to bed."

Katya nodded. Then she shook her head. "Please," she whispered between sobs. "Can I see her?"

The commander propped her against the door frame. He stepped back into the room and turned up the lights, as promised. Olga lay on a simple cot, connected to an IV drip and various monitors. Then the commander nodded at Katya. He killed the light and gently pushed her out the door. When he followed her into the hall, Katya said, "She is breathing without a mask. Does that mean she's OK?"

"Your mother regained consciousness right after we arrived. You weren't called because the doctor said she needed to rest and gave her something to sleep. She has suffered from a moderate cerebral hypoxia. That means brain damage is unlikely. However, her lungs are in poor condition, and I doubt she will ever be able to go out again."

"What? She can't go out? She is going to hate that."

"I know," the commander said quietly. "But she is alive." He added, "Go back to bed now. I'll let you know if there are any changes."

When he turned to go back into the clinic, Katya reached for his sleeve and said, "Sir, I need to speak to you."

"Surely that can wait until tomorrow?" He tugged at his sleeve but Katya didn't let go.

"No. It has to be now, please?"

"OK," the commander relented. "In my quarters."

The commander's room was clean and uncluttered compared to most other spaces in the commune. Katya looked around with unconcealed interest before she remembered that this was the place where her mother had spent many of her nights.

"Please sit." He indicated a stool and took a seat at the edge of the cot.

Katya stared at the bare wall above his head and began, "I'm not sure what Sergej has told you, but it's not true that it was him. I made him do it. But I didn't want anyone to get hurt."

The commander cleared his throat. Katya looked at his face and realized that he didn't seem to know what she was talking about.

"The tracer?" she asked. "You know about the tracer?"

The commander shook his head, and Katya explained, "I was so mad at Mama for interfering. At first, she didn't let me go out. Then she switched partners. She always needed to be in charge, and I felt so helpless. So I asked Sergej if we could rig the tracer so she wouldn't be heard. I just wanted to scare her. I never meant to put her in danger."

The commander stood up, and Katya fell silent. He paced the room in a few, measured strides. Then he came to a halt in front of her and said, "It all makes sense now. Katya, do you realize that you have put the entire team at risk?"

Katya nodded. "I know. I'm sorry. I didn't realize it was so dangerous outside. Mama was always so eager to go."

"You and your friend have willfully tampered with vital equipment to settle a score with your mother. And because of this selfish act, the commune has lost one of its best foragers."

"I'll make it up to you. I'll take her place. That's what she did for me."

"You think you can be trusted to be on a team again?"

"Yes. I'll prove it. Please give me a chance."

The commander resumed his pacing. He finally said, "All right. You take her shifts. I gain nothing by exposing what you did. I feel responsible for the commune, but I also know that all of us are needed. Trust is needed as well. Katya, I only hope you learned something from today."

"I did. Thank you." Katya said.

"You don't need to thank me," the commander replied. "I am putting you into a very difficult position. You and Sergej will have to work very hard to regain my trust. I will hold you to high standards. This is not an easy situation to be in. In fact, it might have been easier for you had I subjected you to some sort of public punishment."

Katya stood up and said, "I understand what you're saying. But I never wanted it to be easy. I promise I will do my best."

"I hope you will," the commander replied and Katya knew she was dismissed.

⊰⊱⊰⊱

"Ivan, I told you to wake me early," Olga chided. She got out of bed and had to steady herself against the wall as she experienced a moment of dizziness.

"You're still recovering. The doctor said to let you sleep as much as possible," the commander replied. "And you don't have to be at the suiting chamber every time Katya goes out."

"I know I don't have to be there every time. But today I need to be there. Sergej has been showing me how to interface the tracers with the Vodnik's GPS so the foragers know when they will be picked up. We'll have the trial run, and I want to be there when the team takes off."

"I would never have imagined you getting excited about technology."

"Well, I need something to be excited about," Olga grumbled as she left.

The noise from the suiting chamber drifted into the corridor outside. Before entering, Olga paused for a moment to catch her breath. It was still difficult to go in there knowing that she couldn't venture any further.

"Olga Evgenyevna, over here!" Sergej called from the equipment rack. As Olga made her way across the room, she not only received many greetings, but also made an effort to return them. She didn't quite know how to respond to the steady stream of support she had received since the day she had been hurt on the mission. Sergej repeatedly assured her that it was a sign of respect, but Olga couldn't quite shake her old habit of second-guessing people's motives.

"Olga, two of the tracers are continuously picking up signals from the shuttle, even outside the selected range. I've just installed replacement transmitters. Nearly done," Sergej said.

"I'm glad we're finally ready to try them out," Olga said. "Who gets the two new ones?"

"Igor and Katya," Sergej replied and handed her the tracers. Looking up at her face, he added, "But no worries, the new ones are fine. I've tested them."

"I'll drop them off." After she delivered Igor's tracer, Olga went to see her daughter.

Katya, already suited up, was chatting with Alexej Vadimovitch. In the last few weeks, her body had acquired more muscle tone and her face had scarred heavily. She seemed relaxed and confident. At her mother's approach, Katya's posture stiffened.

"Mama," she said. "You've come to see me off."

"Yes," Olga replied. She handed over the tracer. Her fingers itched to check Katya's breather, but she made an effort to keep her distance. "And of course we're testing the new system. That's quite exciting."

Katya shrugged. "Well, Sergej seems to think linking the tracers to the GPS will make a difference. I personally don't see the point, but what do I know about technology?"

"More than I do," Olga replied. "And our combined knowledge only compares to a small fraction of Sergej's. If he thinks the new tracers are promising, I think so, too."

"That's something I can agree with," Katya said. Then she turned to Alexej with a smile. "I'm sure you're all glad that Mama and I can agree on a number of issues lately."

Olga wondered if she and Katya would ever lose the awkwardness they had with one another. At least they now treated each other with a tad more compassion. On an impulse, she stepped forward and pulled her daughter into a hug, "Good luck, Katyusha," she whispered.

Olga was surprised to hear a reply: "Thank you, Mama. Good luck to you too."

Compassion can get you in a great deal of trouble. And if women, by nature, have more compassion, does that also mean they will have more trouble?

NATURAL LAW

by Alfred D. Byrd

2

When the exit from the United Nations mission opened ahead of Cassandra, three police officers led her into a crowd of waiting reporters. Camerabots and holoprompters disoriented her, numb from her arrest; reporters' voices made a Babel in her ears.

From this, however, the high-pitched, imperious voice of the star reporter of Achilles Cluster Network News reached her clearly. "In a startling development, UN Domestic Security has taken into custody Cassandra Meihua Lin, Commissioner of Trade for the Natural Humans and granddaughter of former Secretary General Lin, as a rapidly unfolding scandal . . ."

As the cordon of officers moved her away from the star reporter, Cassandra felt anger stab through her numbness. *No one ever lets me forget whose granddaughter I am.* After a moment she thought, *Though just now he might like to forget whose grandfather he is.*

As she neared a black cruiser representing to her both safety and degradation, microphones darted towards her face. The officers swatted them like flies away from her. A din of questions, reaching her ears, rose to a crescendo as her cordon reached the cruiser.

One question caught her ear. "Ms. Lin, how do you feel knowing that the conduct of which you're accused has imperiled a trillion-Econ colonization effort?"

The officers shoved her into the cruiser's temporary shelter. Numb again, she shook her head, thinking, *I did the right thing.*

⋰⋱⋰⋱

1

Six months earlier, as she had entered her office in the United Nations Mission to the Vestal Republic, her secretary greeted her with a dazzling smile. "Ms. Lin, the commissioner and the procurator want to see you at once in the procurator's office."

Cassandra smiled thinly at the secretary. "Don't think that they'll get rid of me, Charlene. I'll return to make your life miserable."

En route to the procurator's office, however, Cassandra pondered Charlene's reason for hope. Cassandra had spent the past three years in working her way up the United Nations' hierarchy at Vesta, just as she had previously spent three-year stints in working her way up hierarchies on Antarctica and on the Moon. It was her time for a transfer.

Charlene does need a rest. Cassandra had a well-earned reputation for working her underlings hard. It scarcely comforted them that she worked twice as hard as they.

How else can I get anyone to take me seriously? Because of her family name, all believed either that she would work miracles, or that all of her accomplishments were due to kinship. Her having been graduated *summa cum laude* from Yale Law School and having earned a string of commendations on the job awed no one. *Maybe someday I'll make a name for myself.*

As for a transfer, she told herself, *At least, if I get one, I'll also get a furlough home.* She recalled fondly her family's mansion in the Traditional Chinese enclave of Seattle, an incomparable view of Mount Rainier from formal gardens...

⊗⊖⊗

In the procurator's office, the Commissioner of Trade, her immediate supervisor, and the United Nations Procurator of the Vestal Republic, her ultimate supervisor at the mission, greeted her with identical grins. Both men were cut from International cloth: a complexion of pale bronze and Polynesian features from a millennium of interracial marriage, and bland clothing and hairstyles from a passion for conformity. Cassandra suspected that the two men found her Traditional Chinese background—not to mention her workaholism and outspokenness—anomalous. She swept her gaze across the procurator's desk, ostentatiously bare but for a tiny potted prickly pear. This she eyed disdainfully; her coworkers called the cactus "Cassandra." "How may I help you, sirs?"

"Good news, Ms. Lin!" the procurator said, annoyingly cheerful. "You're up for a promotion."

Her eyes widened. "Promotion, sir?"

Her immediate supervisor fielded the question. "You do my job now, Sandy. Only—" his grin brightened—"elsewhere."

She gave him her most dazzling grin in return. "No one else can do the job that you do, sir." In her mind's depths she heard her grandfather say, *Sheathe your tongue's sword, Meihua, lest you stab yourself with it.* "Where will I go, sir?" she asked the procurator.

He glanced up at his office's powder-blue ceiling. "Are you familiar with the Natural Humans?"

She frowned. "The back-to-nature society at Achilles Cluster—the cult that won the generation ship to 71 Ophiuci?"

He nodded. "Though please put matters diplomatically around them. The Natural Humans believe in keeping our species pure. Freedom of the body from nanotechnology, freedom of the genome from gene replacements, or, worse, artificial or animal-derived genes. By the Natural Humans' standards, Ms. Lin, you're unclean."

Smiling tightly, she said, "My own people find me clean enough, sir. I can assure you of all of my genes' being human."

Again her immediate supervisor spoke for the procurator. "Could you confirm, though, that none of your ancestors had gene-replacement therapy? And what of nanos, Sandy? An average woman of your weight likely carries over a kilo of them. Dental-hygiene nanos, health-maintenance nanos, depilation nanos, feminine-protection nanos—"

"I'm aware of what I'm carrying, sir," Cassandra replied stiffly. *Barbarian! No Traditional Chinese man would discuss a lady's nanos with her.*

"The commissioner's point, Ms. Lin," the procurator said slowly, "is that you'll need sensitivity and tact to deal with the Natural Humans. Your status as a member of a Traditional People may give you insights into them, but your prejudices may hinder communication with them."

"In any case, Sandy," the commissioner said, "your assignment will be brief. Nine months from now, the Natural Humans will leave the Solar System. A successful performance among them may put you on a fast track to a procurator's chair."

"It's bad luck, Ms. Lin," the procurator said, "that there's no time for a furlough home before you leave here for Achilles Cluster. On the other hand, we'll throw you a splendid going-away party."

"Thank you, sir." *Every mission where I've worked has thrown me a splendid party. My coworkers couldn't wait to see me go.*

♋♋♋

2

Inside the cruiser, stares from the officers seated across from Cassandra replaced questions from reporters. The officer on her left, a man of a pale Nordic type no longer on Earth, met her with a face expressionless but for a curl of thin lips eloquent with contempt. The officer in the middle, a burly International man, wore this openly on every feature. The officer on her right, though, a thin, dark woman with a Hindu's mark on her forehead, gave Cassandra a wink and a subtle thumbs up.

A thirty-three per cent approval rating, Cassandra thought. *My polls are rising.*

೮ೞೞನಿ

At headquarters of Domestic Security, the officers marched her through a second gauntlet of reporters outside the building's main entrance. Although not having to answer their questions cheered her briefly, relief vanished within Domestic Security's processing center. There, in a centuries-old system to dehumanize and intimidate suspects, she was booked, fingerprinted, retinally scanned, holographed, and deprived of personal possessions. The officers led her on to an examination room bristling with medical implements. She had no hope that these were for show.

"Since you're suspected of smuggling genetic technology, ma'am," the Nordic guard said coldly, "we must search you for evidence of it and remove your nanos."

It gave her some comfort that, during the search and removal, the two male officers left her alone with the Hindu officer. It gave Cassandra somewhat more comfort that the Hindu officer was gentle and distracted her with continuous banter from probing by the implements. At the procedure's end, Cassandra even forced a wan smile when the other woman said, "Now, ma'am, you qualify as a Natural Human."

Pity, Cassandra thought. *Just now the Natural Humans are hardly eager to own me.*

೮ೞೞನಿ

1

The flight from Vesta to Achilles Cluster had been so quick that Cassandra wondered how much the chance nearness of the two sets of worlds in their orbits had influenced her selection for her new position. She found the Achillean asteroids, caught in one of Jupiter's Trojan points, lovely, festooned with lights on their surfaces and circled with further lights of orbital habitats. Over asteroids and habitats presided the mysterious gibbous disk of Jupiter itself, far off to one side of the cluster.

When Cassandra's shuttle passed the growing generation ship, it seemed to her untutored eye just a gigantic tin can. *Of course, so does every other habitat.* She smiled tightly at the motto *HUMANITAS SICUT CREATA* emblazoned on the generation ship, and recognized the Natural Humans' current home when she glimpsed the motto again on another otherwise featureless tin can. The shuttle took her, however, not there, but to a nearby administrative wheel. *Afraid of my uncleanness?* she thought sourly to unseen Natural Humans.

⋇⋇⋇

It had puzzled her that they needed a new commissioner of trade just nine months before departure into interstellar space. Provisioning the generation ship, she had learned en route to her new assignment, had fallen far behind schedule; her predecessor had collapsed under the strain of trying to make up time. If Cassandra missed a planetary alignment not to recur for centuries, the ship could not use optimal slingshot maneuvers during its launch, and a thousand-year voyage would become centuries longer and billions of Econs more expensive.

The kind of job for which I was born, Cassandra thought on the administrative wheel as she drove herself and her underlings relentlessly through sixteen-hour workdays week after week. At first her underlings were mere functionaries to her; only Larry, her personal aide, a harried, somewhat pedantic blond young man, became to her a real person. He had a marked tendency, which she barely tolerated, to shower her with unsought information, some of it mere gossip.

Even the Natural Humans whom Cassandra had come to Achilles Cluster to serve formed but a stream of vaguely perceived faces passing her desk with requests. In rare moments of reflection, she recalled those faces as asymmetrical, their deficiencies corrected with such antiquated prostheses as spectacles and braces.

Larry tried to explain these devices to her. "The prostheses are part of the Natural Humans' 'Humanity as created' philosophy, ma'am. Genetic material, as the medium of Nature's creativity, must be free to express Nature's vision. Persons whose genes leave them at a disadvantage beside other humans must live with mechanical aids as the price of Nature's freedom. Thus, even nanos, as products of bioengineering, offend the Natural Humans."

I'll keep my nanos, thank you. Giddy with fatigue, Cassandra replied to Larry, "I'll defend to the death the Natural Humans' right to wear glasses—around another star." She perceived his dry chuckle as obsequious, not appreciative, but welcomed it nonetheless.

જી ભ્ર

In her rush to get provisioning on schedule, she ignored many legitimate claims on her time. One of these took the form of frequent emails from a Dr. Guttagong, the United Nations-appointed head of the launch-preparation medical team. In lurid terms he warned her of a medical nightmare among the Natural Humans, a major injustice against many in their community. He refused to discuss specifics of this nightmare with anyone but her.

Time after time Cassandra replied to the doctor that medical matters lay outside her jurisdiction and that he should bring injustices to the attention of Domestic Security. Each time the doctor said that only Cassandra could solve the problem.

At last she brought the doctor's requests delicately to Larry's attention to learn from him any discrete tidbit that might help her decide whether to draw the doctor's strange behavior to his superiors' attention. "What kind of medical crisis can wait 'til a commissioner of trade finds time to deal with it?"

Larry shook his head. "I've heard no rumor of any urgent medical problems among the Natural Humans, and I think that I would've heard of such problems if there were any. As for Dr. Guttagong, he came highly recommended; and his superiors, colleagues, and assistants are happy with him, by all reports. You should grant him an interview, ma'am. You're catching up rapidly on provisioning, and it'd be intriguing to learn why he insists on dealing only with you."

&CR&D&

Cassandra saw Dr. Guttagong, at his insistence, alone in her office. He was a thin, intense young man as obviously a Traditional Thai as she was a Traditional Chinese. Giving him a thin smile, she said, "How can I help you, Doctor?"

"Ms. Lin, do you understand that, by implementing the policies of the United Nations and the Natural Humans, you'll wreck families and cause hundreds of persons lasting psychological harm?"

She narrowed her eyes at the doctor's allegation. "You have five minutes to make your case."

&CR&D&

2

From her cell Cassandra had called the mission's Commissioner of Legal Affairs. He, after dithering, referred her to a private attorney. "This woman," he said, "has a reputation for winning hopeless cases."

Cassandra, thanking her fellow commissioner gravely, wondered whether his recommendation should comfort her.

&CR&D&

The winner of hopeless cases was, as a holoscreen revealed to Cassandra, a short, thin, middle-aged woman whose shock of reddish hair and sharp features resembled a fox's. *Foxes, according to folklore,* Cassandra thought darkly, *are associated with witchcraft. Still, it may take a witch to get me off.*

Counselor Houlihan seemed to Cassandra eager to fight the United Nations court system. "Yours, Ms. Lin, was a crime of conscience deserving reward, not punishment. Although facts may be against you, justice is on your side."

"Sadly for me, a judge will look at facts," Cassandra muttered. "I really did falsify a manifest and conceal—"

Houlihan waved the admissions away. "You tried to help distressed persons and fulfill the spirit, if not the letter, of the law. Public opinion, properly informed, will support you. Never doubt that public opinion sways judges!

"We can arrange your defense later, though. Today we face an arraignment, where we'll learn what charges the public prosecutor will bring against you."

I know an arraignment's purpose, Cassandra thought with irritation. She kept this within her. She knew that anyone who acts as her own lawyer has a fool for a client.

⊰ⱤⱤⱤⱤ⊱

Some time later, officers took her down an oddly bare set of stairs to a cruiser. After a short ride and a trip up a second set of stairs, also oddly bare, she reached a sitting room where Houlihan awaited her. Rising and shaking Cassandra's hand, the defense attorney said, "Now, Ms. Lin, the important thing about this appearance is that you present the proper image to the Press—"

Something clicked in Cassandra's mind. "I saw no reporters on the way here."

Houlihan frowned. "No reporters? This is a top story—"

A bailiff called the two women into a courtroom. Its gallery was bare; besides Cassandra, Houlihan, and the bailiff, it held only a black-robed judge and a ferret-like man whom Cassandra took as the public prosecutor. When Houlihan objected to the absence of spectators, the judge shook his head. "At the prosecution's request, this hearing will be in camera."

"Outrageous!" Houlihan shouted. "The public has a right to know the charges—"

"The prosecution is filing no charges," the prosecutor said. "I am, though, petitioning the court for Ms. Lin to be held as a material witness to matters of international security."

Houlihan wore a look of stupefaction. "If I don't know the charges against my client, how can I prepare her defense?"

The judge smiled thinly. "If there are no charges against your client, she needs no defense. The prosecution's motion is granted. Ms. Lin is remanded to the custody of Domestic Security."

CR∞∞

As the officers led Cassandra out of the courtroom, Houlihan shook her head. "I don't know whether you're being lynched or let off."

Cassandra gave her a wan smile. "Maybe both."

CR∞∞

1

Dr. Guttagong had taken longer than five minutes to explain his problem to Cassandra. Fascinated with it, she forgave him his wordiness.

"Let me see if I understand you, Doctor. The Natural Humans want to purge humanity of all nanos and unnatural genes. To reach this goal while circumstances forced them to live among the genetically and somatically corrupted, they've been willing to accept into their community anyone who is currently free of nanos and hasn't been genetically modified since birth, even though such a person might carry genetic modifications from an ancestor."

The doctor nodded. "They hoped to use such persons, however flawed, as missionaries for the Cause. It needed their money and their skills, you see. Thus, such persons entered the community without genetic screening as an outer breeding population that could aid the certifiably clean in convincing the rest of humanity to stop the spread of uncleanness."

It's good that I went to law school. "Now, though, that the Natural Humans have won the generation ship, it's suddenly imperative to do genetic screening to ensure that no unclean person will come aboard?"

Dr. Guttagong smiled thinly. "If you could return to Eden, would you take the Serpent with you?"

Cassandra chuckled. "So the Natural Humans have asked you to do genetic screening, and many who'd hoped to go on the voyage will be left behind."

The doctor's nostrils flared. "You're trivializing the problem. It's not a faceless 'many' who'll be left behind. It's men and women, boys and girls who'll be parted from their loved ones for the rest of their lives, or lose the chance for a new life, all because of a fanatical notion of species purity—"

"I hope, Doctor, that you didn't say so to the Natural Humans." As the doctor's face fell, Cassandra gathered that he had indeed spoken indiscreetly. "At a guess, they told you that you were interfering in matters not concerning you."

"Your guess is good," the doctor muttered.

"Now you want me to help you. Your hope of my help is optimistic, to say the least. First, Doctor, even if I am my grandfather's descendent, the Natural Humans are no more likely to heed me than they are you. Second, they have the right to determine the membership of their community and of the generation ship's crew. It's my duty to uphold that right."

The doctor took a deep breath and let it out slowly. "It's not *talking* to them that I want you to do."

Cassandra eyed him narrowly. "What, then?"

"If I hadn't spoken my mind to the Natural Humans' elders, I could've falsified the results of genetic screening so that so-called 'unclean' could have gone on the mission. Now that the elders know my feelings, they'll have their own technicians, perfectly capable of spotting deception, double-check my work.

"My sole chance now of helping the unclean is to reverse their genetic modifications before I formally screen them. Reversal would be easy enough to do—I'd run a secret preliminary screening on a patient and inject him or her with the right gene-replacement retrovirus; the virus would remove the modified gene or replace it with its ancestral equivalent, and the patient's immune system would clear the virus. But—"

Cassandra shook her head. "Why would the elders object to your using retroviruses to replace non-human genes with ancestral ones?"

The doctor sneered. "Because you can't atone for sin with sin. As I was saying, the elders are alert for me to try such a trick. They screen all of my orders and scan me for retroviruses whenever I return to the habitat. Now, I need someone who can falsify manifests and is too powerful to face a customs inspection—"

Cassandra was torn between astonishment and outrage. "You're asking me to break the law?"

The doctor stared at her. "I'm asking you to save relationships."

"Out of the question! I ought to turn you in to Domestic Security for even suggesting such a thing."

Dr. Guttagong again gave her a thin smile. "You can easily be pitiless when you've had no contact with those who are going to be hurt by the elders' decision. I made recordings of my interviews with the unclean, though. Maybe when you view them you'll change your mind."

Cassandra met the doctor's thin smile with a level gaze. "Don't think that I'm moved by sob stories."

കൈലോഹ

2

Back in her cell Cassandra received commercial nanos to replace the custom-made ones removed from her. She accepted the nanos in gratitude at not having to learn to use a toothbrush and dental floss—or primitive items even more terrifying than they.

Gratitude became dismay when Computer informed her of a personal call from Earth. *It must be someone from the family telling me that I've disgraced it. My relatives will wish that they could bring back flogging for what I've done.*

Dismay became horror when she learned that the caller was her grandfather himself. The former secretary general seemed to her a tired, elderly man who had trouble focusing on the screen. In a slow, dry voice, he said, "It seems, Meihua, that you have become someone who takes things into her own hands. Without consulting with your superiors or considering the repercussions of your acts on your family, you did what you willed.

"Now what you did in secret has become public. No one can foretell the consequences of it, for you, for those whom you tried to help, or for those whose decisions you fought. You stepped outside the system that brought you swift promotions. Now it is unclear whether it will take you back.

"You must bear the consequences of your acts, even if they bring you imprisonment. It would do neither the family nor you any good for me to try to clear your name of its stain. You will either have to live with it—or erase it yourself."

When the holoscreen went blank, Cassandra grew aware of hot tears coursing down her cheeks. *On the whole,* she thought with a strange, brittle calmness, *flogging would have been far gentler than that speech was.* As a drowning person might clutch at straws, she clutched at her grandfather's implied injunction for her to erase her own stain. *No matter how long it takes, sir, I'll make you proud of me again.*

Ϩϩ€€

1

To satisfy Larry's curiosity about Dr. Guttagong, Cassandra had told her aide that the doctor was misinformed of the kind of medical equipment allowed aboard the generation ship, and that she would see no more of him. Larry looked skeptical, but made no comment.

True to his promise to her, Dr. Guttagong sent Cassandra files of his interviews with Natural Humans who, because of genetic modifications to their ancestors, would be denied berths aboard the generation ship. Cassandra at first ignored the files; then, when the doctor pestered her with more emails, she glanced at the files with the intention of being unmoved by their message.

Her intention failed to survive contact with the unclean. The first of these, a woman as normal in appearance as Cassandra was, sat by her relatives, a plain man going bald and a pretty young girl. In simple, but moving tones, the woman said, "I have faith in my people's mission. It's through no fault of my daughter and me that we'll be excluded from it. I can't tell you of the pain that separation from my husband will cause me—" she glanced at the somber-faced man—"or my daughter." The girl blinked back tears.

The mother did tell of this pain at length, as did the other unclean whose pleas for help Dr. Guttagong had recorded. As the parade of asymmetrical, downcast faces went on, Cassandra at first rationalized an inability to aid the unclean. Over time, however, she grew angry at the Natural Humans' elders. *They're just cutting their own throats by leaving dedicated crewpersons behind.*

She could not recall when she had come to see that it would be her own inaction that left them behind. With a sigh, but also with a feeling of hope, she thought, *Could getting them aboard be the kind of job for which I was born?*

೮೩౪౪

Arranging behind Larry's back a meeting with her personal tempter, she asked Dr. Guttagong, "What do you need me to

do?" When he told her about his grandiose plans for smuggling gene-replacement technology aboard the Natural Humans' habitat, she nearly lost her resolve to help him; then she firmly said, "To reduce our chances of being caught, you and I must keep our plan simple. Can you get all that you need into a single shipment?"

He pondered her question a moment. "We can get the equipment for injecting retroviruses into a single shipment. The retroviruses themselves, though, must be carried through customs in a form preserving their activity. For our purposes, I propose transporting them inside nanos in a human host." He smirked. "Both of the Natural Humans' unpardonable sins in one neat package."

Cassandra smiled tightly. "Carrying the package, I get to be both Serpent and forbidden fruit?"

ᘓᑕᘛᘉᑐᘔ

Obtaining the equipment required only her submitting a dummy order to a shipper and a false manifest to the receiver. Obtaining the retroviruses, however, required her to make a special trip to another habitat to a colleague of Dr. Guttagong's who had agreed to manufacture them for him. Aboard a shuttle, Cassandra thought, *No one back at Vesta could believe the Prickly Pear capable of risking her career for compassion.*

When she learned that Dr. Guttagong's colleague had hidden the retroviruses within personal-hygiene nanos, Cassandra failed to suppress a wry smile. *I get to be clean even while I'm unclean.*

When she reached customs aboard the Natural Humans' habitat, she felt, absurdly, that her load of illicit nanos would glare on the customs inspectors' sensors. Evidently unwilling to defile themselves with someone known to be as unclean as she, the customs inspectors waved her past them. Strolling through a parklike cityscape from an innocent past, she headed for Dr. Guttagong's office with the intention that, after that day, she would never again think of him, or of retroviruses.

⊱⊰⊱⊰⊱⊰

2

Shortly after the call from Cassandra's grandfather, Houlihan forced herself into Cassandra's cell. "I've never seen Domestic Security so hard-nosed about letting a lawyer see her client," the attorney said as she settled onto a stool across from Cassandra's cot. "It's as if they're trying to deny your very existence."

Cassandra shook her head. "They're taking a cue from my family." She told Houlihan about the former secretary general's call.

Houlihan, narrowing her eyes, frowned. "I can't understand his attitude. You'd think that helping a member of his family would be part of his culture."

"By his lights, he is helping me. Facing the consequences of one's action and overcoming them is a high Neo-Confucian virtue. That one might serve time in prison to do so is incidental to the benefits to one's soul."

"He and I are on opposite sides of the fence. It worries me that the public prosecutor, by declaring you a material witness, has kept you incommunicado. You can't get your story to the public. Just now there's nothing but rumors for it to go on. The latest is that you're being held for your own protection..."

"Well, I'm being held to protect someone. But whom?"

Houlihan grinned at her. "That's the question, isn't it? There are clues as to whom you're protecting. Did you see on the news that Domestic Security trotted out Dr. Guttagong for a staged press conference? He admitted to errors of medical judgment that might keep some members of the Natural Humans from making the voyage. He apologized to them and then was whisked from the podium before the Press could question him."

Cassandra had seen only a sound-byte from the doctor's speech. "Did he say anything about me?"

Houlihan shook her head. "It's as if everyone in the government is downplaying what went on. The public prosecutor announced that you and Dr. Guttagong had violated no UN laws and that you, because of diplomatic immunity, can't be prosecuted for violating laws of the Natural Humans, though you might be disciplined for abuse of office. The Natural Humans announced that they're considering filing charges against Dr. Guttagong, but won't do so before an executive session of the elders. Clearly, though, they suspect you of having smuggled illegal, by their laws, genetic technology into their habitat. I need to know, if I'm to defend you, did you do so?"

Cassandra nodded.

Houlihan pursed her lips. "Smuggling would explain your full body-cavity search." Cassandra felt sick at public knowledge of her humiliation, but Houlihan gave her a lopsided smile. "Don't worry, Ms. Lin! The officers are keeping that aspect of your arrest secret. I learned of it from one of your arresting officers, a Sergeant Indira Chandra, who, it seems, actually performed the search. She refused to discuss its results with me. Did she find anything?"

"If she didn't," Cassandra muttered, "it wasn't for lack of trying." *Guttagong told me that he'd removed everything, but with him who knows?*

"Hm. One thing that impresses me is that there's been no mention of postponing the launch—"

Cassandra laughed harshly. "The ship will leave on schedule no matter what. Billions of Econs fall into the Sun if the ship stays here, and powerful agencies and firms fall into the Sun with them. The Natural Humans will go as crew, if only because it's too late to replace them, and because to select another crew would be to admit making a mistake in choosing the first one."

"Too," Houlihan added, "a major embarrassment will leave the Solar System."

Cassandra nodded, and then felt horror. "It'd make perfect sense, politically, to do nothing till the ship passes the point of recall, and prosecute Dr. Guttagong and me then."

Houlihan smiled. "Never fear. If they do, I'll get you off."

రజ ⚭ ఎ

1

O nly once she had transferred the gene-replacement retroviruses to Dr. Guttagong had Cassandra considered her acts' consequences. She saw then that persons receiving an unforeseen berth on the generation ship might exchange gloom for a joy puzzling to their families and friends among the Natural Humans. Even worse, the beneficiaries of gene replacement might show their benefactors gratitude. *No good deed,* Cassandra thought darkly, *goes unpunished.*

ოჳ⊂ჳჄდგა

T o calm herself, Cassandra arranged, again behind Larry's back, another clandestine meeting with Dr. Guttagong. He was beaming. "I can't tell you how much satisfaction it gave me to help those patients. There's joy in their eyes, they greet me with smiles—"

His nonchalance horrified Cassandra. "Doctor, doesn't it worry you that radical changes in your patients' behavior could rouse the elders' suspicions?"

He frowned, puzzled. "Surely no one can question happiness."

Cassandra closed her eyes and pinched the bridge of her nose. *Which of us is more naïve—you, or me for letting myself get carried away with your enthusiasm?* "Doctor, you can't rely on the UN and the Natural Humans to accept a *fait accompli.* You must stress to your patients the need for secrecy."

He shrugged. "I'll try, but a city on a hill can't be hidden."

ოჳ⊂ჳჄდგა

H is words were accurate. Soon, in meetings, Cassandra's staff began to discuss the unexpectedly low percentage of Natural Humans rejected from the generation ship's crew for genetic anomalies. Cassandra feigned just normal interest in the meetings, but recognized their topic as a sign of danger to her, to the doctor, and to his patients.

Larry began to regale her with items from newscasts. "Did you see, ma'am, that story on the Natural Humans' network about persons who once feared being declared unclean now being certified clean? The network interviewed the mission's medical team to learn the reason for their luck, but that Dr. Guttagong who came to see you was unwilling to speculate on it. He seemed nervous to me."

Fool, Cassandra thought of the doctor, *why did you commit a crime without making a convincing lie to cover it up?*

She lowered her head into her hands. *I'm the greater fool for having trusted him.*

⁊⊰⊱⊱

The next morning, when she entered her office, Larry said, "The network is reporting anonymous calls now, ma'am. The callers claim to have received Dr. Guttagong's help in overcoming their genetic deficiencies. This doesn't have anything to do with his contacts with you, does it?"

Cassandra shook her head, but felt powerless to forestall disaster. Watching the newscasts herself, she learned that the Natural Humans' attorney general had announced an investigation into violations of import laws. Shortly afterwards, the scandal reached the outside world when Achilles Cluster Network News announced "shocking indications of corruption on the interstellar colonization mission."

Even if Guttagong's patients betray him, Cassandra thought, *maybe he'll protect me.*

The thought shaming her, she shook her head. Events had, in any case, spun out of her control.

⁊⊰⊱⊱

2

With no warning, Cassandra received a summons to the United Nations Circuit Court. She barely had time to call Houlihan before guards took her from her cell and shoved her into a cruiser, which delivered her to the steps of the courthouse where she had learned her status as a material witness. Houlihan met her outside the courtroom, but the bailiff barred the attorney's entrance.

"As the judge told you previously, counselor," the bailiff said, "since no charges have been filed against your client, she needs no defense."

　　　　　

In the courtroom Cassandra met only the judge and the public prosecutor from her previous hearing. To her bewilderment, the prosecutor began to talk of an event in the news.

"Have you heard, Ms. Lin, that the procurator of one of the nations in the Kuiper Cloud just committed suicide? We're unsure whether his death was due to personal reasons or to the hardship of his assignment. I tend to believe the latter. It's far from the Sun there, and most of the settlers are outcasts, either by their own choice, or because of cultural practices or genetic modifications illegal Downsystem. It was a shame to lose the procurator. It's hard for the UN to find qualified personnel to serve out there."

Cassandra felt faint. She had heard of Ultima Thule as punishment duty. *I'm hardly such a child that I need ask how the news concerns me.*

The judge at once confirmed her suspicion. "The UN requests you, Ms. Lin, to take this difficult assignment."

She smiled thinly at him. "If I recall correctly, our personnel take six months in hibernation aboard a freighter to reach Ultima Thule. I'd be out of communication for three months after the launch. By then the ship will have built up so much momentum that to turn it around would bust the mission's budget. The UN would have to let the voyage go on."

The prosecutor, grinning, nodded. "Thanks to you, the launch will be on time. No one can deny that you deserve this promotion."

"What of Dr. Guttagong?"

The judge closed his eyes and rubbed his eyelids. "He and his colleague volunteered for duty as medical officers aboard comet-charting missions to the Oort Cloud. Ten years out, ten years there, ten years back."

Cassandra felt horror. "My crime was worse than theirs! It's unfair—"

The prosecutor shook his head. "As I've said, Ms. Lin, no crime was committed. You and Dr. Guttagong merely tried to implement policy by your best judgment. It may please you to know that all of the Natural Humans will leave aboard the generation ship, regardless of the state of their DNA. The elders consented to this arrangement just this morning."

"I see," Cassandra said coldly. "Was their consent like Dr. Guttagong's?"

The judge smiled wryly. "We require your response to the offer of a promotion, Ms. Lin."

"What if I decline it?"

The prosecutor shrugged. "You remain a material witness for the next six months. Unless, of course, your Ms. Houlihan forces public hearings. Capable woman, that. Inconvenient stories would come out—yours, the United Nations', the Natural Humans' . . ."

She thought of her own story and foresaw its end in her return in disgrace to Seattle. She thought of the United Nations' story and burned with zeal to expose the incompetent or corrupt officials who had awarded the generation ship to the Natural Humans. Her zeal burned brighter at the thought of exposing their elders—

If I expose them, all whom I've tried to help will lose a dream, and my sacrifice would be in vain.

With an effort of will, Cassandra said, "I accept."

The judge seemed to her suddenly weary of the proceedings. "Everything concerning your association with the Natural Humans, your arrest, and your detention is under this court's seal. Prepare at once to depart for your next post. You may have a limited amount of time to record your good-byes."

"Just understand," the prosecutor said, "that they're subject to editing."

⁓❧ὧ⁊

1

T he accounts in the Press of a scandal among the Natural Humans had led to its inevitable conclusion: an investigation by United Nations Domestic Security of possible violations of international law. While Cassandra, at her apartment or at her desk in the Mission, watched with numb horror the events unfolding on the holoscreen, the police sealed the Natural Humans' habitat. Lurid accounts of misdeeds there, all of them based on guesswork, but some astonishingly accurate, came from reporters and from anchorpersons. Cassandra ignored puzzled and then angry queries from Larry and from her other underlings and coworkers as she hung on the newscasters' every word. Soon the holowall displayed dramatic footage of guards leading Dr. Guttagong and his staff to black cruisers.

"Sources within Domestic Security confirm that the arrest of a high-ranking official in the UN Mission itself is imminent," the latest reporter announced portentously.

No need to ask who that is, Cassandra thought bleakly. She decided that she owed her staff an explanation, but, meeting a horizon of faces staring at her, she understood that no explanation was required. Some of the faces were openly contemptuous of her, others seemed to her piteous, and only a couple—the faces of junior officials who, she suspected, would always be junior—showed her support. It hurt her that Larry refused to meet her gaze. *At least you'll get more time off now.*

She determined to leave her job with dignity. Thus, she was packing her desk's contents neatly away when she glimpsed motion on its far side. Looking up, she met the gazes of three officers of

Domestic Security. The centermost of them, a tall, blond man, said, "Ms. Lin, you're under arrest."

ଔ୯ଽଊ୪

2

At last, in another examination room, Cassandra eyed something disturbingly like a coffin. *Maybe the shape is convenient for shipping me,* she thought wanly. At Computer's instructions, she began to lower herself, undressed, into a black pool of nanos half-filling the coffin, and quelled her squeamishness at watching them crawl up her legs. *It's just like falling asleep in a bathtub,* previous deep-space voyagers had told her, *if you don't mind one filled with ice water.*

As she kept lowering herself into the coffin, and the nanos crawled over her hips, she thought, *I wonder whether Grandfather arranged my new posting for me. It's just the kind of solution that he'd like—punishment and a chance for redemption in a neat package. What I make of it is up to me.*

She lowered the back of her head onto a padded rest and felt the cold wave of nanos creep across her breasts and onto her throat. She could hardly concentrate now, but dimly envisioned Ultima Thule's squabbling misfit cultures. *I need to do something spectacular among them to earn a trip back to Earth. Bringing them peace with one another and reconciliation with the rest of humanity might be enough.*

As the wave of nanos, reaching her eyes, submerged her vision and consciousness together, she thought, with a touch of humor, *The kind of job for which I was born.*

Women want children; it's a fact of nature. What will a woman who wants a child do to get one when certain aspects of child-bearing are regulated by the state?

BABY, BE MINE

by Susan Tsui

Baby, Be Mine
Mine Alone
Mother to Daughter
Body and Soul
Baby, Be Mine

There are rows of them, babies. All waiting to be born. I place my hand against the side of one tank. The glass is smooth and sticky beneath my sweaty palm. Inside it is dark, better to simulate a womb, I've been told. Still I think that if I look closely enough through the glass I can make out ten fingers and ten toes. At this stage, would there be a heart yet? I want to hear a heart beat. "This is what I want," I say. Divorce or no divorce. Screw my ex. "This is what I've always wanted." I turn to Pamela. She stands there, hands clasped over her purse, smiling sadly. Pamela with her tall stature and hard edges is a formidable-looking woman, even when her dark skin is not silhouetted in blood red light. Just the kind of tough, no-nonsense lawyer I need.

"Can you make that happen?" I ask her.

Pamela presses one hand to the tank, alongside mine. "We can try."

☙❧☙❧

"I'm sorry, Mrs. Eng, but we've had this discussion before. We can't help you."

I stare at the woman sitting at the glass desk across from me. Brown hair with strawberry-blond highlights. How old is she, I wonder. Twenties, thirties? Younger than I. Has she had her babies yet? Empty mahogany bookshelves fan out behind her. An endless herstory waiting to be filled.

"Can't or won't?" I ask. Beside me, Pamela starts to go through her briefcase. She's gearing up, ready to serve.

"We won't pay to have your baby born in a nutrient-tank," the woman says. "Nutrient-tanks are not medically necessary."

"I have an autoimmune disease. I can't have my baby any other way," I reply.

"That's not true. As your insurance provider, we are more than willing to pay for immunosuppression therapy."

"Which could harm my baby."

The woman tilts her head. "It is a risk." She shrugs.

This woman has never had children, never wanted them, I think. A woman who wanted children would never shrug at a risk. She is perfect for her job.

Pamela takes her cue, leans forward, slaps a sheet of paper down. "I don't think you understand," Pamela says. Her words are clipped, professional. I admire her. "My client is serving notice. Mrs. Eng is willing to take this company to court."

This woman, this stranger, my obstacle, smiles. "Please do."

03CR80

The judge is a man. He is a short, fat man with a silver comb-over and bespectacled eyes. It shouldn't matter. Yet somehow it does. Perhaps I only find it strange because I have been dealing so far with women. He looks over my file, flips through a few pages, glares at me over the brim of his glasses from on high, glares down with equal disdain at my opponent, and sighs. "Are you sure you want to go through with this?"

I stand up, force myself to look up at him on his high perch. Beside me, Pamela also rises. "I'm sure," I say.

CRITICAL

"**W**ould you consider a vasectomy a medically necessary procedure?" Pamela asks.

I watch the president of my insurance company smile. His teeth are showing. I can't remember if that's a good sign or bad. The flash of a reporter's camera glints off those teeth. Unlike the judge, he is charming and handsome, with a square jaw and auburn hair. The word debonair comes to mind. I wonder if my ex-husband will be seeing this in tomorrow's paper. I wonder what he would make of me trying to have a child on my own.

"That depends," the president replies. He continues to flash his pearly whites.

"But you cover a vasectomy," Pamela points out. She leans forward onto the arm of the witness stand, almost flirting with him. She has one finger twirled around a curly lock of her hair.

"Yes," he tells her chest.

"You won't cover a nutrient-tank."

"No."

"Is it because my client's a woman?"

"It's because your client has the right to the morning after pill and an abortion. A man does not. There is a world of difference between trying to get pregnant and preventing pregnancy." The president seems very self-satisfied at his answer.

"So you object because you consider pregnancy a disease and prevention medically necessary."

The president's smile falters. Pamela's only brightens.

CRITICAL

"**I**f both parties will please rise." The judge sounds bored, tired. A job like this must take its toll, I think. After years of this, does he now consider every argument a petty one? Around me cameras flash and news reporters hold up their styluses, ready to enter the verdict. My baby, my private medical and emotional issues, will become today's 6 PM entertainment.

What will the people see when they watch? A short diminutive Chinese woman in high heels and serious expression, a fighter in the court room waiting to potentially make history, or a mother trying to have a child? Surface or depth? What would I see if I were anyone but me?

"Obviously this is a very important issue," the judge continues. "Both sides have valid arguments, but the law here is clear. An insurance company must be willing to pay for some method of conception, but there is nothing explicitly stating what method has to be covered or that all methods must be covered. I'm sorry, Mrs. Eng, but I must rule against you. You may, of course, appeal."

☙❧

"I'm sorry."

I glance up in surprise. I did not expect to find my ex-husband waiting for me on the marble courthouse steps, much less with an apology on his lips. I should have known he liked his entertainment live.

"Thank you," I say.

"I'm willing to pay for the nutrient-tank," he says.

I blink. What? "Why?" I ask.

"Because, I want a baby, too," he says.

We're divorced. "What's the catch?"

He smirks. "I want you to give it my last name. It doesn't even have to be a boy, but I do want to be involved in raising it."

I look at this man, my ex-husband: the person I couldn't even share an apartment with, the man who refers to my baby as an it. He never understood.

"No," I say.

I stroll past his shocked expression. I will earn this baby on my own.

In a world in which lifespan used to be a great equalizer, what happens when the balance is upset?

MAYFLY

by Gary Kloster

There was a boy sleeping in Edda's bed, maybe twenty at best, long, lean and beautiful. She blinked at him while her brain lurched towards sentience, pulled her hand carefully away from his thigh and sat up. The movement brought the grainy haze in her head into focus and turned it into a nail of pain that hammered itself neatly between her eyes. Biting her lip to stopper a curse, Edda rubbed her fingertips gently over her temples and put it together. *Sojourner*. The countdown started. The celebration. The boys and the booze. *I'm too old for this*, Edda thought, and she slipped out of bed and padded to the bathroom.

She blamed Kendra. Kendra, who had brought the boys, the bottles of rum, the sweet cannicake, and passed them around like party favors. Edda dry swallowed two happy-wakes and sighed. The pills would quickly clear her head, but not her bed, and while Kendra had dished out the temptation, she was the one who had taken it. Now it was up to her to gently shoo this mayfly from her sheets. In the mirror, the rumpled sheets stirred, and Edda watched the boy as he sat up and flashed a brilliant smile at her.

"Morning, Doc."

"Mmmumph." In her head, there were memories, tumbled and sticky with rum and lust, but nothing like a name. She watched him stretch, smooth skin sliding over muscle. How long had it been since she'd last been with a man? Fifty years? More? That long at least. *Excepting last night.* Whatever, it had been a long time, and now she was staring, not shooing, and he was smiling, smug.

"Well," he said, posing himself for her on the bed. "What do you think? Before breakfast, or after?"

Very smug. But they're like that when they're young, aren't they? Edda sighed, plucked a tie from the counter, and used it to pull the shining white curtain of her hair into a pony tail. It made the girl in the mirror look younger, younger even than the boy on the bed, which annoyed her. But it got her hair out of the way.

"Before," she said, and walked back to bed, her headache washed away by the same rising rush of lust that drowned her conscience.

ଔଔ୫ଔ୬ଔ

"What'd you call this? A crepe? It's good. I've never had one."

Edda dropped her plate into the sink, ran her damp hands over the worn fabric of her nightshirt. *Why did I let him stay?* she wondered. *Will feeding him make me feel less guilty? Or do I just want an after?* She looked over her shoulder, watched his pretty lips slip into a smile. *Is it worth this?* Every time he parted those lips and spoke, it was a reminder of the gap between them, of the inequality of years and power. Dwelling on that, she missed what he said next.

"What?"

"The count. For *Sojourner*? It's going?"

His almond eyes—Sanun, his name was Sanun—were bright, interested. For the first time in something beyond her body or her food. Years of fighting for the project, battling through the bureaucracy for the money, had made her forget the wonder that her work could stir. Out in the world, people actually cared about going to the stars, about humankind's first chance to colonize an alien world. She smiled a little, feeling better about letting him stay.

"Yes, it's going. In five days—well, four and a half now, *Sojourner* will make the leap to Hathor."

"That long?"

"The fold itself is instantaneous. So five days isn't so much to cross over a hundred light years," she said. *Impatient youth.* "For a mass that big, to cross that far, the fold field generator has to . . ." Edda trailed off. After all this time, it still frustrated her to try to explain how her creation worked without using math. "It's like it needs time to charge."

"But it'll work? It'll really get to Hathor?"

Edda looked at him, wondering about the anxious thread in his voice. He almost sounded more worried about this than she was. "It'll make it. Or I've wasted over a century."

"That's good." Sanun set down his fork, his plate empty. "That long?" He stared at the shining-snow conceit of her hair. "How—"

"Two hundred and thirty-six." Edda didn't let herself forget, didn't stumble over the numbers. It seemed sacrilegious to take her years for granted.

"I've never met a woman that old," he said.

"I was already seventy-four when they first developed the Ankh. A lot of women that old didn't survive implantation." *But tried it anyway, though they knew it would probably kill them. The Ankh felt like it was killing me too, that first year. But we took it in anyway, let it wrap is viral hooks into our genes. How could we not?*

"Seventy-four? With wrinkles and all?" He smiled, but she heard a tiny trace of disbelief in his teasing.

"Come here." She took his hand and pulled him up, led him to the living room and the screen that hung over the fireplace. Her fingers stroked across the controls embedded in its frame and it came alive, pictures flashing across it as she spun through the image files until she found the image she wanted.

The frame showed a couple, standing arm-in-arm in a forest. Their broad smiles spread wrinkles across their faces, a topography of years, and their hair was silvery grey. Edda didn't look at them, ignored them. It was a long time ago, and she'd buried those ghosts. Mostly. Instead she watched Sanun as he looked from the picture to her, watched him shake his head.

"I can see it, in the eyes and . . . I don't know. Something." He reached out a hand, hesitantly, and when she didn't move, he stroked it along the firm line of her jaw. "How long did it take you to change back?"

"Three years." Three years, and her body had become young again, healthy, strong. Like it had been. Like it would now be, forever. And so the face in the mirror had turned back into the girl she thought she had left in high school.

"Cool," he said, his fingers trailing slowly down across the sensitive skin of her neck.

Cool. He had told her he was twenty. Just done with puberty. For him, to have your body warp so radically, so quickly, must seem natural. She caught his hand and stopped his caress. "Don't."

"Sorry," he said, pulling his hand back, confused but trying to hide it. He looked back at the picture, trying to change the subject. "Who's the guy?"

Jason. "My husband." He had gotten her through the change, had held her through the pain, had laughed at her exasperation over looking like a damned *teenager.* Had laughed too when she'd modded her hair white, to remind the world that she wasn't young. He had been so in love with her, so happy for her, even after all the male Ankh trials failed, even after it had become obvious that he was never going to share in her rebirth.

Beside her, Sanun cleared his throat. "That must have been harsh."

Harsh. Suddenly, she wanted him out. He was too young, too raw, too ignorant. The bit of affection she had felt for him after his flash of interest in *Sojourner* was gone. It was time to kick his pert ass out, and she was framing a polite way to do that when there was a quiet tap at her door.

Edda turned toward the sound, wondering why the house hadn't alerted her about company, and then Sanun brushed past her. He pulled open the door and the bright morning sun spilled in past three silhouettes. Three men, and Edda went still as the world took on the sharp shades of adrenaline around her.

The man in the lead stepped forward, into her home. A little stooped, he was barely taller than Edda, and his hair and beard were as white as hers. His skin was thin and spotted with age, and his eyes were nested in a map of lines. But they were excited, triumphant. "Doctor Edda Wolfe. I'm Harrison. I need to talk to you about your ship."

⋆⊰⊱⋆

They let her change, but sent Sanun with her. To watch her, she supposed, though the boy mostly kept his back to her while they both silently dressed. Too guilty to meet her eyes, too ashamed of his seduction and betrayal. *I wonder what he did to my security.*

Edda glanced toward her dresser and the simple jewelry box that sat atop it. With him standing that way, facing the corner as he pulled up his pants, she could have tried for it. But even if she overcame the boy, there were the others. Two centuries in academia had done little to prepare her for commando actions, and at least two of the men out there had peacemaker training. More than likely, Sanun's guilt would be more helpful to her than any half-assed offensives. And that guilt would be erased the moment she hurt him. Physically.

So Edda dressed slowly, letting him finish first, leaving him to turn and watch her or stand staring at the wall. She pulled up her pants and slipped her feet into her trainers, took a breath. *Confused, hurt, betrayed, and scared . . . but trying to be brave. Like a child. For a child.* Her expression set, she looked up to him.

Sanun blinked and twisted under her gaze and his big hands clenched by his side. "Doc, I, I just—" He stopped, looked to the door and cleared his throat. "Harrison's waiting."

"I suppose he is," she said, quietly enough that the boy had to step a little closer to hear. "I guess we shouldn't make him wait, when you've done so much to bring him here. To let him have me."

"Doc—Dr. Wolfe," he struggled, his face darkening. "We're not patrys. We just—"

Without a knock the door popped open, and one of Harrison's companions stood looking at them with dark, flat eyes. "Done?" It wasn't really a question. The man was probably only a decade older than Sanun, still so young to her, but no child. A peacemaker, she was sure, and he had a coiled readiness in him that made her smooth her face and nod. Pity would be a bad card to play with this one. "Then go," he said, and waited until she had passed before following her, close enough that his presence was a clear threat behind her. In the living room, Harrison was waiting.

He stood before the screen, staring up at it, sipping a cup of her coffee. The other man was out of sight, obscured by the half-shut door to her office. Edda could hear him moving in there, though, could hear the soft tap of fingers on a keypad. She took a step in that direction, and a hand closed on her shoulder, firm as stone.

"Jules." Harrison hadn't turned from the picture, but the old man shook his head, and Edda felt the hand fall from her shoulder. "Let's at least try to be pleasant."

Try to be pleasant. He had been a peacemaker, too, she imagined. How high had he risen before being retired, to speak so quietly with such authority, to veil a threat so calmly? "What do you want?"

"What did he want?" Harrison countered. He turned from the picture and stared at her, the faded blue of his eyes meeting hers.

"To solve an impossible problem."

"Yes." His face shifted into a smile that was hidden by his whiskers. "How do we reach the stars, when the distances are so vast?"

"Remove the distance."

"Fold space. A simple solution to say. A bit harder to implement. He worked on the problem his entire life, without solving it. But you did. But you had more life, didn't you?"

"You're going quite a distance to answer my question," she said.

"*Sojourner.*"

"She's not mine to give."

"She isn't?" he asked. "I want your keys and codes."

"You want my access to *Sojourner's* control system. What good would that do you?" *What good would it do?* Edda's clearance went deep into the system, but it wasn't unlimited. There were checks on what she could do, on what they would be able to do. The symtelligent computer that controlled the ship wouldn't allow dangerous changes, not during the critical launch window. *But am I sure? Like any security, it always seems uncrackable until it fails.*

"There's no need for you to worry about that." The old man shrugged. "It's not your concern. What you do need to know is that we want *Sojourner* to succeed, too, Edda. We just want it to succeed for everyone, not just some."

"Everyone? Or you? Or men like you?" she said, softly. "And Sanun told me you weren't patrys."

"We aren't," said Sanun. "Why not just tell her what we're doing?" The young man ignored Jules's glare, but when Harrison flicked his eyes towards him, his voice slipped from complaint toward apology. "What we're doing isn't wrong. Not really."

"The women who run this world won't agree." Harrison answered the boy, but he was staring back again at Edda. "They can't admit what they've done to us. So they'll just call us terrorists." The old man shook his head. "We're not, Edda. I helped destroy some of the last cells of those fanatics. The patrys wanted dominion, wanted to restore a patriarchy of the worst possible kind. They were wrong, evil. We don't want that. We just want equality."

Over a century fighting for this ship, and now at the end, this. Edda raised her hand, thumb and fingers spread over her eyes as she touched her temples. There was a new ache in her head, entirely different from the hangover she had earlier. "What if I don't want to give you my codes?"

"Then we'll take them," Harrison said. He nodded to Jules, who stepped away from where he had been looming behind Edda to pick up the small case he had carried into the house with him.

Jules unfolded it on the coffee table, and took a ring of dull metal from inside it. "Mempull," he said, holding the ring carefully in his hand.

"Mempull," Edda echoed. *Of course. Harrison said he'd fought the patrys.* That was the last time those things had been used. Legally. To tear out the information that the peacemakers had needed to finally break the terrorists' network.

"We don't need your cooperation." Jules turned the ring in his hands. "All we need is this."

He was right. The machine would pull the codes out of her, would pull out any memory she had that they might want, and leave ruin behind.

"It doesn't have to come to that," said Harrison.

"If I give you what you want. Then you won't hurt me." She tilted her head and met the old man's eyes, but at the edge of her vision she could see Sanun frowning down at the floor. "No, you don't sound like the patrys at all."

"We need those codes. Now. Why are we still talking to her?" Jules's voice was tight, though with impatience or excitement Edda couldn't be sure.

"Keep it in your pants." Edda kept her voice calm, hard, controlled, but she felt the chill-slick fear sweat on her skin. "I can't fight that and won't. And if you stole that and brought it here, to threaten me, then I know how desperate you are. You've already given yourselves a death sentence." From the corner of her eye, she saw Sanun flinch and look away. *Did you know what you were signing up for, Sanun?* "I'll give you my codes. But tell me why."

"You don't need to know," Jules growled, the ring still held tight in his hands.

"Jules," Harrison warned. "But he's right. You don't need to know what we're doing. But I'll tell you why."

He looked up, back at the picture that still glowed over the fireplace. "The Ankh changed everything. You should know that, better than anyone. You've watched it happen. How much change have you seen? You were around when men made up half the population, not the third that we are today. You were here when our opinions mattered. When we had some say in this world. In little more than a century you've seen us go from someone you could respect, could work with and live with and love, to pretty little toys that could amuse you for a night."

Edda felt her body want to shake, felt the mask of detached calm that she had settled over her in the bedroom threaten to slip. More than seeing the mempull, Harrison's words frightened her. He believed in them, and that belief made him desperate.

She looked up at the man in the picture. *Jason. I miss you. You never lost your calm, even to your last. Help me keep mine.* "I have seen it. An entire century of women having more power than men. Unfair, unfair, unfair." Her words sparked fire in Harrison's eyes for the first time, but she raised her hands to hold off his retort. "Nature's unfair, and only the double X's get the fountain of youth. Honestly, I wish it wasn't like that. But whatever it is you're planning, I can't change that, and neither can my ship."

"I think it can. The codes."

His eyes were hard as diamonds, and so Edda kept her peace. Harrison sent for his tech and turned away from her while she gave her codes. The man hovered, his breath warm on the side of her face as he watched her fingers every twitch over the keys. Further away, Jules watched her too, his eyes hard and suspicious.

"Got it," the tech said when she was done, and plucked the tablet from Edda's hands. "I'll check to make sure her input's clean, then I can start. I'll have the menagerie in their sys within a few hours."

"We can vet her input right now."

Edda felt the fear shake her, before her conscious mind had really understood what Jules was saying. She snapped her gaze up, not to that tall man, but to Harrison. And the old man looked back at her, bleakly considering.

"Hey, no. No." Sanun sounded as desperate as Edda felt. "She gave us the codes. We can't do that—"

"We don't have time for lies or tricks. We need the truth, now." Jules looked to his leader. "Right, Harrison?"

"Right," Harrison answered, and his next words trampled over Sanun's protest. "And we have it. Edda knows the price of betrayal.

She might fear for her ship, her dream, but she won't risk over two hundred years of memories. The Ankh makes them all cowards."

"Still—"

"Enough, Jules. This woman invented the fold generators. She gave us the stars. Who knows what else she might accomplish? Sanun, take her to her room and keep her there until we're done."

"Right," the young man said, relief woven in his words.

"I'll stay with them," Jules said.

Damn your peacemaker paranoia. She saw them looking at each other, Sanun and Jules, their eyes both sharp with suspicion. *Leave him to me.* But Edda said nothing, just turned and let them both trail behind her. In her room, she lay on the bed, ignored them, and waited for her chance.

⚜

L ess than two hours, and it came. The door to her bedroom clicked open, and the tech came in to argue, sotto voice, with Jules. Edda lay on her bed, eyes closed, and listened to the buzz of their voices, the tone of their incomprehensible words. *Some difficulty, and they want him to come see. But he doesn't want to, because of his suspicion of me. And because of his opinion of the boy's loyalty. And intelligence.* But Harrison's name was whispered, loud enough to be heard, and Jules turned to the door with the tech.

"Watch her, but for God's sake don't talk to her. Got it?" The boy nodded, and Jules stalked out.

She waited a minute, letting him wonder if she really was asleep, before speaking. "They didn't trust you enough to tell you the truth."

"Please, just keep quiet."

"You didn't know Jules was bringing that thing, did you? You didn't know how dangerous he was. You thought Harrison held him in check."

"I said—"

"The thing is," she continued, quietly rolling over his words, "he does. Harrison controls Jules. He ordered him to bring the mempull. He set you all up for a death sentence. Did he tell you that, before he sent you out to seduce me?"

"No."

"Oh." It was like punching a child, but his ignorance deserved it. She opened her eyes and looked at him, read the shadow of desperation that was on his face. "What's going on, Sanun? What madness have they tangled you in?"

"It's not madness. It's a good plan."

"Really? Is that all they told you?"

"No, damn it, they . . ." He trailed off, frowning at her, recognizing her manipulation, but still so open to it. "You just want to tell me why it's not going to work."

"Yes, I do. Because I think so far you've only been told how everything is going to go right, and I think you've seen how that's already breaking down." She kept her voice soft, pitched for him, and understanding. When she saw the muscles of his jaw finally relax, she could barely keep herself from cheering.

He said, "There's a ship. Out there, near *Sojourner*. They'll use your codes to get into *Sojourner's* system and mess with the external sensors and communications. Let our ship close and board, and keep them from calling for help. Then they'll switch the crews. Our people for yours." He stared up at the ceiling, as if he could trace the ships' intersecting paths out there beyond the orbit of Jupiter. "They've all been trained. Some of them were almost picked for *Sojourner*. They'll make our first colony work. But they won't take the Ankh with them. The women are all young enough that they haven't been treated yet. And they'll wipe all trace of its synthesis from the data files. Harrison says that on Hathor, at least, the balance will be restored."

"Harrison fell off his rocker a long time ago, Sanun. His plan is insane." And gods, it was. Edda bit her lip, thinking through the implications.

"I knew you would say that," Sanun said, but he shifted his gaze back to her, and there was a desperate worry in his eyes. "But tell me why."

"How many reasons do you want?" She stood, staring up at him. "The fold field is extremely delicate. Any mass close to the ship will disrupt its formation, and throw *Sojourner* light years off target. They'll have to get in, switch the crews, and get out within the next day to get to safe distance."

"Which is why we came here today."

"Right. Which might give them the time, if the boarding worked perfectly. But it won't." She shook her head, unbelieving. Sanun, young and naïve, might believe they had a chance, but the old peacemaker was neither of those. "Damn Harrison, he must know how impossible this is. He'll see them all killed, just for what, a gesture? Martyrdom? A new patry war?"

"What do you mean?" And the boy's voice was rising, and Edda snapped her attention back to him, to get him under control.

"The people on the ship won't go easy. I don't care what weapons Harrison gave his people—stunners, tranqs, semi-auts. It doesn't matter if they hit completely by surprise. They're dealing with a crew of earth's best, on a ship they know inside and out. Some will fight back. Time will be lost. People will die." The boy looked at her then, his eyes widening a little. And there it was, the key. "On both sides, people will get hurt and die, and then the fold will happen in the middle of that chaos, and then they'll all die. Who is it, Sanun? Who's on that ship? Who are you doing this for?"

His eyes dropped away from hers, and when he finally gave up the name, it rode a whisper to her. "Lalana. Her name is Lalana. My sister. My twin."

"Listen to me, Sanun. You're in deep here. And so is Lalana. Unless we stop this, now, before Harrison sends that ship in."

"What do you expect me to do?"

His voice was starting to rise again, and Edda reached out and took his hands, made him look down at her, made him focus on her.

"You can ask me for help. I can save Lalana. And you. If you ask for it. I—"

The door swung open and Jules was in the room almost before she could check her tongue. His eyes were burning, and his smile was as hard and humorless as steel. "I told you, you stupid mayfly. Never listen to them. You're not even human to her. You're just a toy, like Harrison said. And you shouldn't let her play with you." A hand dipped to his pocket, and then there was a roll of binding tape in his hand, bright as glass and impossibly strong. "Let her go, and I'll shut her up for you."

For all the indecision on the boy's face, he moved fast. Edda felt his hands take hers and push, sending her stumbling back to land on her bed. *Damn it, close, so close,* and now that chance was gone and Jules was coming at her, to pin her down and bind her and end all her options. Edda gathered herself up, her adrenaline priming her for some futile, desperate last struggle. Then he was lunging forward, falling onto the bed, and she was diving to the side, rolling away, rolling and suddenly free.

On the ground, on her feet, and Jules was lying still on the bed. And standing there, eyes wide, Sanun was looking at him. In his hand, something gleamed, a tiny injector. Edda felt her heart crashing, felt her lungs bursting, and let her breath go, slowly, slowly.

"They gave me this. In case you didn't sleep, in case—"

"Shh," she hissed, waving at him, and then she was at the door, trying to listen over the hammering of her heart. Her pulse eased when she heard no footfalls, no movement, only the distant sound of voices. She swung shut the door, hoping. "I don't think they heard."

"What do we do?" He was looking at her, and every shred of the smugness she had seen in him this morning was gone.

We. Good. "How long will he be out?"

"I'm not sure, an hour, maybe?"

Edda made herself go to the bed, searched the cover for the roll of binding tape and plucked it up. Forcing away the certainty that Jules was just faking it, she took the man's wrists, pushed them together and began to wrap the tape around them. "Go to the door and listen. If you hear someone coming, let me know." Edda kept her voice calm, made herself confident for him as her heart raced again beneath her ribs. She finished taping up Jules and pocketed the roll. *One down. Two to go.* She slipped off the bed beside her dresser and wondered what her chances were.

It's been, what, a year since I last charged this thing? She flipped open her jewelry box, tossed aside bracelets and rings that she never wore to find the flat grey sensor pad beneath. Edda touched it, let it know her, and then the hidden compartment popped open.

"Do you have a gun? They couldn't bring one through this neighborhood, we could—"

"Shh. No guns." *Harrison might not have a gun, but he has something, I'm sure. And whatever it is, he damn well knows how to use it better than me.* From the compartment, Edda lifted out a bracelet, jet-black and shining, carved like a tiny snake. She slipped it on, and felt it shift on her wrist, tighten slightly against her skin in acknowledgment of her touch. The gem-like eyes of the thing flared emerald for a moment, then dulled to amber. *Low charge. But it's not dead.* There went any hope of sending this weapon out on its own. She would have to get close to use it. But at least there was some chance. "Wadjet, ward," she whispered to it, and the eyes dulled to darkness, waiting.

"Whatsit?" Sanun whispered

"Nothing," she answered. "We need to go."

Sanun looked at the wide windows behind her. "Can we—"

"Sealed armor glass. I've got good security." *As long as I don't let the bad guys in myself.* She nodded at the door. "We'll have to sneak out, head for the back door."

"We'll never make it."

"We're not staying here." Edda stepped to him, put her hand on his arm. "We have to stop them before they get into *Sojourner's* system, before they send that ship. Before anyone gets hurt."

His arm twitched beneath her hand. "Yeah." He put his hand on the doorknob, then looked to her. "Stay behind me. I did some martial arts when I was younger. If we're seen, you run. I'll hold them off."

When you were younger. He might last a few seconds against Harrison. She hoped that would be all she needed. "Okay."

Sanun opened the door slowly, slipped silently into the hall, and Edda followed. At the edge of the living room, they stopped to listen to the quiet tap of keys that came from Edda's study. *Is there a chance?* Then Harrison was there, stepping into the room, moving with a grace that belied his years. *No.*

"Go!" shouted Sanun, and he was hurtling across the room, fast and beautiful, launching a kick in a perfect arc at the old peacemaker's head. Harrison barely moved, just nodded his head and flexed his knees a fraction, just enough to let the boy's foot fly over his white hair. As it passed, the old man's hand twitched, and something in his hand flashed in the sunlight that poured in through the windows. Sanun screamed, and fell.

Edda took a step, enough to put her back to the wall. She ignored Sanun's panting breath as he rolled on the floor, focused instead on Harrison as he moved close, focused on the thin knife that gleamed in his hand, bright as diamond. "Please don't," she whispered, and there was no acting in the fear that laced the words.

She had no sense of what he did, how she ended up on the floor with his knee in her back and his hand on her neck. It was over too fast, and she was pinned, helpless, the point of Harrison's tiny knife a bright, blurry star before her wide left eye. "Please, don't," he echoed. "I didn't, did I? And see where that's got us." His grip on her neck tightened, sent a flare of pain through her head like lightning, but she fought against it, reached out and snagged his ankle.

On her wrist, she felt the snake twitch, then it struck. Like a whip, it snapped away from her to wrap itself around Harrison's ankle. At its touch, he moved, lunging back from her, stabbing down. Then he grunted, and crumpled to the floor.

Edda rolled to her side, staring. Harrison lay beside her, an old man fallen. On his leg, pinned to his calf by the knife, Wadjit twitched. Behind him, Sanun lay on the floor, motionless. "Damn me," and she pulled herself up, in time to watch the tech step into the room from her office.

"Shit," he said, sounding tired, and started toward her, moving to block her path to the door. Halfway there and he lurched, stumbled sideways and his head connected with the smooth stone curve of the fireplace mantle with a sound like a book being dropped. He fell, twitching, then still.

"I guess you are dangerous," Edda murmured, staring down at Sanun where he lay, his hand still wrapped around the tech's foot.

"I might be bleeding to death," he said, staring at her, eyes distant.

Edda went to him, carefully stripped him of his crimson-stained pants. She wiped away the blood that coated his inner thigh and examined the cut as he hissed in pain.

"It feels like he cut my balls off. He didn't, did he?"

"No." She folded the clean leg of his pants, pressed it hard against the deep cut. "He was going for your femoral. Got close, but he missed it."

"How do you know?"

"Because you're not dead." Edda took his hands, cold with impending shock, and put them on the makeshift bandage. "Hold on." She ran for the bathroom and came back with a doc-wrap. She shoved his hands away and let the warm nanoweave slither around his leg, nestling over the wound and pulling it shut. In less then a minute, Sanun's color was better, and the chill sweat that had covered him was beginning to dry as the wrap spilled its drugs into his blood. Edda left him to check the others, and to use Jules's tape. She was winding it around Harrison's wrists when Sanun spoke.

"A snake. Jules didn't know you had a snake." He was staring at Wadjit, which curled on the knife that transfixed it. Edda had decided to leave it and the knife alone, since the wound on the old man's leg was only seeping blood slowly. "I thought they were illegal."

"Private ownership of semi-autonomous weapons systems is a grey area in Second Amendment theory." It was the answer, word for word, that Edda had gotten from the ex-girlfriend who had given her the bracelet decades ago. When the patry wars were still hot. Before Harrison and the other peacemakers had won. "How are you feeling?"

"Drugged." He closed his eyes. "What are you doing?"

"I'm going to run to the neighbors and borrow a phone, since you buggered mine, and I'm not touching my terminal and messing with whatever they were trying to do. I'll be back soon."

"Wait." He pushed himself up to stare at her, his beautiful face marked with the pain that bled through the drugs.

"I have to go, Sanun. I have to tell control about Harrison's ship before they move it."

"I know. Just promise me first. Promise me that you were telling the truth."

"Promise?" Fear and pain aged him, showed her the shadow of what his face would be in scant decades. She stared, and then it clicked. She was safe now. He wasn't. "Sanun, I'll protect you."

"Not me. Lalana. I'm doing this for her. I did this whole damn thing for her. She was the one who talked about it, how unfair it was to me and all the other men, how unfair it was to her that she would never get anywhere when all the other women had more experience . . ." He trailed off, pleading for reassurance.

Oh, gods preserve me from the young and stupid. "Sanun, it will be all right. I'll do what I can. I'll protect your sister too."

"She didn't know. We didn't know. I did this for her. I'm helping you for her. She didn't understand. She knew it was dangerous, but she didn't understand."

"I know she didn't. I know you didn't. That's why I told you Harrison's lies. Now—"

"No. Not Harrison. We never really trusted him. But she wanted to take a chance, and I said I would help. But I didn't know. That picture . . ." He looked at the image of the old couple that still glowed in the frame.

Despite the urgent tension that twisted through her, she stopped and stared up at herself as she had once been, as she would never be again. "What about the picture?"

"You were old. I've never seen a woman like that. I knew, without the Ankh, that she would get old, but I didn't *know* it, didn't understand it until I saw your picture. She'll get old. She'll die."

"Your sister."

"My twin." His eyes turned from the picture to her. "I've always known this wouldn't last for me. That I'd get old, that I'd change. That I'd die. But not her, and knowing that, that made it okay. Better, at least."

"But not if this worked."

"Yeah. Even if you're wrong, and Harrison is right, even if they take *Sojourner*, then she still loses. She'll get old, and die. And she doesn't have to. And she shouldn't have to, just because it won't work for me."

"My husband told me something like that once. A long time ago." *And maybe I'm sorry I thought that you were stupid.* Edda went to the door and swung it open, looked away from the bright bar of sunlight at him. "She won't understand, you know. But I'll talk to her. And the council."

"Thank you," he said and settled back; in the sun, his face smoothed back to fleeting youth.

"Thank you," she answered, then stepped out into the day and began to run.

This is the second story to look at the choices women can make in the face of war. Are they forced to make those decisions? What is peace worth?

TO THE ALTAR

by Therese Arkenberg

President Amileya Jahensson of the Morbat Republic slumped in the hard armchair behind her desk, staring into the shadows of the Primary Office and trying not to think. She had visited another hospital today, chatting and awarding medals to several wounded soldiers, medals for injuries she could have prevented.

Tomorrow would be worse. Tomorrow the president would dedicate Gold Star Park, the new memorial gardens at the edge of the capital. *Gold Star*—that was an old name, one picked up from the ancient records of the Generation Ships. Knowing the grief was immemorial, timeless, did not make it any better. Not as long as she kept sending forces to Bhitubi, kept sending young men and women to die when instead she could have sent a weapon that would end the war in moments.

End it unconscionably.

End it with bombs that were the ancient weapons of Earth reborn, end it by sparking a rain of fire—she imagined it, bombs plummeting like drops of rain, and each one powerful enough to destroy a city—end it by beginning the end of the world.

Or, even if the Apocalypse could be averted, she would end it by trading for the lives of a few thousand soldiers with a few hundred thousand civilians.

Not her people. Bhitubi people. Her duty was to protect Morbatan citizens, not their enemies.

Amileya Jahanesson's duty lies, like her heart, with all of humanity on Genesis. She had campaigned on that promise, as a peaceful candidate; she had won the election—but the war had started anyway.

The Bhitubi started it. They've asked for it. That you have to bear the cost in your soul—take it to the altar, sister. Amileya's mind spoke the last words in the voice of her Aunt Feliciti, the woman who, taking her in after the death of her mother, first introduced her to the concepts of compassion and duty and sacrifice. She had taught only the sacrifice of oneself for others, though, not the sacrifice of others for others.

She rocked the chair from leg to leg uneasily. The president shouldn't be sitting at her desk, brooding, when there were things to be done, a war going on. She should get some sleep so she could think clearly tomorrow, or she should read some of the reports on her desk, or listen to some of the less-important messages left recorded and waiting on her comscreen.

Amileya's hand reached out and logged into the 'screen. It flashed to life, bright blue with a parade of white characters across it, proclaiming the dates, senders, and summaries of previous messages. She was about to bring up one from the Logistics Board when the screen flashed again, this time bright green. She hadn't seen that color for a while, not since the start of the war—the color of an urgent message, one sent directly to her, bypassing the myriad filters and prioritizers of the president's office. The characters, still white but bolded to stand out against the brighter screen, announced a live message from the Bhitubi front.

໕⊂ঽৡ⊃⊱

The Odinaga kept apart from the rest of the Bhitubi forces, especially on the final nights before their missions. This segregation might be self-imposed, as the nature of their work did lead naturally to some feelings of superiority. Or it might be that the traditional troops avoided them, wary of the warriors who walked, knowingly and willingly, into the arms of Death.

Even so, they were human. Odinaga did many things the night before setting out on their missions: laughing, crying, drinking wine, cigarettes, sex, games. One man sat beneath a lantern in the corner of the tent, flipping through the last pages of a book. Hariah stood at the door, looking into the night, hearing the mumble of wind through the jungle, thinking.

Like many of the Odinaga, she felt some grim satisfaction, as though her mission was already completed. But the larger part of her was unsettled, anxious, determined. She had heard the whispers and knew what some in the camp thought of her: that she was out for revenge, that she was the widow of a murdered man or that she had been raped by Morbatan soldiers. In fact, Hariah was a virgin. Her motivation was nothing so concrete.

It consisted, she thought, of large and equal portions of foolishness and patriotism. Love of country and pigheadedness. Compassion and hubris. Overall, the certainty that she could do good, that she was in the right.

She looked into the star-spotted, jungle-rustling night and tried to think of something different—she would have time for this, plenty of time, tomorrow. But for all the months of her training she had thought of nothing else, and the habit was hard to break now.

"Hariah."

She turned to see Namauh coming down the row of tents. He offered something she couldn't make out in the darkness.

"Your gun," he said.

"I already have one, Captain."

"Not good enough. That pistol's meant for . . . protection." He almost swallowed the word.

He was right. She held out her hand and accepted a compact submachine piece. Longer than her pistol, and heavier too, but not unwieldy. She had practiced with similar arms and knew how to handle it. "Thank you."

"Yes." He turned to go, then hesitated. "Your Guide told me you were taking a solitary mission."

"Yes. I'm going to the camp in the south."

There was only one camp in the south, only one they named that way. She saw Namauh select his next words with care. "Do you have a particular target?"

"Yes."

He frowned. If she had wanted to say more, he knew she would have. And Namauh recognized the respect he owed Odinaga. He asked no more. "Well . . . good luck, then."

"Thank you, Captain."

He left her. She stood looking at the submachine gun. Strange; she hadn't considered before the kinds of weapons she must use.

cଷ ଓଃ ନ ୧ ୨ ଚ ର

A farmer who brought provisions to the Bhitubi camp returned south with an Odinaga in the back of his truck. Hariah lay beneath a tarp on the plastic mesh vegetable packing and listened to the wheels squeak, her head aching from the stench of engine fuel. The submachine gun lay beside her.

Odinaga. It meant *One who goes to the altar.* The Bhitubi had legends of men and women who lay on altars and offered their hearts as gifts for the gods. They were old legends, maybe even from before the Landing, certainly no later than the dark, chaotic years after it.

People spoke of those years after the Landing as if they were the worst Genesis had ever seen. As if superstition was worse than the rational slaughter of a modern war.

The truck rolled to a stop. "Ma'am? We're here."

She took up her gun and leapt from the truckbed. The farmer had halted in a thicket of trees on a ridge rising over the Morbatan camp. Hariah looked over the grid of forest-green tents and swallowed against the feeling of an ocean churning in her stomach.

"I'll leave you now, ma'am." The farmer hesitated until she nodded to him; then he dipped his hat in farewell and climbed back into the truck. She stood motionless on the ridge until the vehicle rounded a bend and she was alone.

Hariah started down the slope along a path that must have been worn by Morbatan soldiers, cleared of rocks and tangled plants. She was able to reach the bottom without stumbling, but during her descent she was clearly visible to anyone in the camp who thought to look.

She had no interest in hiding herself.

Thus she wasn't at all surprised to find half a dozen soldiers in Morbatan uniforms standing at the end of the trail, guns cocked, waiting for her.

She came to them with her hands raised. "Please," she said, "I have something to say to you."

࿐ CRSO ࿐

The call might be live, but her comscreen took its fair time connecting, as Aunt Feliciti would say. Rather than stare at the loading graphic, thinking of where the transmission was coming from and what should be done there, Amileya looked around the walls of her office.

It was a mistake—the north wall was curtained by maps of Bhitubi. The bright red triangle of Tonoti, the capital, caught her eye. It had been designated the prime target for an atomic attack— "to cut the head off the snake," one of her officials had suggested. An old proverb, one she thought might have come, ironically, from the Bhitubi delta originally.

She looked back at the screen and saw the call was connected, and she was being greeted by a Bhitubi woman she had never seen before.

࿐ CRSO ࿐

Hariah was almost glad to be relieved of her gun. And she found she didn't even mind the rifles trained on her, so long as they listened to what she said—which they did, if only from incredulity. She asked, in serviceable if not elegant Morbatan, to speak with their president, she pointed out that she couldn't easily effect an assassination through a comscreen, and when they brought her to their general instead, she told him the same thing. She added that what she had to say could end the war.

He asked her what the hell she was thinking. It was difficult, but she summarized.

He dialed the comscreen, set her before it, and said he couldn't promise anything. The soldiers still stood around her, guns at the ready. She forgot them as soon as the screen connected.

President Amileya Jahensson was a small, black-skinned woman with a fat blue pen caught between her fingers—she shuttled it back and forth in an obvious nervous habit. She looked at the screen and put the pen down.

"Who are you?"

"Hariah, madam. I am here to speak with you on behalf of the Bhitubi."

Amileya's face quivered in a struggle to remain expressionless. "Are you?"

"Not . . . officially, as you would understand it. We do very few things officially here, with bureaucrats or such. You no doubt noticed that in your dealings with us. But that is beside the fact. Madam, our people know your scientists have developed an atomic weapon."

The president's hand clutched the side of her desk as if for balance. "All of you know?"

"Not all, of course. But our commanders do—and I do. Our military keeps no secrets from the Odinaga."

"You're a suicide killer?" Amileya asked bluntly. Her eyes narrowed—Hariah realized she was being studied, but not hostilely. The president of the Morbat Republic, the leader of her enemies, was simply curious.

"I trained with them. For a while I thought I would end my days in a strike against your soldiers. But I have changed my mind."

"You want to live after all?"

"I want to serve my people better than I would by dying, madam. That does not mean I am unwilling to sacrifice. I am willing to offer the greatest sacrifice of all to end this war."

"Not your life, then." Amileya seemed to be thinking aloud. "Your soul?"

"My country," Hariah said. "I came here to ask you to drop the bomb."

For three breaths the tent and the office beyond the comscreen were silent. Then both sides burst into sound at once.

"What the hell are you thinking?" a soldier cried. His look at Hariah was almost furious.

"I wouldn't do that," Amileya said with too much certainty. Hariah remembered what she had said about sacrificing the soul.

"You have not done it so far," she said to the president, "and where has it got you?"

Amileya closed her eyes. "Are you . . . real? Are you really saying this? Do you *mean* it?"

"I know my people. You know us, too—you know what *Odinaga* means. We are willing to die before we surrender—unless we can be pushed to it. We will sacrifice much—but not everything. That is what you have to do. Threaten everything." It was too much, staring at the president's face, at the expression that had broken free of her control and now framed the tightly closed eyes; Hariah shut her own.

"Why would you suggest this?" Amileya asked.

"Because if this war continues, my people will destroy themselves. Already there is not a farmer's child who does not dream of growing into a soldier, or an Odinaga. They are eager to kill, eager to die. And your own soldiers continue with air raids and blockades of our harbors and all the other acts of war. I have come to you because I cannot watch it any longer—not without doing something."

"So you're suggesting I declare nuclear war on your country—out of patriotism?"

"Yes." Hariah opened her eyes.

In the screen, Amileya opened hers as well. "What about civilian losses?"

"If you continue this war, there will be no more Bhitubi civilians."

"You're so certain about . . . all of this."

"Yes."

⋄⋄⋄⋄⋄

Amileya stared at the face of the woman on the screen. The wide brown eyes were steady, almost unblinking. Hariah's full lips were pressed tightly together, the only sign of strain.

Thinking of what this woman suggested, Amileya could only despise her. And yet she was grateful to her, too.

To wipe out the capital of Bhitubi. To kill perhaps hundreds of thousands of innocents, thousands of children. To bring atomic warfare to Genesis. Radiation, leukemia. Even mutations. Devastation in all its forms—war, famine, and plague all in one, and all of them an escort for death, like the four men in the story Aunt Feliciti's church had read every New Year's eve. The story about the end of the world.

To do all that, to bring all that upon her soul, to lay it on the altar—that Amileya Jahensson could not do. It was a burden she couldn't take up. But to have it handed to her . . .

Three years before, her people had elected her for her pacifist platform. Now they were consumed with hate for a nation half a world away. *If this war continues,* the Odinaga had said, *my people will destroy themselves.* So would Amileya's.

She met the gaze of the officer standing at Hariah's shoulder. He had made the call, giving it emergency priority—he knew this was important, and secret; he had bypassed all intermediaries so the decision was only hers. Hers and Hariah's.

"General Connor," Amileya said, "I'm calling Field Commander Wates into my office. Expect orders to move out soon."

"Yes, ma'am." He saluted. His face was expressionless, but the gesture went to her heart.

Hariah's eyes shone.

"Thank you," Amileya told her. As she turned off the comscreen, she remembered that tomorrow she would still have to dedicate Gold Star Park.

Field Commander Wates arrived far sooner than she expected.

"Commander," she said. "A few weeks ago we learned of a new development—the completion of a certain project."

"Sunflower."

"That was the name." She didn't like saying it. Aunt Feliciti once grew sunflowers in her garden. Amileya knew she could never look at that flower again. "Some of the weapons are completed, I believe."

"We have four. All of them more effective than conventional weaponry. Two in particular we thought—"

"Those two are for Tonoti."

"Yes."

"I'm giving you orders to drop the first one."

"Yes, Madam President."

"Keep the other three in reserve. And lastly—I want the rest of the results of project Sunflower to be destroyed. Notes, objects, pictures . . . as if it never existed."

Except for the bombs.

"Yes, Madam President."

"The destruction of project Sunflower must be kept an absolute secret."

"Of course."

"But it must be complete."

He nodded wordlessly.

"You are dismissed."

When he was gone, Amileya Jahensson, who had once been elected as the pacifist candidate for president of the Morbat Republic, laid her head in her arms and cried as if her heart would break. She tried very hard not to think. When the worst of the storm had passed, and her eyes felt dry and empty, she rose and went to prepare for bed. There would be long days ahead, but tomorrow she had a park to dedicate to many lost and precious lives.

ᙥᘓᘔᙣ

"Is there anything we can do for you?" General Connor asked Hariah. His voice was a growl—she knew there was something about her he feared, or perhaps resented—but she thought he meant it sincerely. It was an odd offer, but what would have been normal at a time like this?

"I would like a knife," she said.

They brought her one. A machete, long and a little thicker than she would have liked. Three soldiers escorted her out, and they kept her gun, but they couldn't really be expecting her to turn on them. Not after what she had done.

Hariah walked into the forest surrounding the camp. It was only a little past noon; but the light seemed wrong. It would have been better had it been sunset.

She knelt and raised the knife to her cheek, then angled the blade down. She had not betrayed Bhitubi—never—but she had harmed it. She was willing to atone for that harm with her life.

Long ago, when she became an Odinaga, she had brought her life to the altar. The god she gave it to was no god at all—only her country, her people.

With that thought, Hariah set the knife down. Far better to give her life than to take it. While she lived, there was good she could do here. She knew, at least in part, what was coming. She couldn't prepare her people for it—she didn't believe anyone could—but when it came, she would see that the war ended, that the sacrifice she offered was accepted. And once there was peace, there would come rebuilding, and perhaps she could help with that.

Or she might die in what was coming.

"As it may be, may it be," Hariah whispered. It was part of a psalm she had once heard, a psalm from the records of the Generation Ships. Now she knew what it was for, and understood why the architects of those long-ago ships had wanted it saved.

She rose and walked on. She disappeared into the forests she knew, the land she loved.

We often speak as if knowledge is a wonderful thing; we say that information is the currency of the age. But what happens when someone knows every fact? Do the emotions get lost along the way?

SUSTAIN NOTHING

by Paul Abbamondi

Data flowed into Maurene, unwanted, unneeded, and unending. There were newly registered names, there were updates to city and Fleet blueprints, and there were 5,026 registered wishes on last night's falling star. As well as a plan to assassinate the leader of the Currs.

However, it was her day off, so she pushed the streams of information down and tried losing herself in a trance cine. When that didn't work, she went outside.

As always, Redgather bustled with people. The ornamented streets that ran from Lowtown past Maurene's apartment complex through the market district and up to the overlook were littered with shoppers, teenagers, and families on the go.

She jokingly called the city Reekgather and when she was outside, she remembered why; the stench of so many bodies at once hurt her nose. The AI filters grooming her insides with foremost tenacity surged into action, shutting her sense of smell down.

In Maurene's head, monotone as ever, a news blip sounded: Ayman Fahli Houskmed, earlier learned to be the brains behind an operation to assassinate controversial Currs leader Dougan Morris, was shot down by police mere minutes earlier thanks to an Informant's tip.

A short video clip, already censored for the noon news, played in her netware. The assassin had been caught completely unaware.

Still, Maurene frowned at how long it'd taken. Seven minutes and forty-one seconds; the Informants on shift were sloppy, should've pinged the police a lot faster than that.

"Hey, when's the next Fleet display?"

A man with a taut-looking face and offworld clothes stood next to Maurene, staring her down. Children ages two to five climbed on him like monkeys. Their publicly displayed nicknames and favorite colors scrolled along down her mind as the man gave off attitude. "Um, you broken? I asked when the next show is."

"What? Oh."

Foolishly, Maurene looked down at herself and realized she'd forgotten to change out of uniform before leaving the apartment. In fact, she must've slept in it. She did that sometimes, even on her days off, as if changing out of it was too much like peeling back her own skin.

Off. The notion hurt. In truth, Informants were never not working. Always taking data in, always being asked to spit it back out. Living, breathing bodies of information, Makehouse ad copy had once spouted.

"Blast, she *is* broken," the man said, poking her in the cheek. Maurene remained calm as her skin tightened back into place, knowing that it would just mean aggravation and system-wipes and a dozen more quality control quizzes if she did anything but give the man his answer. Anyone could report an Informant, at any time, thanks to net cafes and their ilk.

"The new display of Fleet theatrics will start at quarter of twelve," Maurene said. "Best view today is on the corner of Sixth and Marucci." She watched him walk away, knowing exactly how much savings he had in the bank and how many times he'd refinanced his mortgage and what inventions he'd tried getting trademarked, and so on. Her netware told her anything and everything.

Maurene didn't linger. She headed back up the stairs to her apartment to change, ignoring the gory details of the assassination outcome, but didn't even get seven steps before they started coming at her again. *They.* People with questions in their eyes, demands on their tongues.

"What are the next four bus pickups for the Redmare?"

"Cadence Vavasseur's cell phone number?"

"Recent deaths?"

Maurene answered everyone and tried moving past, but saw only more eager faces locking onto her. They flew to her red-and-blue uniform like birds, wanting to know more, always more:

"What can I buy my little girl for under three bucks?"

"Can you verify the last credit amount charged to my husband's account?"

"Help me out here?"

Scampering back down the front steps, jostling the curious, Maurene studied the splotches of yellow-orange that were taxis and hopped into the one with the most gas in its tank.

"Where to?" the man up front asked.

Thankfully, the driver didn't yet realize who she was. Or else he'd have been asking everything from how to make more money in this rotten city to what is life really all about and is it true that Informants know who shot Ambassador Blane and onwards? No one ever asked anything about *her.* About Maurene Elizabeth-Marie Keating, a young woman-thing who stopped truly living three years, six months, fourteen days, and one morning ago. Now there was only work and data, informing and smiling. And a semblance of living.

She'd signed the contract; she couldn't go back.

"Kenneth's," Maurene said, and then she relaxed a bit. A change of clothes waited for her at the boutique nine blocks south. A quick check showed there was a forty percent off sale until mid-afternoon. Maybe she'd be wild today, buy an expensive blouse—strangely, it would call less attention to her than what she wore now.

As the taxi snaked through traffic, three combat support skyships soared by overhead, their booms and cackles grabbing attentions like hands. Even the driver looked out his window. The Fleet display. She'd almost forgotten. *Almost.* Readings from her netware told her all about each ship and who was piloting what and how many would do dump-and-burn maneuvers versus loops and who would lead when it came to delta formation and so on. It was all nonsense to her.

"My, that near gave me a headache," the cabbie said.

Maureen knew about those. They came with the data, increasing as the day grew older. She wished she could just shut it off, all of it. If only temporarily.

An advertisement for Makehouse, wafting in her netware, caught her attention. It gave her an idea, a pinch of hope.

"Driver," Maurene said, "take me to the Aurla Building instead."

ଓଛଞ୍ଜ

For Maurene, seeing Redgather's second-tallest building again was halfway painful. She lingered outside on the pavement, staring up at its aetheric height, its enchanting balconies and thousands of unblinking windows, feeling its cold hold on her heart. A young man opened the glass door to the lobby, beckoned her in.

Uncertain, she teetered on the edge of turning back. A packed skyscraper agitated senses one through five. Her netware showed an easy 30,000 people inside working and a few thousand others there just visiting and climbing staircase after staircase to find the best view for miles.

The man she needed to see, however, her once-lover, worked on the sixty-eighth floor. He was currently giving a global presentation on the benefits of Olaf's terraforming.

She knew what a surprise visit like this would do to him. Informants rarely dealt with anyone other than their schedulers; they'd last spoken a few months ago, briefly by phone, terse as terse gets.

Irritated and sensing another incoming wave of pointless data, Maurene hurried inside. She avoided the glass elevators and began her climb skyward. Upping her breathing mods made the ascent easier. There used to be a time when she felt flushed after a short walk outside—she actually missed that.

"The view is spectacular," an athletic-looking woman jogging down the stairs said. Maurene nodded and kept going. The less she talked to the public, the fewer questions were asked. Of course the view was good. She remembered it fondly, the colors and all.

But first, she needed to see Carl.

ა⃝CՋԺ⃝৪⃝

Maurene took a seat in Makehouse & Mine's waiting room. The multidimensional company took up the entire sixty-eighth floor, nabbing every office. She put herself in a meditative state and watched, via netware, Carl Oppenhand's meeting three doors away. When the opportunity to ping his phone showed itself, she did.

Unfortunately for him, he'd forgotten to turn his ringer off.

"What are you doing here?" Carl didn't look or sound angry when he stepped out to see her. Then again, he had always been a master of hiding his emotions. She'd loved him; he'd loved her back . . . maybe. Ever the businessman, he pressed on with a flat face. "Maurene, what?"

She remained seated. "I'd like some downtime," she said matter-of-factly.

"I don't handle schedules." He glanced back at the boardroom, its door open and members waiting. "And you *know* that. So come on, I haven't got the time for this."

She looked up at him, shrugged. "Not that kind of downtime. I'd like to go . . . offline. Maybe just until my shift starts tomorrow." Carl's lean face tightened; it'd been recently worked on, she saw. Cracked skin smoothed out. "You're the only one who can do that, I think. Just for a little bit, that's all."

"No," he replied, half-turning away.

"But—"

"No." He shot her a dismissive look. "It's not like there's a switch or something. It's complicated, okay?"

A gut-twisting silence divided them. Maurene didn't know any words to say against his response. No. Truthfully, she hadn't expected him to agree. She looked hard at the man who had taken her in, saved her from a life on the streets, kissed her, offered her opportunity after opportunity, gave her everything she ever asked for—and now nothing.

A sickness swam in her stomach; her filters pumped down some medicine, checked her stats, did their jobs. She tried to come up with an argument, a word, anything at all, but merely sat on the couch and channeled sad, pathetic, help-me vibes.

It didn't work.

Carl left her sitting, signaled something to the front-desk secretary, and returned to his room of presentation slides, graphed numbers, and greedy old men.

She didn't feel anger under her skin, not yet at least, but there was a wash of disappointment. The sensation brought her back to her first day as an Informant. There had been excitement, a rush unlike any other, knowing that she was going to serve Redgather well, inform, instruct, and instill. The first few questions were trivial, mostly about movie times and celebrity gossip. They continued to worsen. And all day long, no one even acknowledged that she was anything more than a walking, talking bank of information.

She shook her head, trying to forget.

Security had been called. As if she were a criminal breaking in after hours or something. She wasn't about to be escorted out like that, to become part of the afternoon news, a quick blip about an Informant on the brink of breaking.

That wasn't her.

Maurene studied her netware to find the most efficient exit— the emergency one near the women's bathroom—and switched on her breathing mods again. In the other room, Carl prepared to finish his presentation with a three-minute interactive vid.

Maurene waited for her moment, stalled patiently, and before leaving all of Makehouse & Mine behind she set off every printer, fax machine, and telephone on the floor. The screeching of electronics hurt her ears, but in a good way. She left them behind as she climbed to the roof of the building.

ରେଷ୍ଟେ

As she knew it would be, the view over Redgather was spectacular. Before, at street-level, all Maurene saw were buildings and dirty people and trashbots in gutters. They were now invisible, replaced simply with a stretch of elegant rooftops and glittering, gold-limned windows. She took it in like breath.

And the moment was ruined by a string of reports to her scheduler. The subject lines varied: INFORMANT TERRORIZES OFFICE; ELECTRONICS HAYWIRE THANKS TO INFORMANT; INFORMANT #1 SHOULD BE DOWNGRADED TO A PC. Security was on their way up, but she made sure they'd have trouble with every door and elevator keypad.

Agitated, Maurene considered Carl's response. He had said *no*, and he had given off the body language to fully support the dictum. She'd interrupted his meeting, after all. But they'd spent years loving each other, sharing. At this point, she knew the ins and outs of Informants, and it wasn't complicated at all to turn one off for a day. It couldn't be.

Zooming into her netware, Maurene logged into Carl Oppenhand's public files. All passwords everywhere were accessible by Informants. Still, those higher up than her had managed to keep a few items under lock-and-key.

Nothing embarrassing sat in the folders, though: a slew of family photos, a holiday shopping list, some old college report drafts about the implementation of the Amarantes within Fleet compounds, a self-done wiki of terraforming terms, a report on Olaf, the forward-planet. One item, however, caught her attention. A piece of straight text, untouched for a couple of years, hidden deep in a folder innocently titled "back-up logs."

The file wouldn't open for her.

Maurene turned her back on Redgather and sat at the roof's edge, thinking. She ran through a list of saved passwords Carl had

used for a number of other accounts and security issues. None
worked. Whatever he was using for this file, it was personal. That
meant the document was personal, too.

Only as she sat stewing did Maurene notice the date the file
had been created: nearly three years, seven months ago. About the
same time Carl convinced her to sign up to become an Informant.
Curiosity towed her forward.

A status light blinked in her netware. The ubiquitous signal
told her that things were happening in both Lowtown and on a
street north of the Aurla Building. She had the time to read up on
them, but focused rather on guessing Carl's password. She was
determined to figure it out.

Maurene finished absorbing Carl's entire history until the day
he graduated from Mardell. The passkey to the file had to be there;
it just had to be wiggled out of years of personality quizzes and
social network surveys.

She tried the name of Carl's first pet dog, Irvine. Nope. She
punched in his birthday. She tried manipulating his high school
sweetheart's first, middle, and last names. Nope and nope.

Her mind raced with information and questions and up-to-date
news coverage about whatever was going on city-wise. She tried
colors and cars and career nicknames. The file wouldn't open. She
felt frustrated. An Informant was made to know all, and here she
was struggling like a kid unprepared for a test. Uncertainty tickled
her nose, and Maurene put in her own name.

The file opened.

Maurene sank with disappointment. It was just a paragraph of
text, no more than five or six sentences, and all the words were
more about Informants in general than specifically about her. A line
of compressed modified code ended the file. 0708007054321. Her
filters dampened. She'd been hoping for something; she barely
knew what.

Maurene sighed and closed the file, defeated. And then, a part
of her netware clicked and shut off. The data flowing into her fell
like shot birds, disappearing into the depth of her mind. For a
moment, she instinctively tried to struggle with it, to not let it go,

but then she did and found the sensation oddly exhilarating. There was nothing, only her.

Netware gone, Maurene enjoyed the moment.

She stood, still trying to wrap her thoughts around on all the emptiness coming into her. How different the world looked to her now, how much she no longer knew.

Suddenly, behind her, Redgather exploded with a half dozen blasts powerful enough to shake the Aurla Building's foundation. Shouts and screams followed, the *pat-pat-pat* fireworks of gunshots after them.

Maurene shrugged and sat down on the roof's edge, all doors now unlocked, waiting for security to finally find her and arrest her.

ⷭ⳱Ⳳⷭ

Despite all Maurene had known, the billions of information bits cumulated grossly over the years, she now knew nothing and loved it. The security guards transported her back to Lowtown and had her thrown in a jail cell. The room was as empty as her mind. She sat on the floor, back against the wall, smiling.

It gave her great pleasure to get information the old way. She asked everyone who passed her cell, usually the head guard or the lady with the clipboard, and they were always slow to answer, confused at the sight of an Informant popping questions. They attributed it to her breaking.

It turned out that the plan to assassinate that Currs leader was only the springboard for a much larger scheme. Several prominent buildings had been bombed with little success, and from what the desk radio shouted it sounded like mild rioting in the streets. Police were taking care of it. In truth, Maurene had no idea about anything.

The feeling comforted her.

Her upbeat demeanor, however, fell away when Carl Oppenhand appeared outside her cell's bars. He leaned forward, glaring. Here, he looked positively silly in his blue-and-gray Makehouse suit.

"Ah, hello," Maurene said.

"Tell me, Maurene," Carl asked, "why am I seeing you twice in one day when I haven't seen you since the switch?"

Maurene had no answer. "I tried to ask for help. I don't know, I tried."

"Looks like you need it."

"Not really, not now." Maurene looked at her feet, avoiding Carl's eyes. The expression in them hurt more than his words did. "I like it here."

"In here?"

She shrugged.

Carl wrapped a hand around one of the bars, tugging on it. "Makehouse is going to pay your bail. It's not much. You only disrupted several meetings and, despite news reports, were charged for disorderly behavior."

"Thanks," Maurene said.

"Don't." He frowned. "We're going back to my office to sign a few papers, and then you're gone."

"Gone? Gone where?" Maurene found the inspiration to stand. "Isn't there a mini-war going on outside or something?" Seeing Carl's reaction, she regretted saying it.

"You don't *know?*"

For a moment, there was silence. Maurene drifted to the corner of her cell, and Carl watched her every move. He didn't blink. She wondered if he had bought special contacts recently and felt a pang of regret knowing that she couldn't verify it.

When Carl finally spoke again, he sounded calm, collected. It made her nervous. He asked, "Maurene, when does the sale on personalized wallets at Kenneth's end?"

She merely looked at him.

Carl motioned for Maurene to come closer. "How'd you do it?"

"Doesn't matter. Not now, considering I'm fired."

"Tell me."

"No." Maurene turned her back on him, her voice cold. "Just go, Carl. Forget about me, I don't care. You never wanted to talk after the switch, so go riot or blather about pie charts or whatever it is you have left to do today."

She faced the wall until Carl walked away. He did pay her bail using his no-limit Makehouse & Mine credit card. Then he vanished, and her cell door swung open, letting her back out into the unknown.

ಜCಒ8C೦ಐ

The air was suffused with thick smoke, and Maurene couldn't stop the smell of the city as she strolled home. It fingered up her nose, choking her; she tried not to suck it back with deep inhalation, but that breathing came to her naturally now. And that, she had to admit, felt very unnatural.

People stopped to ask questions. She made up answers; some brought out smiles or nods of appreciation, other replies revealed that she was lying . . . or just stupid. Most wanted to know about the terrorist attacks, what Redgather was doing to stop them, and how come the Informants hadn't known about them ahead of time.

She had wondered that as well. Before her netware had gone off, there were eleven Informants shown working. One of them had to have been keeping tabs on the second-in-command brains behind the morning attack on Morris. Unless the bombers had found a way around them, as well as the encroaching street cameras.

Maurene lied herself all the way back to her apartment. Before going inside, she turned and looked over her shoulder. Finally, she *saw* the city, took in its demeanor—and it was brimming with restlessness.

The building across the street, an old bakery that had sat ignored for what seemed like decades, showed blast damage, a pile of bricks and rubble at its front door. A man sat outside it, crying, and she wondered how much money he had lost in the explosion.

Inside, Maurene found her single-room apartment exactly like she last left it: clean and cold. The television was off, the heating unit was off, the fragrance sprayer was off, and she was off.

After changing into pajamas and ordering dinner via the refrigerator's expansive menu, Maurene slumped onto her couch. The material items around her, she saw, only made the place a notch different from her jail cell. She rubbed her arms and stared at the ceiling. Time seemed to creep by, but a glance at the clock revealed otherwise. She paced without walking.

Again, a trance cine did nothing for her. The cines used to block out all the extraneous noise in her head, and now she itched at the silence, the hanging darkness of her mind that wafted back and forth, waiting for something to happen. Her doorbell rang, and without checking who it was, Maurene buzzed them in.

Throwing on a sweatshirt, she realized that she didn't care who was approaching her door. No one had ever come up before without her prior knowledge; this was a new experience.

Two hard knocks on her door. "Maurene," came a voice, nearly ghostly. Carl's. "Let me in, we need to talk." He pounded on the door again.

"Don't break it," she said, pressing the plate so that the door slid open. "I'm going to be short of money soon, you see."

He stepped through the doorway, and Maurene immediately saw something was very wrong. She didn't need her netware to tell her that the expression on his face was not just for her, that something else was bothering him . . . greatly.

She stood by the door and watched him closely. It had only been a handful of hours since Carl had bought her freedom, yet he already looked older, much more tired.

"So why are you here? I thought I was gone."

Carl stared at Maurene for some time, then looked away. "I . . . I need to know how you shut yourself offline."

"Why?"

"Because you ruined *everything*. And I could've left you in that jail cell. One small hint from me, and you'd have been Redgather's scapegoat for sure. Then you would not only have been gone, you'd probably have been dead. Or locked up forever."

Maurene crossed her arms. "What do you mean? You'd do that?"

Carl snorted, a nasty sound that couldn't decide whether to be funny or cruel. "Oh, yes. You see, you're the reason Redgather couldn't stop those bombs from happening. If you'd only gone home and dealt with your job properly, Informants would have picked up on the plot. But no, you had to be *Maurene*, stubborn as always."

Anger rose in her throat, and she nearly slapped him. Then tears began to well up, and Maurene could do nothing to stop them.

"Whatever you did," Carl continued, getting louder, "to shut yourself down, well, the others saw you sign off. All of them. And from what limited data we were able to gather at the office, they immediately followed your history tabs, and one by one they all clicked off. Until there was no one around to know a damned thing."

"Oh."

Maurene stepped into the kitchen to separate herself from Carl, using the overhanging cabinets for their secondary purpose. She wiped her eyes with her sleeve and slumped against the refrigerator door until she felt his hands on her shoulders.

"Look, I didn't mean—"

"Yes, you did!" she shouted, shrugging him off. She turned to face him. "You like hurting me, you always have. Since you got me to sign up for your stupid program. What happened, Carl? I thought we loved each other."

"That was a long time ago."

"Was it?"

"I'm asking for your help, Maurene. The city needs you." Carl leaned closer to her. "You help me, I'll help you. You can have your job back, too. I just need to know how to get everyone back online."

"I don't want my job back," she said.

"Then what?"

Maurene took him by the wrists, held him still. She squared her shoulders and looked him in the eyes: "Control."

Redgather at night lifted Maurene's spirits marginally. There were not as many people out, and the ugliness of the buildings was masked in shadows.

She and Carl shared a cab back to the Aurla Building in silence. She stared out the window, watching lights zip by in a blur.

Everyone had gone home for the day. The sixty-eighth floor stretched out before them, quiet and empty. Carl headed straight for his office; he flicked his computer's monitor on and pulled over a chair for her.

"Okay," he said as Maurene sat down, "show me what you did. Go ahead."

She tried not to give him a look. She didn't have the energy to meet his eyes. "It's not that simple. I can't tell you because I can't remember. When I was doing it, I had my netware's help. I was flying through files." She looked at the mouse. "And now I have to . . . I click this, right?"

He sighed. "Yes, you click it."

It took several attempts, but Maurene managed to open the directory for Carl's public folders. She hadn't realized how many there were, the vanilla squares adding up to at least hundreds, and going through them one by one meant working all night, so she shut her eyes and concentrated.

"It was a text file," she said, embracing a memory, "an old one."

Carl grunted. "I have lots of those."

She sat back, remembering. "You made it around the day I became a . . . well, when I switched."

"Oh, shit." Carl stood. He appeared to be both embarrassed and elated. "Oh, *shit*. That file. I'm such an idiot."

"Sing it loud."

"Well, no," Carl said, sounding flustered. "I mean, I never thought it would work. It was something I had the staff toy with for a little bit. I completely forgot we even tried . . ."

"Thought what wouldn't work?"

"The invisible coding."

Maurene squinted at the screen.

"Um, no. It's invisible." Carl waved his hands around, as if washing down all the air in the room. "The text part is just throwaway. I was worried that, at some point, that the Informants might get . . . out of hand. So Makehouse created something that could be mass mailed to them. It does nothing until the file is closed. Then off goes your system, retrievable only by a manual startup."

Maurene got up from the chair. "And this is something you, somehow, *forgot* about?"

"I guess," he said, shrugging. "It was a long time ago. The company was snowballing then. And it never seemed necessary once the Informants were up and running." Carl seated himself in front of the computer, clicking away. Moved some files this way and that. "You signed Makehouse's contract, Maurene. You know what kind of information you have at your disposal, what you could really do with it if you chose to. Granted, you'd be arrested a second afterward and mem-wiped, but you see the problem that Informants could present."

"I'm not a problem," she said. "I only wanted it all to stop, just for a little bit. You don't know what the headaches are like." Maurene paused, shifted, did anything she could not to let the next words out of her mouth. "And I wanted to see you again. See someone who wasn't using me only for information."

Carl sighed. "We're not like that any more, Maurene. I've got a wife now, a job, things to do . . . all the time. I can't stop because you want to reminisce."

"That's not what I was saying," she said through her teeth.

"Then what?"

"Forget it." She now saw that there had never been much of anything between them, that the offworld times they'd spent together laughing and having picnics in the park and cuddling under bedsheets had never bridged a relationship; he'd wanted her to be an Informant because it would forward his career, and now he'd saved her for the same reason. Their love had existed only in her head. "Okay, I helped you. Your turn."

"First, you need to get back online." Carl led her out of his office and down the hall. They went into the quality control testing room. Though she had only spent an hour or so in it the day she became an Informant, Maurene remembered it well. The room was still cold, and it still had the smell of plastic.

Carl took out a small needle-gun and injected a purple tube into her arm. She yelped, but the pain quickly faded away; her netware flipped on, brightening in her mind, and rushed to raise her defense system as well as feed her the good nutrients and endorphins she was lacking.

"Everything back on?" Carl asked, though he checked the monitor on the counter for confirmation. "Good. Now open your shared programs folder. Deep in it you'll find a program called *Golden.* The icon is a musical note. Run it."

"What?"

"Just do it."

Maurene nodded, but before starting the program she checked its history. Slightly older than the silencing text file. She frowned, realizing how much Carl had kept from the Informants, from her. She ran the program to get the night over with.

Everything in her head shut off. The senses that had been lessened now sprang back to normalcy, and she started to ask about it when a small firefly of a green light blinked in the corner of her eye. Maurene focused on it, and suddenly everything popped back online.

"That's yours," Carl said before she could react. "No other Informants will get the program, and none of them will see when you shut down. A mock you will sit online. Use it at your own discretion."

Maurene ran the program again, shut off, switched back on—it broke her heart.

"Thank you," she said weakly.

"Forget it." Carl looked away. "But don't ever bother me again."

୧◌୨

Maurene ordered a cup of chamomile tea with two sugars, curled up in bed, and caught up with the world.

Completely unaware of the Informants' failing, the brother of Ayman Fahli Houskmed had set into motion the bombings earlier in the day. Police detained him shortly after, and a video capturing the man's rabid spewing of hatred and ignorance was already making the rounds. The video could not be stopped, but Maurene flagged it, just to keep up on who viewed it and from where.

Personalized economy accounts for Redgather, and subsequently terraforming funding as a whole, dropped a few points thanks to the day's events.

Seventeen people were admitted to the hospital suffering from blast wounds. No fatalities.

Stock in Makehouse & Mine faltered.

Her inbox overflowed with messages from the other Informants as Carl manually—and slowly—got them back online. Some were nice, some were mean, and the rest indifferent. She hoped he had deleted the hidden coding, but knew he probably hadn't; he'd always liked having his fail-safes.

Maurene's stint in jail had become public knowledge.

She sighed. Her day off . . . in a nutshell.

But she had what she wanted, and that was control. The very tool that could make living livable. On her walk home she switched off nineteen times—just for a minute, because she could. It was her right. She meant to use it like one.

Carl or control . . . truthfully, both would've made her happy, but one would do for now.

And no matter what he said, the other Informants would figure out what she was doing eventually.

Maurene pulled up a home movie; in it, she was a young girl, bouncing on the couch, laughing and smiling and loving life without even knowing much about it; her father spoke to her from behind the camera. She watched more movies of her once-life, wondering about the what-could-have-beens, before Carl and the switch and a million and one questions, taking in what remained of the time when her biggest concerns were the smallest personal things.

When it became too painful to watch, Maurene rolled over, wrapped her arms around her pillow, and shut off. She fell asleep to the sound of soft sobbing and short breaths—and nothing more.

Is there a difference between choosing to stand in a singular place and agreeing to stand there? What would make a quiet heroine out of any one of us?

THE TRUTH ONE SEES

by Kathy Hurley

Tempest kept a friendly smile on her face while she set the holographic card projectors to shuffle, but it was all she could do not to burst out and ask her client what he was doing here. He wouldn't tell her his name. For that matter, he'd barely spoken five words since he'd walked through the door. His immaculate uniform and epaulets implied highly placed military—the sort of man who should be commanding a spaceship or even a fleet, not standing in the entrance bay of an Interactive Holographic Theater, shifting his weight from foot to foot as if his shoes hurt him.

He was opportunity and risk, both packed into the same tense, broad-shouldered frame.

"You look too young to be a fortune-teller," he said. She noticed that he peered at the control panel closely, as if he expected to find mysteries there. Or maybe it wasn't that he hoped for mysteries. More likely, he was afraid he wouldn't be able to explain them if they appeared.

"I'm not a fortune-teller," she told him gently. "I'm a tarot reader. I connect with your energy and the images on the cards to give you an intuitive view of a situation you're facing. No future is definite, but I can usually see some of the ways in which you might move forward."

"Moving forward. That's all there is, I suppose," he said with a touch of bravado that tried and failed to disguise his nervousness.

Tempest's hands stilled on the controls and she took a breath, centering herself. This client was going to be trouble. Skeptics were hardest to please, because they always held onto their old beliefs and paradigms the longest. This man was skeptical *and* military—a recipe for disaster. Or for a breakthrough, which was the only reason she hadn't already politely refused to read for him.

If the reading went badly wrong, she'd be risking more than just a lost fee. She'd be putting an entire alien race at risk of annihilation, which made her probable fate, being locked up for the rest of her natural lifetime for colluding with said aliens, pale by comparison.

She took another calming breath and held out a remote to the client. It had only one button, but it gave some people a sense of control. "Will you shuffle the cards? If you have a specific question, think of that while you hold down the button. Release it whenever you wish."

He took the remote, turned it upside down and examined it from every angle. "Primitive gadget. I'd have expected something with more bells and whistles." With a raised eyebrow for Tempest, he righted the remote and thumbed the button with more force than was necessary.

Hence, the primitive nature of the *gadget*. Anything more sophisticated, and she'd be replacing them every month. Given that Terra Beta's months were shorter than Earth's, that'd be far too often, and she barely made a living with the tarot readings as it was. Good thing she wasn't in this for the money.

The machine shuffled for what seemed a very long time, images flashing into the middle of the circular room in random order, too fast for the human eye to follow. Finally, the client released the button along with the breath he'd been holding, and the first setting projected into the holo field.

Tempest saw him glance quickly upward, his gaze taking in the projectors placed at intervals near the ceiling and down the walls, arranged to cover all the necessary angles.

"Expensive set-up," he said, and she couldn't tell whether his tone held admiration or scorn. He was right, though; it had been expensive—entire life savings and firstborn-child-as-collateral expensive. It wasn't just the holo equipment, either. She'd had the room designed in such a way that it would hide the temporal interface her alien collaborators had spliced into the projectors, and all without the architect suspecting anything out of the ordinary. It hadn't been easy.

The skeptic in front of her had no way of knowing how much rode on this venture. This whole resort was something new— experimental and risky in a way that not even most of the colony founders realized. They'd envisioned it as the Vegas of Terra Beta, but it was so much more than that.

The founders had no way of knowing they'd built this place right in the middle of an alien city—or at least, in the spot where that city had been before its inhabitants shifted it out of phase to avoid potential conflict with the human intruders. An entire sentient species lived within, among and around Tempest's fellow humans without anyone knowing they were there. Oh, a few stories of odd lights and sounds did tend to surface now and again, but people usually dismissed them as whimsy and imagination.

That only Tempest could see the transdimensional beings was both a help and a hindrance to any possible contact and eventual conciliation between their two races. Perception—at least in humans—was a door that had to be opened slowly, and in its proper time. With people like her present client, it might never be opened at all.

"A desert?" the client asked. "That's it?"

The holographic vista drew Tempest's full attention, and she allowed all surface concerns to fall away. All that mattered now was the needs of the client, and what she saw here.

"Wait just a moment, sir," she said. "There will be more. It helps if you are open to what the spirits want to reveal to you."

"Spirits, tosh," he said. "If you're going to give me the whole fortune-teller treatment, you need a crystal ball, not an IHT."

Slowly, a throne took shape between two stone pillars. On the throne sat an imposing man with a golden flame-shaped crown on his head and a long staff in one hand, topped with a red crystal. As the image filled in detail, the face became recognizable, identical to that of her client, who stared in fascination. As he recognized his own features, he stood a little taller. Tempest fought back a smirk at the way he puffed up, imagining himself a king.

"Well, what's it mean?" he prompted.

The figure on the throne gazed sternly back at him.

"This is yourself—the King of Wands. You are a natural leader, stern but fair. You have commanded men in battle and risked your life for theirs. There is nothing you would not do to protect those under your command," Tempest said.

"Nothing you couldn't have known by pulling up a dossier on me," the client said. "Nice job of the ego stroking, though."

"How could I pull up your dossier, assuming I had one?" Tempest asked. "You wouldn't tell me your name, remember?"

"Well, I suppose I made things a bit easy, with the uniform and the decorations," he said. "But I interrupted. Go on, my dear; don't let me stop you from earning your fee."

Grant me patience. Tempest swallowed down her irritation, focused on the information she was receiving telepathically, and went on. "The image I see on my viewpad is reversed—upside down. I see that your life has been hard, and you have often focused on your career to the exclusion of family and those closest to you. This has led to a split between you and some of your children, one in particular. You have not spoken to your eldest son in several years, and you have sworn that you will not do so until he bends and seeks your forgiveness."

"Where did you hear that? That's a private matter."

Oh, dear. It hadn't taken long to get him riled. She'd have to press on and hope for the best. He stood flushed and fuming while Tempest threw another switch, and the sound of hoofbeats came through the speakers.

The horse that galloped into the scene was white, with flame-red ears, mane and tail. On its back sat a tall figure in golden headgear and armor, a plume of flame erupting from the top of the helm. It charged in at such speed that the client backed up a foot or two before he seemed to remember that the horse and rider weren't solid and couldn't actually touch him. Tempest saw him swallow as the giant horse slid to a halt in front of them, spraying holographic sand.

The figure didn't bother to dismount, but sat facing the king on the throne. On Tempest's viewpad, the Knight of Wands joined the King of Wands, both inverted.

In the hologram, the figure on horseback removed its helm, and Tempest was not surprised to see a younger version of her client. As the two images tried to stare each other down, the client sputtered in outrage.

"You are not my commanding officer," the Knight said to the King. "If you try to pull weight, I'll resign from the squadron. If there are any unfriendlies on Terra Beta, I'll find them my way, and I'll get rid of them. I don't need a washed-up has-been telling me how to run a planetary defense campaign."

Unfriendlies on Terra Beta? Tempest felt her shoulders tense, and shot a quick glance at her client. Fortunately, he hadn't noticed her reaction.

The King of Wands' face flushed in a parody of the client's face at that very moment. "You arrogant pup! I may not be your commanding officer, but by Venus I outrank you, and it doesn't matter where in Stellcorp you transfer, I'll still outrank you. If you don't listen to me, you'll end up getting yourself killed. Waste of a uniform, and waste of company expense credits."

"That's all you care about, wasted credits? What about wasted years? What about Mom?"

"Don't you mention your mother to me," the King roared.

The Knight drew himself up, every bit as cold and stern as the King had appeared at first. "You know what I think, Father? She was smart to get out when she did. She knew what a cold-hearted bastard you are, and she left. And then—"

"Now look here, you little—" the client surged forward, fist raised, and swung at the Knight. Of course, the blow passed right through him.

Tempest backed up slightly, finger poised atop another button—the one that called Security.

The client was breathing hard, his face crimson. Tempest hoped he wouldn't have a stroke. That would be extremely hard to explain, and it would draw unwanted attention to her. People viewed her line of work with prejudice already; the last thing she needed was a lawsuit from some high-ranking military family— much less the catastrophe that would follow if an investigation led to discovery of the aliens and her connection to them. However much she'd like to believe that humans had evolved beyond "kill first and ask questions later," history said differently. This reading said differently.

As she slowed her own breath and calmed her thudding pulse, Tempest keyed the controls, and the holographic desert faded, along with the King and Knight of Wands. A blue sky appeared on the domed ceiling, speckled with clouds, while soothing music played in the background.

She caught a wave of reassurance, and closed her eyes for a moment as the image of the one who'd sent it filled her mind. It steadied her, like a virtual embrace.

When she opened her eyes, she found the client glaring at her from beneath lowered brows. "You ought to be careful who you play games with, Madame Tempest, or whatever your real name is. I don't know how you got the intel or data to replay my last conversation with my son word for word, but that—" he stabbed a finger at the spot where the King and Knight had stood—"that was out of line."

"Sir, I assure you, I don't have any kind of database or dossier on anyone. I have no way to know ahead of time who's going to walk through my door." *Good.* Her voice conveyed nothing but calm.

"And you profess to be able to see the future," the client sneered, mopping his forehead with his sleeve.

"My intuition doesn't work like that," she told him. Even with her natural psychic abilities, she usually didn't see any specific details about a client until after the reading began. It was then that her collaborators used their temporal interface to track quantum decision points and access information from the past, then sync it through to the holo projectors and feed her details mentally.

It hadn't taken a temporal interface to predict that Tempest was in for a rough time today, though; she'd known it the moment this man walked into the IHT.

"Shall we continue, or do you want your money back?" she asked him. She really couldn't afford to refund his credits, but she wasn't willing to waste his time or hers if she wasn't going to be able to help him.

"You've expended so much effort already, you might as well continue." His sarcasm was back, bravado returned in full force.

Should she be relieved or dismayed? Tempest fingered the black tourmaline crystal she kept in her pocket, an Earth-born talisman against negativity. It helped—a little. She firmly centered her awareness again and punched up the next card.

The soothing green countryside now in the holo field held nothing but grass, sky, and a large silver chalice, upside down, dripping water. Tempest's viewpad showed the Ace of Cups, reversed.

Heavens, was there no card in this man's reading that *wasn't* reversed?

"What's this? I suppose you're going to tell me not to cry over spilled milk, or my cup doesn't run over, or some other cliché drivel?"

"No." Tempest felt pity squeeze her chest, and spent a few precious moments trying to tamp down her empathy to a manageable level. The man was lonely and heartbroken, but he wouldn't appreciate it if she put it to him like that. "I will tell you that there is a reason your relationships haven't been emotionally satisfying. Would you find it helpful to know why?"

"Blast away, why don't you?" he said. There went those defenses again—up as high as he could build them. But she sensed something in his manner, some new weakness in his wall.

"You are afraid to love fully because you are afraid to lose the ones you love. You feel unable to allow yourself to be vulnerable, and love demands vulnerability. This is what initially drove your wife away from you, and then your children one by one, and now you find yourself unable to fill the void this has left in your life."

Her client blinked at her for a moment, a stunned look on his face. Then slowly, he began to applaud. "Bravo. Good diagnosis, Madame. Now let me make an intuitive guess about you. You majored in psychology and washed out after a brief time. Then, finding yourself unqualified for any respectable field, you turned to fortunetelling—excuse me, *tarot reading*—in order to make a living. And no doubt you do quite well at it. I'm sure all the young lovelorns find it quite thrilling to come have their cards read by you. And I'm sure many people would be quite happy to cry on your shoulder."

"We aren't here to read my life path, sir," Tempest said. *Quietly, now. Don't give him the rise he's trying for. Just read his cards, and get him out of here safely.* His assessment hurt, though; it came far too close to the mark.

Tempest gave the client her most serene expression, and after a moment—and a little more soothing music—he let the matter drop and nodded to her to continue.

The upside-down chalice disappeared and a flowing stream began to wind its way through the peaceful valley scene. Slowly, a willowy female figure appeared beside the stream, balancing with one foot in the water and the other on the bank. Great white wings formed behind her, flexing gently with her movements. Glowing spheres winked into being over her head and in her hands, and she began to juggle, smoothly and efficiently. Tempest's keypad showed the image of Temperance.

Good. At least, this one wasn't reversed.

The face of the angel took shape, fine features and lustrous black hair marking her as a beauty. Tempest had seen many representations of the Temperance card, and this was by far the prettiest yet. Thank goodness.

"This card—" she began.

"That's my wife!" the client said, in an oddly strangled voice.

Tempest, who'd been admiring the angel, turned to him, her heart pounding again. "Excuse me?" she asked, though she'd heard him just fine the first time.

"You, young lady, are on very dangerous ground," he sputtered. "How dare you pull up pictures of my wife? She killed herself after we separated—but I suppose you know that already. She left me, and then she left me again. Analyze that, Dr. Tarot."

Breathing rhythmically to slow her racing pulse, Tempest reined in the fear. Fear had no place in an intuitive reading. If she allowed it to flow, it would take over.

"I know you loved your wife very much, sir. And I sense that she loved you as much as it is possible for a woman to love a man. She didn't leave you willingly, but when you first separated, she did it because she felt that the only way to help you was to let you go. Her death—was an accident."

Images of the client's wife and how she'd met her end filtered through to Tempest, and she closed her eyes. The angel's deep blue eyes were watching them both with such sorrow that Tempest had to gain a little personal distance in order to tell the client what she needed to convey.

"She killed herself. Didn't your database tell you that?" he asked. His voice was so quiet that Tempest cracked an eye open for a moment to make sure he wasn't about to do something drastic. But the images her collaborators gleaned from the temporal interface pressed in again behind her eyelids, insistent.

"No. She didn't commit suicide. The pressure seal in her cockpit failed, and she died of vacuum exposure. I see it."

"Then how is it that the people who found her ship also found that she wasn't wearing a pressure suit? If she knew something was wrong with her ship, she'd have suited up and used her oxygen tanks as long as possible, hoping for rescue. Or she'd have used the life pod."

The answer came suddenly, and Tempest's eyes snapped open. She met the client's gaze; he was staring at her—hard. "When her pressure seal failed, so did several other systems, during which all data was blanked. That was why the black box failed. Your wife couldn't get to her gear or the pod in time. It was over in seconds. I promise you that." Tears leaked from the corners of Tempest's eyes, and she didn't try to hide them. Let him think she was a consummate actress. It didn't matter.

"Now how in the universe could you know that? How do I know you're not just blowing hot air, trying to make me believe that she—" Words failed him, and he fell silent.

"Don't you believe in Spirit, sir?" Tempest asked, phrasing her next words carefully. "Don't you believe that the spirits of our loved ones live on after their physical deaths, or that there are other beings, every bit as sentient as ourselves, who inhabit parallel dimensions? Why couldn't there be life after death?"

"I've never believed that sort of claptrap. If there are other beings in the redundant dimensions, I've never met one. I'd need proof. Can you give me proof, Madame Tempest?"

She could, yes. But how would he react if she did?

"Your wife had one last message for you." The Tarot angel spoke quietly, drawing both their gazes. "She was coming back to you when it happened. She wanted reconciliation. If you go to the shipyard, they will grant you access to her ship. You will find a message pad jammed into the space beneath the pilot's chair and the deck panel. It fell from her hand and wedged there when they auto-docked the ship, and there it has rested these last few years. Go soon, William, before they begin to dismantle the ship for parts. Perhaps this will help you regain your balance."

The client—William—gaped at the angel, his mouth opening and closing like a dying fish. His face turned several different shades of red before it paled to white. For a moment, Tempest thought he might pass out. She put out a hand, but he shrugged it off.

"She always loved you, William. Tell the children what really happened, and don't allow this pain and separation to continue." The Temperance angel with his wife's face blew him a kiss then faded from view.

Silence filled the IHT for several moments, after which soft pipe music began to play, soothing and mournful at the same time.

"Sir? Are you all right?" Tempest asked cautiously.

"Finish it. Just finish it," he whispered, still staring at the place where the angel had stood. He looked shattered.

Blinking back her own tears, Tempest worked the controls, and the last card came up in the center of the hologram field.

A hooded figure walked toward them through a dark forest. Moonlight shone through leafless trees, dappling a forest floor with varying spots of darkness. As Tempest and William watched, the figure folded back its hood, revealing a visage that changed from moment to moment. It was pale as Death, the card image on Tempest's viewpad. As they watched, the face changed to that of a skull, its eerie dignity not at all lessened by its lack of flesh.

It turned toward William, and he drew his chin up and straightened his shoulders, military firm.

"I'm ready," he said to Death. By his expression, he'd forgotten all about the holographic projectors, forgotten Tempest, forgotten everything but the scene in front of him. "Take me to her."

"No. It is not your time," Death said. "I am not here to tell you of your passage beyond the veil. I am here to tell you that it is time for a different journey—a journey of transformation. Go to the shipyards and find your truth. Bear that truth forward into the rest of your life, so that when I come for you again, you will be at peace."

The figure put up a bony hand and replaced its hood, then turned away. As it moved into the holographic forest, Death began to fragment, pulling apart into hundreds of small pieces, each piece taking on shape and light, until it became a flight of moths, silver and gleaming in the moonlight.

Then the moths faded, too, until the forest lay silent and thick with mystery—as silent as William, who stood motionless except for the tears running down his square-jawed face.

Tempest keyed the lights, and the forest winked out, revealing the plain, round walls of the IHT. Still without comment, William wiped his face and handed his credit chit to Tempest, who ran it through the machine and allowed the automatic timer to calculate how much to charge for the time spent on the reading.

"Whatever it comes to, double it," he said quietly.

"Sir?" Tempest asked, not sure she'd heard him correctly.

"Double it. Either you have the most sophisticated surveillance equipment I've ever seen, or you're a bona-fide psychic intuitive. I didn't think they existed, except in dim Earth history. If I find what you tell me I'll find at the shipyard, I'll come back. If not, I won't bother you again. But if I do come back . . . maybe next time you can convince me to believe in unicorns."

There it was—the reason she did any of this. It happened so slowly, one person at a time, but that was how such things started. The tiny spark of change that had just begun in this one man could spread to others, and maybe one day, many more hearts and minds would open. Then, and only then, would the rest of humankind look upon the true wonders of this planet they'd claimed as their own.

William took back his credit chit, spun on his heel, military-precise, and left.

When she was sure he'd gone, Tempest sighed and began to switch off the projectors. It took very little time to shut down the theater and make her way to her living quarters, but by the time she reached them, she was exhausted. Sometimes the readings were like that; some took more out of her than others, and today's had been intense.

Moments after she'd reached her quarters and dropped into an easy chair, she sat watching, rapt as always as the dark-haired, blue-eyed Magician from the Tarot began to materialize beside her. When he'd matched his phase to hers, he moved behind her and began to massage the tension from her shoulders.

"That went well, did it not?" he asked, long fingers kneading gently.

"Better than I thought it might," Tempest admitted. "Ah, that feels good."

"That was my intent." She could hear the smile in his voice, and she willingly relaxed into him and let their energies mingle.

She'd been amazed when she arrived on Terra Beta and saw beings that no one else could see, simultaneously terrified and thrilled when those beings discovered her ability and asked her for help. But the greatest wonder by far had come when she'd fallen in love with one of them, and he with her.

That they could be together at all was a revelation. That he could communicate with her telepathically was only one of the many benefits they'd discovered thus far. It was precisely because of her psychic gifts that she could see into other dimensions; had that not been the case, she'd have been as blind as the other humans on Terra Beta. Feeling the Magician's touch and the warmth of his regard, she couldn't imagine life without him, no matter the risks they took daily to be together.

"You are a wonder," Tempest said, turning to face him after several minutes of quiet bliss. "Do you think we'll ever be able to reveal the truth about your existence on this planet? There are still those like William, determined to be skeptical until something happens to convince them otherwise. Or like the son he drove away, ready to kill whatever scares them."

"Who can tell?" the Magician asked, though it wasn't really a question. "On first inspection, the truth one sees isn't always *the* truth. But perhaps one day people will begin to look beyond the surface, as you do."

"Then I'll wait for that day," Tempest said. "In the meantime, will you drop the costume? I prefer what I see to really *be* the truth."

"And that is why we need your help so badly." With a broad smile, he touched a button at his waist and shed the image of the Magician as if he'd peeled off a garment, his native form emitting light until she was nearly dazzled by opalescence and blue flame. He looked like something out of an Earth legend she'd read once, though Tempest couldn't quite place it. Here on Terra Beta, his species called themselves the People of Light.

Whatever they were, at least his people hadn't tried to kill hers when they arrived to colonize the planet. The time of first contact would have to come eventually, but before it could happen, humans would have to accept the notion that alternate dimensions held life forms as valid as their own. In the meantime, Tempest and the Magician had a lot of work to do.

There are no lengths to which a mother would not go to protect and sustain her child. The instinct may be universal.

MATER LUNA

by William Highsmith

Lunar Colony: Yr2280, Aug 10

Sherrie Meyer touched down in the *ANZI Cargo II* at the lunar commercial port. Her ship was assigned to the Australia/New Zealand/Indochina sector of Commerce Park, the lunar entrepreneurial incubator facility. She presented payments and credentials to the Lunar Union's customs officer.

"We have no cargo this time. We're carrying only private medications and food."

The customs officer's jaw dropped. No one landed without cargo. "Why the hell—"

"We were threatened and didn't report it," said Sherrie. "I know that's improper, but it was a medical emergency."

"Who threatened you?"

"It was a threat against all flights. Our insurer withdrew their cargo policy. The news stories—"

"I saw those stories, but I'm not buying yours." The agent looked at her ID card. "Dr. Sherrie Meyer, ANZI, director of the ore collection robot program." He looked at her. "Here's the problem, Dr. Meyer. Your ship is officially drydocked Earthside, yet it's here."

Sherrie cringed. "Please!"

"Relax. I can help you. Too many officials are going on vacation Earthside, and I'm convinced they will not return. They're taking all their personal effects."

Sherrie looked at him with relief. "You understand the situation. Good."

"The Lunar Union gnashed its teeth explaining why the moonbase's water generation project failed, crippling our food production. But where's the sense of urgency to end dependency on Earth?"

"What do you want?" asked Sherrie.

"I'll sign your certificates if you'll take me back with you."

"You may call me Sherrie." She held out her hand, welcoming her unintended partner, hoping he was more friend than enemy.

"You may call me *relieved,*" said the customs officer, taking her hand. "My name is Winston."

ﾟ￿￿ﾟ

Burani: Alien Lunar Colony, Yr10080

"How about there?" asked Pala, the science counselor of the Buran ship *Kafa.*

"Looks good," said Yopa, the ship's mate and pilot. A forward robotic scout had chosen this area of alien artifacts as a second alternative site on the blue planet's moon nine months ago. Yopa looked at the planet through the viewer and smiled on her starboard side, so that Pala could see.

"She's pretty, isn't she?" asked Pala. "Unfortunately she has a nasty temperament. She's poison to us . . . nuclear radiation."

Yopa frowned astern.

"We'll recommend robotic exploitation of the planet until it's safe," said Pala. "The moon is useful now."

"Shall I awaken our other mates?" asked Yopa.

"Three polar orbits, first, for environmental measurements. Then touchdown by that enclosed pavilion."

ℭ𝔊𝔅𝔊℥

Pala oozed slowly onto the moon's surface through a ship's extrusion port. An artificial organic material coated her outer body, protecting her from the hostile environment and the yellow star. Once on the surface, she congealed enough to convey herself along the surface. She confirmed her environmental measurements and conducted a final crew-safety check.

"Roust the other mates," she said. Yopa left her pilot's station in the *Kafa* to start the awakening process. While waiting for the others, Pala considered the value of the polar regions of the moon. The forward-scout's brief survey indicated that the poles were rich in captive volatile gases and would make a prosperous way station for other missions.

Xenobiologist Lula and mechanic exemplar Kana surfaced, followed by the medical doctor and the materials scientist. The few others would surface as needed. Yopa did not leave her ship, ever. She was the shipkeeper, ship's mate, and pilot.

"Why here, Pala?" asked Lula. "The poles are more interesting for exploitation."

"I trust that the aliens chose this site after due consideration."

"Had it nothing to do with the alien artifacts here?"

"You know me too well," said Pala with a rare double smile.

"Isn't this curious?" asked Lula. "A five-building village, connected by a hub-and-spoke monorail. Do you suppose these aliens had a cold temperament?"

"The structures seem weak. Perhaps the aliens hedged their bets against one disaster killing them all."

"This building serves only as a meeting pavilion," said Lula. She glided around the pavilion, trying to understand it. The transparent perimeter enclosed footprints with signs. "Ah, this is a museum as well. They were bipeds. They preserved their first footsteps here." She pointed to other impressions in the soil. "That is the touchdown area with the ship's standard of stripes and decahedrons."

"They were sentimental beings," said Pala. "Good for them."

ങ(ങ80)ൽ

"**S**weetie, I'm back."

Sherrie gathered her daughter from her godmother's apartment and took the monorail to Commerce Park Infirmary. Sherrie's story to the customs officer was not entirely a lie. Her daughter, Kera, had a low-grade fever that had earned the name *lunacy*. It was a common virus, easily treated on Earth, but persistent in the colony's artificial atmosphere. It was dangerous for preteens like Kera. During Sherrie's trip to Earth, she had tracked down the rare medication needed and obtained a large quantity of food and water.

Sherrie handed a medicine vial to her physician. "This is for Kera."

"Where did you get this?" he asked. "The drug company no longer makes it. Too little sales volume."

"I'll give you five more if you don't ask."

The physician knew a good deal when he heard one. "Ask what? I'm glad you didn't take her to Earth. Spaceflight is dangerous for lunatic children . . . forgive the term."

"I'm used to it. Those vials cost me a third of my savings," she said, to seal the deal of silence.

"I'll use them wisely," he said. "They're a godsend for several residents here."

"Um, would you tutor me in cryogenics in return?" asked Sherrie. "The mechanics of it are a cakewalk for me. But I don't know the practical medical aspects of it."

"Okay, but—"

"Don't ask."

"Fine. If you're thinking about fooling around with cryogenics, I expect you can operate this." He held up an atomizer and smiled. "Put the fluid in here and completely coat the inside of Kera's mouth, then get her horizontal quickly. I'll collect the information you need."

CR
ಶಿ

Burani: Alien Lunar Colony, Yr10080

"This moon tells the star-system's true history, since it has little atmosphere or weather to hide past events," said Pala. "If this moon has a history of radiation, then the planet's radiation is natural."

She deployed a twenty-meter sensor into the moon's surface, which transmitted its findings to Yopa's computer for comparison with the planet's data. The computer returned the results quickly.

"It was the aliens," said Pala. "They're sentimental, yet spoiled the planet with radiation?" She sighed deeply. "So it was. Still, their moon is rich."

"We must understand them before we leave," said Lula.

"I want to understand them, too," said Yopa, from her place at the ship's piloting console.

Pala instructed Yopa to send the soundings to Bura with an early recommendation to prepare for tunneling a city deep within the planet, below the radioactive shell, should they choose to exploit it with anything but robots.

Yopa then surprised her mates. She had detected a brief radio transmission from the direction of the third building from the pavilion. "Ku-ku-ku, kaah-kaah-kaah, ku-ku-ku," she said, imitating the transmission vocally. "It's a code of some sort."

ಶಿ

Lunar Colony, Aug 12

"Damn."

"What's wrong, Mom?" asked Kera.

"You look so much better today," said Sherrie. "How are you feeling?"

"Good. What's wrong?"

"It's becoming more difficult to be on Luna and Earth at the same time, dear." Sherrie sent a message to the ANZI home office in Melbourne; it would be re-sent through six anonymous relays, terminating at her Earth home, and relayed again from there. She let all voice calls go to her recorder because of the delay in Earth-moon-Earth communications.

"I'm afraid of Earth," said Kera.

"Who isn't? But there you don't have to buy oxygen. And it's lonely for you here, isn't it, with so few friends?"

Kera's face showed her panic. "Not if you're with me. You'll *always* be with me, won't you?"

"Come here. Of course I will." Sherrie hugged Kera snugly. "I'm going to a meeting. Would you rather visit Godmother Beth or come with me?"

"I'll go with you," Kera said quickly.

♋☪♋

"**W**e're in a precarious position," said Sherrie. "If my company figures out what I'm up to, they'll remotely disable the ship."

Winston looked at Kera, who was sipping on her water bottle. "May I speak in front of the little a-n-g-e-l?"

Kera snorted water. "Y-e-s, d-o-r-k."

Winston's face turned red. "In my opinion, you have only a few days before you're noticed. You belong here, but you're not behaving normally."

"I have the excuse of nursing Kera back to health," she said.

"That helps. Let's plan for a late evening departure in the next week or so. I'll nose around for the best time. Um, the flight will go unnoticed, officially, if I bring my buddy Martin into the plan—"

"I don't know—"

"He can alter records that I have no access to. It would be sad to get halfway home, only to have the ship disabled."

"Okay, that makes sense."

"I'll give you a two-hour notice," said Winston.

Burani: Alien Lunar Colony, Yr10080

"I detest these buildings," said Pala, "They're disorienting, angular monstrosities."

Pala's comment amused Lula. "We know what our mothers teach us, *Sacha*: organic buildings with few partitions. These aliens' mothers taught them angular buildings and many partitions."

"Could it be that they were not social?"

"I doubt that's possible for sentient beings. Perhaps there are technical explanations."

Pala tried to imagine people sentimental enough to save their first footsteps, but distancing themselves from one another. "*Ku!* Space travel was new to them. Perhaps they were not skilled in the building arts and space transport."

"Perhaps," said Lula.

"They were such little people, weren't they?" asked Pala, looking at the first alien body they had encountered, which was somewhat decomposed by the oxygen that had been in the room.

"They suffered from a skeletal design. They could not tolerate the smallest disruption in their support systems for oxygen, food and water."

"Why did they bother with spaceflight?" wondered the physician. "It was too risky for them."

Lula rippled. "They were explorers—" She then remembered the radioactive shell around the blue planet. "—but short-sighted."

ભ૯ૠ૬૦૪૦

Lunar Colony, Aug 13

"Sweetie, how do you feel?" Sherrie touched Kera's forehead.
　　　　"I'm fine, Mom. I'm hungry."
"Good. What color food do you want?"
"Yellow. I feel yellow today."

"That sounds good. What flavor?"

"Lasagna-flavored. Aren't you having anything? You look bad."

"Thank you so much," said Sherrie. "I'll have blue later."

"You always get blue," said Kera.

Sherrie put the coloring and flavoring in the packet, heated the food and plated it for Kera. While Kera tested her appetite and stomach, Sherrie noticed a news clip on the muted video screen. She clicked it off to protect Kera from the images.

"Back in a sec." Sherrie went into the common room.

She turned on the viewer, and her heart sank. The newscaster reported deadly violence in Indochina and India. New Burma and Thailand were exchanging blows, as were Assam-Indian Republic and India. Other conflicts were brewing in Eastern Europe, Brazil, Nicaragua, and North Africa.

"Armaments have advanced far faster than we can manage them," said the commentator. "We find ourselves back in the early middle ages, where cheap, devastating weapons enable any thug with a few loyal men to be king for a season."

To Sherrie, starving on the moon was gaining in its appeal. She decided to continue her planning, knowing she could pull out at anytime.

ভ৩৪৪০ব

Burani: Alien Lunar Colony, Yr10080

"What have we here?" Lula picked up a printed book from a shelf in a residential apartment in the colony. "*Ku*, I think this is a child's picture dictionary. Big ideas explained for untutored minds. Just what a xenobiologist needs to understand aliens."

"Lovely," said Pala. "Yopa, add this to the official documents list for Bura."

"They interest me," said Lula. "I'd like copies for our ship for idle times."

Lula rocked on the floor while she toured the book. Then she formed feet and stood straight up.

"What?" asked Pala. "What?"

"Perhaps this is a book of myths rather than a dictionary."

"That is useful, too."

Lula sighed. "Wishful thinking. It is a picture dictionary. It explains much."

"What stood you up on feet?"

"The blue planet has sexual reproduction predominately, if the pictures are any indication."

"Not unusual," said Pala.

"Bear with me, mate. It seems that the only groupings for mates are pairs."

"Interesting!" said Pala. "What else?"

"What else? Bura has societies of mates. Pairing is the worst sort of lonely, even-numbered grouping that—"

"Lula! Listen to yourself. Do you remember your academy paper? You fretted that xenobiologists were too invested in their own design."

"Yes, I said that," said Lula, turning a bit monochromatic.

"We find pairings of sentient beings awkward, but if all the universe were like Bura, then why would we leave home to search for something else? For minerals? Stores of oxygen? Boring."

"You're right. Irrational. *Ku!*"

രുന്മ8Dഇ

Luna Colony, Aug 14

"Mom, you're skipping your meal again? What's wrong? The pantry is full of food and water from your trip to Earth."

"Who's the mommy here?" asked Sherrie. "I'll finish the meal I started yesterday, after I watch the news."

"Okay, but that was from the day before yesterday. Promise?"

"Promise." Sherrie hated lying to Kera. Some adult decisions were beyond understanding for young minds. Food had to be saved for Kera, in case the primary plan of leaving the moon fell apart.

"May I watch, too? I haven't seen my shows in a week."

"No. That's an executive order. The news these days is not for young eyes. They mix news flashes with children's shows."

"Okay. I don't want anymore nightmares."

"Good girl. Oops . . . a message." Sherrie received a text message from Winston.

Time is ripe, two hours. Meet me at Moon-o-Rail Crossing.

Sherrie put down her phone. "Sweetheart . . ." Her voice dripped with portent.

"No, already?"

"It's time."

Kera didn't argue. Sherrie had on her *it's time to trust Mommy* face.

Sherrie wolfed down one meal. She then executed a part of the plan she had kept from Winston. She sent an urgent message to her three closest friends, informing them that they had two hours to meet her at the crossing, if they wished to leave with her. They were the only ones to whom she entrusted her daughter's life— Kera's godmother, godfather, and godaunt.

Sherrie gathered her package of favorite possessions and took a car to the crossing, with Kera in tears. Earth was a vague memory for Kera. Luna was her home.

Winston was waiting for Sherrie nervously.

ɞⱭℰᴏ

Burani: Alien Lunar Colony, Yr10080

Mechanic exemplar Kana revived the monorail and outfitted the cars for Buran girth.

"The beacon haunts me," said Yopa to her mates at the third alien building. "Please, for your ship's mate?"

"It haunts me, too," said Lula, "even though it calls aliens who can no longer answer."

"We'll go," said Pala. "Yopa, we've noticed your love of the blue planet by the many images and dirges you've entered into the ship's journal. This planet I now call *Yopahu*, Yopa loves."

"If you were in the ship, you'd see my tears," said Yopa.

CRThe Buran crew approached the beacon's source with trepidation. The colony was a long-dead experiment, but the Burani suddenly felt unnerved. Just outside the corner room identified by Yopa, the Burani arrived in time for a simple mechanical device to activate, which startled them. Kana viewed the gadget and smiled.

"It's a valve powered by the star, probably actuated by the surface and interior temperature gradient. It vents the room opposite this wall as needed, for what purpose I do not know."

"It is a thermostat?" asked Yopa from the ship.

Kana laughed. "Yes, our shipkeeper speaks more clearly. It is perhaps 10,000 years old and still working, the loveliest gadget I've seen here."

The Burani entered the building and then the room opposite the thermostat, carefully, to avoid spoiling whatever plan had begun so long ago. The room had a double door to protect it from the outside.

Pala entered first and found a child of the blue planet sprawled on the floor and tethered, but her body was not corrupt, like the others' had been.

Pinned to the wall near the child was an extensive set of notes on paper, which included a photograph of the child and hand sketches. On the floor below the note was a large bound book of engineering drawings. Pala realized slowly that the note was meant for her. It was a note drawn in such a way that any physical scientist with vision could understand it. She examined the book of drawings and decided it was a gift of knowledge, detailed findings about valuable ores on the moon. As with the child's note, there was a visual lexicon understandable by mining engineers anywhere.

"This child is special," said Pala. "We've seen what became of the others." Over the last few days, the Burani had found nearly 700 others in a gruesome scene of corrupt flesh in many rooms of the five buildings searched so far.

The Burani resealed the door until they arrived at a plan for the child.

ಲ೧ಙ೧೩

Luna Colony, Aug 14

Sherrie arrived at Moon-o-Rail Crossing with a grim child in tow. Winston's friend joined him as Sherrie approached.

"There are three others coming, I think," said Sherrie.

"What?" Winston was outraged.

"You added Martin to the mix," she said. She looked at Martin. "And I'm glad you did. Now I have done the same."

"Martin has a purpose. What about yours?"

"They love my daughter. I believe I have a few Brownie points coming for supplying a spaceship, don't you think?"

Winston sighed deeply. "Yes, of course. I'm sorry. I hope they arrive soon. We're—"

"Look, they're here."

Kera's god-relatives arrived with hastily arranged luggage.

"Hi, sweetie," said Kera's godfather.

"We're going to Earth. I'm scared."

"Of course you are. I'm terrified, happy and grief-stricken, all at the same time."

Sherrie was distracted by light from the Earthside window. While the others made introductions, Sherrie checked the news on her phone. A special bulletin knocked her back onto her heels.

"Oh my God," said Sherrie. She showed the others the phone and covered Kera's eyes and ears. A grim reporter described the event.

☙❦☙

". . . escalating rapidly from conventional limited-range bioweapons and smart robotic explosive devices to illegal atomic weapons. Worldwide panic has seized every nation, as each atomic power considers its options to step into the nuclear fray, offensively, defensively or preemptively. The United Nations is obviously ill-equipped—"

☙❦☙

The broadcast feed went off the air. Sherrie cried out and looked out the Earth-side window. She could see more evidence of the disaster with unaided eyes.

"Every vehicle flying over Earth will be shot down without warning," said Winston.

"I would not take my daughter there, anyway," said Sherrie. "Thank God we waited. Um, you can take the ship if you wish . . . no takers?"

The refugees sealed their grief with hugs and kisses and returned to their tiny apartments. A deadly light show continued for several hours.

☙❦☙

Burani: Alien Lunar Colony, Yr10080

"The note is a recipe for warming the child," said Pala. "The sketches describe water, through obvious depictions of hydrogen and oxygen, and uses water to describe a temperature scale, by indicating the freezing and boiling points. The moon's cycle defines a time scale. So now we know the phases and rates of warming the child. Additional sketches show the composition of gases and fluids she needs." Pala smiled. "She sketched herself holding the child."

"These aliens were careless, but they're growing on me," said Lula. "I suppose that is not a professional sentiment for a xenobiologist."

"That is a Buran sentiment," said Yopa. "Her mother gave her a beacon and a hope for life. The child is the last representative of her race, her planet. Did she dream of her mother while frozen like a polar *corci* bird all these years? Lula, is the mother not Buran?"

"You have convinced me," said Lula. "To say she is not Buran, because of her manner of mating, is to say we are Buran only because of it."

"What will we do?" asked Yopa. "Our mission here soon ends."

"I've just informed the mission director of the prospects for the planet and moon and made our recommendations towards colonization," said Pala. "Now we await direction from the forward-scout for our next mission, at least three months away, perhaps a year. We have time to consider the child's situation as pleases us. We can learn their language and read their literature."

Lula formed arms and hands and clapped her hands to her sides in pleasure. "Now the fun begins. This is why we explore."

‹₃∾₴∾₸›

Luna Colony, Aug 15

Sherrie stood in line at the port with about two-thirds of the colony's residents, awaiting the provisions cargo ship from Earth.

"Do you think it will come?" asked the nervous man ahead of her. He was a contract mechanic Sherrie had worked with on her ore-processing robot project.

"Honestly, Mark, I don't think the consortium will make new deliveries anytime soon; it might not even exist now. But I hope the shipment already in progress will continue. Cargo ships take a three-day journey to save fuel, so one should have been in space when the nukes began to fly."

"Oh."

"Who knows? Maybe the consortium had contingency plans for this and will—"

"There's your answer," said Mark, pointing to the message board.

"Postponed?" asked Sherrie. "No, recalled. At least there's someone left alive to recall the ship. Maybe the Associate Director will have new information about this in today's community meeting."

಄ಲ૨ౠ౦ಜಜ

"We have hope that the consortium will resume their deliveries in a few days," said the colony's Associate Director, addressing the colonists. "We're now receiving sporadic shortwave transmissions from various parts of the globe. But I'm not optimistic about Earth's long-term prospects."

The crowd responded with a stunned silence.

"I'm sorry," said the Associate Director. "We have little reliable news, so there's still hope."

"The Director General was one of the suspicious vacationers," whispered Winston. Sherrie nodded.

"Obviously, we must take conservation measures."

"Not the Director General," said Winston. "He's eating real food, now, on Earth. He's probably hunkered down in a well-provisioned bunker."

"Shhhh," said Sherrie.

The Associate Director kept speaking. "Fuel is not a major concern since we use only solar power, but water, food and oxygen should be treated as precious."

"How do you conserve oxygen?" asked Winston.

"Shut up, please," said Sherrie.

"Some of you may be wondering how to conserve oxygen."

Winston started to comment, but thought better of it.

"Obviously, we must breathe, but we can avoid exerting ourselves, and halt non-critical work projects, especially those using stored oxygen. I imagine you'll want to spend this time with your families."

"Sherrie, would you like a guy around to help out? I'm—"

Sherrie's jaw dropped at that suggestion. "No, Winston. I want to spend the time with Kera."

"I just thought . . . I hoped—"

"I'm sorry."

"Frankly," the Associate Director went on, "I'm more concerned about water. I'll send messages to each household with conservation suggestions. Some of them may seem awful, but we've no choice. Some in our community have expressed concern about thuggery, but is there one among us who would kill a child or a child's parent for the sake of one more week of life? That is no way to leave this world. And to end on a positive note, we hope and pray that pockets of civilization will soon make themselves known, and that the shipments will resume soon. Thank you."

"I'm glad the Director General is gone," said Sherrie, as the Associate Director left the podium. "I like this guy. Good luck, Winston. I'm sorry you're not more prepared, but as he said, we're only talking about weeks of life."

ⒸⓇⓈⓄ

Sherrie continued underfeeding herself. She reckoned her private water supply would far outlast her food. The food was Kera's. She agonized over the tradeoff of leaving Kera alone and extending her own life by eating. However, she did not want Kera to suffer starvation weeks later.

"You know which is the last parcel of food, right, Kera?"

"Yes, Mom. They'll come with more food, won't they?"

"I'm sure of it, right after you use the last parcel, but it *must* be the last one to work."

"I know, Mom."

"And what must you do before you take the last meal, or if you have difficulty breathing?"

"Strap the mask over my mouth."

"And?"

"Hold it there for one minute. Then I can have the food."

"Right. Mask first, food second."

Sherrie attached some papers to the wall by Kera's bed and put other documents on the floor. "Do not move these, Kera, ever."

"I know, Mom."

CRESO

Kera's physician had come through with the cryogenics information. Sherrie borrowed a tank of diluted hydrogen sulfide gas from ANZI's storage and further diluted it. She reckoned that being abandoned on the moon to die was sufficient payment for the tank. She added to the tank the six-percent gaseous mixture suggested by the physician.

She fabricated a valve to couple the gas mask to the tank. It would release the gas mixture and a narcotic when Kera pressed the mask to her face. The narcotic would put Kera to sleep quickly while unpleasant things happened to her body. A drop in the tank pressure would activate a mechanism to control the room temperature.

Sherrie had spent much time considering the design and materials for this mechanism, as it needed to survive possibly for several years. She used exotic coatings and materials from her robotics lab for the vent, including self-healing and self-cleaning nanotube seals.

The last food container was empty. It was a memory aid to help Kera remember what to do. She would never have a chance to open it. Sherrie activated a solar-powered SOS signal with a low duty cycle, twenty-four transmissions per day, that would start when the mask was used. She constructed a similar system for her own room, without the elaborate starting mechanisms, since she'd activate it manually.

CRESO

The day came when Sherrie had difficulty raising herself up from her bed. She cuddled Kera for many hours, urgently kissing her face, eyes and hands, and whispering into her ears. "Remember, the last food packet—"

"—is marked *last*. I know, Mom. Is this goodbye?"

"For now, my love . . . for now." Sherrie did not want Kera to have to deal with her mother's body. She left for another apartment she had prepared in advance and sealed it. She took the mask with a smile on her face. Her mother had said she would never have use for a mechanical engineering degree.

ෞ෬෫෨

Burani: Alien Lunar Colony, Yr10080

"*Kafa* is ship-shape," said Pala. "We have no official duties until the forward-scout contacts us. We look forward to learning the common alien language so that we may enjoy their documents and literature. We'll visit the remaining residential areas, which by their repetition, offer little new."

"The alien child is never off my mind," said Yopa. "I'd visit her if I could, but a ship's mate never leaves her ship."

Pala also was moved by the child's circumstances. "Mate, we'll leave the child for our sisters to manage a few thousand years from now, so—"

"I know. That will be a painful moment," said Yopa.

"Mechanic exemplar fortified the mechanisms created elegantly in haste by the child's mother. She added redundancy to further protect the child. She is safe."

"Thank you, Captain." Yopa used an extravagant honorific that touched Pala deeply.

ෞ෬෫෨

"Is it her?" asked Pala.

Lula consulted her digital copy of the alien child's effects, the sketch of the resourceful mother holding her daughter. "This sketch is artless, but I believe she is the child's mother. Her own beacon failed, else we would have found her sooner."

Lula had found the slightly emaciated body a few apartments from the child. "That she is frozen in the same manner as the child speaks volumes. We've found no others so preserved among the colonists."

Pala nodded. "More evidence that a cataclysm occurred. Only this woman's gifts in the mechanical arts and her resourcefulness allowed her to prepare quickly."

"Why is she emaciated and not her child?" asked Lula.

"I look to our xenobiologist for that answer," said Pala with a smile.

"We must revive them," said Yopa from the ship. "Now that there is mother and child, we must."

"To what end?" asked Pala. "Raise them up and leave them alone on this barren moon, only to starve?"

"We can teach them to synthesize nourishment."

"And then? In a few years, they will die, and the journey of their planet with them. These strange aliens, mother and child, do not have the completeness required of this race to procreate."

"That is not *precisely* true," said Lula.

The medical doctor nodded in agreement.

"Better that we leave them for the exploitation crew to choose their fate. They will have sufficient time . . . uf . . . *what* is not precisely true?" Pala smiled at her own slowness to hear.

"That these aliens cannot procreate," said Lula.

"You've seen evidence that they have this capability?"

"I've seen evidence that they do not . . . but, mate, we can give it to them."

"That can be done?"

"On this moon, no. But on our ship, there will be time."

"You've been listening to our ship's mate, have you?" said Pala with a smile.

"She has her charms, especially when her eyes are forward."

"I agree," said Pala, "but now I must write a most artful report for Bura. *We are so sorry. We only imagined the frozen aliens. Their star is blinding.*"

Lula laughed. "We will make our apologizes at our leisure and without deceit. Bura will receive them long after we are dead."

ೞ୧୨ඔ൚

Burani: Deep Space, Yr10081

"Kera's waking, again. She's hallucinating from the narcotic after all these years . . . imagine."

Kera's eyes shot open. She thought she heard her mother's voice. She lay on an oval table, nauseated and confused. To her right was her mother. To her left was a cartoon monster. It had at least two eyes, and probably more if the creature had a decent modicum of symmetry. Its body was shaped like a squat rutabaga with no limbs. Then it reshaped itself to resemble a human, if a very frightening one.

Kera snapped her eyes closed. She knew she was dead. She remembered eating her last meal, an extravagant treat on the moon—a loaf of steaming-hot buttered Italian bread, cakes, ice cream, grape juice, cream cheese on crackers, spread out on a long walnut table . . . all from that tiny last box of food.

Kera became confused. *Dying hallucinations*, she thought. *Mother poisoned me to spare me from suffering starvation, and I took it gladly, though it burned in my throat. There is no one like my mother.* Kera sighed her last breath, she thought, feeling closure. One tear rolled down her cheek for her mother. Then she felt her mother's distinctive soft touch on her face and felt familiar lips kissing her ear.

"Kera, I'd like to introduce you to Yopa," said the death-dream, imitating her mother. "She loves you so much." Sherrie whispered softly in Kera's ear, her warm breath like the breath of life. "I love you, too."

"Oh, Mom!" Kera's face showed nausea as she put her hand over her mouth. Sherrie held out a bowl for her.

"I'm sorry, honey. I overdid it a little with the narcotic, but I was ready for you this time." Sherrie turned to Yopa. "I'm sorry you had to see that again."

"See what again?" asked Yopa.

Women always need things to nurture, things to treasure. Sometimes those things are each other.

A PEARL OF GREAT PRICE

by Leslie Brown

My sister Saralyn held her newest baby up to the vidscreen and tickled him to make him giggle. She then took me on a tour of her new house, built pueblo-style in the New Phoenix complex. The message was clear. Come home to the Prez and all this could be yours. The vid ended with my mother and sisters waving goodbye with the hands of their various offspring. I clicked off the screen.

"If you are finished, you should dress for dinner," Fayleen said. I glanced over at her and blinked at her resplendent costume. The organic silk dress fitted her like a glove with padded grommets around each spike emerging from her exoskeleton. Rose-hued opalites were glued to the carapace around each of her eight eyes, each stone worth an orbiting biosphere. I didn't know if it was her own jewelry or supplied to her for the duration of the mission. The entire effect was exactly what she wanted to achieve: a rich Risian matron attending the renowned gem auction on the luxury space liner *Seventh Daughter*. To me, she looked like a four armed spider-armadillo in an evening dress. I grunted assent to her comment and went reluctantly to my closet.

"Wear the red dress," she said. Ignoring her, I continued to push the button that revolved my extensive wardrobe. A thin arm reached gently over my shoulder and stopped the display at the red dress. Sullenly I pulled it out. I was in disgrace because of some impulsive behavior on my last mission. Fayleen had been given absolute authority over me. One slip-up and I was out of the Protectors' Bait and Lure program. I would be sent back to Earth, never to leave Sanctuary or the Prez, as we humans called it, a combination of Preserve and Reservation. Now, that would make my sisters happy.

I put on the dress, or rather the wisp of silk that passed as a dress. Culturally, it spoke volumes. It left my breasts bare, criss-crossed underneath by straps. This signified to all that I trusted my owner enough to protect me even though I displayed my tempting flesh in public. It also served to showcase my real and cosmetic scars, designed to show that I had been tortured at one time and knew the Way of Pain. This would have any potential kidnappers positively salivating when they saw me, set out like the main course at a buffet. It also highlighted the warm tones of my brown skin and contrasted nicely with my black hair.

I glanced again at Fayleen. This was our first mission together, and I was taking a big leap of faith that she could indeed protect me. The sign of Protection tattooed between my eyebrows meant nothing in the big wide universe. While she had been briefed about my sordid history, my boss had declined to tell me her background.

"When you know your partners' qualifications ahead of time, you almost always judge your own abilities to be superior and then decide to operate solo." Mushall had still been angry at me when he said this, but the ring of truth had stung anyway.

"Here is your leash." I took the object from Fayleen. It was studded with the same jewels as those around her eyes. I clipped it around my neck without comment. I walked over and handed the other end to my new partner. She blinked at my sudden cooperation, but said nothing. She keyed the door open and we promenaded out into the corridor. *Seventh Daughter* was one of the most expensive liners running the Arms, and it showed, everywhere. The corridors were completely covered by a projecting holosystem. We were walking through a rainforest. The scent of flowers drifted to us, and silver, bat-like creatures flew about our heads. The transport tube was disguised as the polished trunk of a sabat tree. A solid piece of wood dissolved into a mist before us, and we entered the tube.

"Reception hall," said Fayleen. We started to move so gently that we didn't have to brace our legs. The doors slid open on a glittering spectacle. The holos in the hall were designed to make it seem as if we were inside a huge fire emerald. The green flames flickered up and down the walls, following the facet lines. I tried to look sophisticated, the pet that has been everywhere and seen everything, but I paused in consternation at my first sight of the melanti delegation. Normally a slim, beige-colored twig of a being, the melanti were mosaiced with jewels, applied like Fayleen's directly onto their skin. I laughed involuntarily. All the patterns created by the gems directed the viewer's attention to the melanti's genitals, which were decorated with the largest and flashiest gems. Fayleen gave a warning tug on my leash.

"Careful, Hadass Mendoza, they are sensitive about certain matters." In my new spirit of cooperation, I blanked my expression and concentrated on following Fayleen, using my most graceful walk. She was greeted by a curleep, an old friend apparently. It might even be another agent. I wouldn't put it past Mushall to plant other operatives and not tell me.

"Fayleen, my darling, you look breathtaking. And a human pet, no less. How amazing!" The curleep and I regarded each other. As a pet, I was not supposed to speak unless invited. I sank into the comfortable kneeling position that pets were supposed to assume when their owner was stationary. The curleep flared all the gills along its chest, a gesture that meant it was impressed. "She must have cost you a fortune! The scarred ones don't usually leave Sanctuary ever again."

I bit my lip to stave off a scathing reply. The curleep would not have understood my ire anyway, had I expressed it. Besides, it was not of interest. That species' penchant was for gossip, not torture. I ceased to listen to it and scanned the crowd instead. There were veshai, always suspect, as well as some others with potential. I needed to keep in mind that any species could be greedy enough to broker Way of Pain slaves.

My attention was caught abruptly by another human, not a pet, but a player. He wore a re-creation of an old-style tuxedo and had a single sapphire glued between his eyes to indicate that he was a buyer of gems like the rest of the glittering throng. I looked around for his protection and found them quickly, a trio of barlak mercenaries positioned at a discreet distance from their employer. He was talking to a veshai and, as if he felt my glance, looked over in my direction. It took him a millisecond to register my species, my mode of attire and the leash connecting me to Fayleen. A mixture of disgust and pity crossed his handsome face before he turned back to his conversation partner. I bristled in spite of myself. The days of involuntary servitude were over. He should know I was here of my own free will and being paid for it. Did he think we all had the wherewithal to travel the galaxy as players? I remembered the real reason I was here and laughed inwardly with pleasure. Already I was deep in my role and taking offence at the reaction of ignorant humans.

"Excuse me, Shazit." It was the ignorant human.

"You are excused, Shazim." I looked up at him from under my fringe of black hair and made no move to stand up. He glanced over at Fayleen, who was still deep in conversation with the curleep, allowing me a moment of privacy.

"Are you in distress, Shazit?"

"Do I look like I am in distress?"

"I'll be blunt then. You have a leash around your neck, you have obviously been physically abused in the past, and this arm of the galaxy has a particularly bad reputation for humans disappearing. I can help you." I decided to relent. The poor neb seemed sincere.

"I assure you, Shazim, I am here of my own free will, under contract and being paid quite well for it. I trust my employer to protect me." His manner changed; and I knew he was shifting from pity to disgust; I began to relish our conversation.

"Then perhaps I can convince you to find another way to make a living. What you are doing here demeans humans in the eyes of the rest of the galaxy." He was cold and disapproving. I began to feel like a Jane Austen heroine. I blinked innocent eyes up at him.

"How so, Shazim?"

"Only fifty years ago, we were everyone's meat. We couldn't set foot off Earth without being taken and sold to creatures that would breed us against our will and torture our offspring. What you do here reminds them that we were once at their mercy and encourages those who long for the old ways, when they had a species that could endure pain."

I felt a gentle tug on my leash. Fayleen had finished and wanted to move on. She was asking if it were important that I talk to this human. I answered her by rising gracefully to my feet.

"I notice you were talking to a veshai, a species that tortures for recreation. How can you forgive it and not me?" I was pleased to see red creep up from under his collar into his face. I decided to wrap this little interview up. "I don't have the money or influence to be a player like you. To get off Sanctuary and into space, I had to become a pet. I'll do whatever my employer asks of me. Now, if you will excuse me?"

He stepped back and nodded to me impassively. "You're excused, Shazit."

I joined Fayleen, and we strolled across the room.

"Was that important?" she asked softly, her way of inquiring as to whether or not the player was a contact.

"No, just some self-righteous prig who wanted to save me from myself. He thought I was demeaning the species."

She swiveled several eyes towards me. "Did he offend you, then?"

"No, but I get tired of the arrogance of people like him. They think that everyone else has the same choices, the same opportunities they do. He was born and raised in the Dasha Enclave; I can tell by his accent. They think they're privileged because they deal with aliens on an equal basis, being the business face of the Prez. They have no idea that they are regarded as nothing more than trained monkeys by the rest of the galaxy."

Fayleen paused to nod at an acquaintance and took a drink from a passing mobile tray. "Is that how you think I regard you? As a trained monkey?"

"I have no idea, Fayleen, you've never said." I helped myself to a drink from a tray in violation of protocol. Fayleen was supposed to hand it to me first, but I was thirsty and didn't feel like asking permission to drink. The pink stem on the glass indicated that it contained no intoxicants and was suitable for Class Four stomachs.

She blinked several eyes at me again. "I was part of the Kandai rescue."

That shut me up. The Kandai episode had happened 200 years ago, but Fayleen's life span could be ten times that. If she was telling the truth, and there was no reason why she should lie about this, then she was partly responsible for saving half the human race. When it looked like the Pangovernment of the Seven Arms was about to declare humans a protected species, it was open season on us, with everyone and his brother trying to snatch up humans for their private zoos. In a series of lightning quick raids on Earth, 10,000 people had been kidnapped from their homes and spirited away to Kandai, a slaver clearinghouse on a biosphere orbiting a gas giant. When they came back for more, the Pangovernment forces were waiting for them and, in the ensuing battle, most of Earth got crisped. Meanwhile, a second strike force rescued the people at Kandai. Of the millions of people on earth, only about 20,000 had been saved. We were placed on an untouched continent and protected with orbiting weapons platforms and warships.

I was at a rare loss for words, but nothing I could say would be appropriate. I bowed my head to Fayleen.

"I think it is time to view the merchandise," said Fayleen, breaking the awkward silence, and we made our way to the three-dimensional holos of the jewels to be auctioned. The actual jewels would not arrive until *Seventh Daughter* met the sellers' ships in a predetermined hyperdrive pocket. Only ships supplied with the right coordinates would be able to pause in that spot, thus providing impenetrable security for the auction. It also created a terrific opportunity for another sort of auction, and it was my organization's suspicion that the annual jewel auction was used as a cover to sell human slaves.

My job was to find out where the slaves were on *Seventh Daughter* during the auction, because they had to pass through this ship to enter another: our large mass stabilized the pocket; all visiting ships linked to us. If possible, I was to tag a slave or two so that they could be traced and we could nail both the sellers and the buyers. For once, my temptingly scarred body was not a trap for overconfident kidnappers. However, this mission presented far more difficulties than the usual bait and lure.

"This one is lovely," said Fayleen, pointing to a square-cut harmony stone.

"How much money do you have?" I asked incredulously. Was she going to bid on it?

"Enough for this, I think. I do so like the way harmony stones vibrate when next to the skin. I may have a chance to wear it before I have to turn it in."

"Nothing wrong with treating yourself," I murmured.

"Do you do that ever? Treat yourself?"

I looked at her in surprise. "Sure, all the time."

"I was wondering. We are on a luxury ship with funds at our disposal. Yet you show no interest in the beautiful clothing supplied to you, nor the delicacies that can be ordered from the kitchen. You don't even soak in the massage tub, but take a shower instead."

"I'm working," I said, but it sounded feeble even to me.

"Contrary to what you think, I do not know your history. I think I am missing some important pieces, withheld by your previous employer to protect you. That does a disservice to both of us, I think. You appear to be punishing yourself by not allowing yourself to enjoy pleasurable things. I have been on similar adventures with other humans. They did not behave like you." All eight eyes were on me, and that made me uncomfortable.

"I'm unique, Fayleen. I like to stay focused on the job, not let things like treats and toys distract me."

"Fair enough, Hadass. Yet, if you were to allow a treat to distract you, which one of these jewels would you pick?"

I smiled at her game. Would my choice tell her something about my psyche? Fine, I would play.

"That one," I said pointing.

"The pearl? That's an Earth treasure, it is not?"

"Yes, that is from home. It appeals to me because it is created when an irritant like a grain of sand gets inside a mollusk's tender parts. It protects itself by building the smooth pearl around the bit of grit."

"Are you the grit or the pearl?" she asked.

"I had not realized we were talking in metaphors, Fayleen." Her reply was interrupted by the auctioneer, a large and hairy brachan.

"Shazims and Shazits, the viewing is coming to a close. I thank you for your courtesy and invite you to the auction at the start of the seventh bhal. Please obtain bidder chip from one of our employees at the tables next to the refreshments."

Fayleen drifted gracefully over to the registration tables, and the leash necessitated that I follow her. She was served immediately, and we took our leave of the throng. We waited until we were in our quarters and she had activated the jamming device before we spoke.

"Let me review our timetable," I said. "We enter the pocket in a bhal, and the buyers are invited back to the hall in two bhals to bid. So, between the time we enter the pocket and the end of the auction should be about four bhals, based the number of jewels to be sold. That is my window to find where the human slaves are, get a few to agree to be tagged and get out undetected."

"And no heroic rescues, Hadass. Not only would that put us in danger from the slavers, but also from the jewel auctioneers who may be knowing participants."

"Understood, Fayleen. In and out, quiet as a mouse."

Fayleen made a strange noise between a hiccup and a chirp that I interpreted to be a snort of disbelief. I set about preparing myself for my mission. I would be traveling the hallways in a deck cleaning 'bot until I found the humans. Then I would use the ventilation shafts. I had a device to neutralize the sensors installed to detect the motion of anything but shaft cleaning 'bots. I would be giving out the signal of the smaller shaft 'bot as well as a distorted version of my mass. I packed five trackers, meant to be swallowed. They would not activate in a slave until five bhals had passed after initial contact with stomach acid. Finally, I had an extremely sensitive detector calibrated to detect the ketones in human exhalations. Oh, and a filter mask, so I wouldn't set off my own detector.

In case I was caught, I was wearing a pet outfit and had no weapons of any kind. My devices were concealed as pet jewelry. I had several plausible to implausible explanations for my activities depending on how and where I might be caught. They would not save me, but they might protect Fayleen.

We felt the curious deceleration as the ship went sideways into a hyperspace pocket. We were too insulated by our location to hear or feel the linking tubes from smaller ships clang against our hull. Fayleen took one of her mobile travel cases and expanded it into a very reasonable facsimile of a deck cleaning 'bot. I slipped inside it and made myself as comfortable as I could on my hands and knees. I inserted the mouth guard that had the directional controls so I could keep my hands free for the ketone detector. Fayleen made no comment as she opened the door of her quarters and gave me the all-clear signal. Perhaps her species did not believe in wishing anyone luck.

I trundled along the hallway, keeping close to the wall as a cleaning 'bot would and peering out through a narrow slit. The air intake was working fine and kept me cool. I made my way to the cargo hold level, where I was sure the humans would be held somewhere in the maze of holds and storage rooms. Far away from any legitimate human passengers who might confuse the detector, I slipped on the mask and turned the detector on. It lit up immediately. I followed the directional arrows to a closed door. I called up a holo map with a flip of my tongue and studied it as it hovered a few inches from my eyes. There was a small storage room on the other side of the door with easy access to the cargo hold that served as the connection hub for all the ships.

Using the map, I backtracked to the vent that led to a shaft servicing the room. I pivoted the cleaning 'bot in a circle to check for company in the corridor and then slipped out. The vent plate opened easily, and I neutralized the motion sensors around its lip. There were two openings to the storage room, one at floor level and the other at the ceiling. I slipped magnetic adhesive on my hands and toes and spidered up the shaft so that I could peer out the upper opening.

Even before I reached the opening, I could hear them: faint whimpers and the shifting in discomfort of a number of bodies. There were at least forty people in the room. Most were lying down. I could see one guard from my angle but that didn't mean there weren't more. I worked my way back down the vertical shaft and then crawled half the length of the room along a horizontal shaft to reach the floor-level port. A man was lying with his head quite close to the port. His neck was a mass of scars from the Way of Pain. I made a 'hist' at him, softly.

Slaves learn not to react visibly to anything in case it draws the attention of the slavers. He turned his head slightly until his eyes met mine. Casually he rolled on his side so that his face was close to the port grating.

"I'm a Protector," I whispered to him softly. "I need your help."

"Mine? The Protectors are in desperate straits, then," he whispered back. "Are you here to rescue us?"

"Not immediately. I need you to swallow a delayed tracker so we can shut down the whole operation. I don't have the manpower to help you now, but we can rescue you once you are with your new owner."

He stared at me, and I couldn't read his expression. Many were brainwashed, learning to like the Way of Pain. He could easily call the guard on me, but I had to chance it. "On one condition," he said, licking dry lips.

"I can promise nothing."

"Then you get no cooperation."

"What do you want?"

"Take my baby with you. Now." Once he said it aloud, he could no longer hide the terrible mixture of hope and desperation in his eyes. He rolled back slightly so that I could see the blonde woman lying beside him, a very young baby asleep or unconscious on her chest.

"Impossible. It would give me away." My mouth was dry, too. Terrible memories were hammering at the closed door at the back of my mind.

"They drugged her. Her name is Pearl. Pearl Bennett. Take her and I'll take your tracker. So will my wife."

I looked at the pretty, decorative chrono on my wrist. The auction would be ending in fifteen decibhals, and this doomed family would be leaving with new owners. I made a decision and to hell with the consequences.

"I can unscrew the grate from this side. Are there any more guards besides that one?"

"No, he's the only one and he's listening to vion music in his helmet."

Vion music induced a mild stupor. Perfect. I unscrewed the grate and turned it sideways to pull inside the port. I passed the man the trackers.

"Swallow them. Now push the baby to me."

The man turned to his wife and took the baby from her. She moaned, but did not wake. How terrible that she would not get to say good-bye. The warm, limp mass was in my hands, but I had to put her down to re-attach the vent. When I was done, I looked back at the man. He held the tracker between two fingers and swallowed it as I watched. Although I didn't ask him to, he opened his mouth wide to show it was on its way to his stomach.

"Your name?" I mouthed at him.

"Charles Bennett. Snatched from Dasha ten years ago. My wife is from a breeding colony. I've called her Angela."

I nodded my understanding of his world. "Pearl?"

"Pearl."

I looked at my chrono. Time was almost up. I held the baby to my chest with one arm which made crawling very difficult. The cleaning 'bot was where I had left it, and I laid Pearl between my knees. I was half a deck away from our quarters when a general alarm went off.

"What the hell?" I whispered. I couldn't believe they would have missed one baby so soon. The noise made the baby stir against my knees, and I absently made soothing noises as I continued towards our quarters. I thought I could hear shouting in the hallway. I really didn't think this had anything to do with me.

I rounded the corner and halted. Two humans and two barlak mercenaries were in the process of blowing the lock. There was a bright flash and then they were forcing the door open. I sidled the 'bot closer, trying to see if Fayleen was inside.

I heard loud voices, and Fayleen's higher tones answering back.

"Where is she, where's your pet?"

"She's out. She wanted to explore the ship's common areas."

There was a meaty noise, and I feared that Fayleen had been struck. Her carapace was tough and once she was curled in a protective ball, it was very hard to hurt her. However, if she had been caught by surprise and was standing, her throat and gut were very vulnerable.

"I won't let her be hurt. Leave her alone." Fayleen was still in her role, maintaining our cover. In her place, I'd be trying to inflict as much damage as I could by now, determined to go down fighting. That was what had gotten me in trouble on my last mission. But now it was more than just me who would suffer the consequences: I had a baby to protect. If I had left Pearl with her parents, I could be out there helping Fayleen. Pearl could have been saved later when we rescued her parents. What had I been thinking? I had to stop being impulse-driven all the time, because now it was getting someone hurt. Again.

"Hurt her? We're here to liberate the silly bitch. Boss's orders."

Liberators? Boss's orders? Could this have something to do with that human prig I met at the viewing reception?

"She doesn't need liberating. I'm paying her to be my pet." Fayleen did a perfect job of acting the bewildered Risian matron. I winced as there was another cracking noise and a trill of pain from Fayleen. At that moment, Pearl woke up and started a gasping wailing. I snatched her up from between my knees and started bouncing her in my arms, the way I had seen my sisters calm their offspring. Pearl wasn't having any of it and started crying in earnest.

The cleaning 'bot rocked and the top casing was wrenched off. The humans and barlaks stared down at me in disbelief, pulse weapons pointing at me. Hiding under a bed was one thing but being found in a cleaning 'bot was another. I decided to follow Fayleen's lead and stay in my role.

"Don't hurt me," I whimpered. They had to see me as a helpless pet and lower their guard. Pearl had subsided now and was back in her semi-comatose state.

"A baby? The boss didn't say anything about a baby." This was a tall, blond man with an acne-pocked face.

"She's mine. Please don't hurt her." I got to my feet slowly and stepped out of the cleaning 'bot. I glanced past their shoulders into our quarters and saw Fayleen lying on the floor in front of the small sofa. "Fayleen! What did you do to her?"

"Taught her a lesson: humans are not pets."

Her chest was moving with her gasps; she wasn't dead. The second human, a short man with dark hair, spoke for the first time.

"What were you doing in that cleaning 'bot?"

"Hiding. It was Fayleen's idea." If I seemed to be a dimwit, they wouldn't demand more answers. It seemed the second human agreed with this theory.

"Bring her with us, the baby too. Let the boss decide."

The barlaks didn't hesitate, and I was lifted to my feet with one of their hands under each elbow. They hustled me down the corridor, and I kept a tight grip on Pearl. We passed some crew members, knocked out by pulse pistols. Our direction was taking us towards the cargo holds. At a joining of corridors we met up with a group of humans. Mr. Dasha Enclave was in the lead. He glanced at me, barely registering me as an entity and then did a double take when he saw the baby.

"Where did the baby come from?" he asked the shorter human in my group.

"Had it with her. Thought you'd want both."

"Yeah." He turned to me. "You're being liberated, little miss pet. You probably don't have the brains to appreciate what we're doing for you, but your kid will in time."

"Where are you taking us?" I asked in a tiny voice.

"We have our own sanctuary, run by humans, not by patronizing aliens. We're taking you there along with other humans we're in the process of rescuing."

I needed to salvage this huge screw-up somehow. The only solution I could see chanced revealing my identity, but I didn't have time to think of anything else.

"When slavers think they are going to be caught with cargo, they kill them and vanish. A couple of gas pellets usually do the trick."

Dasha Enclave stared at me blankly. "How do you know?"

"You're wasting time. They've probably been killed already."

He didn't reply, but gestured to his men to get a move on. Without any contradictory instructions, my two barlak escorts continued to half carry me behind the crowd. We reached the cargo hold, but the door was already open. I could hear Dasha Enclave swearing bitterly. Reluctantly I peered over several shoulders and could see the bare feet of several prone slaves.

"Bring the pet up here." Dasha Enclave sounded murderous. I was dragged forward. Now I could see all the way into the compartment. They were all dead, gassed by the look of their twisted, purple faces. The Bennetts were still by the floor vent port. Charles's fingertips were resting against the port's grate.

"How did you know?" Each word was spat out.

"I'm a Protector." In for a penny, in for a pound.

"You, a Protector? You're a silly frivolous pet, not worth the space you take up."

I stared at him and watched it sink in. He was pompous, not stupid.

"You were here to save them, weren't you? Then we came and fucked it up." He rubbed his face with one hand, oblivious to the fact that they were all standing around, empty-handed, about to be caught. They were criminally stupid, but they were humans, and I had to get them moving.

"You imagine yourself a hero, don't you?" I said. "Why work so slowly, so incrementally, while humans are dying all over the galaxy? You have to act now before the human race dwindles and vanishes. Have you rescued many people so far?"

"We found a ship transporting ten slaves. We killed the slavers, took the ship for our own. We heard about this setup, got the coordinates from a jewel merchant. We were going to save them all." He looked like a disappointed child who had just been told there was no Santa.

"One lived." I lifted Pearl up slightly, then resettled her. "But you can't have her. I want her to grow up in Sanctuary."

"How are you going to stop me from taking her?" he asked. He still didn't take me seriously.

"You've got a large number of seriously pissed *Seventh Daughter* crewbeings and auction house employees converging on this spot. Now you can waste time fighting with me for Pearl and finding out what a Protector is capable of, or you can save yourselves. Live to fight another day, as they say." I was bluffing, of course. Holding a baby, I'd need a pulse pistol to be truly effective, but Dasha Enclave was rattled, full of self-doubt. Killing a human at this point would be a bit hypocritical.

"We're taking these people with us," he informed his men. "We'll bury them in a place that's free."

I restrained myself from rolling my eyes with great difficulty.

"You'd better hurry then," I said.

The bodies were collected efficiently and hustled down one of the many identical docking tubes on the departure deck. Dasha Enclave was the last down the tube and he paused. "Come with us."

"I've got a job, thanks." *But maybe not much longer,* I thought, cupping Pearl's skull with one hand.

"I'm sorry," he said vaguely.

"Don't apologize to *me*," I said unkindly and watched him seal the tube behind him. In the bowels of his ship were two bodies with tracking devices in them that would go off in a few hours. I would be seeing Dasha Enclave again.

⋙⋘

The Risian doctor had mended Fayleen's carapace well. I could barely see where the seam was, but I knew that the damage had rendered Fayleen unbearably ugly to her fellow Risians. She was recuperating in a bed at the Oberlac station when I dropped in to check on her before heading back to Earth. Pearl was being babysat by two doting Protector colleagues on the small transport that was taking us home.

"Fayleen . . ." I began. If I hadn't had to protect Pearl, I could have prevented her pain by giving myself up to the rebels that much sooner.

"Stop, Hadass. I have no wish to indulge your desire to assume responsibility for everything that does not go well. I am fine."

"Your carapace . . ." I tried again.

"I am years past my last mating dance. I assure you it bothers me not in the slightest. I hear you are returning to the Prez."

"I have custody of Pearl. I want to raise her among humans."

"And what of your work?"

"I'll still be training others. I won't be bored."

"Are you certain you are not atoning for the death of Pearl's parents by dedicating your life to her well-being?"

"Even with my tendency to blame myself for everything that goes wrong, I can't shoulder that. I never saw Dasha Enclave/Seth

Rogers coming. He escaped the round-up, you know, had a bolthole ready."

"So I heard. He will surface eventually." Fayleen paused. It was the first time in our short acquaintance that I saw her carefully choose her words. Usually she knew exactly what she wanted to say to me. "Had events in your life been slightly different, you would have been working for Rogers, killing everything in your path to free humans. Mushall called me on live-vid. He told me you lost a son to slavers."

I snarled inwardly at my interfering boss. "He tell you the whole story?"

"No, he said he would leave that to you."

"Figures. It's not something I'm proud of."

"There are many life lessons that are painful to acquire." The eight eyes were unblinking. She wasn't going to let me go without the story.

I sighed. "I rebelled as a teen against the whole cruel, oppressive system. Somehow that rebellion got detoured into drugs and a pregnancy by a father whose identity escapes me. When I was hurting for drugs, I sold my baby for money to buy more." I waited for the shock and disgust, but those eyes were still unblinking.

"How did you end up as a Protector?"

"A long road with family and friends helping along the way. Mushall accuses me on a regular basis of using my job to search for my son, and he's not entirely wrong. I screwed up my last mission on a breeding colony by charging in to look for him without waiting for backup. Of course he wasn't there. But that's not why I rescued Pearl. I saw the look in her father's eyes and couldn't leave her. But yes, there's atonement too. I can give Pearl a good life now, the life my son should have had."

"Hadass Mendoza, giving up? I do not see that, as yet. You can call on me for any assistance you might need."

I bowed my head in gratitude. It was no small offer. I had found out just how high-ranking my partner was, courtesy of my own live-vid with Chief Warden Mushall, who was very upset at me for letting my partner get her carapace cracked. Fayleen opened a drawer in the table beside her bed and pulled out a box. "I have a gift for you."

"I don't deserve a gift, Fayleen."

"Open it."

I took the box and slid it open. The enormous pearl from the auction nestled in a cushion of webbird silk. I laughed. "You bid on it on my say-so? I guess we'll have to give it back."

"I bought it with my own money. It is for you and Pearl, to remind you of me." Fayleen preened slightly under my speechless regard.

"Fayleen, it's too much. I can't accept it."

"You can and will. In twenty of your Earth years, if you are still uncomfortable with owning it, have your daughter bring it to me on Risia. You may come too, of course."

I laughed and tucked the priceless treasure in my belt pouch. Daughter. I liked the sound of that. I reached out and touched fingertips respectfully with a being far wiser than I would ever be and then went to collect my child.

This is the third story asking what choices a woman can make in the face of war, and the answer is a very different one.

DARK MIRRORS

by John Walters

Her face and arms bore the yellow marks of old bruises and the purple marks of new ones; her left forefinger and middle finger were in rough splints of cardboard and tape; the half-centimeter-thick bright red scar of a recently-healed cut ran from her right temple to the top of her nose near the corner of her left eye. Add to all this a hard, determined expression that suggested she wouldn't take shit from anyone, and she looked like a fighter, a brawler, a troublemaker.

But Margaret Keller knew she was anything but that.

The loose gray prison coveralls made her appear diminutive, like a little girl. She *was* very thin, abnormally so. Her scalp could be seen through her light brown hair; obviously much of the hair had fallen out. The hard work, scanty food, derision and beatings were telling on her. But she held her head defiantly high; she had kept herself together through it all.

Margaret, despite herself, was impressed. However, she assumed a calm, cold, professional air as she said, "Bethany Williamson?" and when the woman nodded, "Sit down."

They were in the mess hall, a small table with obscenities carved into its gray Formica surface between them. Prisoners shuffled to and fro, with wide frightened eyes glancing around as if already in the line of fire. The guards watching them were whispering intently together in a corner. They, too, would be called up, as soon as the last prisoner had left.

"Do you want my decision now?" asked Bethany. "I thought I had another day."

"Your decision?"

Bethany smiled ironically. "Service or dismemberment: aren't those the options?"

Momentarily taken aback, Margaret quickly recovered her poise. "Those are your choices, yes. Do you need another day to decide?"

Bethany slowly shook her head.

"How long have you been here?" Margaret asked.

Bethany smiled again, though her eyes narrowed and her jaw tightened. "I'm sure you in your fancy uniform, all clean and polished and obviously more than well-fed, have access to my file. You don't need to be asking me any questions like that."

"Don't you dare get insubordinate with me . . ."

"Or else what? I have been here for a year, three months, and seventeen days, and I have been beaten and abused on almost every one of those days. I was ripped away from my parents, my school, and everything else from my former life. I am about to be cut up and used as spare parts for wounded soldiers. There's nothing you can threaten me with that can make any difference to me." The hard look remained, but a teardrop formed in the corner of her right eye, though it did not trickle down.

Margaret forced the twinge of sympathy out of her conscious mind as if it were an enemy, but then adopted a more solicitous tone. "All right, all right. It seems we got off on the wrong foot."

"Is there a right foot? I don't think so. I'm a condemned woman." Bethany stood up.

"Please sit down."

"No."

They stared at each other for a long time, as if in mental combat. Finally Margaret nodded at a guard, who led Bethany away.

ⓢⓇⓈ

For her next interview with Bethany, Margaret went down to her cell.

The section guard was a short, stocky woman with a clean-shaven head, thick lower lip, and a pasty complexion. "That's murderer's row. It's been almost cleaned out," the guard said. "There're just a few prisoners left. Some are unaccounted for, though. They're trying to hide to avoid service. It could be dangerous if they find you. I can come with you if you want."

"I'll be all right." To emphasize the point Margaret pulled out her pistol, checked that it was loaded, and put it away again. "By the way, what is she doing down there with murderers?"

The guard shrugged. "They don't like her kind much. Maybe the warden thought it would break her. Anyway, there are maps on the guard post walls in case you get lost. There're a lot of corridors."

Margaret descended a flight of stairs and turned left into a wide but low-ceilinged hallway. The cells on either side were vacant; her footsteps echoed loudly in the empty spaces. Since the facility was being shut down, regular cleaning had stopped. Humidity beaded on the graffiti-covered walls and then trickled down in rivulets to form puddles on the muddy floor. Black specks of mold had begun to grow in the corners of the ceiling. Cockroaches were everywhere; Margaret saw an occasional rat as well. The air smelled musty from the damp, rotting mattresses.

After having navigated the maze of corridors for a quarter of an hour, Margaret became convinced she was lost and was just about to try to find her way back, when she spotted Bethany alone in her cell, sitting on the edge of the lower bunk reading a book.

Once again a burst of sympathy erupted from somewhere within; once again Margaret stifled it and sent it back where it came from. She reminded herself that she despised Bethany and everything she stood for, and she resented the circumstance that forced her into this hellhole to deal with her. Bethany had turned her back on her people; she *deserved* the dismemberment. At least then she could be of some use.

But even as she thought these things, Margaret wondered whether these were her own thoughts or whether others had implanted them in her. Things had taken such a crazy turn that she didn't know what to believe any more. But whenever she became confused, she thought of her husband and son, both early casualties of the war. Her husband she remembered as he had looked the day he left for the last time: balding, with gray hair at the temples, but sharp and strong and determined in his uniform. Her son, however, she could never picture as an adult. She saw him as a toddler, running into her arms with a big smile to be scooped up and hugged, or grade school age either in bed with one of his myriad childhood illnesses, or pale and thin, playing basketball at a nearby park with his friends. Though he had never been very healthy, when the conflict began he had wanted to enlist right away; he was rejected at first and was only allowed to join up after several defeats had been suffered and the medical checkup consisted of feeling you to see if you were still warm. He had been thrilled to be a part of it all, but he hadn't lasted a week once he was out on the field.

A part of her desperately wanted to consider it Bethany's fault that they were dead, but another part of her knew that it was not true, that what she had done had made no difference one way or the other.

Margaret remembered Bethany's photograph from her file: long, thick, straight, shining hair, round almost chubby face, big smile, large light brown eyes full of trust and confidence. She had looked like a completely different person. She had been a seventeen-year-old university student majoring in pharmacology when the draft law had been amended to make the minimum age fifteen instead of eighteen and to include women as well as men. She had immediately filed for conscientious objector status, on secular moral grounds rather than theological. In her statement, she had quoted Jesus, Buddha, Gandhi, Thoreau, and others, but by then it hadn't mattered what personal convictions she'd held: conscientious objection had been officially abolished. The choices had been military service or prison.

Bethany heard Margaret's footsteps and looked up. Without enthusiasm, she said, "Well, look who's here. What brings you to my humble home?"

Margaret stood on the other side of the bars. "We're alone. We can talk."

Bethany threw the book on the bed. "Twenty-year-old almanac. Not much in the prison library. I have nothing to say to you."

Margaret wanted to shout, to order her, to force her somehow to listen, but she knew it wouldn't work. "Just give me a few minutes, please."

"I suppose I can spare a few minutes. Don't threaten me."

"I won't." Margaret slipped the key-card into the slot and went inside; when she swung the door behind her, she left it open a few centimeters.

"Aren't you afraid I'm going to try to run?"

"No." Margaret sat down on the lone stool. The strong smell of the mattress combined with the stench of the filthy open toilet in the corner almost made her gag, but she managed to control the impulse. "Have you heard much recent news, Bethany?"

Bethany chuckled humorlessly. "Just rumors. I'm denied newspapers, magazines, and TV. Does the war go on?"

Margaret nodded.

"And how goes it for our side?"

"Please don't be sarcastic with me. If you know nothing else, you know it goes poorly. Otherwise why would we be conscripting prisoners into military service?"

"Or butchering them if they refuse."

"That's just supposed to be a threat to scare you into fighting."

"It's real enough to me, isn't it? And I'm still not fighting."

"Why are you so stubborn?"

"Why should I explain myself again? What's the point?"

"Sorry. Sorry." This was not how Margaret wanted things to go. "Let me give you a brief summary of what's been happening out there."

Bethany cautiously nodded. "All right."

"Around the time of your incarceration, after the fiasco with the tactical nukes, more ships landed, and we planned another major offensive."

"Now that the depleted ranks were swelled with female cannon fodder."

Margaret ignored the comment and continued, "We had been developing a new type of weapon, a hand-held laser. We thought it would turn the tide. But as soon as we attacked, they retaliated with lasers that were more powerful than ours. It was another rout. We lost a lot of troops. A lot."

"I'm sorry for them."

"Are you? You're certainly safer inside than out there."

"That's not why I'm here."

Margaret sighed. "All right. Well, we had still never actually *seen* them—they still used those robotic dolls that were obvious imitations of *us*—but the assumption was that somewhere in those ships there must be something of flesh and blood, or some kind of biological life, anyway, and so somebody proposed that we try to hit them with bacteriological warfare—try to burn them out from the inside. We tried it. We threw everything we could think of at them. Only it didn't work. And when we were done, they unleashed a plague that destroyed about half the world's remaining population."

"So everything you hit them with, they send back at you, only more so."

"That's the way it's been so far. As a matter of fact, a group of mathematicians put all the data into a computer, and as close as they can figure it, whatever we do to them, they do exactly double back to us."

"Did they *ever* initiate an attack?"

"At first we were convinced that they had started it all, back when they were just circling the Earth and the missiles began to fly. But upon further analysis, we think maybe our automatic orbiting defense system may have fired the first shot."

"So they have only been countering your moves."

"It seems so. I got up close to one of their ships once. It was many-sided, like a cut diamond or something, and it was dark. But the strangest thing was how reflective it was. I could see myself and everything else around as if in a huge mirror. And that's like what they seem to be doing in the war: they reflect and magnify everything we do."

"You should have done nothing."

"It's too late for that now."

"Too late for you. Not for me."

"You still have no compassion for your fellow humans? Remember, these are not people we're fighting, but something else, something—alien."

"What's the difference? Obviously they're intelligent. And anyway, is it doing any good to fight them?"

"Look, I know how you feel. You're right: I've read your file, I've read transcripts of interviews, I've traced your family history as far back as I could."

Bethany smiled, still without warmth. "Why would you be so interested in one little conscientious objector? No one has cared until now. I've been thrown in with these crazy-ass wackos and forgotten."

Margaret raised her hands in a gesture of futility. "We're bolstering armies with prisoners, old folks, pre-teens, the insane— anyone we can grab. But we know it won't do any good. Face-to-face, or I guess I should say face to no-face, we know we're no match for them. So we've been brainstorming, trying to come up with something unusual, unconventional, something wild and unexpected we could try. And that's when we thought of you."

"Me?" For the first time since Margaret had met her, an unguarded emotion crossed Bethany's face: surprise.

"Well, not just you. People like you."

"I was led to believe I was unique. An anomaly, an abnormality."

"No. There are quite a few others, both men and women."

"And they are all willing, like me, to be dismembered rather than fight?"

"Yes."

"If that doesn't beat everything. You isolated us from each other to break down our wills, to make us think that we were all alone. Unity would only strengthen our convictions, right?"

"That's right. Only now . . . Only now . . . ."

Comprehension lit up Bethany's face. "You want to send us to them. You're hoping they'll mirror the way *we* feel. If they do, they'll stop fighting. They might even pack up and go home."

Margaret nodded. "We want to surrender, to plead for mercy, but there's no one to surrender to. We figure if we send you to them, they might pick up our intentions."

For a moment Bethany was incredulous, then she started to cry. "You bastards! You bastards! After all I've been through— after all *we've* been through—you ask us to walk right out to the enemy and try to save the world!"

"I'm sorry," Margaret said. "I—"

Wiping her tear-stained face, with a chuckle that sounded like a sob, Bethany said, "This must have killed you. This must have just killed an old military warhorse like you to come here and tell me this."

In her confusion of emotions Margaret was finding it hard to keep her composure. "It . . . it's a last resort."

"Meaning that if you had your way you'd blow them to hell first, right?"

"We've been trying to defend our country, our world."

"But it hasn't worked." Bethany grabbed some toilet paper and wiped her eyes, blew her nose. "Have you talked to the others? What do they say?"

"What do *you* say?"

"I say, why should I? You say, either I do this or I'll be torn to pieces. Forget it. You're not worth saving. Let *them* have this messed-up world. Maybe they'll do better with it than we have."

"It's not like that."

"What do you mean?"

"I mean the dismemberment. It was just a threat. We never intended to do it."

"What?"

"We had to know who was sincere and who was just a coward."

Bethany shook her head in disbelief. "You still don't understand, do you? Maybe you never will."

"I'm trying to."

"And if you're not going to cut us up if we refuse to help, what *are* you going to do with us?"

"Nothing."

"Nothing?"

"We realized for this to have any chance to work it must be sincere—completely voluntary. As of this moment, you are a free woman, whether you choose to help us or not."

"You're kidding. Do you mean I can just walk out that cell door and out of this prison and never look back?"

"Yes. Well, you'd have to come with me to the warden's office first to sign some forms."

Bethany sat motionless, still as a statue, her jaw set in a frown of concentration, rivulets of tears gleaming on her cheeks. Finally she spoke in a low voice. "If we did this, there would be no tricks, right? No hidden bombs or bugs on us, no backstabbing them if they drop their weapons."

"No."

"You powers-that-be are behind it? You're willing to back it for the long term?"

"Yes."

"What's your name? You never told me your name."

"Margaret Keller."

"Are you, Margaret, personally, willing to unequivocally turn your sword into a plowshare? Figuratively speaking, of course."

Margaret hesitated before saying, "Yes."

"I see. You'll do it, but reluctantly. I guess that's the best that can be expected at this stage. How soon are you planning to try it?"

"As soon as possible. As soon as we assemble the team. Volunteers are being sought out around the world, everywhere

where ships have landed. When everyone is ready, we'll synchronize the advance."

Bethany thought again for a time and then said, "I miss my mother. I want to go home."

"That's understandable."

"Can we leave now?"

"All right."

Margaret swung the door open, and Bethany stepped gingerly through, as if unsure whether she really had permission to do so or not. She waited for Margaret to come alongside her before she went farther.

Margaret hesitated. "Uh . . . I seem to have lost my sense of direction. Which way?"

"This way. Come on." They turned right towards an intersection of corridors. Some of the ceiling fixtures ahead had been smashed, so that part of the hall was in shadow, and part washed in pale yellow light.

They had gone only a few steps when five women in gray prison coveralls appeared from around a corner and blocked their way. Two were black, one looked Hispanic, and two were white. They all brandished makeshift weapons: steel pipes from bunk frames, and metal scraps shaped like knives, taped at one end for a handle and sharpened at the other.

A tall, heavy-set black woman tapped her pipe rhythmically on the palm of her hand. "Where you goin', Bethy?" she said. "We haven't said goodbye yet."

"Back off," Margaret said. "My business is only with Bethany. Stay out of it."

The woman continued the thump of pipe on palm. "Well, our business is with Bethany, too. And if you don't want some of it yourself, *you'd* better back off. Don't you know what she is? She's a coward."

"No, Emma," said Bethany. "I'm not a coward. I'm willing to be dismembered. You're the ones who ran away."

Emma gripped her pipe with both hands and raised it over her head. "Why, you bitch!"

Bethany began to walk slowly towards the prisoners. "It's natural to be scared, Emma. Everyone's scared. Even those who pretend they're not."

Emma half-lowered the pipe and said, "Don't be callin' *me* a coward."

"All right. I'm sorry. Please let us pass."

For a moment, Margaret was mesmerized. She had considered Bethany a coward, nothing more, yet here she was advancing on women who had already announced their intention of thrashing or possibly even killing her. And the women, spellbound by her boldness, were slowly stepping back, and even lowering their weapons. It looked like they would make it past the prisoners unscathed.

But then Margaret's training reasserted itself. Bethany was a part of the larger plan now, and too valuable to take a chance with. She drew her pistol, held it at arm's length, and shouted, "I said back off! Do it now!"

The Hispanic woman shouted, "She's got a gun!" They all raised their weapons again, as if they were going to charge Margaret.

Five deafening shots boomed through the corridor.

For a timeless moment Margaret became disoriented and imagined herself on a battlefield, with bombs exploding, bullets flying, smoke filling the air, and all around the stench of burning flesh.

Then there was a long silence.

When her vision cleared, Margaret saw that four of the women lay still on the floor, shots to the head having killed them instantly. Emma, however, was bleeding from the chest, and more blood gathered between her lips and flowed down her cheek; Bethany sat in the mud and blood, cradling Emma's head in her lap, looking into Emma's frightened eyes.

Margaret's arm fell to her side; the pistol dropped to the floor with a loud clatter. Then the only sound was Emma's quiet bubbling cough.

From a distant corridor came shouts and footfalls.

Bethany raised her head and looked at Margaret. "You don't deserve it," she said. "You don't deserve to be saved."

಍ଓଔ

For months the enemy had been dormant.

The time had come.

The plain was littered with the debris of old battles: crumpled and rusting vehicles, shattered weapons, bits and shreds of materials and components of the robotic soldiers the enemy used to fight for them. In the distance, at the edge of the sere hills, sat three of the enemy's dark, multifaceted ships.

Some people were milling about, some standing still; some were talking, some silent. They were men and women, young and old, black, brown, and white, tall and short, fat and thin, some bald and some with hair down to their waists, some with tattoos, some with bangles and beads and necklaces and bracelets and earrings and nose rings and rings in their lips; some were formally dressed and some casually, some sported clothes with wild flamboyant colors, and some were scarcely dressed at all.

It was almost time to start. Margaret hurried through the crowd, searching.

Then she saw her, standing by herself, gazing at the dark ships. She wore brown leather sandals, blue jeans, and a pink blouse. The scar and bruise-marks were still on her face, but she looked healthier, more robust, like she'd been eating well and had filled out.

"Bethany."

Margaret had expected bitterness and animosity, but Bethany merely smiled. "Oh. Hello."

"What made you change your mind?"

"Well, it's true what I said, that you don't deserve to be saved. But then, none of us do."

"You must hate me."

"No. How could I walk out now with these others if I did?"

"I came to say . . ." Margaret's voice broke; she hesitated and tried again. "I came to say I'm sorry."

"There were times at the prison, after they had worked me over, that I wanted to kill them, too."

"But I . . ."

"It's all right." Bethany hugged her, and kissed her cheek. "Come. Walk with me."

Margaret shook her head. "I can't."

"Why?"

"I have responsibilities. No, that's not the reason. I guess I'm not ready." Margaret felt the urge to cover up her confusion, so she turned and left the crowd. A three-story-high platform had been erected from which military personnel could view the outcome of the event; she rode the lift to the top.

She spotted Bethany's pink blouse; she was still standing where Margaret had left her.

The signal was given. The people below began to move slowly forward, some walking hand-in-hand, some alone, and some in groups.

Beyond, the dark ships waited.

Who decides what constitutes "human"? And if the people who are being judged don't agree with the judgment, what are the results?

A BIRD IN THE HAND

by Douglas Smith

"**D**id you check the electrodes and restraints again?"

A male voice, she thought. *Hard, sharp.*

"Yes, doctor. I didn't like being in there with her."

Different voice, but male again. This one sounded nervous.

"I wonder what she'll be?" the first voice asked.

Only two of them? She kept her eyes closed, listening.

"Something beautiful, I think. She certainly is now."

Where was she? She tried moving. The structure under her swayed slightly, creaking. Some kind of table.

"Stay focused, Steen. She's one of them."

"We don't know for sure," the one called Steen replied.

Her arms were strapped down. She was wearing a short gown. She felt cold metal under her bare legs and more straps. Something soft and plastic pulled at a corner of her mouth.

"Look at the readings, man! Have they been wrong yet?"

"No. No, they haven't," Steen admitted.

"Hopefully, she'll be a predator of some type," Voice One continued. "A bear, a wolf, a big cat—any of those would have the most *theatrical* effect with the Department of Justice."

Her eyelids fluttered open. She quickly shut them, blinded.

"Dim the lights, Steen. Our subject awakes."

The light dropped. She tried again, blinking until her eyes adjusted. Five feet above her hung a lattice of metal bars. Mounted on the bars, a video camera focused on her. Above that, beside fluorescent tubes, a half dozen spotlights stabbed down.

"Miss . . ." Voice One began. Papers shuffled. "Hoyl. Lilith Hoyl. You are with us again, are you not?"

Where were they? With an effort, she turned her head to the right. Pain seared up her neck into the back of her skull. More bars and another video camera stood about two feet away. Six feet beyond, filing cabinets lined a pale yellow wall on either side of a large closed window. She fought her head around to the left. Again, a crosshatch of bars. Fifteen feet past the bars, a row of wooden tables with computer screens stood against another wall.

She was in a cage.

Footsteps. Two male figures walked into her line of vision. One was tall, thin, with sharp, pointed features. Number One. The other, short and plump, round and soft, hovered at his elbow. Steen.

"My name is Dr. Lindstrom," the tall one said. "This is Dr. Steen." Steen gave a nervous smile and a little wave. Lindstrom froze him with a glare, and he reddened.

"Wh—" she tried, but her throat wouldn't respond.

"Squeezing the bulb under your right hand will dispense water from the tube in your mouth," Lindstrom said.

Squeeze. Water, warm and acrid, but ambrosia at the moment, flowed down her throat. "What's happening to me?" she croaked.

"Your government, Miss Hoyl, has chosen you to demonstrate the efficacy of a revolutionary advance in the field of law enforcement," Lindstrom said, watching her closely.

"What? Law enforcement?" she murmured.

"You will participate in the final test of a product we have developed to assist our police to identify certain individuals in our society."

"What are you talking about?" *Damn it*, she thought. *Focus. Gain control.*

"The Heroka, Miss Hoyl," Lindstrom said, his eyes still locked on her. "Don't feign innocence. We know what you are."

She struggled to clear her head. "The what?"

Lindstrom's jaws muscles worked as he approached the cage. "The Heroka. A race of shape shifters. Monsters who assume animal forms to prey upon us." The lights above sparkled on a spray of spittle from his words. "Freaks. Mutants. Travesties of God's design. And you are one of them." He stopped a pace from the cage.

Electrified? She squeezed the bulb again, taking another swallow. The acrid taste remained. "Shape shifters? You're chasing . . . werewolves?" She fought a rush of panic.

"Were-*beasts*, actually," Steen corrected. "We know that your kind can be many different animals."

"What we are chasing, Miss Hoyl, are murderers." Lindstrom's voice broke on the last word, and the anger drained from his face. "Murderers," he whispered, turning away to walk slowly to the tables.

A sad, gentle smile flickered over Steen's face, as if unsure it would be welcomed. He stepped to her cage. "Dr. Lindstrom's son was with CSIS," he whispered, "in a special unit formed to capture Heroka subjects for, uh, scientific purposes. The creatures killed him and several others in an ambush last year."

"I guess they don't like being captured for, uh, scientific purposes," she replied quietly. Steen looked puzzled. She shook her head. "Never mind. You're serious? Shape shifters? So why haven't I heard of these things in the news, in the papers, anywhere?"

"Dr. Lindstrom says the government wants to avoid a panic."

And keep any scientific finds to themselves, she thought. "What's this got to do with me?" Her voice trembled.

Lindstrom turned back to face her. "Spare me the denials. We've known of the Heroka for years." He straightened, again in command of himself. "Early tests on captured subjects identified certain physiological differences in your race. Irregular alpha wave patterns and unusual infrared auras."

"It's not my race," she said.

He ignored her. "We have since developed devices to detect these differences. These scanners, Miss Hoyl, enable us to identify the monsters that walk among us." He leaned forward. "And they identified *you* as one of those monsters."

She squeezed and swallowed again. "You've made a mistake."

Steen consulted a manila folder. "Oh, no. Your readings are all positive." He smiled, as if this should please her. "Now, some are borderline." His eyebrows swooped down towards plump cheeks, almost swallowing his beady eyes as he checked something. "But within established tolerances," he finished happily.

"Enough," Lindstrom sighed, waving Steen back with a flick of his hand. "Recognizing the menace the Heroka represent, the DOJ plans to initiate special measures for their capture."

"I thought you were worried about panic," she said. "Bringing legislation before Parliament to track down were-creatures, not to mention their trials, might attract some attention, don't you think?"

Lindstrom smiled. "We need no legislation. Justice will invoke the War Measures Act, citing the Heroka as a threat to national security. And they intend no public trials."

Just your private tests, she thought, shivering.

Lindstrom went on. "Unfortunately, Justice contends scanner readings will be inadmissible as evidence. That is where you play a role. We have developed a drug that triggers a specific chemical reaction in the brain, releasing an enzyme unique to the Heroka and forcing a transformation. In short, Miss Hoyl, it obliges you to assume your animal form, whatever that may be."

Lindstrom walked to the monitors, conferring with Steen in a whisper. Apparently satisfied, he turned back, smiling.

Never knew a snake could smile, she thought.

"You will receive our drug, while these computers monitor your transformation, and video cameras record it for posterity. This will convince Justice that a reliable method now exists for proving the existence of the Heroka in the courtroom."

"What!?" she exploded, straining against the straps. "You doped and kidnapped me, stripped me and strapped me onto a table in a cage. Now you're giving me some weird fucking drug? Are you nuts? Are you crazy?"

Lindstrom's smile broadened. "Very good. Adrenaline speeds the assimilation of the drug into your system. We shouldn't have long to wait," he said, checking the monitors again.

"You mean . . ." she began.

Steen nodded, smiling. "The drug is soluble in water. We placed it in your drinking supply." She dropped the bulb. He shuffled closer. "Oral delivery will allow undercover field agents to test suspects more easily. Dr. Lindstrom says that makes it much more marketable," he said in a conspiratorial tone.

"Shut up, Steen," Lindstrom snapped.

"Why do you need me?" she snarled. "You've already caught some of these things. Use them to test your goddamn drug."

Steen paled. Lindstrom spoke. "CSIS makes very few subjects available to us, and then only briefly. Once our drug prompts a change, they remove the creature to another facility." He paused. "You see, CSIS performs tests of their own, to determine the effectiveness of various weapons against the transformed Heroka." He smiled. "Regrettably, such tests do not lend themselves to reuse of the same subject."

She felt nausea rise in her. Steen avoided her eyes. *They're right*, she thought. *Monsters do walk among us.*

"How much has she taken?" Lindstrom asked.

Steen waddled out of sight. She heard a fingernail tapping against glass. "My goodness, nearly 107 cc's." Steen returned to stare wide-eyed at her. "That should be more than sufficient. The maximum any prior subject required was seventy-five."

Lindstrom's brow creased. "At twice her body mass." He walked to a monitor. "Steen, look at these scanner readings."

Steen waddled over. "Why, they've dropped, into the range of possible error." He turned to look at her, blinking. "We generally don't classify such levels as a positive I.D."

"You mean your fancy scanners are finally getting it right, saying that I'm human?" she asked. "Nice toys they give you. You guys buy wholesale or something?"

Lindstrom ignored her, grabbing the folder from Steen and pulling him over to the table. Whispering, they consulted the papers and occasionally the monitors. Finally, Steen stepped away, nervously wiping his hands on his lab coat.

Lindstrom stood silent for several heartbeats then looked up, smiling. She had the impression he was trying to be charming.

"Miss Hoyl," he said, "the possibility exists, it appears, that we acted in error. Naturally, should this be true, we would effect your immediate release and a swift return to your residence. For this to occur, however, I must ask for your assistance in eliminating some final doubts that remain."

"Fuck you," she replied.

Lindstrom seemed unperturbed. "Allow me to point out that you are not in the most opportune position to negotiate."

"Do you get paid by the syllable?"

His smile faded. "Is that a 'no'?"

She glared at him. "What's the deal?"

"Ingest another 100 cc's," he said.

Steen looked startled. "That's over three times the maximum we've ever used." He scribbled on his folder. "Per kilo of body mass, she'll ingest five times more than any other subject."

"Is this stuff toxic?" she asked.

Steen fingered his folder. "Well, not at those levels."

"But I'm getting close, right?" she said. Steen nodded. She bit her lip. "And if I cooperate?"

Lindstrom shrugged. "Assuming you retain human form, you will receive our most sincere and humble apologies. A CSIS operative will escort you from this facility, blindfolded I'm afraid, to your home and release you." He ended with a smile that she wanted to punctuate with a fist.

He's lying, she thought. They had said too much. Lindstrom would have CSIS kill her once she was out of Steen's sight. "That's it?" she snarled. "I could have you tossed in jail."

Lindstrom shrugged again. "Officially, this lab does not exist. We do not exist. The CSIS unit that hunts the Heroka does not exist. Against whom, precisely, would you bring your charges?"

She stared at him. "Never mind. I just want out. Okay."

Lindstrom raised an eyebrow. "Then you agree?"

She nodded. Lindstrom motioned, and Steen approached the bars. "Miss Hoyl, I'll regulate the flow of the liquid into your mouth tube, releasing about twenty-five cc's each time. Swallow that, and then nod. I'll then release the next amount."

"Yeah, yeah. Let's rock and roll."

Steen shuffled out of view. "All right," he called.

Fighting an urge to gag as the liquid flowed into her mouth, she swallowed and nodded. With each repetition, Lindstrom grew glummer, alternating his attention between her and the monitors.

Steen walked back into view. "She's taken two hundred and eleven cc's."

Lindstrom stared at the monitors, and then slammed his hand down on the table. "The readings have stabilized even further. She now shows as clearly human. Those idiot field agents must have fouled up using the damn scanners." He glared at them both.

"Those units have been in the field for quite some time," Steen offered. "Perhaps they need adjustment."

"Yeah, you should probably service them every hundred were-beasts or so," she said. "Now, this bird wants to fly."

Lindstrom glared, but made no move to release her.

Steen moved closer to him. "Doctor," he said quietly, "she's not one of them. You can't blame her for . . . for what happened."

Lindstrom swallowed, then nodded. "Very well," he said, moving to a keyboard. He tapped some keys then turned to look at her. "I assume we won't encounter any unpleasantness upon your release?"

"Look, I'm half your size, I'm a woman, and there're two of you. Plus I'll bet you have guards outside the door. I just want to go home." Her voice caught on the last word.

Lindstrom considered this, then nodded. He tapped some more keys. A high-pitched hum dropping rapidly in frequency caught her attention then fell below her hearing. *The electric field on the bars*, she thought. He tapped again. The straps fell away.

She pulled the plastic tube from her mouth and the electrodes from her arms and neck. Pain screamed from every muscle as she sat up on the table. She swung her legs over the side. More tapping, then the sound of released air and a metallic click. The cage door swung open.

Sliding off the table, she took a shaky step toward the cage door. Lindstrom turned from the keyboard and shoved his right hand in the pocket of his lab coat. *He has a gun*, she thought.

"Carefully, Miss Hoyl," he said, watching her closely. "We wouldn't want you to fall and hurt yourself."

"Yeah, right," she said, "especially after you've treated me so nicely."

As Steen brought a chair, and she settled slowly into it, Lindstrom removed his hand and visibly relaxed. Steen hovered over her. "Can I get you anything, Miss Hoyl?"

"My clothes and my purse, please."

Steen looked at Lindstrom, who nodded. As the little man walked over to a filing cabinet, she looked around the room, seeing for the first time the two walls that had been out of her view. One held a heavy metal door with a series of dead bolts. The other wall had a smaller door, slightly ajar.

Steen returned with her clothes and purse. "You can change in the washroom outside. I'll call security to take you home."

She flashed a hundred-watt smile. "I need a while to recover."

"Certainly," he said, blushing. "Please, take your time."

"Could I have a glass of water?"

He nodded and turned away. From her purse, she removed a tube of lip balm. Pushing a large amount of the stick out, she began applying it to her lips, peeking from under half-closed eyelids. Lindstrom sat staring at a folder. Steen was pouring her water. She bit off the tip of the stick and swallowed. The lip balm was back in her purse when Steen returned. Taking the glass from him, she smiled. "Tell me," she said in a low voice. "Am I now in some Department of Justice database as one of these creatures?"

"Oh no! All of our research is stored on this system right here," Steen said quietly, pointing to a unit under the table of monitors. "We don't want others to have access to our work. We do our own backup, too." He patted the pocket of his lab coat where she could see an outline of what she guessed was a USB drive.

"No assistants?" she asked. He shook his head.

"How do you manufacture and store the drug?"

He winked and nodded toward the small open door. "Our lab. We store all samples in a temperature-control unit in there."

"Quite the setup." She then added in a normal level of voice, "Well, I'm ready to go home now." She tweaked Steen's plump cheek. "Thanks for the hospitality."

As the little man reddened and began to speak, she drew a sharp nail quickly along the soft skin under his jaw. A thin line of red appeared. Steen gave a little cry.

"Oops!" she said. "Sorry. I scraped you."

Lindstrom straightened from where he had been reading and put his hand into his pocket. "What's wrong?" he snapped.

"Oh, nothing," Steen tittered. "Just an accident. I'm sure Miss . . ." Steen's face went blank. He staggered back a step.

Lindstrom swore and stood, struggling to pull the gun free.

In a single flowing motion, she leapt from the chair to close the space between them. A snap kick to his groin dropped Lindstrom to his knees. One of her hands slashed scarlet furrows across his neck; the other raked his face, slicing a cheek and an eyeball. He opened his mouth, but only a choking, gurgling sound escaped. His head hit the floor with an audible crack.

She spun around. Steen sat slumped in the chair she'd left, arms hanging like wet towels, breathing in short gasps. His head was tilted sideways, saliva dripping from his mouth, his eyes locked on her. She put a finger on Lindstrom's carotid, then checked that all the door bolts were in place. Apparently, Lindstrom and Steen preferred privacy to having guards readily available.

Taking her purse, she moved to the computer. Lindstrom had left it on, so log-in security was not an issue. She selected a menu option labeled "Test Subjects," then chose "Name Search." It felt strange typing his name. She'd never done that before.

"No match" flashed on the screen. Other spellings brought the same result. Scanning the data on various victims, she noted that most didn't show names. And he wouldn't have told them. Not him. He wouldn't have said anything. She stood up. Better follow her orders. She removed the hard drive from the server and put it into her purse. Steen's eyes followed her.

"Wondering what happened, Steeny? Well, Lindstrom's dead, and you're dying, from the snake venom I use for nail polish on special dates. Your cut was small, compared to this garbage." She kicked Lindstrom's body. "So you'll live a while longer."

She climbed on a table to disconnect the smoke detector and the heat sensor on the sprinkler system. In the cage, she removed the storage card from both cameras. Pulling the backup drive from Steen's pocket, she dropped it and the camera cards into her purse.

"You were right, by the way. I am Heroka." She watched his eyes widen. "So why didn't I shift? Well, you made an assumption. Unfortunately—for you—a wrong one." She began opening filing drawers, throwing the contents onto the floor.

Stopping at a cabinet labeled "Test Subjects," she bit her lip. She had to know for sure. Wrenching open the drawer, she began pulling out folders. Each had photos of captured Heroka. Many faces were familiar, but none was his. The photos showed the Heroka as human, then in changed forms, in what appeared to be a series of weapons tests. An autopsy report ended each file.

She was nearly through all the folders. Maybe she was wrong. *Sky Mother, please let me be wrong.*

She found him staring at her from the next-to-last folder. Found the eyes she'd wake to on those too rare mornings as he lay watching her. Found his mouth that knew hers so well. Found what they did to him, to that body that had held her, loved her, so often but never enough. Found the pictures of how he died.

The folder and its contents dropped from her hands. She threw her head back and screamed a scream no human throat could ever produce. Stumbling to Lindstrom's corpse, she fell to her knees to claw and beat at his face. Finally, the rise and fall of her hands slowed, then stopped.

She rose and walked to Steen. Lifting a bloody hand, she struck him across the side of the head. "Murderers!" she shouted. His limp body slid from the chair. She stood swaying over him. "Murderers," she whispered.

Sobbing, she ran into the next room. Equipment and bottles covered a row of tables. She seized and hurled a container against the wall, then overturned each table. Ripping open the doors to two large refrigeration units, she began pulling out bottles, smashing them on the floor.

She stopped. Holding the last bottle in her hand, she staggered back against the wall and slid to the floor, crying quietly. She had to take a sample back. Her people needed to know what CSIS had. He'd want her to do that. She broke down again, clutching the bottle to her chest. It hurt so much. She never thought he could hurt her, but oh god, this hurt.

Her sobbing stopped. She sat motionless then rose, moving like an automaton. The last bottle in her hand, she returned to stand over Steen.

"Figure it out yet, you little bastard? We have two forms, human and animal. One is our natural state. Most of us live as humans but can shift to animal form. But even we have freaks. Like my tribe. Our natural form is animal. We're rare, even among the Heroka."

And she was the rarest. A freak among freaks. But he never treated her that way. She fought her tears.

"We shift to become human. As humans, we show the same readings on your scanners as other Heroka. That's why you picked me out." Putting the bottle in her purse, she removed a perfume atomizer.

"We set you up. We knew that CSIS was working on a shift agent and that you'd eventually succeed, because we had."

Steen's eyes widened. Walking up and down, she released a mist over the papers scattered on the floor, avoiding looking at one particular file.

"Our shift agent lets us hold a change longer. I took some, to keep my human form during the unconsciousness we knew would follow my capture."

I was used to taking it, she thought. *To be with him. To be normal.*

Unlatching the single window, she pulled it open. Good. No bars. She threw the screen on the floor.

"When I recognized a familiar taste in the water, I gladly drank up. We worried that you wouldn't give me your drug in time, that I wouldn't be able to maintain my shift. Your drug let me keep my human form. The scanner readings dropped because you'd made me more human." She looked out the window. Ten or more stories below, armed guards paced a walled courtyard.

"Can't . . . escape," Steen rasped.

She smiled sadly. "After you released me, I took a drug to counteract both shift agents, to allow me to return to my normal form." *Normal?* Only for her, for she was unique. "Wondering what I am?"

She laid the purse under the window. "Legend says that the Hoyl was the only creature in Eden not to eat of the forbidden fruit that Adam offered to all the animals. We, the Heroka, also choose not to eat of this fruit, the world of man, your destruction of species, your rape of our Garden."

The chemical spray now soaked the papers littering the floor. Striking a match, she looked at Steen. Tears streaked his fat cheeks.

"In that legend, the Hoyl was a phoenix. It does not know death. Fire consumes it in its nest, leaving an egg from which hatches full-grown a new Hoyl." She dropped the match. The fire raced across the floor to lick at the walls and furniture.

Would that I could be reborn, memories erased, she thought.

She let her cotton gown fall to the floor. The flames rose, and smoke grew thick, but Steen did not close his eyes.

Naked, she cried out in another voice. "You, who seek to bind us, look upon that which you would cage. Behold the Hoyl!" Raising her arms, she threw back her head. The change began. Her head narrowed and sharpened. Neck arched and shoulders broadened. Legs turned backwards, lengthened and thickened. Her tears dried, and the aching pain in her heart grew dim. She looked down at her skin, flickering now with a thousand colors and lights, until she burned brighter than the flames.

Though dying, Steen's face held a terror of another sort as the Hoyl looked down on him.

See me, little mouse! Taller than a man, plumage of shimmering crystal, talons of sharpened ivory, beak a scarlet scythe under eyes of flame. I am the Hoyl.

She seized the purse in a claw and leapt to the window. Perched upon the sill, the Hoyl turned back to the room.

Flames ran and skipped up the walls. Steen lay gazing at her. His lips moved to form one word. "Beautiful," he whispered, then his eyes closed.

She stared at him, but he did not move again. Her golden eyes fell on a picture lying on the floor, flames tasting its edges. The picture of a man, somehow familiar, gazed back at her. A feeling washed over her that she could not describe, and an alien thought winged through her alien mind: *Beautiful.*

Fire consumed his image, and he faded from her vision and her thoughts. Then with a rush of air and wings, she left the room behind, as the ashes danced across the floor.

ABOUT THE AUTHORS

Paul Abbamondi reads and writes speculative fiction compulsively from somewhere in New Jersey. His short stories have appeared in *Shimmer, Farrago's Wainscot*, and *Kaleidotrope,* as well as other fine markets, and he enjoys all things weird. In his spare time, he draws comics and wastes too many late night hours on videogames. You can send him e-mails at *pdabbamondi@gmail.com*. He likes e-mails.

Aimee C. Amodio was eleven when she told her parents she wanted to grow up to be a writer. She may not consider herself "grown up" but she does do that writing thing on a regular basis. Aimee lives in the Pacific Northwest with two neurotic dogs (they take after their mother). Visit her at *www.newroticgirl.com*.

Therese Arkenberg is a student ast Carroll University in Wisconsin. Her work has appeared in *Beneath Ceaseless Skies* and the anthologies *All About Eve, Things We Are Not, Thoughtcrime Experiments,* and *Sword and Sorceress XXIV*. Her novella, "Aqua Vitae," has been accepted by WolfSinger Publications for a 2011 release. Several of her short stories are also available at *AnthologyBuilder.com*.

Leslie Brown is a research technician working in the Alzheimer's field. She has previously published stories in *On Spec, Strange Horizons*, and in several anthologies including *Sails and Sorcery, Escape Clause,* and in *Warrior Wisewoman 2*. This story is a sequel of sorts to "Preservation of the Species," *On Spec,* Fall 2000: her heroine still had unfinished business. Leslie's website is at *www.leslie-brown.com.*

Alfred D. Byrd has a bachelor's degree in Medical Technology from Michigan State University and a master's degree in Microbiology from the University of Kentucky. He has worked for the past more than twenty years as a research analyst in a plant genetics laboratory at the University of Kentucky. "Natural Law" was his first professional sale, but a story sold later has since appeared in *Quest for Atlantis: Legends of a Lost Continent.* He has also published by print-on-demand several works of fantasy, science fiction, Appalachian regional fiction, and Christian theology available online.

Gwendolyn Clare is a New Englander transplanted to North Carolina. She has a BA in Ecology, a BS in Geophysics, and is currently working to add another acronym to her collection. When she's not living out of a tent in the desert or a hammock in the rainforest, she enjoys practicing martial arts and writing speculative fiction. Her short stories have sold to *Asimov's, Flash Ficiton Online,* and *Abyss and Apex,* among others.

Bruce Golden's short stories have garnered several awards and more than 80 sales across seven countries. *Asimov's Science Ficiton* described his second novel: "If Mickey Spillane had collaborated with both Frederick Pohl and Philip K. Dick, he might have produced Bruce Golden's *Better Than Chocolate*." His latest book, *Evergreen*, takes readers to an alien world full of ancient secrets and a strange intelligence, populated with characters motivated by revenge, redemption, and obsession, on a quest to find the City of God.

William Highsmith has sold stories over the last year to *Flash Fiction Online, Abyss & Apex*, the *Thoughtcrime Experiments* anthology, and the *Butterfly Affects* anthology. He also has published various technical articles and documents. He is a software engineer and tech writer in the telecom industry.

Kathy Hurley lives near Boise, Idaho, with her husband and two daughters. She owns and operates a business called Pookatales Press, through which she produces handmade miniature books for collectors. She also reads tarot professionally.

Swapna Kishore is a software consultant and lives in Bangalore, India. She also writes speculative fiction. Recent publication credits include *Nature (Futures), Ideomancer, Ray Gun Revival*, and *Expanded Horizons*. Her website is at www.swapnawrites.com.

Gary Kloster lives in the Midwest with his wife and two daughters. His writing gets worked in around his efforts as a stay-at-home dad and the sole representative of the Y-chromosome in a house full of genius-grade XX's. You can find more of his work in *Baen's Universe*, the twenty-fifth volume of the Writers of the Future anthology, and forthcoming in *Fantasy Magazine*. He also adds occasionally to the internet's clutter at *www.garykloster.com*.

Susanne Martin lives on a small island on the Canadian West Coast and works for the community newspaper. Her writing has appeared in various magazines and newspapers as well the British anthologies *In the Shadow of the Red Queen* and *Spooked*.

Melissa Mead is from upstate New York, and a member of the Carpe Libris writers group. She has sold stories to *Sword and Sorceress 23* and *24, The Lorelei Signal, Electric Velocipede*, and others.

Al Onia pursues the sense of wonder in his fiction since discovering Jules Verne and Robert Heinlein in grade 4 and in the real world as a geophysicist. He has published fantasy and science fiction in Marion *Zimmer Bradley's Fantasy Magazine, On Spec,* and the Canadian SF anthology *North of Infinity*. He is a member of the Imaginative Fiction Writers Association, and lives in Calgary, Alberta, with his wife Sandra.

Jennifer R. Povey is in her mid thirties, and lives in Northern Virginia with her husband. She writes a variety of speculative fiction, whilst following current affairs and occasionally indulging in horse riding and role-playing games. She was a contributor to *Warrior Wisewoman 2*.

Joel Richards has published one novel, *Pindharee* (Tor), but is mainly a short fiction writer. His stories have appeared in *Asimov's*, *Amazing*, and a number of original anthologies, including Terry Carr's *Universe* (14 and 17), Harry Turtledove's *Alternate Generals II*, and Roger Zelazny's *Warriors of Blood and Dream*.

Douglas Smith's stories have appeared in over a hundred magazines and anthologies in twenty-nine countries and twenty-four languages, including *InterZone*, *Amazing Stories*, *Cicada*, *Baen's Universe*, *Weird Tales*, *The Mammoth Book of Best New Horror*, *Postscripts*, *On Spec*, and *The Third Alternative*, as well as anthologies from Penguin, DAW, and others. He was a John W. Campbell Award finalist for best new writer and has twice won the Canadian Aurora Award. He has two collections of short fiction, *Impossibilia* (PS Publishing, UK, 2008) and *Chimerascope* (ChiZine Publications, Canada, 2010). A short film based on his story "By Her Hand, She Draws You Down" will appear in 2010.

Susan Tsui resides in New York with her husband and near her family. She holds an MFA from Goddard College, and her previous publishing credits include stories in *Expanded Horizons* and *Mind Flights*. Her website is at *www.susantsui.com/blog*.

John Walters is an American writer, a Clarion graduate and member of SFWA, currently living in Greece with his Greek wife and five sons. He has had stories published in *Talebones*, *Altair*, *GUD*, and other magazines and anthologies.

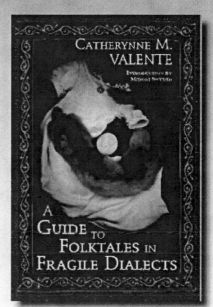
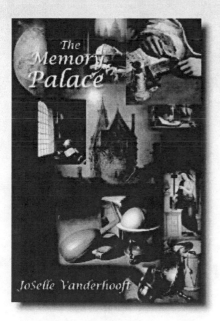

LaVergne, TN USA
06 October 2010
199814LV00006B/19/P